The Happy Chip

The Happy Chip

DENNIS MEREDITH

Glyphus

For information about this title or to order other books and/or electronic media, contact the publisher:

Glyphus, L.L.C.
4159 Summit Rd., Purlear, NC 28665
www.glyphus.com
editor@glyphus.com

Library of Congress Control Number: 2015917055

ISBNs: 9781939118226 Print
         9781939118202 Kindle
         9781939118219 ePub

Printed in the United States of America

Cover and Interior design: 1106 Design

To Greg

Also By Dennis Meredith

Fiction

The Rainbow Virus (RainbowVirus.com)

Wormholes: A Novel (WormholesaNovel.com)

Solomon's Freedom (SolomonsFreedom.com)

The Cerulean's Secret (CeruleansSecret.com)

Nonfiction

Explaining Research: How to Reach Key Audiences to Advance Your Work (ExplainingResearch.com)

CHAPTER 1

J ames Preston shoved open the apartment building's heavy oak door and stepped out into an icy wind that whipped the driving rain down the gloomy Boston street. His thin raincoat gave little protection from either the cold or the downpour. He huddled against the weather, thoroughly chilled . . . grinning like a total idiot.

After all, he'd just enjoyed about the most incredible first date ever!

It started with first meeting the incandescently beautiful Darlene, followed by their cozy dinner in which they discovered they had tons of stuff in common. They'd totally clicked. During intimate after-dinner drinks at her place, they even agreed to sync their Happy Chip data—unheard of on a first date. Even one where the very expensive dating service Happy Resonance predicted would be a perfect match. And they'd discovered, delightfully, that each registered a stunningly high physiological reaction to the other. Their sex would be incredible!

It was awesome to feel so great after weeks of going through his crazy roller-coaster moods. He'd suffered the blackest funk one minute and a top-of-the-world elation the next. He'd guessed it was just all the crap at work, some run-ins with so-called friends, and worries over the date.

But now he almost skipped down the rain-slick steps, not even caring what the lean, dark-haired man standing at the curb with the umbrella thought. In fact, Preston decided maybe he'd ask the guy if he could borrow his umbrella and do the goofy, fun, *Singin'-in-the-Rain* dance from the old movie. He checked his watch. It was midnight, and the trains were still running. He decided he'd better head for the entrance to the subway's Green Line down the block. Maybe he would just do a little jig along the way.

He'd walked only a few hundred yards along the deserted block in the swirling deluge, when the pouring rain and the street were lit by headlights from a car approaching behind him. Maybe it was a taxi. Yeah, he should take a taxi. He was feeling too terrific to let the mood fade, getting soaked, waiting for a train, and coping with the drunks and rowdies and bums on subways at night.

A smile still on his face, he turned toward the headlights, and realized it was not a cab, but a van with a Parker Plumbing sign. The side door slid open, and he found himself staring at a muscular bald-shaven man crouched in the van and dressed in black.

Before he could say anything, a sound behind him—the whoosh of a closing umbrella—made him start to turn. But powerful hands gripped his head from behind, and a vicious, expert twist snapped his neck, killing him instantly. His mouth gaped open, his dead-glassy eyes wide with a remnant horror of his death, as the rain washed down his face in a final, tragic baptism.

Before his body could crumple to the ground, the killer grabbed him beneath his arms, and together with the man in black, they shoved him into the van.

The killer picked up the umbrella, quickly scanned the street, saw no witnesses who would also need to be dispatched, and climbed in.

"Go," he said simply to the driver, and the van lurched away, winding through back streets for a dozen miles into an industrial area and to a warehouse where an overhead door slid up to admit it.

The driver, a sandy-haired mercenary with carefully groomed face stubble, slid out of the van and opened the back door.

Waiting for them with a gurney was Thomas Beale, a small, stooped man dressed in a blue plastic apron. He wore a surgical cap, a plastic face shield and blood-stained surgical gloves.

"Any problems?" Beale asked.

"Clean kill, clean extraction," replied the driver cocking his head nonchalantly. The two other mercenaries in the back hefted Preston's limp body onto the gurney and helped wheel the corpse into a large, clear, plastic tent awash in the glare of floodlights. They lifted the corpse onto a blood-encrusted stainless steel autopsy table. Nearby sat other smaller tables piled with scalpels, saws, and other surgical instruments, all clotted with dried blood.

The three mercenaries sat wearily down outside the tent on folding chairs, one lighting a cigarette.

"You need to do this fast," the driver told Beale through the plastic wall. "By the time we get this one to the chopper, it will be three a.m. We have to finish the mission before dawn."

"It'll take whatever time it takes!" snapped Beale, quickly cutting away the corpse's clothes, leaving Preston's pale, fleshy body lying naked and inert under the light. "Besides, your mission's not finished until you get all the subjects. That's only nine. There's one left . . . the Kelley woman."

"Not our fuckin' problem!" spat the driver. "That's the recon team's job, and you know goddamned well she's disappeared. They say she hasn't been to work in a week, hasn't used credit cards, hasn't seen any family, friends . . . fuckin' gone. Somehow, she must have known some of the other subjects, and found out about the loony behaviors, the suicides."

Beale made an annoyed face behind the blood-spattered plastic shield, but said nothing. He picked up a small box with a glowing screen and carefully began to scan Preston's body, scrutinizing the display.

"She's probably dead, anyway," he mumbled distractedly. He stopped his scan at Preston's chest. "Shit!" he exclaimed to himself. "The chip lodged in the damned heart. Why couldn't it be in a damned extremity!"

"What do you mean she's probably dead?" The driver parted the plastic, taking care to stay clear of any blood spatter. "You mean she killed herself? What's with the subjects committing suicide, anyway?"

"Above your pay grade," said Beale, still scanning the chest.

"*So, is there a fuckin' suicide chip inside me? In them?*" he demanded, pointing at the other two men.

"Not to worry, soldier. It's not the same chip," said Beale tersely.

"Why should I believe you?"

"Because I'm the goddamned director of research for NeoHappy, and I know what chips we've put in people!"

"And *you* know we mercenaries carry big damned guns and know how to use them, right?"

Beale straightened up and glared at the driver. "Okay, I'm impressed. I'll need help. Suit up. I've got to crack his chest."

"Oh, *hell,* no!" said the driver, looking over at the other two expectantly.

They both shrugged, and the mercenary who had murdered Preston said, "Dude, you're team leader. We did the kill, the extraction. We moved the body."

Their argument was interrupted by the whine of a surgical saw, which lowered in pitch as Beale forced the saw down to slice into Preston's breast bone.

Beale looked up from his task, snapping, "Okay, you want out of here on schedule, you got to get a little messy."

The driver muttered a curse, quickly donned the same garb as Beale, and pushed his way into the plastic tent. He smelled the cloying metallic-fleshy odor of blood, but he was used to that smell.

He took up a rib spreader and jammed it into the gaping incision in the corpse's chest, ratcheting it open. With the dull snap of cracking ribs, the incision into the chest cavity widened to reveal Preston's inert, pale yellow heart. Beale scanned the small box over the heart and nodded his head. "Yeah, the chip's there."

Taking up a scalpel, he quickly sliced through the arteries feeding the heart and lifted the organ out of the corpse's blood-filled chest, dropping it into a tray beside the table. Again, he used the scanner on the excised heart, now only a lump of dead muscle.

"Yup, got it." He dropped the heart into a plastic bag. Marked it with Preston's name and pitched it into a cooler, onto a pile of similar flesh-filled bags.

"Let's get him wrapped," said Beale, and he and the driver slid a body bag under the corpse, enveloped it, and zipped up the bag.

The other mercenaries had rolled the gurney into place and they quickly loaded the body into the van.

• • •

The Black Hawk helicopter was already spinning up its rotors, whipping the icy rain into a furious gale, when the van rolled up to its open passenger bay door. The two mercenaries hauled Preston's plastic-shrouded body out of the van and dumped it onto a pile of other body bags in the helicopter. They climbed in, followed by the driver, who'd parked the van near the helicopter's hangar.

Its door slid shut, and the helicopter roared into the onyx-black sky, its landing lights flashing, and swooped out over the storm-roiled waters of the Atlantic Ocean. The three men donned headsets and settled in, lounging casually against the pile of body bags. One bag shifted slightly, and the nearest man shoved it back into place.

"How far?" asked one. "This ain't exactly the most comfortable ride."

"I want to get well into the offshore currents."

"Hell, that'll take an hour!" shouted the other man.

"Yeah, well, the currents will keep the bodies from washing onshore, and we got hungry friends out there. Great Whites."

The other two settled into a bored sulk, one folding his arms for a nap on the body bags, until the sandy-haired leader slipped into a harness, clipped its safety line to a ring in the ceiling, and directed the others to do the same.

They heaved open the hovering helicopter's metal door, and rolled the nearest body to the edge. The leader raised a hand to stop their progress and hauled out a shotgun, waving the other two away. He leveled the gun at the body bag, careful to aim it out the open door. A thunderous shotgun blast rang in their ears, even over the noise of the storm and the helicopter.

"Helps them sink. Attracts the sharks," shouted the leader, motioning for the others to roll the shredded, bloody bag out the door, watching it flutter down the beam of the helicopter's searchlight into the surging sea. Eight more times shotgun-blasted bags rolled out the door, until, despite the whipping wind, the helicopter bay was filled with the organic stench of dead flesh.

Finally, they hauled up buckets of seawater, sluicing down the floor to rinse away remnants of blood and tissue, and slammed the door shut.

"Bleach the shit out of this copter when we get back," instructed the leader, giving another command to the pilot through the headset. The helicopter surged forward into a swooping turn in the pitch-dark toward the mainland.

CHAPTER 2

Brad Davis nearly collided with a matronly woman, as he walked into the glass-domed atrium lobby of the NeoHappy, Inc. headquarters. He'd been staring up at the massive, transparent globe suspended high in the three-story space, the morning light shining through it from the skylights.

The glimmering sphere was studded with long, winding filaments and pierced with apertures connecting to a maze of glass pipes and chambers. Electronic circuitry jammed the globe's interior, surrounding the chambers. A profusion of twinkling lights traced what were probably the pathways of electrons through the circuitry. The effect was of a massive, high-tech Christmas tree ornament.

So that's what a Happy Chip looks like enormously magnified, he thought. Millions and millions of people had the actual chips, each the size of a cell, injected into them. He'd studied photomicrographs of the chip when he'd explored the NeoHappy website, but this sculpture really revealed what an amazing technical achievement the nanochip was.

And just *maybe* he'd get a chance to write the biography of the scientific virtuoso who invented it! He took off his glasses and rubbed his eyes, tired from a day reading up on the company, cramming for the interview. Unfortunately, contacts irritated his eyes, so he wore rimless

glasses, which made him look like more of a geek than he really was, even given his sallow complexion, skinny frame, and somewhat out-of-control mop of reddish hair.

He announced himself to the stocky, rather intimidating receptionist sitting beneath the giant sculpture. She actually looked like a female wrestler, he thought. He wondered whether even this hulking woman ever got nervous, with the massive structure looming overhead. Seemingly at ease, though, she checked the schedule and peered at him with slightly narrowed eyes, saying with some mild reproof, "I have you down for half-an-hour from now. Is that correct?"

"Uh . . . well . . . I am a little early. I'll just sit and wait." His premature arrival made him look overeager, but he *was* eager. He noticed that the woman glanced with some unspoken signal at a hulking blue-blazered guard, who regarded him with a stern, perhaps even suspicious, stare. The atrium contained a cadre of such guards, who patrolled the long gallery.

This company employed some serious security, unlike the many other high-tech firms Brad had visited in researching his articles. He wondered why. After about twenty-five minutes, the guard approached him.

"Sir, you can go up now. You can sign in at the desk." The security man escorted him to the elevator, using a key card to access the top-floor executive offices.

As he rode up with Brad, the man stood feet-apart, hands folded in front of him, staring impassively and silently straight ahead. A bulge in his jacket told Brad the guard wore a shoulder holster.

The doors opened into a thickly carpeted foyer, where a trim, middle-aged woman sat behind a chrome-and-glass desk. Her desk sign read Irene Crawford, and lettered on the cherry paneling above her was the NeoHappy slogan, "Knowledge for the Best Life You Can Live."

The guard disappeared back into the elevator, and the woman said cheerily, "Mr. Davis, if you don't mind, Marty is running a little behind. Can you wait a moment? Can I get you something to drink? Coffee? Soft drink?"

Brad declined, fearing he would manage to spill something, he was so jittery about the meeting. He settled into one of the foyer's leather armchairs and tried to calm himself by taking the time to check his bank account on his smartphone. But that act was far from calming. The corporate PR guy still hadn't deposited the damned payment for the CEO's speech he'd ghosted. He *needed* the money. Annie wouldn't get her paycheck until next week, and there were overdue bills.

"Hi, I'm Marty," said a voice startling him. He jammed the phone into his coat pocket, looking up to see that famous, smiling, boyish face that had become nearly ubiquitous on TV and the web. He struggled to his feet and shook the hand that was offered.

"Brad Davis," he answered back, realizing that his coat and tie made him embarrassingly overdressed compared to the khakis, polo shirt, and sneakers that Fallon wore.

"C'mon in. I'm sure Jenny offered you something to drink. You sure you don't want anything? I'm having a vitamin water."

Again Brad declined, following the slightly built, multibillionaire techno-genius into a huge office strewn with papers, computer stations, and electronic parts. One wall held massive display screens, and another was covered by a shelf full of models of the company's products. He recognized some, particularly the implantable clinical blood analyzer that had launched the company.

But what surprised Brad, and slightly intimidated him, was that the office also held three other people, all with tablet computers in front of them, sitting around a large conference table.

This interview would be something of a grilling, he realized with trepidation. The three stood and introduced themselves: Mindy Carroll, a perky, animated young woman who headed corporate communications; John McClellan, the towering, balding company lawyer; and Clair Roberson, a bright-eyed, long-haired, twenty-something, who was Mindy's assistant. He only knew Carroll through the e-mails they had exchanged when she'd queried him about writing the biography.

"I've read your books, your articles. *Really* liked them," said Fallon, gesturing for Brad to sit at the head of the table and settling into one of the chairs, leaning back and propping his feet on the chair beside him. He took up a tablet computer, sliding his finger across the screen, flipping through what Brad recognized as a collection of his magazine and web pieces.

"Well, thanks," said Brad.

"I like your biography of the Harvard biologist . . . Melville. And the book on gene therapy. And the pieces for *Scientific American* and the *New York Times Magazine*. And I see from your resume you've done corporate writing."

"Speeches and so forth. Freelancers need to take all kinds of jobs to stay solvent."

"And I see you're born and bred in Boston."

"My mom calls me a Green Line baby," said Brad, referring to the Boston trolley lines that extended westward from downtown. "Born at Brigham and Women's Hospital. Grew up in Brookline. My folks lived there until they moved to California. Went to college and learned science writing at Boston University. Heck, I first met my future wife at a performance of the Newton Community Theater. She was in the cast and I met her at the cast party. And our two daughters were born at Brigham. Now we live in Newton." Brad willed himself to shut the hell up. He was rattling . . . and rattled.

"Yeah, one of my kids was born at Brigham," said Fallon. He continued swiping through document screens on the tablet. "Wow! Two tours in Afghanistan," he said.

Now Brad became less loquacious. "Yes, out of high school." A silence settled on the room. Brad didn't talk about the experience, other than to acknowledge it. He could only share details with Annie. She'd done two tours as an Army ER nurse in a forward surgical team in Afghanistan. So, only she could fully understand the soul-shaking experience. It was one of many bonds between them.

Fallon seemed to sense his reluctance to talk. "Well, thank you for your service," he said.

Brad nodded, saying nothing.

Fallon set down the tablet, took his feet off the chair and leaned forward. "So, what do you think about the project?" He gave Brad a disarmingly intense look.

Brad had read about Fallon's signature style—seemingly offhanded, but then zeroing in on a target to try to rattle them. He knew the tactic because he used a version of it in hostile interviews, to poke the interviewee to see what new facts would spill out.

"Well, it sounds really exciting, from what Mindy has told me," he said, recovering from the mention of his service.

Fallon leaned forward even more. "So, why should *you* write my biography?"

"Because I'm good." Now they were on a topic Brad was confident about. He *was* a good writer.

Fallon laughed at Brad's boast, thankfully not thinking it arrogant. "Okay, well, what if I said it's too early for me to write my memoir?"

Now Brad clicked into his freelancer's sell-the-assignment mode, another comfortable place for a writer/pitchman.

"I'd say it should be the first of several memoirs—not *the* memoir." Brad leaned forward, grinning. In addition to persuading this famous billionaire that the book should be written, he wanted to show him that this writer had done his research. "Y'know, the whole world wants to know your story. How you started grad work at MIT in nanofluidics, nanoelectronics, and molecular engineering. How you founded your company to build nanomachines at twenty-five. Then built your first nanofluidic analyzer. And how you then bet *everything you had* on the Happy Chip. And how you went round and round with the FDA about approval. I read the transcripts of the review hearings. And finally, how the chip just went viral. Y'know, by the time the book comes out, most everybody will be chipped."

Mindy chimed in. "Marty did have his doubts about the project," she said to Brad. "He's modest. But our Executive Vice President, Lawrence Lundgren, convinced him it's critical to the company. And to getting his position out there, given the critics of the chip and the controversy it caused before it was finally accepted."

"Are you chipped?" asked Fallon abruptly. Brad took it as a sign that he'd passed whatever initial test Fallon had been giving him.

"Well . . . no . . . haven't had the money or time to—"

"If you decide to take on the project, we'll chip you as part of the deal. And we'll pay for the app and Happy Ratings subscription, of course. We're all chipped here. Then you'll be able to see for yourself how . . . well . . . *happy* everybody is with their chips."

One phrase riveted Brad's attention: *"If you decide to take on the project . . ."* It triggered his internal assignment detector! Every poverty-stricken freelancer had one, and it pretty reliably detected whether an editor was about to hand out a paying assignment. Until Fallon had uttered that phrase, Brad thought he was just one of many prospects being interviewed for the gig!

"Well, sure, that would be terrific," he replied, trying to stay cool. Now Fallon had managed to rattle him, even beyond his initial jitters.

"Okay, then," said Fallon. "Let's just spend a little time making sure we're compatible. Then if we are, Mindy and John can work out contractual details."

Brad tried to tamp down his growing excitement. He took a deep breath to settle himself. He needed to ask a key question, without seeming too money-grubbing.

"Well, I do need to ask about one detail that's kind of important. The writing fee."

Brad determined not to let the lure of the project and Fallon's charisma divert him from his prime objective of thickening the thin financial ice he and his wife Annie were skating on. For too long Annie had been the chief breadwinner, with her nurse's salary and benefits. She had been more than tolerant of his love of the journalistic juggling act of freelancing—pitching editors, investigating and writing fascinating science stories; and unfortunately of waiting and *waiting* for payment. She understood his excitement at watching geneticists pinpoint a lethal cancer gene, or tracking jaguars with conservationists in Central America. But it was a financially precarious profession and brought no benefits.

"Ah, yes, the financial consideration," said Fallon, leaning back in his chair.

"Writing a book will take at least a year, probably more," declared Brad. "It's a time I almost certainly won't be doing any other projects."

Mindy tapped on her tablet screen, consulted the result and gave an answer. "I did research on the standard fees for a book like this. I talked to Lawrence . . ."

Brad steeled himself for the news that he would have to spend at least a year with little income.

Mindy continued. " . . . Fees run a max of two dollars a word. But Lawrence insisted that we make it *really* worth your while. And, he pointed out we would expect your complete commitment. So, we'll give four dollars a word. Plus expenses, of course."

Awesome! thought Brad. He struggled to keep himself from leaping up and dancing around the room. "And what length do you think?" He switched on his mental freelance income calculator.

"Oh, we're thinking a hundred thousand words . . ."

Brad's mental calculator melted! He tried to focus on the rest of what she was saying, but *Four hundred thousand dollars!* His shock meant that at first he didn't grasp the import of Carroll's recitation of the payment schedule.

". . . a hundred thousand on signing, another two hundred when you deliver a satisfactory manuscript, and the last hundred when it's published . . ."

A hundred thousand dollars up front! Brad wondered whether hugging the woman would be out of line. He wondered whether he should try to hug this Lundgren guy when he met him.

". . . and the fee's a guarantee against half the royalties."

The last word boosted his excitement even more. *Royalties!* This wouldn't be just a work-for-hire project! He'd also be a coauthor on the book contract, and the book would likely be a bestseller! And a movie!

"So, you okay with that?" asked Fallon.

"Uh . . . well . . . sure . . . that would be fine," Brad choked out.

McClellan the lawyer chimed in. "I'll have a contract drawn up. You'll want your agent or lawyer to check it over, of course. And there will be a standard nondisclosure agreement. You'll also be party to the contract with the publisher, when the bidding is over. I should mention that Marty's giving his share of the advance and his royalties to charity."

Brad restrained himself from declaring that his favorite charity would be the *Davis Family Trust for Solvency-at-Last!*

"So, let's take a walk, show you the place, have some lunch," said Fallon, standing and heading toward the door. Brad barely had time to shoo the dollar signs from his mind and follow.

• • •

As Fallon led Brad through the main corridor of the sprawling chip fabrication plant, Fallon recited the mouth-filling technical term with a prideful smile: "Nanofluidic electrodynamic opto-biosensor." No doubt he had said it countless times before, but it was his shining technical achievement. He explained the term. "That's what the 'neo' in NeoHappy stands for. It's initials. But you knew that, right?"

He stopped so they could peer through the corridor's windows into fluorescent-lit, ultraclean rooms bustling with workers shrouded in pristine white suits, masks, and caps. Some technicians stood over the beige consoles of complex nanofabrication machines, intently manipulating the controls. Others peered through microscopes examining the nanofluidic chips.

"Sure, I knew that," said Brad. "I spent quite a bit of time on your website. But I find it's always good to hear information from the original source." His voice was slightly muffled, because he and Fallon both wore masks and the other clean-room garb, even though they wouldn't be entering the labs.

"Okay, so, then you know that 'nanofluidic' means the chip contains infinitesimal pumps and chambers for circulating blood plasma into the sensors. 'Electrodynamic' means that the whole chip is powered by electricity generated by the flexing of a crystal as the blood flows past it. It's called the piezoelectric effect. And 'opto-biosensor' means the chip has sensors made of tiny lasers and biological circuits to detect and measure the blood hormones."

He continued down the corridor to the next clean room. "Here's where we fabricate the brains of the chip . . . synthetic biological analyzers made of self-assembling proteins that process those measurements and send them to a smartphone. The chip has a very cool graphene nano-antenna for transmitting, since the signals otherwise wouldn't penetrate to the surface. Once the chip is injected into somebody, the nano-antenna unfurls and self-directs itself toward the skin surface."

"Tell me about the idea for the Happy Chip," said Brad, as they strolled to the next labs. "Where did you get it? Why do you think it's important? How did it make you feel?"

These questions were a subtle test of Fallon's willingness to open up. He and Fallon were already an hour into the tour, and so far Fallon's talk had been overwhelmingly technical. He had enthusiastically spouted details of the machines and the fabrication processes.

But if Brad was to write this biography, he *really* needed to know whether Fallon would let him probe beyond the enthusiastic engineer, into the personal history and thoughts of this man whose story he was hired to tell. He was remembering a fellow science writer who'd had to return a badly needed advance, because the scientist refused to reveal his innermost thoughts.

Fallon's answer was only somewhat reassuring. "Yeah, I get you," he said, waving his hand deprecatingly. "You'll want the inside stuff. The personal stuff. We'll get to that. I'm a private guy, though, so I won't be real comfortable with it, I warn you."

Shortly, they shed their isolation suits and were sitting in the spacious atrium of the employees' cafeteria, with trays of food, and surrounded by workers having lunch. There were a few suits and ties, but the people's garb mostly reflected Fallon's casual style.

Fallon leaned forward, talking eagerly, as he ate his sandwich, periodically waving to passing workers as they greeted him.

"Okay, well, I got the idea for the Happy Chip when I was fiddling on my laptop one day, looking for something on Amazon. A book, I think. I suddenly realized *everybody* collects and analyzes data about us. Amazon, Facebook, Netflix, banks, marketers . . . everybody knows what we like, *except us!*"

He waved the sandwich in the air, dislodging a bit of lettuce. "I wondered why couldn't people collect their own data about themselves, to help them really measure what they like, what they don't like. So, I thought, 'I've got this nanoscale technology that can measure chemicals in the body, so why not hormones?' Hormone levels reflect how happy or sad or excited we are. So that was the start."

"And you ran with the idea?"

"Well, only walked at first." Fallon chuckled. "I went and talked with our engineers. I talked to a whole bunch of medical types. They all said we couldn't possibly measure hormone levels in real time. I talked to computer people. They said that getting that much data from a nanochip to a computer was a humongous problem. They all said it wasn't possible." He smiled and shook his head.

"So?"

"I decided they were wrong. So, I put everything we had into developing the Happy Chip. It had to measure and transmit data on all the relevant hormones—cortisol, adrenaline, testosterone, oxytocin, leptin, thyroid, estrogen, dopamine—all of them. Once we actually had a working prototype, that's when my engineers got all excited and started percolating ideas. We were working for days on end. My wife threatened to send in guards to drag me home to sleep. But the engineers were going nuts. They said, 'Hell, how about measuring blood pressure, heart rate and temperature?' So, we added all those measurements. We built them all into the chip. And we had physiologists figure out what we could do with the data—how we could give people a precise measure of how they felt."

"But that was just data."

"Right. Raw data doesn't help anybody. We needed an app to process it and make it useful for people. That's where Gregor Kalinsky came in. He's a software genius. Some said, 'That Russian is crazy, and don't go anywhere near him.' Others said he's shady as hell, which he is. And you never know whether he'll agree to help you or throw you out a window. But he's crazy-*smart*. So, I went to see him and didn't get thrown out a window. We put him together with the engineers and the medical people, and he came up with the Happy App."

"That's the one on your smartphone that interprets the data?"

"Yup, you'll love it! The chip has a short-range Bluetooth wireless connection to the phone. The app crunches the raw data and gives you a real-time personal measure of how much you like or don't like something. So, for example, you scan the bar code on a bottle of beer you're going to drink. You drink it, and the app gives you a score of how much you liked it, based on how much it pumps up your hormones and heart rate, and so forth. And as you try different beers, it scores which one really gives you the most pleasure. And the same goes for other products . . . songs, restaurants, even people, jobs, apartments . . . anything at all."

Brad smiled to himself in some relief. This guy would be easy to work with! He was no self-important, egotistic CEO. And he had that what-the-hell attitude that made for a fascinating character. Brad could foresee a fun, productive year interviewing Fallon, exploring the company, and writing Marty's biography.

He continued the test, quipping, "As they say in the commercials, 'But wait, there's more!' Right?"

"Oh, yeah, baby," said Fallon, high-fiving a passing employee. "Then we created the Happy Ratings service. The app draws data from the Happy Ratings database of people's physiological reactions to thousands of products and services, and it suggests what others might make you happier. Like a beer you haven't tried or a movie you didn't know about. And even people who aren't chipped can subscribe to Happy Ratings. It's so far beyond other ratings services . . . like *Consumer Reports* on steroids. It's really become the best true measure of what people like and don't like . . . better than any survey or review."

"How many people are chipped now, and how many Happy Ratings subscribers?"

"I'd say over a hundred million chipped worldwide, and maybe half-a-billion subscribers to the database."

"Wow, I had no idea."

Fallon leaned back, his smile becoming puckish. "Um . . . now on a more personal note, I'm sure you've heard of the chip's Intimate Pleasures feature."

"Uh . . . yeah . . . but I was a little reluctant to talk about—"

But Fallon wasn't reluctant. He continued. "Two people can sync their chips, so each can measure how much they like the other. It breaks down barriers between people. Hey, and if they have sex, they can measure just how much the other really enjoys a position, or a toy, or a sexy piece of clothes. When that came out, this dating service, Happy Resonance, licensed the technology. Jeez, they've already got hundreds of thousands of subscribers."

"I read on the web site that the personal uses have gone beyond sex."

"Yeah, all the media went nuts over the Intimate Pleasures feature. But last year, we started working with therapists. They're using the chip to improve treatment for depression and other mood disorders. For example, the chip tells them exactly how depressed a patient is, or how fearful. The therapist uses that to prescribe a better therapy! And the weight-loss people are using the chip to monitor hormone levels to help people stay on their diets. They can track hormones that govern hunger and fat storage and make it easier for people to lose weight. Cool, huh?"

Now, Brad had to find out how Fallon would react when he got poked a bit. "Yeah, that's the good stuff. But I also read that the feds went after you over privacy concerns."

"We took care of those." Fallon waved his hand dismissively, but smiling. "You know that Kalinsky's company is also expert on data security. So, we got his people to create security systems that keep individual data absolutely private. So the user can choose to delete the real-time readings on his device, to store them in the cloud, and/or let them feed into the anonymous Happy Ratings database. Those cloud servers use the same firewalls and security protection that the military uses. The ratings data are totally anonymized. We couldn't get hold of a particular Joe Six-Pack's data even if we wanted to. In fact, we invited white-hat hackers to try and breach the system. Nobody's done it yet!"

"But sticking a chip in people. It's invasive." It was yet another poke at Fallon, this one more provocative.

"We solved that, too," said Fallon, still smiling tolerantly. He likely knew he was being tested. "I'll give you the clinical studies we submitted to the FDA. Only after we did tons of animal studies did we go into human clinical trials. The animal studies showed that the chip has no effect on the body. It's nearly invisible to the immune system, like some viruses. But we did an even better job than nature. Our chip is enveloped in a fatty lipid layer, which our guys developed. Once the chip's injected, it just sticks benignly to a venous wall somewhere in the body and stays there."

"Okay, all this discussion is great, but you know I'll want lots more details. And I need to emphasize that this is your *biography*, not a science book, so you'll have to really open up to me. And I'll want access to the people who've influenced your life. And, of course, access to facilities and background information on the company."

"Yeah, I understand. I've had a pretty boring personal life, but you can talk to people about it. And this was only a quick look at our stuff," said Fallon, finishing the last bite of his sandwich and standing up, grinning and sticking out a hand, which Brad shook. "You'll get it all, maybe more than you want. But I'm convinced you're the one to write my story."

CHAPTER 3

Brad leaned against the lamp post outside the school, his expression changing like a partly cloudy day. First, the sun would come out; that is, he would relish the massive infusion of cash that was to come his way. Then a cloud would pass by. He would remember the old adage "If something is too good to be true, it probably is."

Yes, the money was incredible. And yes, Fallon had passed his test of being a cooperative, interesting subject.

But yes, he also had to do some necessary-but-agonizing due diligence. During a cloudy moment, he remembered the case of another fellow writer, Al Jessup. A highly reputable journalist, Jessup agreed to do a long magazine piece on an amazing new Alzheimer's drug. The piece was published and made a big splash. Then Jessup found out all the research was a hoax, to con investors. He ended up as the main subject of an expose in *The New York Times,* and a long, cautionary piece in the *Columbia Journalism Review.* Now, Jessup's career was ruined. He worked as a night copy editor for a small daily in Connecticut.

But any clouds totally evaporated at one of Brad's favorite sights—that of his bubbly little girls bursting from the school door. They brought the sunshine, the five-year-old Sarah and seven-year-old Sally.

Here they came, holding little hands as always; Sally the serious older sister helping little Sarah down the stairs. And Sarah jumping with both feet down step by step, always the little comic, wearing those ridiculous red-spangle-decorated Crocs and hilarious fluffy-dog hat. Their smiles brightened his day, as they scurried to meet him, and the group-hug was delicious. They chattered the entire walk home about their day—Sarah learning her letters, and Sally making a jungle diorama *with tigers!* Brad happily basked in the chatter; it was pure sparkling joy for his soul.

He opened the door to their small apartment very, very quietly, giving the girls an exaggerated "shhhh." The girls were fairly successful at being quiet. Sarah giggled and did her "little tiny tippy-toe" down the hall to the living room, and Sally managed to grab away Sarah's backpack before it whacked the hall table.

Quiet was necessary. Annie had come off a twelve-hour night shift at Boston General Hospital and had done the grocery shopping. She was no doubt still trying to get some sleep in, before the girls got home. And since their bedroom was just off the front entrance, the slightest noise of them coming home might wake her.

After taking off their coats, fixing the girls a snack, and settling them in to doing homework, Brad tore a page from his notebook and scribbled "ASK ME ABOUT $400,000!!!!!" on it. He folded it and got a piece of tape. He was going to tape it inside the bedroom door. But when he entered the darkened room, Annie stirred and rolled over to peer sleepily at him.

"Hey, you," she purred, pulling back her tangle of curly blond hair to reveal an oval face that looked like Sally's—her large brown eyes trying to open, to come awake. She smiled and stretched her roundly petite body beneath the sheet.

"Hey, sweetie," he whispered back. He crawled in beside her, spooning. "I've got something to wake you up."

She chuckled and snuggled back against him. "You just wait till the girls are asleep. Then I'd like very much if you would give me your wake-up."

He loved that soft, silken voice of hers. He'd first heard that voice when she sang in a performance of *Phantom of the Opera* at the Newton

Community Theater. He remembered thinking how wonderful that voice would sound singing lullabies to children.

Smiling at the memory, he swept her hair away from the back of her neck and kissed it, breathing in her warm, delicious aroma. With difficulty, he brought himself back to the great news at hand.

"Actually, you'll want this wake-up now. Read this." He held the note in front of her, and she unfolded it and squinted to read by the light from the open doorway. It took a moment for the sentence to register. When it did, she executed a vigorous bounce on the bed to turn to face him, eyes wide.

"*What!? Ask you about four hundred thousand dollars!?*" She read the note again. "Okay, Bradley, what about four hundred thousand dollars?"

"I got the NeoHappy book assignment! And that's the fee! And we get a hundred thousand dollars advance!"

"*Holy sh . . .*" she started to say, then remembered they had made a pact to watch their language for the girls' sake. "*Cow! Cow! Cow!*" she shouted, kissing him hard.

She leaped from the bed and into the bathroom. As she washed her face and slipped on her robe, he began excitedly spouting the details of his interview, and tour and lunch with Fallon. He decided to save the cloudy part for later. He dearly wanted to give them a rare moment of pure joy and celebration.

They hurried down the hall, to try to explain "Daddy's amazing new job" to the girls. Sarah and Sally didn't exactly understand, but they knew that Mommy and Daddy were very, very happy.

That night they celebrated with a rare dinner out, at the Super 88 oriental market food court, their favorite. The market's cavernous interior—lined with cluttered family-run food stalls and spartan tables and chairs—was comfortably homey. But the place boasted the best, cheapest oriental food around. As the girls attacked heaping plastic containers of lo mein, Brad and Annie continued to talk about the project and how it would advance his career and shore up their precarious finances.

The celebration was helping to evaporate Brad's worries about the need for checking the company out. After all, this was NeoHappy,

Inc., for God's sake. There was absolutely no possibility of fraud here. Given how intense the media coverage had been, one of the phalanx of hard-nosed reporters covering the company would have ferreted it out.

It was Annie who expressed the first doubt, but not about the company.

"They're going to chip you?" she asked dubiously, brow furrowing.

"Well, yeah, it's so I can see what's great about the Happy Chip. It'll be fine. I'd always thought about us doing it, anyway, if we ever had the money."

"Us?"

"You've seen all the articles about how in synch couples get once they're both chipped." He grinned with only a hint of a suggestive leer.

"In synch. Well . . ." She trailed off, screwing up her delicate features and cocking her head back and forth in her trademark I'm-not-so-sure expression. He recognized it from when he declared he wanted to take up scuba diving. She'd been proven right when he got a severe sinus infection just taking the scuba pool course.

"Millions of people—" he began.

"I want to see the clinical data," she interrupted. "I've heard about the studies, the FDA approval, the raves. But I want to see what the studies have said."

"You don't want somebody with more expertise to check it out?" he asked.

He immediately cringed. He'd made a serious tactical error. She wanted to become just such an expert. She wanted to earn a doctoral degree and become a nurse practitioner, but when they got married out of college and Sally came along, she decided being an RN was a more financially logical choice. He tried to recover.

"It'll be your call," he said. "I'll get you all the data. We won't make a decision until you're happy about this. But, you know that if I don't get chipped, that's kind of a sign I'm not really committed to the project."

"I get that," she said tersely. "But I just want to make sure."

He put his arm around her. "This could make some big changes in our lives. You could get into Boston General's doctoral program. We could look for a house."

She smiled tolerantly at her overeager husband. "You know I'll still like you a little bit if you go ahead with the chipping," she joked. "And, yes, you *know* how much I've wanted to be a nurse practitioner."

At that, they postponed further discussion. The girls needed help counting how many of the coveted, super-tender dumplings they had left and dividing them up equally. Brad liked to test their arithmetic by trying to give himself an extra dumpling or two, but the indignant girls called him on it every time.

By now, he had dismissed the due-diligence cloud. And Annie would take care of any remaining cloud about the chip itself. The sun had come out to stay.

CHAPTER 4

Whoa!, Brad breathed to himself, as he walked out of the NeoHappy lawyer John McClellan's office, slightly overwhelmed, clutching a hefty pile of documents. The balding vest-suited lawyer, sitting behind his massive walnut desk, had loaded Brad with a thick employee manual, a freelance writing contract, a nondisclosure agreement, and a sample publishing contract.

The sample contract was solid evidence that McClellan expected a heated bidding war by publishers for the book, and that McLellan and Fallon would try to pretty much dictate the terms of the resulting contract. Brad mused on the fact that, for such a laid-back wunderkind, Marty Fallon had hired some pretty aggressive executives.

Those executives included communication director Mindy Carroll, who walked beside him, ticking off Brad's immediate future schedule.

"Once you've signed the writing contract and NDA, we'll issue you an electronic badge, with appropriate access," she said. "We'll get you an account on the company's internal intranet, and we'll also put you through the standard orientation we give new employees. And we'll work out an interview schedule with Marty. Oh yeah, and we'll get you chipped."

"Sounds great, but if you don't mind, I'll need some things," said Brad. The due-diligence cloud had reappeared over the last few days, although it was now only a wisp of its former self. "I'll need time to absorb these documents and get a lawyer to look at them. And I'd like the scientific papers and FDA submissions on the chip. Before I get chipped, I need to understand more about the technology and its impacts."

"Sure, sure, of course," said Carroll. "We'll give you full access to all the documents you need. There's a little caveat, though. But it shouldn't be a problem for you, since of course you're writing Marty's biography and not so much a company profile. We'll have to limit your access to technical reports and data on our future technology and products. We can't let you see proprietary data, and so forth. But, like I said, that should be no big deal. It's just technical details on new chip technology. And Marty will give you an overview of where the company is going."

The cloud thickened slightly. Brad didn't like clients to keep secrets. True, they were trade secrets that companies had good reason to keep. And he was still pretty comfortable with the deal. But he decided that he would keep his investigative reporter's antennae fully deployed, to detect anything that seemed hinky.

• • •

Lawrence Lundgren fixed his glare on the white-coated Thomas Beale, as he commanded, "Look, you need to find out quick what the hell went wrong with these chips and how to fix it!"

Lundgren looked distinctly out of place among the white-coated scientists, in his bespoke pinstripe suit with the wine-colored silk tie and light blue shirt. His six-foot-two height, meticulously coiffed silver hair and permanent, slightly disdainful expression also gave him a natural ability to intimidate people, which he used to good effect.

To Beale's deep annoyance, Lundgren had showed up unannounced in the equipment-crowded laboratory and inserted himself into the group observing the dissection of James Preston's heart.

Beale, the research team leader, was not ready to tolerate Lundgren's bullshit. He was bone-tired after dissecting nine murdered corpses the night before and then laboriously taking down the makeshift autopsy tent and scrubbing away all traces of the blood-soaked dissections.

"Larry, here's the deal . . ." said Beale, slicing into the pale muscle of the lifeless heart. " . . . It'll take several days to surgically extract the subjects' chips and their sequestration chambers, even with all of us working on them. A week to run diagnostics, and a *year* to carry out simulations and analysis."

Guided by the radio-frequency scanner, Beale pinpointed and carved out a tiny sliver of Preston's coronary artery and moved it from the scanner to a microscope. Placing the sliver on the microscope stage, he dialed up the magnification. The microscope's monitor screen showed a string of tiny globular chips clinging to the artery wall. The nanospheres looked like opalescent pearls attached to the smooth surface.

Lundgren loomed impatiently over him. "Well, at least tell me how we can possibly move forward with the second-generation system!"

Beale didn't answer, as he intently tweaked the micromanipulator joystick to bring its tiny pincers to clasp the nanospheres and transfer them to a petri dish. When finished, he coldly regarded Lundgren.

"Oh, what the hell," he said resignedly. "Might as well go ahead and test the version two chips with GPS. We're fairly sure we understand the malfunctions in these chips, just from the telemetry data."

Beale stood back and motioned for the other scientists to crowd in for a better look at the screen. He said to them, "Okay, that shows you the general extraction procedure. Divide up the other tissue samples and do the same. Let me know if you have problems."

"You're fairly sure you understand?!" exclaimed Lundgren, clutching Beale's arm and guiding him away from the group. "We've got nine dead subjects . . . a tenth if we find the Kelley woman. God damn, she was the *worst* one we could have possibly lost! A company employee! And even losing her, you still want to go ahead with another trial based on a '*fairly sure*'?"

Beale yanked his arm away. The stooped, balding man was the antithesis of Lundgren, a head shorter and with a permanent hangdog expression on his thin, middle-aged face. But he was not intimidated by the imposing Lundgren.

"Fairly sure is all we've got now, *Larry*." He uttered Lundgren's nickname with barely disguised exasperation. "Yeah, we do need to go immediately to a new clinical trial. You know animals won't work. And we still have to do covert human trials, to ensure the system works before we applied to the FDA. And we agreed that this is a *hundred-billion-dollar* bet worth making."

"If you'd had the GPS tracking chip in the first prototype, we'd have located all the live subjects. And as for the ones who committed suicide—we could have gotten to them early enough to extract their chips."

"You know goddamned well the GPS circuit wasn't ready." Beale's jaw tightened. He'd had about enough of this abrasive pain in the ass.

"And what about deniability?"

"You've got deniability, *Larry*. There's no records linking you to this. And confidentiality is guaranteed. The team here is solid. They know what would happen if they leaked anything about the testing. The Coronado Security field group is also solid. They get paid to keep their mouths shut. You just worry about the funding, okay?"

Lundgren nodded. "We're good on funding. I've got five corporate data contracts in place and more coming. And I've got a big operational contract."

"Operational? What the hell does that mean?"

"You'll know when you need to."

"Well, then if you're going to stonewall, get the hell out of my laboratory," spat Beale, turning back to the researchers.

CHAPTER 5

"**D**o you really *have* to track the injection?" asked Brad clenching his fists as he lay on the clinic table, watching the technician prepare the chip injector.

"Yup, we need to know where it goes," said the dark-haired young woman, carefully lowering the combination ultrasound scanner/chip injector onto Brad's arm. "We want to make sure it's in a vein to accurately measure hormone levels, blood pressure, and so forth."

Despite the technician's merry chatter, Brad still tensed. After all, his arm was strapped to an extension jutting from the table. However, the "Happy Chamber," as it was labeled, did feel like a happy place, decorated in bright colors and with piped-in upbeat tunes—currently Johnny Nash's "I Can See Clearly Now."

Peering at the ultrasound scanner screen, the technician continued.

"We've done a zillion of these. I know the whole thing looks a little intimidating, but we just want to ensure the chip stays in the venous system."

"And if it doesn't?"

"Oh, the chip is harmless wherever it ends up. If we get a rare misplacement, we just inactivate the chip's transmitter and go again with another chip. Your vein is looking good, here. See?" She pointed to the scanner's screen showing the black-and-white image of Brad's arm, his vein registering in stark white.

"And where does it go in the vein?"

"Actually, just about anywhere. It doesn't really matter. It just attaches itself wherever it finds a vessel wall—usually in the arm, and that's fine. Okay, just relax. You won't even feel it. We're up to . . . I think . . . one hundred and thirty-four million chips implanted. And we've never had a client even wince."

"Well, my wife read all the scientific papers, the FDA reports, and so forth. And she said it looked okay."

She smiled as she positioned the injection needle. "Oh, you'll find the chip to be more than okay!" She patted his arm and tapped the screen on the light blue console. Even though Brad's arm had been rubbed with local anesthetic, he felt a touch of pressure. On the ultrasound screen, the tiny dark line of the injector needle entered the image for a moment, then withdrew.

"Done!" exclaimed the technician! "Your chip's in there, right where we want it to be." She turned to the computer console, watching a series of colored bars pop up on its screen. "And *voila*, it's turned itself on and it's transmitting. Want to see something cool?"

The technician moved the injector aside, unstrapped Brad's arm, pressed on a Band-Aid and helped him sit up. She touched an icon on the screen that said "Anxiety Amplitude" and a bar graph popped up, labeled "medium-high."

"That's how nervous I am?"

"Yeah, right now. But just watch yourself relax," she said. Shortly, the bar began to lower, its label changing to "medium," then to "medium-low," then to "low."

"So, that's me relaxing?"

"What's especially cool is that when people see this bar start to go down, it relaxes them even more, making the bar go even lower. Chippers have found this a great way to calm themselves down after a tough day."

"So I'm a *chipper* now," chuckled Brad, rubbing the bandage, then rolling down his sleeve.

"Yup, you're officially a Happy Chipper. Let me have your smartphone, and I'll download the Happy App and activate it. And I'll send the registration information to your e-mail address, along with a link to the online tutorial and instruction manual. I tell ya, you're gonna have a ball with this thing!"

Brad handed over his phone, and the technician fiddled with it for a few minutes, then handed it back. On the menu screen was a new happy-face icon in the company's sky-blue color.

"There ya go. I'd suggest you go through the quick-start procedure, and just play with it. Then you should take the tutorial. The default settings and displays are good, but you'll no doubt want to customize it. The website has a blog and discussion board where people talk about their mods to the system. That's really fun to explore."

She shook Brad's hand and gave him a pat on the back as he headed out the door, his head down, poking at the phone's screen to learn about the hormonal ebb and flow that the chip was reporting from his own body.

The technician made sure he had left the floor. Her smile faded. She returned to the console screen, pressing an icon to bring up a new registration menu. She touched a link that read "NeoHappy Chip, Enhanced version 2.1." After a moment, messages appeared:

"Control interface complete."

"Remote signal strength optimum."

"GPS data acquired."

Moving to a laptop, she brought up a map with a moving red dot that was just leaving the clinic building. She moved the cursor over the dot, and a small window popped up that said "Davis, Bradley." She pulled back to a larger map view, showing a number of red dots moving about the area.

The newest NeoHappy experimental subject had just been recruited.

• • •

"Holy Moley!" Brad sat at his kitchen table, his laptop open, staring unbelieving at the screen. The NeoHappy people moved fast! His bank account showed $100,434.00! He smiled and shook his head. Thanks to the NeoHappy deposit, their account had just gone from a measly $434.00, indicating their paycheck-to-paycheck financial status, to *hot-damn-we-got money* status.

He took out his smartphone, deciding whether to text Annie first or check his hormone levels on the Happy App. Annie, now working a day shift, came first. He sent the message, "We're in the money! $100K in the bank!" She didn't reply immediately, probably busy with patients.

Then he brought up the Happy App to find that his Anxiety Amplitude had dropped to Low, his Pleasure Measure was moving up, and his blood pressure was trending downward. He smiled. Just looking at those numbers did, indeed, make him more relaxed and . . . hey . . . *happier!*

Two days earlier, Annie had spent hours poring over the scientific papers and FDA submissions for the chip. Finally she had sighed, given him a long wrinkled-brow look and shaken her head and said, "Okay. Go ahead. I'll worry, but then I guess that's what I do."

Her brow relaxed, however, when they got the good news from their publishing lawyer, Alan Benson.

"Yeah," he pronounced decisively. "They've really done right by you." They'd met with Benson in his cluttered office in a high-rise downtown. He had delivered a positive verdict on both the freelance contract and the nondisclosure agreement. Benson was also happy that Brad would be a full-fledged coauthor—with the cover reading "by Martin Fallon and Bradley Davis," rather than billed as merely an "also with Bradley Davis."

So, Brad had signed the contracts, delivered them, and gotten chipped the same day.

And now his family was, for the first time, financially secure.

• • •

An hour later, Brad stood eagerly in the long ordering line at the renowned Barry's Village Deli in Newton.

After the terrific news about their bank account, he'd tried to get down to work, compiling background on Fallon and NeoHappy, Inc. But that effort lasted exactly twenty minutes. He was too buzzed to sit at a computer and also far too curious about the functioning of that microscopic chip that now rested somewhere in his body.

After all, this would be research. And after all, he was hungry. And after all, he'd always assumed that Barry's luscious, toasted Reuben sandwich was the best sandwich ever.

He'd worked through the online tutorial and knew the basics of how to operate the Happy App, so he was ready to roll . . . or rather nosh.

Standing at the counter, he entered the diner's name and address, and recorded his order, a Reuben sandwich. Clutching the fragrant bag, he hurried home and popped open an ice cold bottle of his favorite beer, Sam Adams OctoberFest. He scanned the bar code on the bottle as the tutorial directed, and took a drink of the cold tingly brew. Now would begin the long, dedicated process of trying all of Sam Adams brews, to discover his favorite. Or, whether there might be another beer out there that was better.

Now for a bite of sandwich, with its perfect mélange of tender pastrami, melted Swiss cheese, and tart sauerkraut, all slathered with homemade Russian dressing—the delightful concoction barely constrained between two slices of crisp grilled rye. *Yum!*

Propping his smartphone in front of him, he watched with fascination the up-and-down movement of the colored bars labeled "Pleasure Measure," "Satisfaction Action," and other hormonally driven gauges of his reaction to the beer and sandwich. It was so weird to actually see what was going on inside his body at that very moment! He took another healthy bite of the sandwich and watched the bars adjust their height to reflect his enjoyment.

And then a swig of beer, to see the resulting measure.

Finishing the sandwich, he downed the last swig of beer and pressed an icon labeled "Assess."

"Moderate enjoyment of beer. Extreme enjoyment of pastrami sandwich," reported the Happy App. "For recommendations, press 'Make me Happier.'" He touched the appropriate icon and got the Happy Ratings listing of other delis to try, other pastrami sandwiches, other beers.

Cool! he thought. The Happy Ratings were drawn from the massive database on similar measurements from thousands of other area Happy Chippers who'd tried the same foods and beers.

A recommendation popped up that another Boston deli might have a better sandwich—although he doubted it. He scrolled down to a list of other recommended brands of beer. Other Sam Adams brews were there, as he expected, but there were also other brands.

And not only would the app enable him to find the perfect pastrami sandwich for him, and the perfect beer, but just about the perfect *everything*. Over the next weeks, he resolved to capture data on many other experiences in his life, and see where the infinitesimal chip clinging to a venous wall somewhere in his body would lead him.

Ah, what a long and happy process he would undertake in his quests for perfection!

CHAPTER 6

"Hey, you found the place!" exclaimed Marty Fallon, as he opened the door to the massive Georgian-style mansion and thrust out his hand.

Brad shook the hand in relief. He'd been lost until only minutes ago and feared missing this critical first appointment.

He hadn't even been sure he had "found the place" until he saw the sign on the imposing wrought-iron gate warning that trespassers would be arrested and prosecuted. Then the blue-blazered, stone-faced guard confirmed that it was the Fallon estate, as Brad had shown his ID and waited for a thorough search of his embarrassingly road-sand-scarred old Subaru.

"You gave good directions," he told Fallon. "And it was the only place for a mile." Brad had tried to gauge the size of the colonnaded brick mansion. He wanted to describe to Annie how a billionaire lived. But he'd given up guessing how big the house was, with its multistory central house and side wings.

"Yeah, I like the privacy," said Fallon, leading him into the two-story entry hall. "Lisa found the place. It's surrounded by conservation land. She did a whole bunch of restoration on the house and gardens and convinced the landowners around here to sell us more land. C'mon and meet her. She's eager to see you."

They walked down a long hallway, and Brad realized that the mansion was even larger than it seemed from the front. They hiked back through a wing that extended out the back as long as the side wings. Finally, they arrived at a large, sunny, glassed-in garden room. Its colorful confusion of orchids and other flowers gave the room a delicious, sweet fragrance. A trim young woman dressed in jeans and a t-shirt knelt on the tiled floor, digging away in a huge flower pot with a trowel.

"And this is my lovely, brilliant, Harvard-educated wife playing in the dirt!" announced Marty grandly.

"*Sweetheart*," scolded the woman with mock annoyance. "You just had to wait until I was up to my elbows in gardening. And it's not dirt, it's soil!" She stood smiling, pulled off a glove and shook his hand. "I'm Lisa. Please write that my husband invents interesting gadgets but doesn't know the difference between dirt and soil."

"Oh, good, I've just started the project, and I've already got dirt," quipped Brad.

They chatted amiably for a while about the house and its elegant gardens; then Lisa walked with them back through the central part of the house, where Brad met their two children, Mary, 7, and Kevin, 10, both wearing soccer uniforms. Lisa bid goodbye as she shepherded the children out the front door and to a waiting SUV.

Brad thought it rather incongruous that the literally down-to-earth Lisa and the busily chattering children climbed into a large, black SUV accompanied by a military-looking sandy-haired man in a sports jacket that opened briefly to reveal a glimpse of a pistol in a shoulder holster. He closed the SUV door, glancing at Brad with a cool, appraising look. His muscular build and stubbled face looked out of place in the homey, family setting.

"Is he a bodyguard?" Brad couldn't resist asking. "I noticed you had security at the gate, too."

"Yeah, it's a shame we have to do that. But our security director recommended it when we got threats from some nuts who think the chip is a Big Brother kind of thing. We had already convinced the FDA and the public that it wasn't, but no amount of data will satisfy a paranoiac. I thought the security was overkill." Fallon smiled, embarrassed. "Gee, I guess that's not an appropriate word. Anyway, Lawrence insisted on hiring this outside firm that also does foreign security work. Lots of ex-military guys."

They entered Fallon's study, which like his office was dominated by a wall of computer displays, shelves of books, and a desk overflowing with papers and electronic paraphernalia.

Switching on his digital recorder, Brad began the first of what he expected would be dozens of interviews. This was just a scouting expedition. The deeper explorations of Fallon's past would take place over the next year. So he started by asking general questions about Fallon's upbringing and education, and who else he should talk to in Fallon's past.

"Well, fortunately, just about everybody you'll want to talk to is out here. I did undergrad at Harvard, where I met Lisa. Did grad work at MIT. My folks are in Connecticut. Dad's an engineer and Mom's an art historian at Yale. My brother is in New York, a lawyer. And my sister is in Philly, a pediatrician."

"Shoot, and I hoped to get to travel worldwide," said Brad.

"Oh, you will. Quite a bit. At some point, I've got to go to China and the Far East. We're looking at manufacturing and marketing out there. The flight time is a good chance to talk uninterrupted."

After other discussion of his personal background, the talk then turned to the company facilities Brad should tour.

"Well, you should talk to Lawrence," said Fallon. "He can get you wherever you need to go, to see how the company runs. I should tell you he's a pretty security-conscious guy about that kind of thing, and I understand that. There will be places that he'll put off-limits, just because there's proprietary stuff going on."

"If I'm going to really capture the full scope of the company, I should know everything," said Brad. This was a push-back he had to make, to establish that he had necessary requirements to do a credible job. Fallon grew quiet, his expression serious. Brad sensed a tension that hadn't been there before.

"Nevertheless . . ." began Fallon, but he didn't finish the sentence.

CHAPTER 7

Brad stood up with a puzzled shrug behind the desk of the small office he'd been assigned in the basement of the NeoHappy main building.

"Jeez, I'm so glad you're here," he said to the chunky, curly-headed technician who'd arrived at his door. "I rebooted three times, and I tried fiddling with the network settings, but I just couldn't get my laptop into the network." He backed away and let the tech take his place at the desk.

"No problem. There's some security settings you don't know about." He launched into rapid-fire typing with stubby, nail-bitten fingers on the keyboard.

"You handle the network?" asked Brad, making small talk.

The man smiled through a thick bush of a beard. "Yeah, well, I do more than that. The guys at the top said you get special service, so I came on over."

"So, they gave me a big gun."

"Well, sometimes I feel like a starter pistol. Yeah, I run the IT department. Head tech geek. Jim Bell," he said reaching out his meaty hand, his eyes darting back to the screen. Brad shook it, and moved to look over Bell's shoulder at a cascade of indecipherable computer commands resulting from Bell's typing.

"Okay, I may need you a lot," said Brad. "I'll be doing a bunch of library data searches for the book. They also want me to enter my schedule in the online calendar, so they can arrange interviews with Fallon and other people. And it looks like you know your way around the system."

"Book? Fallon?" asked Bell, his eyes still on the screen. "Are you a big-time writer or something?"

"Or something. I'm writing Marty Fallon's biography with him."

Bell stopped typing and looked up at Brad, his eyes widening.

"Wow! That'll be a trip!"

He resumed his rapid-fire typing, and finally leaned back in triumph as the NeoHappy logo—a traditional happy face made from electronic parts—appeared on the screen.

"Tell you what," he said. "I'll buy you a beer, and you tell me all about this book. And then you buy me a beer for fixing your connection."

"Deal," declared Brad. This was a golden opportunity to connect with somebody who knew the inner workings of NeoHappy perhaps better than anyone.

So that evening after dinner with Annie and the girls, Brad found himself sitting in a booth in a noisy, somewhat funky bar in a strip mall near the company headquarters. Bell had brought along two other techs. Freddie was a muscular crew-cut young man, who looked like he'd be at home in a gym full of iron-pumpers; Brendan was his antithesis, a gaunt-faced young man whose skinny arms had never seen a weight heavier than a computer mouse.

Brad took a sip of his complimentary beer and was peppered with the expected questions about doing the biography of their boss:

How would he keep up with the high-energy Fallon? *With difficulty.*

How would he do interviews? *Whenever Fallon had spare moments, meaning that Brad would have to always be on-deck with questions.*

Was it hard to be a freelance writer? *Yes, sometimes like juggling chainsaws and bowling balls.*

They didn't have to ask what Fallon was like. They said they saw him often, and they had all been to his mansion. Fallon held the annual summer office picnic there.

Then, Brad bought the second round, and it was his turn to ask questions. He tried his best to remember the answers, to transcribe later for his notes.

What was it like to work at NeoHappy? *Pretty damned good! Actually, well . . . happy!*

What did he need to know about Fallon that he might not already? *Fallon loves to tinker with toy robots and hobby drones, even though he is a genius at nanofluidics, nanoelectronics, and molecular engineering. The techs chuckled at the memory of walking down the hall, to be buzzed by one of Fallon's quadcopters, zooming overhead on a preprogrammed flight.*

After nearly an hour of back-and-forth, Brad posed what he thought was a routine question. But Bell's guarded answer triggered his reporter's investigative instinct.

He asked, "Given that NeoHappy is such a massive tech company, I'll bet it's got a massive computer network."

"Well, we've got two big server farms, and three supercomputers about as powerful as ones at the national labs," said Bell. "But that's not counting the shadow network . . ." he stopped abruptly, seeming to realize he had said something he shouldn't have. He took a silent drink of his beer, as did the other two techs. Brad recognized a pregnant pause, after experience with hundreds of interviews for freelance articles, even when camouflaged by beer.

"Shadow network?" Brad let the silence linger—a reporter's trick. It generally led people to reveal more than they normally would.

"Uh . . . yeah," said Bell. "We're not supposed to talk about it, but I suppose since you're working for Marty. For particularly sensitive work, the company runs an isolated shadow network with no connections to the outside world."

"Sensitive work?" Again, Brad let silence draw answers out of the techs.

"Well . . . there's labs that are doing proprietary high-risk, high-reward stuff," said Bell, shifting his bulk nervously. "Corporate spies would love to get their hands on it. And they'd love to launch cyberattacks."

"And you're not involved at *all?* The chief IT guy?"

Bell shrugged. Freddie and Brendan took yet another long drink of their beers and gave each other nervous glances that said *we'd better keep our mouths shut.*

40

But Bell continued on. "They hired a guy who'd run secure systems at the CIA Office of Technical Services. I only met him once, when I was one of those interviewing him for the job a couple of years ago. He sometimes e-mails me with questions about our server system."

"So, there's no connections between the systems at all?"

Freddie let out an inadvertent chuckle, and Bell gave him a cautionary look. "Well, Freddie swears that there's back-door access going on to our system, like tapping into our databases. But we never could find any hard evidence."

The techs quickly changed the subject, falling to a discussion among themselves of some arcane technical problem they were having. Brad took it as a sign that he should finish his beer and leave. He said his goodbyes, and Bell and the techs gave him an amicable toast as a sendoff. He'd enjoyed the evening and the company, and Bell would be an incredibly helpful ally in his work on the book.

He arrived home, only slightly inebriated, to find Annie in her robe, reclining on the couch in their tiny living room, intent on her laptop screen. He lifted her legs, sat down and draped them over his lap, beginning a foot rub.

"Girls asleep?"

"Uh huh," she said absently, still scrutinizing the laptop. Then, "Oooh, feels nice," she said of the foot rub.

"You look serious."

"Okay," she answered decisively, snapping the laptop shut.

"Okay what?"

"Okay, I'll get chipped. I've gone over all the research on the chip. Clinical trials, papers, media articles. It looks like a thing that's useful and safe. And even fun."

"Cool!" exclaimed Brad. He pulled out his smartphone to show her the features of his Happy App. He displayed the continually shifting bar graphs showing his real-time hormone measurements. They registered that he was very excited, but also relaxed. "I've been feeling great since I got the chip, and sleeping like a baby," he declared.

He realized with some surprise how true those statements were. He hadn't really thought about it. Then, he grinned eagerly, like the tipsy, young husband that he was.

"Let's start with the sex app!"

• • •

"Okay, you should meet the most important guy in the company . . . ," said Fallon the next day, ". . . besides me, of course!" They had just wrapped up a quick interview session, on Fallon's early childhood, and Fallon led Brad down the long hall of the executive floor. They reached an outer office richly furnished with impressionist paintings, oak-paneled walls, a thick teal-blue carpet, and plush armchairs. The office was also decorated with a stunning administrative assistant who displayed the cheekbones, blond hair, blue eyes, and professional makeup of a *Vogue* cover girl. She smiled a modulated smile, showing perfect white teeth.

"He's waiting for you," she said.

"Great," said Fallon, turning to Brad. "Lawrence Lundgren basically shepherds our products from lab to factory. He came here just before we introduced the first Happy Chip. He's been in the business a long time. So I think he can give you both an outsider's *and* an insider's perspective on the company and its history."

They entered Lundgren's office, whose interior matched the richly furnished decor of the foyer. Lundgren rose from the French antique desk. He also fit with the elegant decor, dressed in a tailored dark blue cashmere suit, light gray shirt and royal blue tie.

Brad and Lundgren shook hands, and Lundgren settled into one of two wingback armchairs across from a brocade couch. The office was a stark contrast to Fallon's cluttered tech-stuffed office, Brad noted.

"Call me Lawrence," Lundgren said upon the introductions, nodding amiably as Fallon described the book project.

With a wave, Fallon departed, leaving Brad and Lundgren to talk.

"So, I'm glad they took my counsel and put you on the project," said Lundgren, as the receptionist appeared carrying a coffee tray. Brad noted the fine China cups and silver coffee service, a contrast to Fallon's coffee maker and ubiquitous insulated coffee mug.

Brad suppressed a surprised look. "Oh . . . well . . . thank you. I didn't know—"

"I was in the initial meetings when Mindy proposed the project. Marty had some doubts. But I felt that a responsibly done biography of him would be important historically." Lundgren leaned forward and took a sip of his coffee. "A *responsibly* done biography," he reiterated with emphasis. "One that highlights Marty Fallon's absolutely central role in the success of this company and its current and future products."

"Well, I think my work speaks to my credibility," said Brad. "And I certainly will do my very best," He felt an indefinable undercurrent in the conversation that made him mildly uneasy.

"Very good," replied Lundgren. "I should add that I wanted to ensure the full commitment and attention of the coauthor. So, when they said they wanted to pay the usual rate for such projects, I insisted that such a rate was inadequate, given what we wanted to achieve."

Right! This guy was responsible for the windfall fee! Brad remembered. But given that Lundgren appeared to be a coolly pragmatic businessman, he must want something, thought Brad. The phrase "quid pro quo" came to mind. But he couldn't put his finger on the "quid" part—what Lundgren might expect of him, other than the best book possible.

"Well, I certainly will make every effort to justify your confidence," he said. "And I deeply appreciate your going to bat for the fee."

Lundgren waved his hand dismissively, as if the amount was but a minor expense. *A business expense*, thought Brad. He felt a little relieved. Corporate types thought nothing of spending big on marketing and advertising. Lundgren probably just considered this a blip in the marketing budget. It was nothing compared to, say, a Super Bowl commercial. So, he put his doubts aside and launched into his interview mode.

"If you don't mind, I'd like to have a bit of an initial interview," he said. "Tell me about Marty and how he brought you to the company."

Lundgren gave forth a self-satisfied smile, leaned back and took a sip of coffee. "I was, as you may know, heavily involved in management positions at several major consumer electronics companies," said Lundgren, going on to describe at length his work at a string of international corporations.

Brad—having prepared himself by reading Lundgren's resume—decided not to ask why he appeared to have hopped from company to company for some two decades. However, Lundgren continued to expound, giving himself glowing reviews at the companies, explaining why he had been such a catch for NeoHappy.

"So, Marty felt it was time for the company to bring someone like you in?" asked Brad.

"Oh, yes. He knew that NeoHappy had an incredible product, and that there would be a massive demand. And he needed somebody to build the manufacturing and distribution infrastructure. And that was me," he said, finishing his coffee. The conversation continued as Lundgren told how he had built NeoHappy from "basically a few very smart people with a revolutionary product" to "a major technological powerhouse."

"And you're responsible for product development?"

"Yes, under Marty's direction, of course. He's the inspiration for all that we do. But I manage the systematic process of taking his ideas and moving it through preclinical animal testing. And then to clinical safety testing, clinical effectiveness testing, FDA approval, and transition to manufacturing as a perfected product."

"And what's in the pipeline for the Happy Chip?"

"Oh, Marty has us doing just incremental improvements now," he said, waving a manicured hand, displaying a large gold ring and an elegant Patek Philippe watch. "Tweaking the chip a bit here and there. We've got to make sure the system is as safe and effective for the consumer as possible before we try any quantum jumps in technology. *Safe and effective.* Those are our watchwords."

CHAPTER 8

"*W*ow!" whispered Annie in the darkness of their bedroom.

"*Double Wow!*" answered Brad.

"Um . . . actually triple," she replied, smiling.

They lay in a delicious, naked embrace, each using one hand to softly stroke the other's skin. In the other hand, each held a smartphone, peering at the screens in rapt fascination.

They kissed softly, then more deeply, still eying the screens that graphically and colorfully registered the hormonal signature of their rising passion. The red Pleasure Measure bars rose inexorably, and the throbbing heart icons on the screen increased in speed. A small blue graph registered rising blood pressures.

With two days off, Annie had gotten chipped that morning and spent the time until Brad came home taking the tutorial. With the girls *finally* in bed, they had shut and locked the bedroom door and activated the Intimate Pleasures function of their Happy Chips.

"*Ooo . . . good . . . better . . . best!*" Annie had whispered, as Brad had found the right spot with his roaming fingers. Sure enough, the bar graph on her smartphone screen registered rising pleasure.

"Let's turn on the audio indicators," murmured Brad. "We won't have to look at the screens." And so they did. Both phones began to emit low tones registering their pleasure levels, the tones increasing in pitch as their pleasure rose.

Annie began to give Brad a special treat, making his pleasure tone—as well as a key anatomical structure—rise quickly.

"Gee, I didn't know how much you liked that," she whispered from below. He nodded enthusiastically, and they shifted positions to offer mutual pleasure.

That night, they explored and experimented for hours, the chip data revealing more than they had ever known about each other's sexual preferences and needs.

And they "pegged the meter" three times, as Annie so aptly put it, finally lying, freshly showered, in exhausted, satisfied embrace.

The next morning Brad padded into the kitchen to find Annie sitting at the kitchen table, sipping her coffee, smiling serenely. The girls were already up, eating their cereal, which Annie had fixed, floating dreamily through the task.

"Hi, husband," she said.

Brad sighed. "Hi, wife. I slept!"

"Me, too. Gooood sleep!" They kissed.

"Well, I sure didn't," grumped Sally, slurping a spoonful of cereal. "What was that music?"

"Uh . . . music?" asked Brad.

"Yeah, *music!* Kept us awake."

Little Sarah sat back from her cereal and demonstrated—starting with a low tone moving up the scale to a high squeal. "Oooooooooaaaaaaaeeeee!"

Brad rubbed his hand over his mouth to keep from laughing. He gave Annie a wide-eyed look. She would have to try to explain this away.

"Uh, sweetie, that was an . . . um . . . ah . . . uh—"

"*Radio* that we had on," Brad said, recovering his composure. "We'll turn it down from now on."

"Pretty weird music," declared Sally, wagging her spoon in the air expressively.

• • •

"Where is he now?" asked Lundgren.

"Home," said Beale, as they stood together in the laboratory's large control room looking over the shoulder of the monitoring technician. He was scrutinizing two screens displaying labels "Bradley Davis" and "Annie Davis." Each screen showed a map with a small red dot, the rising and falling bars of hormone levels, the pulsating heart icon and the small blue icon representing blood pressure.

"And where is she?"

"Home, too. They had a very busy night." Beale chuckled. "The data indicate they made it three times."

"And what did you gentlemen do to help?"

"Well, we gave him a nice dose of testosterone. And adrenaline. And we gave her a lady cocktail of estrogen, testosterone, and adrenaline to help things along."

"No anomalies?"

"No anomalies. The version two-point-one chip is showing a much higher precision of control."

"And during the day?"

"We keep a little adrenaline flowing in him. Keeps him working. A good test of the system. Then we sequester the hormone at night. Her, too."

"And the other subjects?"

"Yes, and all nominal," said Beale as he instructed the technician to sequence through a dozen other screens. A succession of maps and data flashed past, each showing normal levels. "But what if we do get . . . malfunctions? Behavioral anomalies? Like with the others?"

"We've been there, done what was necessary," said Lundgren with a dismissive wave of his hand.

"No, Larry, you haven't been there, done what was necessary. *I have!*" exclaimed Beale, his jaw tightening.

"We'll worry about that if it happens." Lundgren looked at his watch. "I have a luncheon appointment, and afterward a meeting with our client. The very lucrative one."

"Shit, I'm not going to—"

But Lundgren was already walking out the door.

• • •

The crisp fall weather was invigorating, so Brad decided after lunch with Annie to walk from their favorite Boston pizza joint, Nino's, down brick-cobbled Charles Street, past the Public Garden, to the Arlington Street Green Line trolley stop. He'd ridden the Green Line in from Newton with Annie, just to spend a little more time with her before her shift. After all, he now had the luxury of a steady, very lucrative gig.

They sat close together in the booth in the funky little place near the hospital and shared a pizza. Each smiled a little more than usual, unspoken between them the delightful memory of the previous night.

They smiled even more when they had taken out their smartphones, each to record data in the Happy App on Nino's great—and inexpensive—pizza. Those data would meld into the massive Happy Ratings database, yielding a guide to better pizza for all!

Enjoying the memory of a parting kiss and hug that were a little more fervent than usual, he had headed down toward Beacon Street and cut over to Arlington, approaching the luxury Taj Boston Hotel.

He was strolling along, half-a-block from the fortress-like entrance to the condos that were part of the hotel, when a black limo glided past with the rear window down. He was surprised to see Lundgren in the back seat, talking to another man. Brad waved, but Lundgren didn't see him.

Brad quickened his pace after the limo, when it pulled up in front of the Taj condos. He wasn't really sure why he wanted to greet Lundgren—perhaps it was a reporter's curiosity; perhaps just to say hello to the man who had so greatly enriched his bank account.

He had almost reached the limo when Lundgren climbed out, followed by a portly balding man in a pinstripe suit.

They had started into the condo building, when Lundgren turned his head toward Brad approaching and smiling. Surprisingly, he seemed not to register any recognition, quickly ducking through the thick glass doors and disappearing. The portly man followed, and by the time Brad reached the entrance, they were gone.

Maybe Lundgren really hadn't recognized him. Sometimes that happens when you see people out of context. And they'd only met once. But still he was perplexed, nagged by curiosity with maybe a pinch of suspicion.

Still puzzling over the encounter, Brad walked past the condo door to the hotel entrance a hundred feet beyond. He hesitated in front of the revolving hotel door. What should he do? The doorman looked at him expectantly, waiting for him to decide whether to go in or move on.

Yeah, he decided, he should go in, hang around; see what happens. Something didn't seem right. After a decade of interviewing, Brad had learned to read people's body language. Recalling the encounter, he judged that Lundgren had, strangely, hastened his step when he had seen Brad. He also sensed that the portly man had an air of gravitas about him, as if he were a person of power. Something significant was going on between those two. Something that his book research demanded he know about.

He decided to do a stakeout, and he knew just how, because he'd been in the Taj hotel before. He pushed through the revolving door, turning right and entering the hotel's richly paneled bar, with its soft lighting and antique paintings of hunting dogs, naval scenes, and revolutionary-era portraits.

Fortunately, a couple had just vacated one of the tables he wanted, at the windows looking out on Arlington Street and Boston Garden. He sat down and ordered a beer from the crisply uniformed waiter and took out his laptop to do a little work. He had time. And he still had that nagging itch of curiosity.

He'd slowly nursed two beers in tall pilsner glasses and munched a full bowl of complimentary nuts, when the same black limo slid past the window, heading down Arlington Street.

The back window was still down—Lundgren fortunately liked fresh air—and he saw the distinctive silver-haired head in the back.

Showtime! Now Brad would pull a little scam to find out what was going on. He paid the bill and walked onto the street down to the condo entrance. He rehearsed his story in his head, assumed a panicked look, and rushed in.

"Hey!" he exclaimed breathlessly to the concierge. "Mr. Lundgren sent me back to get some papers he left. I'm new. He thought I knew where his meeting was here, but I don't. Can you help me?"

The uniformed man wavered between charity and suspicion. "Well, sir, he was in the corporate suite, of course."

"Of course! Shoulda known that. Where's that?"

"Sir, I'm afraid that without his express permission or a key, I can't let you up."

"Jeez! I'll be in trouble!"

"I'm sorry, sir, but—"

"Look, that's okay. I'll have to get a key from his assistant."

He left quickly but satisfied that he had the intel he wanted: NeoHappy had a corporate condo in the Taj. In itself not unusual. Many corporations had them for posh guests and consultants. But Lundgren had seemed a little too on edge about Brad seeing him there.

Brad filed this bit of intelligence away for later, because now he had a really intriguing interview scheduled late that afternoon, with the eccentric software genius Gregor Kalinsky. Fallon himself had warned Brad that Kalinsky was volatile, maybe even threatening. But the interview was necessary. Kalinsky had developed the first Happy App that transformed the chip's raw data into a guide for people's lives.

He wasn't too surprised that Kalinsky hadn't answered his e-mails. Sometimes eccentrics didn't bother. However, after several calls, when the Russian finally answered, he'd curtly declined to be interviewed, saying in his thick Russian accent. "I do not wish to be involved."

Brad had persisted, emphasizing that he considered himself an independent writer, not an employee of NeoHappy. And he was writing about Fallon, whom Kalinsky had respected enough to agree to work for.

Kalinsky had finally relented, sort of, growling, "If you come, and I don't like you, then I tell you go fock yourself," before hanging up the phone.

CHAPTER 9

Brad stood puzzled before the tenant directory in the nondescript brick-and-glass office building. It was anonymously nestled behind a seedy strip mall in Chelsea. Was this the place?

The address he'd gotten from the NeoHappy records was right. But there was no listing for Kalinsky's oddly named company: *Fignya Khudozhniki* Information Technologies. Suspecting that the foreign name was Russian, Brad had looked up the translation. He'd laughed when he'd read it: "Bullshit Artists." He also smiled when he realized that the company's initials, FKIT, would likely be pronounced as an obscenity.

Shrugging at the lack of directory listing, he climbed the stairs to the second floor, acutely aware that cameras in the stairwell and hallway were trained on him. Finding the gray steel door with yet another camera trained on it, Brad didn't know whether to knock or just go in. Given the company's obvious desire for security, he decided to knock.

"We know you are here. Look directly at camera beside door," commanded a thickly accented voice over a speaker beside the door.

He did so. After a long moment, the door was answered by a tall, brawny middle-aged man whose jowls were carpeted with a thick beard. His unkempt bushy head of hair made him look as if he'd just crawled out of bed. He looked more like a bad-guy wrestler than a software genius. He scratched his belly and scowled.

"I don't know why you come here," he grumped. "I don't know why I let you here." He blocked the door, still not admitting Brad.

"You are Gregor Kalinsky?" It was a necessary question. Brad hadn't found a single photo of Kalinsky anywhere, not even in the NeoHappy database of contractors.

"*Da*, and you are man who screws around on his wife?"

"*What? What the hell do you mean by that? I do not!*"

"I do not talk to man who screws around on his wife. I never screw around on any of my wives."

"Look, I don't know what the hell you are talking about. As I told you in the e-mails and the phone messages, I'm doing a biography of Marty Fallon, and I want it to be right. I want it to include everything. And you were an important part of his success."

The man hmphed. "Important part? I *was* success for him."

"Mr. Kalinsky, you saw my website, the pieces I've written, and my book. I'm an independent writer. I want to learn about your part and your history with Marty."

Kalinsky stood in the doorway for a long moment, positioning himself so he could slam the door in Brad's face.

"You paid by him?"

"Yes, but that doesn't affect what I write. I'm not going to whitewash anything. And if it works out there are skeletons, and the project goes south, so be it." Brad winced to himself. He actually didn't dare let the project flop that was saving his financial ass.

"Okay, you are not whitewashing skeletons even going south. I get it. You come in. You explain why you are not focking some woman beside your wife, and I talk to you."

"Mr. Kalinsky, I—"

But Kalinsky had turned and walked back through a large room crowded with computer workstations. Bent over keyboards or leaning back gazing at the monitors was an odd mix of people. There were skinny, scruffy, tattooed men, many with shaved heads, all with the wary look of criminals. And, there were just-as-scruffy younger men and women, who might look perfectly at home in an MIT dorm. Brad passed one man asleep on the floor, who could have been a younger, thinner clone of Kalinsky. Farther along, a tousle-headed young man and a young, blond woman were peering at a computer monitor festooned with intricate computer code.

They reached Kalinsky's private office, a large space made claustrophobic by a clutter of computer equipment, mounds of paper, and piles of books. Multiple glowing monitors were alive with text, flowcharts, and scrolling computer code.

Kalinsky plumped himself down in a large recliner, but didn't recline. Brad found a chair, removed some papers and sat down.

Kalinsky picked up a wireless keyboard and pecked out some commands.

"We know everything about you, Bradley Davis. My boys are good detectives. They find out everything about anybody who comes through our door. We know you have no money for long time, then a big dump of money from NeoHappy."

"Look, you have no right to—"

"But it looks like you focking around on wife. Last year, when hospital records show your wife at work, your little girls in school, you go every few days to condo in Cambridge. Expensive condo. You do this for weeks. Your phone GPS tell us that. We hacked phone GPS records. At condo, you stay for an hour or so. Condo camera show that. Then you go back to apartment. We check to see if you have freelance assignments that would take you to condo. We hack into places you write for. You don't have freelance assignments. Hah! Then, we see that you buy very expensive antique necklace on eBay. That for your girlfriend who you are focking at condo?"

"*You . . . you*—" Brad sputtered, unable to even form a sentence he was so stunned. These people had rummaged through his life as if there were no firewalls, no security at all!

"You are bad focker," spat Kalinsky. "Your wife, she is nice lady who was in Army on battlefield saving brave soldiers' lives, and now she is saving lives in hospital. And you are cheating on her. *You get out!*"

"No," said Brad, standing up and leaning over Kalinsky's desk, jaw clinched in anger. "I won't. And I'll show you that you aren't as smart as you think you are."

Kalinsky hmphed derisively. "Show me I am not smart . . . that my boys are not smart."

Brad sat back down, his expression still one of smoldering anger.

"About the necklace. Annie had inherited an antique necklace from her grandmother. A gold necklace with diamonds. It had been in the family for generations. Somehow, it got lost. We didn't know how. Maybe the girls were playing with it; maybe Annie had it in her purse at work and it was stolen. She was devastated. She remembered when her grandmother had put it around her neck on her sixteenth birthday. Her grandmother died the next year. I held her when she cried about the necklace. Her grandmother was very special to her."

"And this was necklace you bought?" asked Kalinsky.

"Well, I found a necklace just like it on eBay. Hell, it might even have been the same necklace that the thief was selling. But I couldn't just buy it and give it to Annie. That wouldn't have relieved her guilt. I had to pretend to find it. Anyway, I couldn't afford it. They wanted five thousand dollars."

"So, then, what was going to condo about?"

"There was this rich college kid who lived there. He was flunking some classes where he had to write papers. He wanted me to ghost-write the papers for him. Well, I couldn't do that. But I agreed to coach him on writing, and . . . well . . . it did happen that some of the writing on his papers was mine. He gave me five thousand dollars. And I bought the necklace. And I sort of 'found' it under the couch in the apartment."

"So, you not cheating on wife, eh?"

"No . . . but, I did cheat in helping that kid write his papers. And I did lie to Annie. But I love my wife. Maybe the lying was wrong, but I wanted to make her feel better. You won't tell her."

"No. She feels better, that's good."

"And by the way, from now on you stay the hell out of my records."

Kalinsky opened his hands and shrugged. "If you knew what we do here, you would understand why we investigate you. But yes, we know all we need to about you. We leave our nose out of your business."

"Well, let's start our interview by telling me what exactly you do here."

Kalinsky loosed a belly laugh. "No focking way I tell you! I only tell you we do lots of stuff for different people. Government, companies, universities. I like universities best. No bullshit like government. Especially some parts of US government. Others sometimes okay. No, we just talk about NeoHappy."

Brad nodded and took out his recorder, but Kalinsky emphatically, waved both his wrestler-sized hands. "No recording my voice! Never! And no shooting my picture."

"Sure, fine," said Brad making a conspicuous show of putting his recorder away. As if to demonstrate his acceptance, Kalinsky popped the lever on his recliner and leaned back, bringing up the footrest. "Damn bad back I got," he said. "Too much time hunched over at computer. You go ahead."

Brad did go ahead, asking Kalinsky questions about how he'd immigrated to America to become a programmer. And how he'd gotten a job at MIT, where he met Fallon. And how Fallon had asked him to create the Happy App. As Kalinsky talked on in his rumbling accented voice, Brad scribbled furiously, aware that his notes were the only record he would have of what could be his only chance to talk to the eccentric Russian.

Kalinsky concluded by saying, "Finally, I turn over code to Marty. My guys help him secure the hell out of Happy Rating data system. Then I focking leave!"

"Why?"

"I finish."

"But you were friends with Marty. And the company was going to really explode."

"Explode? Hah! Yes, company going to explode." Kalinsky slammed the recliner down and leaned forward. "That motherfocker make it explode!"

"Marty Fallon?"

"*Nyet*. Lundgren. He want to fock with my code. I tell him code is *my code* and no focking going on."

"What did he want to do?"

"He never tell. But I hate him, fancy-suit focker. So, my guys make all the code bulletproof. I think Lundgren might want to hack private, personal data on people. I know how to make bulletproof code. I tell Marty, 'Okay, I will fix code so personal data behind firewall. But I also attach logic bomb.'"

"Logic bomb?"

"Well, code had firewall protecting personal data of people. Only anonymous data go to Happy Ratings. Anybody try to steal personal data, alarm go out to FBI, FDA, every-focking-body!" Now Kalinsky cackled and slapped his hands on the desk. "But *then* also, my guys put in secret logic bomb that will *kill whole focking system!* Then after I leave, I send them e-mail telling them I rig whole system so if Lundgren fock with it, whole system crash permanent!" He made an explosion sound, laughing heartily.

"What did they think?"

"Marty was a little pissed, but Lundgren, he go nuts. He almost have stroke! I keep hoping he does!"

"Why didn't you like Lundgren?"

"I don't talk about Lundgren beyond saying he is motherfocker. I don't want his trouble for me."

"What do you mean 'his trouble'?"

"You find out yourself." Kalinsky heaved his bulk out of his recliner. "I have things to do. You can go now."

"Can I get back to you with more questions?"

Kalinsky chuckled and headed out the door. "Oh, yeah, sure, you can give me any questions. I not answer them. We are done. Don't come back."

He led Brad through the computer room and to the front door, opening it, waiting for Brad to go through, and slamming it behind him.

• • •

As Brad drove back into Boston, two memories kept resonating with one another, like microphone feedback, generating an annoying brain-buzz of curiosity. The memories were Kalinsky's expressions of utter hatred of Lundgren and Brad's own unsettling earlier encounter with Lundgren in Boston. The only way to at least reduce the buzz, he decided, was to figure out what Lundgren was up to.

Before picking up Annie after her shift, he had time to go by NeoHappy to do . . . *something*. He had no idea what, but he'd found out long ago that plunging himself blindly into a problem often revealed a solution. He took the plunge.

He walked into the building, passing under the massive glass sculpture. Now the hulking guard merely nodded and smiled, since Brad was now officially part of the corporate team. He used his access card to go to the executive floor. On the way up in the elevator, as he'd hoped, a plan began to form, thanks to his investigative reporter's instinct.

He stopped at the receptionist Irene Crawford's desk, asking whether Lundgren was in. The answer was no, which set up the next phase.

He strode down the hall into Lundgren's outer office, and the decorative blond assistant smiled vaguely at him.

"Uh, I wonder if you can help me," he said, smiling back and shaking his head, knitting his brow in embarrassment. "I was using one of the company limos, and I found this." He pulled out his smartphone. "I know that Mr. Lundgren was using the limo before me, and I wanted to return the phone."

"Well, Mr. Lundgren isn't in right now. But I know he still had his phone with him. So, it isn't his."

"Oh. Well, it must belong to the other gentleman who was with him. Look, I don't want to bother Mr. Lundgren. And I'm not exactly authorized to use the limo, so I just wanted to return the phone quietly."

The assistant smiled again. "No, I can take it and return it." She held out her manicured hand. *A glitch!* thought Brad. *How to put her off without seeming to put her off, in which case she'd report the incident to Lundgren.*

"Gee, well, I do know the gentleman. Mr. Lundgren introduced me to him earlier, outside the Taj. So, he'd see it as a favor if I returned the phone directly. You know how it is?"

The woman held her hand out for a long moment, a dubious expression shadowing her face. Finally, she withdrew her hand, then nodded. She knew the value of good personal service.

"I understand," she replied smoothly.

"The thing is, I can't remember his name. It's—" Marty paused, making his best mortified-underling expression. There was another silence, while the woman judged whether to give the information.

"Bailey," she finally said.

"Ah! Yes! Mr. Bailey! Thank you! And his first name is Kevin."

"Frederick."

"Of course! Fred! So sorry to bother you! Thank you so much!"

Brad waved the phone and left quickly, before she changed her mind. Back in his cubbyhole, he Googled Frederick Bailey. The search listing showed a movie director, an Australian botanist . . . they certainly weren't the ones.

But as he scrolled down, a more likely prospect came up. A Frederick Bailey was an executive vice president for American Brands, a huge food conglomerate. Grocery shelves were crammed full of snacks, frozen dinners, drinks, and other products from American Brands. And, the corporation owned several major fast food chains. He did an image search, and among the thumbnails was the familiar image of the portly, balding man who had gone into the hotel with Lundgren.

His curiosity-buzz, unfortunately, only grew louder. What was the EVP of NeoHappy—which was supposedly independent of corporate influence—doing with a bigwig from one of the biggest food corporations in the world? And why was he so cagey about it?

CHAPTER 10

The next afternoon, Brad slid into a booth across from the IT guy, Jim Bell, in the same bar they'd had drinks at before. But now, at Brad's request, they were seated at the back of the room, where they wouldn't be noticed or disturbed.

Bell looked puzzled, especially so because Brad hadn't sent him an e-mail asking to meet, but ducked into his office on the pretext of having a computer question.

They ordered beers, and when they were delivered, each lowered his head. A naive observer would have thought they were praying, but their heads were really bowed over their smartphones, entering data on the beer and the bar into their Happy Apps.

"So, how's it going?" asked Bell after the digital benediction. "Everything okay? The chip okay?"

"Yeah, but that's not it. Here's a question that opens a door you might not want opened. And I'll understand."

"Okay," said Bell dubiously, taking a sip of his beer, glancing at his smartphone.

"I saw Lundgren the other day downtown. He was meeting with a guy who's an executive vice president at American Brands. You know it?"

"No. What is it?"

"It's a huge food company. I mean massive."

Brad brought up the web site on his smartphone and slid it over to Bell, who took several minutes scanning through the products and subsidiaries, pausing occasionally to drink his beer. He handed the phone back.

"So?"

"Why is the head of NeoHappy meeting with a big shot at a food conglomerate?"

"How the heck should I know? Maybe they're just buddies."

"Lundgren? Buddies? Seriously?"

"Well, then, maybe NeoHappy's going to do some kind of partnership."

"What kind of partnership could NeoHappy possibly want to do with a food corporation? There's no advertising on the Happy Rating site, right?"

"None. That's a big no-no. I helped implement the new website, and somebody suggested the design should allow for advertising. The webmaster reacted like they were suggesting posting kiddie porn. There's even a statement on the site that Happy Ratings has no corporate affiliation."

"Okay, back to my question. Why meet with a corporate exec?"

Bell finished his beer and sat back in the booth, turning his smartphone over in his fingers, looking around the bar absently, brow knitted. Then abruptly something appeared to dawn on him. He threw his head back, mouth open peering at the ceiling.

"*Ahhhh, shit! Of course!*" he exclaimed. A woman with children at a nearby table stared at him indignantly. He ducked his head in apology.

"What?" asked Brad.

Bell rubbed his face and groaned. "Oh, man! Oh, man! I should have realized. I knew there was something!"

"*What?!*" demanded Brad.

Bell leaned forward, looking around, and whispered conspiratorially, "I'm not going to say anything else until I know for certain what the deal is. I've got some stuff to find out. I'll see you back here tomorrow."

"C'mon, tell me what's going on," Brad pleaded.

But Bell waved him away, got up and quickly left the bar.

That night, Brad and Annie had a quiet dinner, and afterward played with the girls, happily lounging on the old couch, hearing Sarah tell stories about her collection of toy horses, and reading with Sally. However, the moment the clock showed bedtime, they did a no-nonsense, quick, tuck-in-and-tell-a-story that signaled it was *really* bedtime.

They also decided it was a *serious* bedtime for Mommy and Daddy. Their clothes shed, nestled in bed, their smartphones on, and the volumes turned down, they again gave each other delightful connubial bliss. But afterward, nestled in each other's arms, while Annie drifted off to sleep, Brad lay there wide awake. He was haunted by Bell's panicked reaction to his news about Lundgren.

• • •

Lundgren paced his office, sipping from a crystal glass of fifty-year-old Glenmorangie scotch, waiting for his assistant to notify him that she'd reached Beale. Finally, her silken voice sounded over his phone speaker, and Beale came on.

"Did Davis go see Kalinsky?" demanded Lundgren.

"Yeah, his GPS tracking shows he's pretty much followed the interview schedule on his calendar."

"'Pretty much?' What the hell does that mean?"

"Nothing unexpected really. He's going to a bar near headquarters. He went to Boston General to pick up his wife. He did stop at a hotel downtown. The Taj. He was there for some time."

"He stopped? He didn't just pass it? How long did he stay?"

"Maybe an hour."

"An hour. You're sure?"

"GPS doesn't lie. Does it mean anything?"

"Not anything you need to know about. Get more leverage on him."

Beale paused, the silence signaling he was trying to process the command. "Larry, you don't mean the children? I thought you weren't going to do that."

"The wife may not be enough, if it comes down to leverage."

"Yeah, but the children!"

"May I remind you what we've already done?"

Lundgren punched the phone button to hang up just as Beale exclaimed "Jesus, Larry, we—!"

• • •

Brad sat back in the richly padded leather seat of Fallon's private Boeing 767 and peered out the airplane window, watching the suburban landscape around Hanscom Field drop away. He took a sip of his latte from an insulated mug with the NeoHappy logo. Fallon sat across from him, talking on the phone, but signaled to Brad with a wink and nod that he would be off shortly.

The plan for the trip had crystallized quickly. Early the previous afternoon, Fallon's assistant, Irene Crawford, had appeared at the doorway to his small office, asking, "Can you take a trip on short notice? Marty's leaving late this afternoon to meet with some electronics subcontractors. It gives you a good five hours in the air each way for interviewing, and you'll stay overnight in his California house. It's nice and quiet. It's in the Napa Valley."

Brad had hesitated, knitting his brow. He had family responsibilities. But he knew he couldn't pass up the chance for such a long uninterrupted interview time; and also a look at Fallon in action, and at home in another setting.

"I'm supposed to take care of my daughters while my wife is doing night shifts. She's a nurse."

Irene smiled comfortingly. "Not to worry. We have a delightful lady who is a nanny for executives who run into family conflicts. Her name is Dora, and you will just love her. I checked just in case, and she's available the whole time you'll be gone."

Relieved, he'd phoned Annie to make sure it was okay. It wasn't quite.

"You mean just leave the girls with a stranger and take off across the country?" Annie had queried in a scolding tone.

"Sweetheart, I'm sure she's okay. The top executives use her. We can ask for references, if you want."

"*We'll* be the only references here," declared Annie. "Get her resume. We'll talk to her when she comes. See if she passes muster. Okay?"

Brad was prepared to protest. But then he remembered that Annie's reaction was colored by the scalding memory of the many abused children she had seen at Boston General. Caution was safest, he concluded, both regarding the babysitter and his wife. So, he agreed to abide by her decision, even a veto.

That afternoon, their doorbell had rung, and they'd opened the door to meet the smiling, grandmotherly Dora. Her silver hair was done up in a homey bun, and she wore a reassuringly modest house dress and sensible shoes. As they'd chatted, Annie tried to be subtle about the cross-examination. Dora told about her past experience, not only as a sitter, but a mother and grandmother. And a nurse. The last bit of information, plus her extensive resume, produced a slight softening of Annie's guarded expression.

Brad and Annie conferred in the bedroom, as Dora pulled some toys out of her "magic bag," to the delight of toy-junkies Sally and Sarah.

"Seems nice enough," said Annie. "I'd really rather we'd had time to schedule Bonnie or Sadie. The kids know them."

"I'm sorry there wasn't time. And she is a nurse."

Annie sighed. "Well, okay. She seems sweet. I just wonder about people who are that sweet."

Brad took her reluctant agreement as a confirmed yes, and they proceeded to give Dora instructions on the girls' schedule. Their confidence was bolstered by the fact that Dora took detailed notes on her tablet computer.

So, now, lounging on the private jet, Brad felt little guilt. He could concentrate on making the trip productive, trying to elicit as much information as possible for the book.

Indeed, during the hours of the flight, over wine and a dinner prepared by Fallon's chef, he had recorded a rich trove of information and stories about Fallon's growing up in Boston, his education at MIT, and especially the challenges and controversies of starting his company. Throughout, Brad took notes about people to talk to, facts to check, points to follow up on.

The flight was an hour out of San Francisco, when the talk turned to the eccentric software wizard, Gregor Kalinsky.

"Yeah, Gregor was . . . and is . . . a hoot," said Fallon, shaking his head and smiling. "He was difficult for most people to work with, both at MIT and after he started working for us. His . . . well . . . prickly personality probably came from his background in Russia, which he never talked about. But I respected his boundaries. And his distinctive personality and working style. People had trouble with that, too. But heck, I'd hang out with him all night to work on programming after all the other folks on the software team had run screaming."

"And when Lundgren came in they didn't get along?"

Fallon chuckled. "They had their differences."

Brad decided to be blunt. "More than 'differences'. Kalinsky hates his guts. He says Lundgren wanted to do something underhanded with the app's code."

"Well, Lawrence said all he wanted to do was to understand it, so he could make sure it was properly structured. And I think he knew Gregor wouldn't stay with the company. He told me he'd seen too many times when programmers left without documenting their code, and the company was left with just a black box." Fallon waved his hand dismissively. "And in the end, it was really a clash of personalities. Jeez, all you have to do is look at those two, and you could predict that."

"And the logic bomb?"

"Yes *that*." Fallon stopped smiling. "It's there. And, yeah, it's nuclear. It does seal the personal data completely from accessing or tampering. And we couldn't do anything about it. Lawrence was ready to start a lawsuit, but I know Gregor. He would never, *ever* sabotage the viability of his code. So, I talked Lawrence out of it."

"By the way, I saw him at the Taj, going into NeoHappy's condo—"

"Condo?" Fallon asked, brow wrinkled in puzzlement.

"Yes, he was with a guy who turned out to be Frederick Bailey. He's with American Brands."

"We don't have a condo at the Taj," Fallon said, shaking his head in puzzlement. "And I don't know of any business Lawrence would have with American Brands. I'm sure it was a social thing."

Fallon grew silent, his mood darkening, so Brad decided that, to preserve their amity during the trip, he'd drop the subject.

"Well, maybe it was," said Brad, deciding not to mention his reporter's suspicion.

The talk turned to the clinical testing of the chip, and the contentious FDA approval process. Fallon's mood became even more somber. He abruptly said he was tired and wanted to take a nap before they landed.

He retired to one of the jet's bedrooms, leaving Brad to go over his notes and wonder whether Fallon's ignorance of the condo and Lundgren's meeting with Bailey were real or just an evasion. His curiosity brain-buzz was getting annoyingly loud.

His buzz faded into the background, when he experienced the exhilarating way they traveled to Fallon's Napa Valley house. Alighting from the jet, they piled into a luxurious helicopter that whisked them out over the San Francisco skyline at dusk.

During that flight, Fallon was back to his energetic self, rested, and perhaps having filed away the question about the condo. An enthusiastic host, he eagerly pointed out the sights, as they sped northward out of the city and over the rolling landscape of vineyards and handsome wineries.

By the time they landed on the helipad at Fallon's sprawling, Spanish-style mansion, softly illuminated by glowing landscape lighting, Brad's fatigue had overcome him. He was only interested in being shown to his bedroom. Unlike Fallon, he was jet-lagged, still on East coast time.

As he sank into slumber, he speculated sleepily that this house, so different from the Boston mansion, might reflect a kind of multiple personality thing with Fallon—a man who changed personas according to circumstances.

• • •

Dora looked up and nodded with a warm smile, as Annie emerged from the kitchen with her canvas bag holding her dinner and other paraphernalia. The grandmotherly woman was sitting on the couch, reading to Sarah, who nestled happily against her, immersed in the adventures of the baby elephants in the children's book that Dora had brought with her.

Sally played on the floor with a picture puzzle from Dora's magic bag. Dora had declared that her bag held all manner of treats for "children who eat healthy foods and brush their teeth and go to bed."

"Thanks so much," said Annie, pulling on her coat. "This trip is so important to Brad for the book. And the book is so important to him . . . to us . . . and it was a great chance for him to get together with Mr. Fallon."

"Oh, dear, think nothing of it," said Dora, hugging Sarah to her. "It's always such a joy to take care of babies like these. I'm just glad the company needs me. I don't get to see my own grandbabies near enough."

Annie kissed Sarah on the forehead, knelt down and gave Sally a hug and a kiss, and hurried out the door.

Dora finished reading the book to Sarah, cleared the dinner dishes, and put away the leftovers. She pulled out an iPad with a cartoon letter-learning game, which immediately fascinated Sarah, and helped Sally work the puzzle.

After an hour, her cell phone rang, and she answered it, looking out the window, her smile replaced by a coldly resolute expression.

"Okay, bring up the ice cream," she said. "Then wait outside, and we'll bring them down."

She turned to the children, her smile returning and said in a merry, lilting voice. "I have the most marvelous news, little ones! A friend of mine is bringing us ice cream! Isn't that wonderful?"

• • •

Standing by the pool, a safe distance from the helipad, a haggard-looking Brad watched the helicopter lift off and bank out over the rolling wooded hills of the Mendocino wine country, headed for San Francisco. He'd been awake since four a.m. local time, typing away on his laptop in an ornate four-poster bed in the luxurious mansion.

The early rising came after a night of not sleeping a wink. He couldn't figure out why he was uneasy. Maybe it was just the pressure of the book, of being away from Annie and the girls, of the over-the-top, opulent luxury he was immersed in. Or, maybe it was some deeper dread that he couldn't quite place.

There was something going on with Fallon. At seven a.m., he'd met the normally jovial billionaire for breakfast on the patio under the massive oak tree. Fallon was cordial, but again subdued as he'd been the night before. Something was bothering him. Brad couldn't tell whether it was Brad's presence, or a business or personal matter.

They'd had eggs Florentine, warm, crisp croissants, fresh-squeezed orange juice, and richly aromatic Vietnamese coffee . . . all exquisitely prepared by Fallon's personal chef.

After small talk about the house and vineyards, Fallon said, "Well, I called Lawrence this morning about some business, and I asked him about the condo. He said he bought the place a couple of months ago, to give our visiting managers a place to stay that would be nicer than a hotel. He'd added it to the facilities inventory, but hadn't brought it up for discussion. He wanted to get solid data on whether it was cost-effective before including it in an executive meeting agenda for discussion."

"Okay," said Brad, trying to maintain an offhanded tone.

"And he said he'd known Bailey from when he ran a company that produced food-processing machinery. Bailey was in town, and they had lunch at the condo, since it wasn't being used."

"Okay," said Brad again. He decided not to bring up that he'd encountered Lundgren and Bailey after lunchtime was long past.

"Okay, well then, I've got to get going."

And he did, leaving Brad to his own journalistic business. He'd called Annie as soon as he knew she'd be awake.

He reached her at home, asking, "The babies okay?"

"Uh, sure. I got home in time to walk them to school. Dora said they'd been good girls for her. But the girls said something funny on the way to school."

"Funny ha ha?"

"Funny *strange*. Sarah said somebody had brought ice cream to the apartment."

"Maybe one of her friends. That was nice."

"Well, yeah, but then Sally said they got really tired after they had the ice cream and fell asleep. And it was well before their usual bedtime."

"Well, maybe they just had a really busy day. Our little girls play very hard, you know."

"Maybe. But it was strange. Anyway, we won't use her again. I called Sadie, and she can watch the kids tonight."

"Don't worry, sweetheart. Marty said we'll be home late this evening, so I'll be there for the overnight."

Brad had settled in with his laptop in the spacious living room, organizing his notes and doing more research on Fallon. After an hour, his cell phone rang again.

"Please hold for Mr. Lundgren," said the refined voice of his assistant.

"Mr. Davis," said Lundgren in the chillingly matter-of-fact tone that a boss would use before dressing down a subordinate.

"Hi . . . Lawrence." Brad was not sure he should use Lundgren's first name after that cold greeting.

"Mr. Davis, do you know what the cornerstone of effective corporate functioning is?"

"Well—"

"*Trust*, Mr. Davis. Trust among its employees. You have compromised trust in several ways."

"Well, I'm sorry if—"

"Marty mentioned that you had seen me at the Taj condominium with Mr. Bailey. Subsequently, I learned that you took it upon yourself to begin some sort of investigation."

"Well, when I saw you—"

"My assistant tells me you approached her with some story about a lost cell phone in my limousine. And when she was talking to the condominium concierge about another matter, he mentioned that some man had come in asking for access. Was that you?"

"Yes."

"Mr. Davis, trust is critical to my relationship with Marty. And by insinuating yourself in this matter, you have interfered with our relationship. And, you have raised significant doubts about whether you can be trusted with a project that involves your deep involvement with this company."

Brad's heart began to race. He had to think fast. He could feel the book deal slipping away, their bank account emptying out.

"May I explain?" he asked.

"Please do."

"In fact, you're quite right, Lawrence, trust is very much involved here. My objective was to ensure your trust in me."

"Oh, really," said Lundgren disdainfully.

"Yes. When I saw you on the sidewalk, I knew that you'd seen me. But you proceeded into the building without acknowledging it. I thought about it quite a while, and I realized that I may have interfered with some very important and sensitive company business you were conducting. In doing this book, I very much want to stay out of your way, because I understand the key role you play in the company. As I see it, my job is to do a book that will help the company, but also to be trusted to keep the company's interests in mind."

"Indeed, it is."

"So, in my very clumsy way, sir, I just wanted to find out, without bothering you, what boundaries I need to respect to maintain your trust. I deeply apologize for any inconvenience it has caused you."

There was a long pause. *Had Lundgren bought the bullshit?* Brad wondered.

"Well, not that I owe you an explanation, but I did not greet you on the street because frankly, I didn't recall who you were. I meet a great many people, and we'd only seen each other briefly, and in the context of the office. And I was in a hurry. Mr. Bailey was due at a conference in New York, and we only had a limited amount of time to catch up on our friendship. And, Mr. Davis, you are not exactly at the top of my agenda."

"I understand completely, and again I apologize."

"In the future, Mr. Davis, please restrict yourself to matters that concern you as regards the project you have been assigned to carry out."

"I certainly will, sir."

Lundgren ended the call with no goodbye.

Brad took himself out to the flagstone patio, to settle his nerves and mull over what had just happened. The maid appeared with an offer of lunch, which he took. Munching on a perfectly prepared lobster salad, sipping the Fallon vineyard wine, he gazed out across the rolling landscape of the winery without really seeing it.

First, he managed to get beyond the panic of possibly losing the book contract. He realized that Lundgren couldn't get him fired without making a big deal about the condo and the Bailey incident. And Lundgren didn't want to do that.

Lundgren also wouldn't have him fired because, Brad decided, Lundgren's story was bullshit. Just as Brad's story, and apology, had been bullshit.

This was a chess game between two experienced bullshitters, he decided. He had his chessmen; Lundgren had his.

Brad spent the next hour plotting out as many strategies as he could think of to figure out what to do next. They ranged from doing nothing, to abandoning the project, to doing what his training at BU taught him—investigate.

Finally he decided on the last, even though it was the most dangerous. And, since it entailed continuing to conspire with Jim Bell, it meant putting the IT guy in the middle of the chess game—maybe as a pawn. He gave long thought to the possibility that he would put Bell in danger. But finally, he decided to call Bell, telling him the whole story about seeing Lundgren with Bailey, and the call he'd just received from Lundgren.

Bell's answer was terse, cryptic. "Well, I did some checking," he said. "It's what I thought. But not over the phone. See you when you get back."

After lunch, Marty's helicopter roared into sight, landing long enough for Brad to board, and in an hour, they had taken off from San Francisco International. Brad resolved to be upbeat during the flight, to try to alleviate any dubious feelings Fallon might have toward him. He asked Fallon to tell war stories about his efforts to build the company and overcome regulatory and technical obstacles. Fallon was in his element, and even happier to tell stories about Lisa and his children, Mary and Kevin.

"Jeez, why a Harvard-educated woman deigned to marry an MIT geek from the wrong end of Massachusetts Avenue, I'll never know," he'd joked.

Their relationship had been recemented, if it was ever cracked. But still, Brad wondered whether Fallon had been just a little too ready to accept, and pass on, Lundgren's answers about the condo. Was Fallon a player in this chess game, as well?

CHAPTER 11

"Like I said, the business with Lundgren was what I thought," said Bell, his expression grim, ignoring his full mug of beer and his Happy App. Again, they sat at a back booth in the bar, largely hidden from view.

"Well, you took off the other day like a bat out of hell," said Brad. His beer was still full, too, no more than a prop for their conversation. "It must be bad."

Bell leaned in, his voice lowering to a whisper. "They've been altering the Happy Ratings to favor certain brands."

"*What?* How do you know?"

"Well, when we talked last time, I remembered that they brought in a programmer to do an upgrade to the NeoHappy software. I thought he was from outside, but I later found out he's really an employee of the proprietary research group. The secret guys . . . the ones running the shadow network. I thought it was odd at the time but now I understand why. I managed to get into the code. It took me a solid day to find the subroutine. He added a back-door control subroutine to the Happy Ratings software."

Brad shook his head. "No. No. That can't be. Kalinsky told me the personal records were bulletproof. He even put a logic bomb in so that they couldn't be tampered with."

Bell smiled and shook his head in disgust. "They didn't touch the personal data part. They knew better. They fixed the ratings algorithm so they could selectively adjust ratings . . . how chippers measure their enjoyment of different products. See, that software component is not behind Kalinsky's firewall. It's controlled by the Happy Ratings people, and Lundgren runs that. You get what all this means?"

Brad sat back, rolling his eyes. "So, Lundgren's people can manipulate the numbers reflecting how much somebody likes a specific brand."

"*Hell, yes!*" exclaimed Bell.

"So a corporation like American Brands pays Lundgren big bucks under the table. And he has his guys boost the measurements for all their products. And that means the chippers get higher personal ratings for those products. *And*, it means higher ratings go into the Happy Ratings database. So, subscribers buy more of the company's potato chips or cereal or beer . . . whatever . . . and the company make tons more money."

"You got it."

Now Brad slapped the table in frustration. "But there's no way to prove any of this, unless somebody hacks into the system and gets that code. Then it becomes an arcane technical issue that would get all tangled and complicated. Nobody would understand it."

Bell chuckled in satisfaction. "Yeah, well, we can absolutely prove it so that everybody would understand," said Bell. "The proof is in the pudding, in this case, the drinking."

"What do you—"

But Bell had already left the booth, returning shortly with two young men. One had a crew cut, one had long hair in a ponytail. The crew cut man wore a football jersey, and the long-haired one wore a blue blazer. But those were the only differences between them. Their faces were identical.

"I'd like you to meet Don and Ron," said Bell. "They're identical twins I've known since high school. Don's got the crew cut, and Ron's the ponytail. But they both like beer."

"Yes, we do," said Don, grinning.

"And they're both chipped, and they've agreed to take part in an experiment."

"As long as it involves beer," said Ron, identically grinning. Bell slid into the booth beside Brad, and the twins took the seat across from them. Bell signaled the waitress, and ordered an array of bottled beers, two each of four brands, which she brought on a tray.

Bell said to Brad, "American Brands makes all these beers." Then to the twins, "Okay guys, remember, you're just tasting the beers at this point. And since this is an experiment, I'm not telling you what's going on, right?"

"But we get all the beers ultimately," said Ron.

"Absolutely," promised Bell. He set an identical brand of beer in front of each twin. "Don, you scan the product code before you take a drink. Ron, you take a drink first, then scan the code."

"Ah ha!" said Brad. "So for Don, the Happy Ratings system knows the beer brand *before* he drinks, but for Ron, the system doesn't know the brand until *after* it gives a measure."

"Right," said Bell. "If the app is unbiased, their Pleasure Measures should be identical. After all, they are identical twins. But if it is biased, scanning the product bar ahead of time should give that twin, Don, a higher reading."

"Okay guys, proceed." The twins did as ordered, then slid their smartphones across to Bell and Brad.

"Damn!" exclaimed Brad. "The system reports a 20 percent higher Pleasure Measure when the system *knows the brand beforehand!"*

"Man, that sucks!" complained Don. "This thing is rigged."

"Yes, but you can't let it out," said Bell. "Let's keep going."

The twins worked their way through all four brands, and in each case when the product code was scanned first, the American Brands beer showed a higher Pleasure Measure reading.

As a comparison, they called for four beers not from American Brands. With each of those, the twins' Pleasure Measures were the same, regardless of whether the code was scanned before or after the drinking.

"Smoking gun," said Brad, recording the numbers on his laptop and saving them in his notes.

At the end, the table was covered with beer bottles, which the twins began to happily finish off. As they drank, Brad warned them, "Look, this is a really big deal. You have to promise not to tell *anybody* about this. These are really big-time people, and if they find out before we're ready, we could all be in deep shit."

The twins nodded heartily as they drank, and Brad and Bell moved to another table.

"What we do next is gather more data," said Bell. "There's a national twins organization. I checked. We could get them to test every product American Brands makes. We could take the data to the FBI, the SEC, and—"

"No, not yet," cautioned Brad, shaking his head cautiously. "I think there's more going on here than just money. I just feel it. There's a classic saying among journalists, 'follow the money.' I'm sure there's more coming in than just from American Brands. So, we find that out. And then we find out where it's going. Is it just lining people's pockets? Or is it being used for something else? Remember your history? Like Watergate? Like all the times congressmen bribed people using campaign money?"

"Yeah, the secret money was funding bad stuff in all those cases. And how do we find that out?

"Well, I'm going to start with finding out which corporations the money came from. I think I know a way to do that. And I need you to do a little hacking."

● ● ●

"I *love* corporate malfeasance!" exclaimed *Boston World* reporter Sam Pritchett, opening his laptop and donning his reading glasses, as they sat in the Starbucks near the newspaper's offices.

The gangly, rail-thin, balding reporter was the perfect collaborator for Brad. He had been nominated for a Pulitzer Prize twice, and won once—all for articles exposing corporate crime.

"Well, as I said, there may be a major story here," said Brad. "I'm willing to give you the financial part. But I need to investigate the technology and cover whatever I find. I know they screwed around with their software. And I just have a hunch something more is going on there. Until you agree to that deal, I can't tell you which corporation it is, or—"

"Oh, I already know which corporation," said Pritchett, grinning. "NeoHappy, right?"

Brad startled, but only for an instant. "Hmph. Should've known," he said resignedly.

"You remember what I taught you about investigative reporting at BU? A reporter never goes into see a source cold. I found out the scuttlebutt at BU. Everybody there has heard that you signed a contract to write a book about Marty Fallon. Is he involved? Is it their technology? Is it the chip? Jesus, my kids are chipped. Is it—"

"Don't know any of that. I've just found out something is going on. But I need you to help me figure it out, at least the money side. I need your research department."

"Yeah, well, you know the drill, Brad."

"What do you mean?"

"Anything I find out independently, I am free to go with."

"Sam, I brought this to you. You can't—"

"You only alerted me to something hinky at NeoHappy, Brad. You didn't say what. If I figure it out, the story is mine." Pritchett got up to leave. The aggressive reporter wasn't about to give Brad an inch.

"Sam, you can't. There may be lives at stake. You really want to be responsible for deaths?" Brad was exaggerating—he thought. So far, it was just a corporate scam. But he had to rein Pritchett in.

Pritchett stood towering over him for a moment, scowling. Then shook his head and sat back down.

"Okay, if I find out this is just a white-collar financial crime and you lied, I'm running with it myself. I'll put a request in to our research department. What exactly do you want?"

"A list of the major consumer product conglomerates that have shown bumps in sales over the last, say, couple of years. Not just gradual rises, but sudden bumps. And I need to know what products in each company have shown bumps. And if possible, I'd like to know the corporate VP in charge of each product."

"Jesus, does this involve a lot of players?"

"Maybe."

"What next, then?"

"Just give me the names."

"You get names; I get the full story, right? Otherwise, no deal."

Brad took a deep breath. It was a wary dance between them. But he'd have to trust Pritchett because the reporter had the newspaper's business database. Finally, Brad nodded.

"Yeah, you're in, but you have to hold publication until I say."

Pritchett chuckled. "We'll see. But you've got to be straight with me." He began pecking away on his laptop. "If you are, I can give you more than just corporation names. I know the stock analysts who follow the companies and the individual brands. They can tell me whether any sales bumps are unexpected or unexplained."

"That would be incredibly helpful, and if you can give me some time to—"

"Hey, listen, I won't give you a lot of time. Sure, my editors are going to approve this. But newspaper budgets are tight as hell these days. So, they're going to want me to be proactive as hell. So, if we find significant anomalies, I'll give you maybe a week, because that's what the editors will probably give me. Then we're putting our own team on it."

"Sam, just remember . . . life and death. And I'm vulnerable as hell. And there are other people who are also vulnerable."

"I'm just giving you the realities, here." Pritchett slapped the laptop shut and picked up his coffee. "I can tell my editors you'll move as fast as possible. But they're editors, and they answer to the publisher, and the publisher answers to corporate, and corporate likes a healthy bottom line. And these days our bottom line has just about flat-lined."

"Well, you've got your worries, I've got mine."

Pritchett drained his coffee and leaned forward over the table, peering over his glasses at Brad.

"There's another elephant here . . . in fact, a whole herd. Advertisers. If it turns out these shenanigans involve any of our major advertisers, you'd better damned well have the goods on them. Frankly, the bean counters know that uncovering a nasty piece of business by a big-bucks advertiser would cost us more than we'd get in revenue. They don't give a shit about journalism, or prizes, or whatnot. Their business is to keep us in business, got it?"

• • •

Frowning in concentration, Jim Bell bent over the iPad, swiping his finger across its screen, scrolling through Lundgren's calendar. He and Brad sat once more in the back booth in the bar, which had become something of a headquarters for their sleuthing.

"Jim, how did you get this?" asked Brad, watching the appointments scroll by on the screen. "Is this going to get you in trouble?"

Bell ignored him, and Brad couldn't figure whether it was because the techie was so intent on scrutinizing the calendar, or because he didn't want to answer the question.

"There's blacked-out appointments here, here, here, here . . ." said Bell, sliding the iPad over to Brad, pointing them out.

"Are you risking getting in trouble?" asked Brad again, this time more insistently.

"Okay, okay, *yes, I could get in trouble.* Sure, I'm the sysadmin, so I could get access to the system. But I had to do some tweaking to erase any evidence that I'd accessed his calendar."

Brad shot him a worried look, then turned back to scrutinizing the iPad. He took notes on his own tablet, listing the dates and times of the blackouts.

"Ah, this one . . . this one is important. This is when he met with Bailey at the Taj. I wonder if—"

"Ahead of you, Brad. You want to know whether Lundgren was at the Taj at other blacked-out times." Bell typed a command, and another calendar came up. "This is the schedule for the company's executive limos. They record all their trips and who used the cars. I cross-correlated the blackouts with Lundgren's calendar. During blacked-out periods on his calendar, he took a couple of dozen trips to the Taj condo over the last year."

"Okay, those are data that we'll put into the mix. But that doesn't tell us who Lundgren was meeting with."

"Can't help you there."

"Not to worry. I've got some information coming from my contact at the *World*. And I think I've got a plan to use it, that is, if Annie is game."

"*World?*" Bell yanked the iPad back and sat straight up in his seat. "Damn! You never told me you were going to the papers! Jesus, I could get fired, prosecuted for releasing company data! *What the hell were you thinking?*"

"I was thinking that we needed more data. And they could provide it. And if we get backed into a corner, we can threaten to release what we know. Jim, you're a source. Reporters will never reveal a source."

"*Shit!*" Bell spat. "*You're not a reporter! You're an employee!* Look, you signed an NDA. And I'm an employee! I've got a contract that says I can't release proprietary information." He stood up, jamming the iPad into his satchel and raising a hand in resignation. "I am fuckin' outta here!"

He hauled himself out of the booth and bolted from the bar, leaving Brad feeling very, very alone.

• • •

Annie sat at their kitchen table, phone in hand, her posture erect to help her come across as more official. Her open laptop sat before her, with the list from Pritchett of companies that had seen abrupt, major bumps in sales.

"Hello, this is the accounting office at NeoHappy," she said in a crisp, business-like tone. "We've mistakenly received a receipt for some additional charges after checkout at a hotel here in Boston. It should have come to your office. I'm sure you like to keep those . . . okay . . . thanks."

"Who's that?" whispered Brad. He had his laptop open as well, surfing the web for more information on the Pritchett list.

"Latour, Inc., the hair-care-products company," she whispered back. "This is the VP's office. Name is Stanton."

She shrugged resignedly at the lack of success so far. Her hour of playing the role of a NeoHappy accounting clerk had yielded only one hit so far, out of a dozen calls. But it was an important hit: a VP at Bountiful Group, a company that owned several chain restaurants. He had visited in Boston exactly when Lundgren made one of his jaunts to the Taj. He was a prime candidate to be a "paying customer" in Lundgren's scheme.

She waited for Stanton's assistant to come back on the line, her expression grim when Brad wasn't looking. She was remembering their tense exchange when Brad told her of Lundgren's under-the-table dealings. As if that news weren't disconcerting enough, then he told her that he was scheming with Bell to investigate the conspiracy, and contacting Pritchett at the *Boston World*.

"Listen, I'll try to support you," she'd told him unhappily. "But you're risking everything by pursuing this, you know? Your reputation, our finances, being sued, even being sent to jail."

"But you understand why I'm doing it."

She shook her head in bewilderment. "I'm trying. Okay, I get that you couldn't live with yourself if you didn't pursue it."

"I love you, you know."

"Yup, and I deserve it." She smiled, but for only a moment. "But I can't help thinking about what could happen to the girls, not to mention to us."

"But to just walk away—"

"I know, I know. We're stuck . . . trapped. The money, the contract, the NDA. And I get that, if you just drop it, *when* the underhanded stuff he's doing invariably comes out, you'd be accused of being an accessory. Maybe charged with obstruction of justice. The police, the FBI . . . everybody . . . will know you knew." So Annie had ultimately talked herself into going along.

Stanton's assistant came back on the line. "Yes," Annie said. "Yes, it is for the Four Seasons. Right. Can I check that date again? Okay, just let me know the person and a fax number to send the receipt, and I'll send it along. Okay. Bye."

She looked up triumphantly. "Albert Stanton stayed at the Four Seasons, right near the Taj, when Lundgren was there. Another possible conspirator!"

Over the next hours, she tracked down three more corporate vice presidents who had met with Lundgren over the previous year and whose products had shown a significant bump in sales.

"Okay, that's a start," Brad had said as she prepared for her shift, and he got ready to fetch the girls from school. "Now, it gets tougher. I've got to trace the money through NeoHappy."

• • •

"I really don't know why the hell I'm doing this." Bell stood beside the booth in the bar. He had appeared at the appointed time, but just stood there, shifting from one foot to the other.

"Look, I'll understand if you want out," said Brad. "I know you're risking your job, even getting sued."

"*Shit!*" Bell finally exclaimed, sighing and sitting down and opening his laptop. "Okay, for starters, when I poked around in the financials, I found something weird. NeoHappy has been buying duplicate scientific equipment," he said.

"Like what?"

Bell turned his laptop and slid it across the booth table to Brad. "Electron microscopes, chip fabrication systems, and so forth. You see that when they did an order, *two* of each machines were ordered. This started a couple of years ago. Why would we need two of everything?" He answered his own question. "I talked to the purchasing office director, and he said Lundgren wanted backups."

"Sounds reasonable. Those things probably take time to get," said Brad scrutinizing the list of equipment on the screen.

"Maybe. But they were shipped to separate addresses. The purchasing guy said one of each duplicate machine went to a warehouse outside the city."

"Okay, again that sounds reasonable."

"Yeah, maybe. But here's the real kicker. The second machines shipped to that address were *not* paid for from the regular equipment accounts. The money came from what the purchasing guy called a 'contingency account.'"

"And where did that money come from?"

"He didn't ask."

"*He didn't ask?* I mean keeping track of money was his business, right?"

"He said he frankly didn't want to know, in fact. But I did get him to show me the account documents and the purchase orders. You're not gonna like this."

"What?"

"The original account had Marty Fallon's signature on it. And both he and Lundgren signed the purchase orders."

Brad leaned back and closed his eyes. He pictured his future. It was bleak. "So Marty's involved. But where the money came from is a dead-end."

"Well, not quite. I went to the accounting director. I lied and got what I needed. So, you see, I'm neck-deep in this shit now. I told her we had to resolve some computer issues with the accounting system."

"So, you got in."

"Yeah, she gave me their password to review the contingency account. It was a Cayman Islands account. Lundgren told her it was revenue from overseas ventures that for technical reasons couldn't be deposited directly into the corporate budget."

"Technical reasons?"

"Yeah, sounds fishy, and the accounting director wouldn't really say so, but I got the idea she thought it sounded fishy, too. But accountants worry more about funds disappearing . . . embezzlement . . . than money coming in. So, she didn't pursue it. Besides, Lundgren's a pretty intimidating guy."

"Show me the account," said Brad, sliding Bell's computer back to him. Bell typed some commands and slid the computer back. The screen showed a list of deposits. Brad scanned it and blew out a whistle.

"Damn. These names are familiar. The Bountiful Group, Boehlert Chemicals, Latour, Inc., and several others. These match the companies whose VPs have met with Lundgren. Okay, this is odd." He turned the screen so that Bell could see it. "All the other companies show single deposits of half-a-million. But American Brands shows *two* separate deposits of half-a-million each. The latest one just a few days ago."

"For what, do you think?"

"Don't know. Maybe for an extra service of some kind. Over and above tweaking the ratings."

"Well, for half-a-million, it had to be something special."

"Okay," said Brad. "We've got a handle on the money. We need to see where the second machines are going."

"Well, the number of that warehouse is not listed in the company directory, but I found it on an invoice. I didn't want to call. You're the one who's trained in journalism. You know more about what to ask."

Brad took a deep breath. After a long pause to prepare himself, he nodded.

Bell brought up on his laptop the invoice with the phone number on it, and turned it so Brad could punch the number in on his phone.

"Warehouse," said the female voice that answered.

"Hello," said Brad. "I'm trying to reach the NeoHappy facility."

"This is a NeoHappy warehouse. How can I help you?"

"I've got a delivery to make. I need directions."

There was a long pause, then "Sir, this is a restricted facility. We don't give out directions over the phone. You'll have to contact the NeoHappy purchasing manager who made the order. They'll give you whatever information you need."

"Well, I'm on the road. I've got the equipment in the truck. If you could just—"

"I'm sorry sir. You have to go through the purchasing manager." The woman hung up the phone.

"That was odd," said Brad, sitting back in the seat, frowning in puzzlement. "They seem to be pretty cagey. I want to see this warehouse. If it's empty, we've got Lundgren and Fallon cold for embezzlement."

But even as he said it, Brad knew simple embezzlement wasn't likely the case. Fallon was a billionaire. Lundgren was probably rich as hell, too. Something else was going on.

• • •

Lundgren did not rise to greet Brad; did not offer to shake hands. He gestured for Brad to sit down, the expanse of his antique desk between them.

"So, are things going well with the book?" he asked, leaning back in his leather armchair.

The chess game continues, Brad thought. *Lundgren will use this meeting to exert his authority over me.*

"Things are going great," he said. "I've had good access to Marty. We just spent time on a California trip doing interviews. And I'm interviewing people who he knew growing up and at MIT. I've found some terrific background in the company archives."

"So, you're on track?"

"Sure. I've got enough to start writing sample chapters for a book proposal—"

"I just hope you're up to the quality needed."

"I hope so, too."

"Y'know, we had quite a few applicants for your job. We reviewed about a dozen names and portfolios. But Marty and the management group listened to me, in the end, when I advocated for you."

"Well, that's very—"

"And it's the reason they'll listen to me if I recommend firing you."

Brad felt his heart rate rise. Lundgren was laying the groundwork for canning him! He wondered what his Happy App would register.

"I don't understand, why—"

"Not only because of your inserting yourself into my business at the hotel, I have it on good authority that you are spending a great deal of time with our information technology director."

"I'm asking him technical questions . . . how to access databases and so forth."

"Well, if I have any inkling that you are collecting unauthorized information . . . just remember that the NDA agreement you signed not only means you can be fired, but you can also be sued for leaking corporate data. In fact, you may be prosecuted."

Brad decided the best defense was an offense. "So, you're saying you were doing business at the hotel, not social?"

Lundgren stiffened and paused very briefly, but ignored the question. "Look, we're doing critically important work here; developing products that will make people's lives happier and more productive. And I'm in charge of that work. I will not allow our progress to be endangered by the compromise of proprietary information. I would like to see this book project go ahead for the good of the company and for Marty's. But unless I can be assured that you are restricting your research to that required for Marty's biography, I will have you terminated."

Lundgren emphasized the word "terminated" in an oddly threatening way that was more than professionally unsettling. Brad sat silent for a long moment, his jaw clenched. He was trying to figure out what Lundgren really knew and how to answer him when Lundgren gave a dismissive wave of his hand signaling that the meeting was over. He picked up his phone and asked his assistant about plans for an engineering meeting. Brad got up and left.

Brad sat immersed in thought in his small office with the door closed for an hour, wrestling with the many implications of Lundgren's threats. As was a journalistic habit, he took notes to himself on a yellow pad, charting his reasoning.

He could lose the money for his family, damage his reputation, and be sued or even prosecuted. He could cause Bell to suffer the same fate.

But then his conscience took over, impelled by his journalist's training. He and Bell did have strong evidence that Lundgren, and maybe even Fallon, were up to no good. Strong, but not irrefutable. Lundgren was clever, and had likely begun taking steps to protect himself and his scam. But on the other hand, he was also arrogant, so he might well believe he'd solved the problem with his threats. In either case, his attack on Brad did show he was worried.

And yet again, Brad was nagged by the suspicion that those corrupt activities involved more than embezzlement. After all, they were very wealthy men already; why would they want more money?

So, the choice was clear-cut: whether to retreat to certain safety or advance toward an uncertain, perhaps dangerous, future.

Brad made a call. He wouldn't proceed without Annie's blessing; it was her life, too. But if she agreed, he would yield to that same compulsive curiosity that drove the scientists he'd written about for a decade.

He needed to know more.

CHAPTER 12

B rad had driven for an hour out beyond the Route 485 loop that circled Boston. With Bell beside him scrutinizing the Google Map on his tablet, they had navigated the narrow rural road, reaching an unmarked driveway that wound away through the forest.

They'd driven up the driveway for a quarter mile, stopping only when a guardhouse came into view. Bell switched to a satellite image of the area, zooming in. He showed the screen to Brad. It revealed a sprawling building beyond the guard station, set amid an expanse of forest. The building was surrounded by a large parking lot. It actually consisted of two interconnected buildings, with the roof of the larger section covered by many white dots.

"Okay, this is the place, but I don't want to risk dealing with a guard," said Brad. "We're going to have to get a look at it from another angle."

So, they backtracked using the map to navigate the narrow roads, until they estimated that they had reached a border of the property safely opposite the guarded entrance. Brad parked the car, and they began to push through the thickets of trees and vines, crunching gingerly through the carpet of autumn leaves.

Making their way laboriously in the direction indicated by the map, they finally reached their destination and crouched behind a large, lichen-encrusted boulder. They ducked down just as a golf cart carrying two armed men sped into view along the back of the building. The men were scanning the forest, with one saying something over a walkie-talkie.

"Okay, this is clearly not a warehouse," whispered Bell as they peered through the thicket of trees and a chain link fence topped by razor wire.

Before them loomed a huge windowless brick building, with a parking lot filled with cars. "Armed guards don't patrol warehouses."

"And they don't have surveillance," said Brad, pointing out an array of video cameras mounted along the edge of the roof.

"Or vents," said Bell, pointing at tall white metal exhaust vents jutting from the roof.

"I thought so," said Brad. "Those are the dots we saw on the satellite image. This is a lab, not just a warehouse. They're the kinds of exhaust vents I've seen before on lab buildings. So, the smaller section must be offices, and this section is the lab."

Brad pointed his smartphone at the building and snapped a series of photos, scanning across it left to right. Later, he'd stitch them into a panoramic view they could scrutinize for details.

They backed away from the boulder, until they were safely out of sight of the building, then turned and made their way back to the car.

"What next?" asked Bell.

"Hell if I know," said Brad flipping through the images, shaking his head. "I'm going to keep working on the book as usual. You carry on, too. We've got to be damned careful. They are doing some kind of research in there that they don't want anybody to know about . . . not even other people in the company."

• • •

"The little shit is sitting in the woods on the north side of the lab!" exclaimed Beale into the phone. He leaned in to look at the computer screen showing a map with a red dot labeled "Davis, Bradley."

"Well, I guess my warning didn't work," said Lundgren. "Is Bell with him?"

"Not sure. Bell's got an old version two-point-zero chip. No GPS. We don't have eyes on them. And we can't send guards out there, or we'll let on we know his position."

"But Bell's chip has the control capability. We could affect him if we wanted to."

"Of course, Larry. It's a two-point-zero chip." Beale moved away from the technician monitoring Brad's position and whispered into the phone, "Y'know, just one touch of a button and Davis wouldn't be a problem anymore . . . permanently. He's got the terminal reservoir."

"Hell, not now! Not with him right there by the lab! Are you insane?"

"Okay, Larry, but we could pick a time and place that won't arouse suspicion. At home at night in bed, for example. Right in front of his family. They'd be witnesses. These things happen. Young people die sometimes."

"Look, there's another reason I don't want to do Davis. I just finalized a financial arrangement with Bailey. He's Executive Vice President of American Brands. He wants to be CEO."

"God damn. You don't mean—"

"We've got the capability. We might as well monetize it."

"*Monetize?* Hah, Larry, you sure know how to use jargon to talk about murder-for-hire."

"I'll come by tonight. Just have our trusted guys there. We'll start the process."

"Sure, start monetizing to amortize our investment," said Beale sarcastically.

There was a long pause while Lundgren decided whether to ignore the near-insubordination. Finally, he said, "So, let's not use the chip on Davis . . . yet. And there's still Bell. We have hormonal control over him. And we still don't know exactly what they know. Or think they know. Call Coronado Security. Tell the operative to put a tail on Davis and Bell. Also, tell him we might instruct him to take action, on either or both."

"Jesus, that Coronado guy is fucking scary," said Beale. "You didn't see how they killed the clinical trial subjects."

"It shows he's also capable of doing what we need done," said Lundgren, hanging up.

• • •

Brad leaned against his favorite lamppost, waiting for the girls. Today, though, his attention wasn't riveted happily on the school door, but on his smartphone screen. He'd set a Google Alert to catch any news about American Brands or Frederick Bailey.

The Alert had yielded some hits—deeply disturbing ones. Reuters News Agency reported that John Parker, the CEO of American Brands, had experienced some kind of public breakdown at a big corporate dinner the night before. The Reuters report said he'd been hospitalized. And a piece on the *Forbes* website reported that the executive vice president, Frederick Bailey, had taken over day-to-day management temporarily.

Had Lundgren caused this breakdown? If so, how? Could it be related to the Happy Chip? And what should he do about the warning from Lundgren? And what about the warehouse that was really a laboratory?

He was deep in clouded, distracted thought, when he heard the scrape of shoes on pavement behind him. His growing paranoia made him flinch and whirl to face a ragged young woman, her face smudged with dirt, a moth-eaten wool cap pulled low over an unkempt mop of brown hair.

"Hey," she said in a raspy voice. The organic odor of dirty clothes and an unbathed body wafted from her. She stood hunched over, as if fearing that someone was about to hit her. She looked up at him with rheumy brown eyes. Tear stains had eroded paths down her soiled cheeks.

"I'm sorry?" queried Brad, taking a step back. "What do you want?" It was very strange to see a street person here in the suburbs. They preferred downtown, where they could shelter in the subway and hang out in fast-food joints.

"Take out your wallet like you're giving me money."

"What? What are you talking about?"

The woman glanced around fearfully, the whites of her eyes contrasting with the dark face. "I'm going to tell you about NeoHappy. I worked there. They experimented on me. Phyllis Kelley. Now, take out your wallet and hand me a dollar. Like I'm panhandling."

"NeoHappy? You know me?"

"Of course. I read you're doing Marty Fallon's biography. I tracked you. You need to know what I know. But dammit, hurry up! I think you're being followed. I saw a guy. He's around the corner now getting a coffee. He'll be back in a minute."

Brad shook his head, but took out his wallet and extracted a dollar, handing it to the woman.

"Look, I don't understand—" he started to say, but stopped when he felt a cell phone slip into his hand as she took the bill.

"I'll call you," she rasped. "*Oh, God! Not again!*" she moaned to herself, slumping over before recovering and slouching away.

The girls appeared, and he took their hands and walked to the car. But today, he was ignoring their happy chatter; instead he was trying to look around for somebody following him. It was hard to pick anybody out, there were so many people on the street. He buckled the girls into their car seats and climbed into the driver's seat. Maybe he'd try a bit of slightly reckless maneuvering, which wouldn't be noticed among Boston's slightly loony drivers, but which might give him a clue.

He pulled the car out of the parking lot, turned right, drove half-a-block and immediately did a u-turn in the middle, cutting off a van, whose driver honked. He watched in the mirror. Behind him, a black suv did the same.

• • •

The disposable cell phone the street woman had given him rang late that night, rousing Brad from the blackness of a deep sleep. He rubbed his face to become clear enough to answer. He looked groggily over at the empty side of the bed, remembering that Annie was on a night shift. So the call would not disturb her, either in the sleep sense or in the worry sense. She would certainly grasp that he was being contacted by somebody with dangerous information, and he wanted her to have as much deniability as possible.

"Phyllis?" he asked.

"Don't use my name. Are you alone?" she asked.

"Yes. Look, I checked the NeoHappy employee directory. You're not in it. I asked a guy in IT to check your name, too. He said you've never been an employee. So, I'm not going to—"

"I didn't work at the main lab. I worked in one that's off-site . . . that's secret."

"Where is this lab? What does it look like?"

"Can you record this conversation?"

"Well, yes. I have a connector to a recorder."

"Okay, set it up and record. But only store the file on your laptop, behind a password. Okay?"

"Yeah, sure," said Brad rolling out of bed to rummage through his bag on the small table in the corner that constituted his office. He came up with the digital recorder and a connector and attached it to the phone. He switched on the recorder. "I'm recording. Still there?"

"Yes, look, I can't talk long. They may have bugged your place, so just listen and give short answers."

"No, first you answer my questions. Prove to me you know about the . . . thing you said."

"Okay, but from now on, short answers."

"Okay! All right!" Brad was teetering between believing this woman and dismissing her as a loon. But then she launched into a precise description of the laboratory building he and Bell had reconnoitered, complete with its location and what the guardhouse looked like.

She ended by asking, "You know about the version two chip?"

"No."

"You chipped?"

"Yes."

"When?"

"About a week ago."

"*Shit! Shit!* Then they probably gave you the new version two-point-one. Your chip has GPS tracking. So, they know where you are at all times. And it's a sequestration chip."

"Sequestration? I don't—"

"A goddamned *control* chip! It sequesters . . . isolates and stores hormones . . . and can release them in a burst. Don't say anything. Just 'yes' if you understand."

Brad's hand began to tremble. A *control* chip. So they were controlling his hormone levels, not just monitoring them!

"Yes. But Jesus, what—"

"Don't say anything else, just listen. They can use that control to make you do things you wouldn't otherwise do. They were testing it on me. I think it has other capabilities, but I'm not sure what. They killed the others."

"Others?"

"Maybe a dozen. More, maybe."

A dozen murders! He thought. *It could not possibly be, even for Lundgren! And especially not Fallon!*

"We have to meet," he whispered. "I just can't do this over the phone. I need to see you in person."

"Absolutely not! Too risky. They know exactly where you are, and there's somebody tailing you. They're looking to kill me, and the guy following you would do that in a heartbeat. They've tried their best using my chip to blast me with hormones, maybe with other drugs that made me suicidal. The chip has reservoirs. If I hadn't known what they were doing, I would have already been driven to kill myself. *Others did!*"

"We have to meet. I won't proceed unless we do."

She breathed a painful moan, whispering "*Oh, dear God!*" Clearly, she was under some kind of traumatic stress. He couldn't tell without meeting her whether it was her own demons or those induced by the chip. Finally, she seemed to recover enough to answer.

"I'll figure something out." The line went dead.

• • •

Brad waited in the Park Street Station, checking the GPS map on his phone. The arrow icon pinpointed him as being in the station, which meant that the NeoHappy people had his location, too. He smiled wryly and shook his head at the irony of calling these bastards "Happy." He nervously paced the narrow platform, breathing the familiar funky-sweet aroma of Boston's subways, listening to the sonorous voice of the announcer.

Scanning the platform surreptitiously, he noticed a couple of men who could be following him. He moved down the platform to see whether they would stick close. They casually moved, too. He had to lose them.

Phyllis had instructed him what to do, so he watched for the right train to pull in from the Charles Street station. Finally, heralded by a rush of air and the screech of metal wheels on rails, it slid into view.

This was the one he'd been looking for. A yellow sticky-note was attached to the last window of the last car. Its door opened, people exited, then others began streaming in. He waited until the last instant and slipped into the car. One of the two guys, a short man in a brown leather jacket, slipped in the next car down. Then at the last instant, Brad leaped out again, leaving the man in the car as the doors closed and the train accelerated away into the tunnel. An old trick, but it worked. One guy left.

He did the same with the next car, quickly slipping in and out. This time the remaining man followed him in, but was ready to slip out as he did. Still on the platform, the man studiously avoided looking at Brad, to preserve the illusion that he wasn't following him. Phyllis was smart, though. She'd told him how to give this guy the slip. She knew the guy would assume Brad was going to pull the in-and-out trick again.

But he didn't. At the last instant, he boarded the fourth train after the one with the paper signal, as Phyllis had instructed. Now he stayed on, watching as the train left the station, the frustrated man standing on the platform.

He was certain he had no other tails. The other passengers either had their heads bowed over the screens of their smartphones and e-readers, or stared blankly ahead with the usual bored riding-the-subway look.

They were paying little attention as the slight young man with the reddish hair carrying a large bag got on, sitting in the most distant seat he could find. They also took little note as a rather disreputable young woman with tattered clothes navigated the swaying car, hunched over, to sit down beside him.

"How do you feel?" she whispered, as the car lurched along, heading south, periodically rolling into one station after another—South Station, Broadway, Bradley . . .

"Look, how do I know you're not crazy?" Brad whispered to her. "How do I know you're not just some fired employee who carries a grudge?"

"Tell me how the hell you feel. Then we'll talk."

"I feel fine."

"Then they haven't started. They still think you're useful."

"Started what? What would I feel otherwise?"

"Suicidal. You'd feel like getting off this train and jumping in front of the next one. That's how I feel. Constantly." At that moment, the train reached the Kennedy Museum stop, and the doors opened.

Brad wondered whether he'd have to restrain this woman. "You're sure this isn't just . . . well . . . a mental problem you have?"

Phyllis smiled grimly and rubbed her grimy temples, shaking her head. "Okay, here's what happened. Turn on your recorder."

Brad took out his digital recorder and pressed the record button. She took it and held it up to her lips, so she wouldn't be heard. Some of the other riders looked at the pair curiously.

"They told me they wanted me to test a new chip. So, they injected it, and everything seemed fine at first. Then the sky fell in on me. I'd go up sky-high . . . feeling great . . . then I'd crash. Deep, deep depression. I was all over the place. Highs and lows. I figured something was bad wrong. I decided to find out who else was in this trial, to see if it was just me."

"And you found out?"

"Yes. I got access to the clinical records and found the list of experimental subjects. At that point the engineers hadn't realized anything was wrong with the new chips. The others weren't due to come in for evaluation for a few days. So, I called some of the others. They were in a bad way, all of them. Same thing as me. Then I called one guy, and his roommate answered. He'd committed suicide. Shot himself in the head."

"Jesus!"

"Then I checked on all of them. There were three suicides . . . one poisoning, a second jumped off a building, and third hanged himself."

"Why didn't you go to the police?"

"Well, by that time, the company had sent out the security goons. The scientists had realized that their trial had gone to shit. They had a guy watching me. I tried like hell to act like nothing was wrong." She stopped and grimaced. "Oh, man. Another wave." She bent over and moaned, then recovered. The middle-aged man next to her pointedly got up and moved. "They're blasting the shit out of me." She recovered a bit and said, "Anyway, before I managed to get out of there, I hacked into the database file on the clinical trial, read the research protocol document."

"On the new chip? The version two?"

"Yeah, the intro explained everything. They were trying to develop a chip that could *control* people's mental state, not just *monitor* it. The version two is not just one chip, but a system, a series of components. There's the control chip itself. But also there are separate reservoirs that can grab specific hormones from the bloodstream, and store them . . . sequestration, they call it. And the chip controls the release of the hormones. But what scared the shit out of me was that there are other reservoirs."

"Containing what?" Brad realized they didn't have much time before the train reached the end of the line at Braintree. They would have to get off and switch to the inbound train. He wasn't sure he could keep her from bolting.

"Well, I know that one reservoir contains a pleasure chemical. It's a molecular form of dopamine that crosses the blood-brain barrier. It can trigger the brain's pleasure centers. If they let that loose, it could bliss you out! But then there's other different reservoirs. They put different ones into different people. They could put any drug they wanted into a reservoir. And they can inject new reservoirs whenever they want, to continue the dosage or add a new drug."

Brad sat up, watching the train pull into another station, trying to absorb what he was hearing. "Why the hell would they develop a control chip?"

"The research protocol said there was a civilian use. Imagine if people could control their own moods, their energy levels. *Everybody* would buy one."

"Yeah, and they'd end up like those lab rats that press the lever to get cocaine and ignore food and water until they die."

"Yeah, they figured that would be a problem. That's one way they rationalized building in a remote control using the cell network. They're

controlling my chip now. That's why I'm going through this hell. And you can be damned sure they've been controlling yours."

"Oh, my God!" exclaimed Brad, drawing stares from the other passengers. He recalled his recent daytime feelings of energy, of euphoria, his deep contentment and relaxation at night. He remembered the amazing sex with Annie.

Phyllis shook her head in sympathy and continued. "But the main applications—the main reason they gave it remote control—were industrial, military. Imagine if you could control workers or soldiers to relax totally when they were off-duty, not to have any anxiety. Then, in the factory or in battle, they could be juiced to work or fight like demons . . . never get tired."

"Okay, so their objective in these trials was to secretly test this chip on people, which is illegal."

"*Illegal as hell!* But they needed to have the system already perfected when they did start animal trials, then on to clinical trials. They didn't want the FDA to see the sausage being made—a prototype chip that might glitch . . . hell, did glitch! And the only way they could be sure it worked was clandestine human trials. We all signed stringent NDAs. And they gave us fifty thousand bucks up front, with another fifty when the trial was done. They never told us what the chip did. But for a hundred thousand bucks, people will accept all kinds of risks."

"Did they think there would be glitches?"

"They sure as hell didn't expect the chip to malfunction so badly . . . people going nuts, killing themselves. But their security goons covered it up by making those they could reach disappear. And those they couldn't . . . the suicides and nut cases . . . well . . . the security people managed to hide those subjects' participation in the trials . . . getting their computers, tossing their apartments, and so forth."

The train reached Braintree, and they got off, walking over to the inbound train. But Phyllis stopped before boarding the train back to Boston. "Look, I'm pretty sure I know how to block the chip's function, at least temporarily."

"How?"

"I'm not telling you. They know where you are. If they catch you, they'll force you to tell. I guarantee it. And I need this advantage." She waved him off. "I need you to get on that train and get as far away from me as possible. Unless you do, I'm dead. And if they catch you with me, you're dead."

Brad hesitated, but slipped onto the subway train as the door closed. As the train pulled away, he watched Phyllis slump onto a bench huddled over, her head bowed.

CHAPTER 13

Brad exited the train at Park Street Station and followed the crowd upstairs to the Green Line. He was tempted to check his stress level on his Happy App, as he stood waiting at the yellow stripe for the next trolley. He was sure it was high. He needed this comforting ride on the familiar trolley—hearing the dinging of its bell as it arrived; feeling the gentle sway of the car as it wound its way through the narrow, ancient tunnel blackened with venerable age. And anticipating the enjoyment of the trolley emerging from the tunnel into the bright New England autumn day, to rattle into the suburbs toward West Newton.

He needed home. Some time at home would give him perspective on the incredible story he'd just heard. He'd figure out what to do next.

He realized he had to scan the station for his tails. *Oh, Jesus!* he exclaimed to himself. Over by a column stood the familiar short man in the brown leather jacket! Eyeing Brad, he was speaking into a cell phone.

Suddenly Brad's heart began pounding so hard it seemed about to burst from his chest. White-hot panic smothered him. His eyes widened with utter horror, his mouth gaped open, he staggered forward across the tracks in front of a stopped trolley.

"OH GOD! OH GOD!" he cried, catching himself from falling and staggering back against a support pillar, turning and embracing its cold surface. The fear clawed at his gut, and he groaned and thrashed, as if his flailing could rid himself of it.

"NO! STOP!" he shouted. The nearby subway musician, thinking he meant her, stopped playing her guitar, staring at him with startled round eyes. The crowd around him shrank away, leaving him the center of a circle of frightened people. A little girl began to cry.

The fear gave way to a smothering shroud of the blackest depression that penetrated to his soul, the most bone-deep feeling of hopelessness he'd ever known. He sank to the grimy brick floor, sobbing and clutching his head.

"OH PLEASE! OH NO!" He curled himself into a ball, moaning.

After what seemed an eternity of torture, a broad Boston accent above him asked him what his problem was. Through eyes veiled in tears, he saw a large figure in a tan uniform, a badge, a wide leather belt holding a pistol. Powerful arms lifted him up. The searing panic returned and he lashed out violently against the arms, yelling maniacally. He felt his hands being wrenched behind his back, metal cuffs clamping hard around his wrists, being hauled through the crowd.

He kicked and thrashed. *This man was trying to kill him!* Panic ripped through him like a lightning bolt.

"*Nuh . . . nuh . . .*" he grunted. "*You want to kill . . . you're trying to . . .*"

"Pal, you need help," the deep voice said. "Just try to stay calm." The voice was joined by others. More uniforms surrounded him. Thrashing wildly, he was dragged up steps into sunlight, a chill wind blowing around him.

More people trying to kill him! Hands lifted his struggling body into the back seat of a car with metal mesh separating the back and front seats. He slumped over onto the cracked brown leather, sobbing, kicking the door and windows as hard as he could. *He needed to escape these killers!* Through the bone-deep panic, a memory worked its way into his consciousness. Of Phyllis, bent over, moaning.

"*Stop! It's the chip! The chip!*" he exclaimed.

"We need to secure him," he heard a voice say.

The car door opened, and massive bodies pinned his legs, and he felt manacles clamping his ankles. He felt a hand in his back pocket, pulling out his wallet.

He heard the muffled voice of a radio call. A voice in the car answered with his name, his address. He heard ". . . No wants, no warrants. This guy is wicked screwed up. Went nuts in the T. No apparent injuries."

"*The chip!*" heard himself exclaim, pleadingly. "*Happy Chip! Please! It did this to me!*"

A voice from the front seat. "Okay, sir, just calm down. We'll get ya help."

Then, the other voice: ". . . yeah . . . yeah . . . okay . . . transport to the station. We'll process him. But alert the psych ward at Boston General."

Now vaulting out of the fear came another emotional wave, now exultation, utter euphoria. "Oh, yeaahh!" he breathed, smiling. "No problem, officer. So gooooood!" He was sailing along on top of the world. Everything was wonderful. He laughed.

The exultation disappeared. The black shroud smothered him again, the unreasoning panic, and he began to sob, slumping over on the seat. Now Phyllis's warning insinuated its way into his conscious. *Use your brain! Fight the feelings! Know that it's them; it's not you!* But that logic fought a losing battle against the terror that was gnawing away at his soul.

"Sir, you're going to have to calm down," he heard from the front seat. Then he heard the two cops talking to each other: About a Patriots game. Taking the kids that weekend. He couldn't understand how people could talk about just mundane things when his world was collapsing in on him. *When they were taking him to his death!*

Alternating waves of fear, exhilaration, and depression crashed against one another in his body, as beefy men in uniforms hauled him from the car, sat him into a black plastic chair and strapped him in. He was vaguely aware of a video camera trained on him, as he was strapped in. He continued to struggle, as he was wheeled into a large waiting room, then down a hall under fluorescent lights.

Suddenly, all emotion simply deserted him, except for utter fatigue. He slumped over, unable to move.

He felt a cuff tighten around his arm. They were taking his blood pressure. Something cold on his chest. A stethoscope. A needle prick in his arm roused him from his fatigued stupor. He flinched.

"We're just drawing your blood, sir," said a female voice. "Nothing to be afraid of." Then: "This one's for psych," said the female voice. "We won't process him."

He was left in a corner facing a wall, slumped over. He didn't know how long he stayed there. Every ounce of energy was drained from him. He was an empty husk.

"Mr. Davis?" asked another female voice. He looked up to see a young woman in a police uniform. "Mr. Davis? Do you understand me? Sir? Do you know where you are? You're in the police station. You had an episode."

"The chip," he mumbled. "It's the chip."

"Ambulance is coming in now," he heard a male voice behind him say.

He continued to struggle feebly, enduring the remnants of suicidal lows, rapturous highs, and panicked paranoia in which he was certain he would be killed. A cop wheeled him back down the corridor and out to a waiting ambulance. Three men unstrapped him from the chair, strapped him to a gurney and hauled the gurney into its back, doors slammed shut. A white-clad man sat beside him, checking his blood pressure.

After a swerving ride through Boston's winding streets, the ambulance stopped, and the white-coated men slid his gurney out of the ambulance and into the emergency room.

More fluorescent lights passing overhead, more hallways, an elevator, wheeled into a fluorescent-lit room, lifted onto a bed, padded straps fastening his wrists to the rails, a jab in his arm. A warm blanket of tranquil relief settling over him, shrouding the panic, the fear, the elation. But they still lurked, waiting to engulf him again. A nurse's voice came through the enveloping fog.

"Sir, we've given you a sedative. You'll be all right. Just relax."

A moment of resigned clarity emerged through the warm haze of the drug. Now, Lundgren had rendered him powerless, not only physically. Now nobody would believe anything he said. His credibility was gone, shredded by the ravings of a madman . . . him.

. . .

He was immersed in a deep, exhausted sleep when her voice lured him to consciousness. It was that soft, soothing voice he loved.

"Brad, sweetheart? Sweetie? Wake up."

A warm hand on his brow. Then a pat on his shoulder. A kiss on his cheek. He opened his eyes to see her face. Her wonderful face framed by blond ringlets. A smile, but not a happy smile, with creased brow, eyes wide with anxiety. Her voice quavered slightly, but showed the firm calm of a nurse who knew how to handle a patient.

"You had a breakdown. You're safe now. Everything will be fine."

"It was the chip."

She shook her head in puzzlement. "What? What do you mean?"

His voice was thick with the tranquilizer. He took a deep breath, inhaling the subtle tang of hospital air.

"Met a woman who had worked there . . . NeoHappy. A secret laboratory. There was a clinical trial. A new chip . . . controls people . . . controlled her . . . I have it in me . . . makes you crazy with fear, depression, euphoria."

"Sweetheart, they found PCP in your bloodstream. How did it get there? Could somebody have put it in a drink or something?"

"PCP? No . . . the chip."

"Oh, dear," she whispered. "Oh, sweetheart." She took his hand, which was still strapped to the hospital bed. He saw her eyes begin to glisten with tears. She kissed him again on the cheek.

"I'll be back. I just have to talk to the doctors."

She left. Brad realized he had been babbling to her, but the drugs and the emotions that tore at him had robbed him of coherence. A true feeling rose now; not one spawned by the bursts of chemicals coursing through his blood.

Desperation.

. . .

Lundgren's voice on the phone was curt with annoyance. "Did you get him?"

"Yeah," replied Beale. "Our guy reacquired him at Park Street station. We figured he'd take the trolley there. Gave him the full treatment. Our guy said he went nuts. Cops dragged him away. And it was a good thing we included a PCP reservoir. That was the icing on the cake."

"You've got video?"

"Yeah, in the т station. Our guy just sent it. He got Davis's satchel, too"

"Send them both to me."

"You going to send it to the тv stations?"

"No, of course not! That would raise unwanted attention. No, I'll just threaten him with it. Where is he now?"

"gps shows him at Boston General," replied Beale, peering over the shoulder of the technician, whose display screen showed a map of Boston littered with the dots of chip locations. His computer mouse hovered over a dot just south of downtown, the pop-up box reading "Davis, Bradley."

"They took him to the psych ward, I suppose."

"Good bet," said Beale.

"Good. We'll check his computer and see what he knows. Keep up the regimen."

"Well, the pcp reservoir is depleted. Only way to repeat that would be to inject him with new reservoirs."

"Okay, then, if you can get somebody into the hospital, do that. I want him seen as totally unbalanced. I want him suicidal. What's the situation with the American Brands target?"

"Well, gps shows him in Chicago Methodist Hospital."

"The client wants final closure . . . not to risk recovery. Or discovery."

"Kill him? Goddamnit, that's just too dangerous!" exclaimed Beale. "There will be an investigation—"

"And they won't find a thing." As usual, Lundgren hung up without a good-bye.

• • •

"Give me the phone," commanded Annie in her nurse-instructing-a-patient voice. She thrust out her hand insistently, as if asking for a dangerous object from a child. Brad recognized it as distinctive from her friendly-wife voice, but still resisted.

"You don't understand," he said, in a Valium-sedated voice, even as his body trembled with the remnant trauma of vicious highs and lows. He sat on the edge of the bed in their apartment, bent over, clutching the cell phone in his hand, staring at it. "They need to stop this. They need to investigate. The FBI, the FDA. There've been murders."

"Okay, okay. I believe you. But if you call them, they'll check you out and find out you just got out of a psych ward. And that you tested positive for drugs. If they report your calls to the doctors there, they *will* put you back in. After your action in the subway, they'll see you as a danger to yourself and others. I won't be able to persuade them to release you into my care again."

"Pritchett!" exclaimed Brad, desperation coloring his voice, still clutching the phone. "I'll call Sam. He gave me the data on the bumps in product sales. He'll listen. He'll understand. He'll launch an investigation."

"Yes but, Brad, a greedy corporation is a far, far cry from a murderous one that's trying to control people. I don't want you to ruin your reputation, to let you put yourself in further danger."

"Then Jim Bell," said Brad, still not relinquishing the phone. "He'll listen. He knows what kind of people they are."

Annie lowered her hand, a look of resignation on her face. She shook her head, realizing that she couldn't dissuade him from taking some kind of action. This would be the least damaging.

Brad punched in Bell's cell number. She hovered beside him, listening to his side of the conversation, prepared to snatch the phone from him, if necessary.

"Jim there? Oh. You're his girlfriend? Well, why do you have his phone? No . . . no . . . *Oh, dear God!*" The phone fell from Brad's hand, and he covered his face in despair.

Annie picked up the phone. "What happened?"

"He's being taken to the hospital. He tried to commit suicide."

CHAPTER 14

Brad stood for a moment trying to steady himself before entering the waiting room of Boston General's neuroscience intensive care unit. But when he stepped forward, he stumbled slightly, grabbing the door frame, trying to withstand the crippling waves of emotions still washing over him. The heavy doses of Valium barely suppressed the panic, the depression, the elation.

In one of the rows of chairs, he found a petite, tearful young woman sitting with three grim-faced people. One of them introduced herself as Bell's sister Vicki, a sturdy woman with long brown hair. A couple introduced themselves as friends.

"You're Marcia?" he asked the tearful woman. "I'm Brad. I was on the phone. How is he?"

Marcia looked up and shook her head, wiping her eyes with a tissue. "He's alive. He's critical, but the doctors say he's got a good chance. They said the bullet didn't go straight in. Apparently, the gun slipped when he shot, and the bullet passed through the inside of his skull. *Why would he do this?*"

"Can you tell me what led up to . . . it?"

"Well, everything seemed okay. He was worried about work. But he didn't say why. He told me I shouldn't know about it. I didn't know what that meant. Yesterday morning, he woke up screaming. He was so scared! I asked him what was the matter. He just said he didn't know. Then he started saying something about feeling hopeless. He was crying. We have this gun he bought me for when he was traveling . . ." Before she finished, she broke into sobs that racked her body.

Brad sat in a chair across from the group and leaned forward. "We were working on a project together. It might have something to do with it. Could I see him?"

"He's resting now," said Vicki decisively, putting an arm around Marcia and glaring at Brad, an eyebrow raised in suspicion. "The doctor said he shouldn't be disturbed. Besides, how is it possible that what he was doing with computers would have anything to do with his shooting himself? He's a computer guy, for God's sake!"

"Just for a moment. I might be able to help."

"*What is it with you people?*" exclaimed Vicki, her voice thick with anger. "You come around here to ask about work when he's fighting for his life?"

"*We* people?" asked Brad.

"Yes. You're the second guy from work. We let the first guy go in, and he wanted to spend some private time with Jimmy, so we let him. But now you come! Jesus, can't you all leave him alone?"

"What was the guy like?"

"What the hell difference does that make? A big guy. Brush cut. Face stubble. Like he didn't shave for a few days."

Brad sat up in the chair. It could have been the security guy who was at Fallon's house. "Jim would want to talk to me. He'd want to tell me about this guy."

"Rocky Road," said Marcia abruptly, wiping her eyes. Vicki looked at her, with an expression of surprise and annoyance.

"What?" asked Brad.

"That's the code word. You need it to get in to see him. Everybody needs a code word to get in to the ICU. But you can only stay a little while. I'd go with you, but . . ." She couldn't finish the sentence, but began to weep again, as Vicki shook her head in resignation and hugged her.

"Just you don't disturb him!" Vicki warned.

Still fighting vicious waves of emotion that eroded his concentration, Brad pushed through the double doors and into the intensive care unit. The brightly lit room—holding the subtle organic odor of illness—was quiet. Doctors and nurses were going about the business of tending to patients. The room was encircled with glass-walled cubicles holding patients attached to an array of monitors and IV bags.

Brad gave a nurse the code word and was directed to the third bay on the left. He slid open the glass door, and slipped in.

Jim lay in the bed, his head swathed in bandages, from which jutted a device that looked like a bolt. Another tube emerged from his skull, draining a pinkish fluid into a plastic bag. Electrodes snaked from his chest to a heart monitor. He had only a small oxygen tube draped beneath his nose, so if he was awake, he could talk.

Brad leaned over and whispered "Jim? Jim? It's Brad. I know how you're feeling. I am, too. Jim, it's your chip that's doing it."

Bell stirred, groaning quietly, opening his eyes slightly. "Hurting. So bad," his voice slurred.

"It's the chip, Jim! It releases hormones not just monitors them! It's controlling your hormones. And it probably releases drugs. That's what made you so depressed . . . made you try to kill yourself."

Bell showed no evidence that he'd heard. He lifted his left hand and touched his right arm. "Here. Something here."

"What do you mean?"

But Bell's hand dropped to his chest, and his eyes closed.

The door slid open, and a nurse smiled gently and said "I'm afraid you have to leave now, sir. He needs to rest."

Brad made his way back to the waiting room, finding Vicki and the others.

"I'm so sorry, but—" he began.

"Okay, you're sorry," snapped Vicki. "We've established that. Now leave!" She stood up, her body stiff with indignation, and Brad nodded in apology and left.

He stood outside the hospital, taking another four Valiums. Now, guilt was added to his utter fear and abject despair. Why hadn't he called Bell the moment Phyllis Kelley told him about the version 2.0 chip and its devastating power? Why hadn't he warned Bell about the people who might be following him? True, he didn't know that Bell had a version 2.0 chip, but that didn't matter.

He checked his phone for Google Alerts, and the news made him collapse onto the bench near the entry. "Oh, dear God," he whispered to himself.

The first sentences of the Associated Press report read, "American Brands CEO John Parker has died of an apparent heart attack, after being hospitalized when he collapsed at a corporate dinner Wednesday night. A hospital spokesperson said his family was in attendance."

Any wisp of hope Brad had evaporated. Suicide wasn't the only danger from the chip. Somehow, the vicious emotions he was feeling could actually kill him!

But he had no real proof of Lundgren's involvement, and without Bell he was unlikely to get any. He was at the mercy of Lundgren and his murderous whims.

He slumped into a chair and bent over, his head in his hands. A lady wheeling an elderly man into the hospital stopped to ask him if he was okay, and he tried to reassure her. After fifteen minutes trying to think through possibilities with a Valium-fogged, emotion-wracked brain, he stood up as best he could.

The best defense is a good offense, he thought. He would confront Lundgren.

CHAPTER 15

Brad passed beneath the looming globe that was the Happy Chip sculpture, recalling the time when he regarded that object with admiration. Now it was a terrifying Sword of Damocles, hanging over him and millions of other people. He took out his key card and tried it on the elevator. Surprisingly, it worked! The door opened, and the elevator allowed him to access the executive floor.

When he emerged from the elevator, he expected to encounter a guard, but there was only the receptionist, who nodded and smiled her routine smile. He walked down the long hall toward Lundgren's office, but stopped suddenly, leaning against the wall in relieved shock.

He felt fine! In fact, he felt great! It was as if some ponderous, smothering blanket had lifted off him. He remained there, relishing the relief, the feeling of . . . happiness! He realized that, of course, he was being manipulated again, but this time to make him feel good. Ironically, he found himself fighting against this feeling—fighting to maintain his resolve, his concentration on the task at hand—as he had fought the wrenching fear and depression. He had to stay angry, stay focused.

He continued to Lundgren's office, entering to find the elegant assistant, who looked up, smiled and said. "Mr. Davis, he's expecting you. Go right in."

Surprised at first, Brad realized that Lundgren had been a step ahead of him until now, and likely still was. He entered the office to find Lundgren sitting comfortably in one of the armchairs, having coffee and leafing through a sheaf of papers. He motioned for Brad to sit across from him on the couch, but Brad remained standing.

"I thought we'd give you a little rest," said Lundgren, setting the papers down on the coffee table. "You held up quite well, you know. Others didn't do so well."

"You fucker! You almost had me! But you—"

"It's probably best for you that you lower your voice. Wouldn't want my assistant testifying that you're unbalanced, would you? So, let's dispense with the vituperation, shall we? You must realize by now that you've been effectively neutralized. Nobody will believe anything you say. I would suggest that the best course for you is to give up this useless quest and continue your work with Marty uninterrupted. It's best for you. And it's best for Marty and the company."

"I know everything. I've talked with Phyllis Kelley."

"And you have some proof?"

"I do . . . well, I did."

"In your bag? *That* bag?" Lundgren gestured to a shelf in his office. Brad hadn't notice that his bag was sitting there. He rushed over and grabbed it. Lundgren sneered. "Oh, it's been searched. Unfortunately, the recording of your conversation with Miss Kelley did not survive the search. Nor did your notes. You know, it would have been a wise move to back that material up."

"Jim Bell knows about the deals with the companies. You tried to make him commit suicide, but he's alive, God damn you."

"And you're sure about that? That's not what I heard."

Brad stood confused for a moment, then took out his phone and dialed the Boston General neuro ICU. He asked for the charge nurse, and asked about Bell's condition. He heard the answer, and clenched his jaw at the answer. "You son of a bitch, you killed him."

Lundgren merely shrugged. "Unfortunate."

"Is Marty in on this? His signature is on all the documents, along with yours."

Lundgren gave a tolerant smile and sipped his coffee. "I suppose it's fine for you to know. After all, you are discredited. You've heard of an Autopen?"

Brad slumped onto the couch. "You signed all the documents with his signature automatically."

"Should it come to any . . . problem . . . I'll just say that Marty was head of the company. He commanded that I sign the documents. He really didn't tell me what was going on. And, of course, I was preparing to report him to the authorities."

Marty needed to know about this betrayal. Brad bolted from Lundgren's office and ran down the hall, entering Fallon's office. Unlike Lundgren, Fallon didn't feel it necessary to have a decorative assistant to guard his door.

He burst in, to find Fallon leaning back in his chair, sneakered feet on the desk, a laptop open before him. He saw Brad, grinned and slapped the case shut, rising.

"Hey, where've you been the last few days? I thought we'd spend some more time talking at the house. I've made some notes, and—"

"Do you know what Lundgren's been doing?"

Marty looked puzzled. "Lawrence is a busy guy. He does a lot of things."

"You don't know about him contracting with companies to bias the Happy Ratings in their favor? You don't know about the version two chip? You don't know about what it can do . . . *has* done?"

"Well, I do know about the version two chip. Lawrence gave me a presentation. It's more efficient, gives quicker readings. Basically an upgrade."

"No! No! It's more! *It's a controlling chip!* It stores and releases hormones. And it carries drugs. It can control your mental state. They've been testing it on people. I talked to one of them, a woman who worked at the lab. It's caused people to commit suicide. They've killed people to hide it!"

Fallon's eyes went wide with shock, shaking his head in stunned puzzlement. He swung his feet off his desk and stood, his fists on its surface. "Lawrence? Is this true?"

Brad turned to see Lundgren, who had silently come in behind him.

"Yes," said Lundgren. "We've developed an entirely new class of chip. It's quite amazing really. It sequesters and releases hormones. And it carries reservoirs of drugs that can be released at will. People can use it to control their own moods, to rescue themselves from depression. The military can use it to give their soldiers almost superhuman endurance. We would be saving soldiers' lives. No longer would fatigue endanger their fighting ability, their survival. Companies can use it for their employees who work under stress, to make their lives better. It's a revolutionary device!"

"Lawrence, why didn't you tell me about this? Dear God, man, this is so far beyond anything I would have approved—"

"I know. That's why I didn't tell you until we had it done, and it was a fait accompli. And I didn't tell you about the preliminary clinical testing."

"So you *are* testing it on people! Lawrence, this is totally illegal, and unethical. What have you done?"

Lundgren said nothing, calmly punching in a number on his cell phone. He waited for an answer, and said "Go," then hung up. Then, to Fallon:

"I didn't want to tell you under these circumstances. I wanted to privately, persuade you. But Mr. Davis got out of hand. I was afraid you'd react this way. I'm sorry."

"What do you mean—" began Fallon, but abruptly gasped in shocked pain, opened his mouth, slumped onto his desk, and collapsed to the floor.

Brad rushed to him, turning him over. He was not breathing, his eyes staring blankly open. Brad felt for a pulse.

"Guess you'll have to finish his biography without him," said Lundgren coldly. "You've just seen the effects of a bolus of succinylcholine released from a chip reservoir. It's a paralytic agent. Mimics a heart attack very nicely. Then disappears in minutes. You have the same reservoir in you. Bell does, too . . . or rather did. One of our security men, posing as a colleague, injected the chip into him. I'm sparing you for the moment. It would be highly suspect if four people died the same way in such a short time. You, Bell, Marty, Parker at American Brands. But I will kill you, if necessary."

"You killed Marty!" gasped Brad. *"And that's how Bell and Parker died?"*

Lundgren smiled and turned to the door, shouting down the corridor, "My God! Help! Marty's collapsed! Something terrible is wrong!" People began rushing from the other offices, and Lundgren punched in a number on his cell phone, breathlessly telling the person answering of the "terrible, terrible thing that's happened here! We need the doctor here immediately. And call an ambulance!"

Brad still held Fallon in his arms, as Lundgren rushed to their side, kneeling down beside the inert form. Several people helped them lift Fallon's limp body onto the conference table, and Lundgren began to give him chest-compression CPR. Brad stood back, speechless at what had happened, at Lundgren's cold-blooded charade.

The company medical team arrived in minutes. An emergency technician tore open Fallon's shirt and used a portable defibrillator to attempt to restart his heart. The faint whine of the device charging was followed by the jolt of electricity to his body, which jerked slightly. But Fallon remained lifeless, his legs splayed out, his unseeing eyes staring at the ceiling, his chest unmoving. Again and again the technicians tried, but after each jolt, after each jerk of Fallon's body, it remained still.

As they worked, Lundgren backed away, pulling Brad with him. "One phone call and you're the same," he whispered.

"And what if I don't goddamn care what you do to me, you son of a bitch?" spat Brad.

"You should call home," answered Lundgren matter-of-factly, as if he were suggesting they go for lunch. He smiled at the puzzled look on Brad's face. "You know why I recommended you? Because you're malleable, vulnerable. You have a family. The other candidates didn't have families. You'd do anything for your family, wouldn't you?" He moved back to Fallon's side, his face assuming its former mock-anguished expression.

Brad stood paralyzed, his expression showing rising panic, as he realized the import of what Lundgren had just hinted at. He took out his phone and called Annie. The phone rang and rang before going to voice mail. He left a frantic message for her to call him back, and tried again. Again he got voice mail.

He bolted through the door and down the hall to the lobby, punching the elevator button until the door opened.

He had to get home!

CHAPTER 16

Brad burst through the door, finding the apartment ominously dark. He called for Annie, but heard nothing. He ducked into their bedroom and flipped on the light. It was empty, the bedclothes in disarray, as if someone had thrashed about there. He rushed through the living room to the small kitchen. Again, nothing. He heard sobbing from the girls' bedroom and flung open the door.

Annie sat huddled in the corner, her expression mad with fear, her hair hanging over her face. She clutched the girls to her, and they sobbed uncontrollably. Then he realized that Annie held a butcher knife in her hand, its blade poised over the girls.

"Annie, sweetheart, what's wrong?"

Her voice was guttural, almost animal. "We can't . . . live."

"What do you mean?"

"It's all gone. All of it. There's no sense in us living like this."

"No! No! Annie! You can't hurt them! Think of how much you love them—"

"It's hopeless. The pain. I have to stop it for all of us." She gripped the knife bringing it up to the girls' throats.

"Mommy, I feel a hurt inside," whimpered Sally.

Sarah begin to slap herself on the head. "Ooooh, stop! Stop!" she begged in her delicate little-girl voice.

"It will stop," whispered Annie hoarsely. "I'll make it stop."

"Annie, it's the chip inside you. It's making you feel like that. Remember what happened to me? What I told you? It's releasing hormones . . . drugs. Think of the girls! Think of us!"

Annie looked up, confused, tears streaming down her face, gasping and opening and closing her mouth in soundless agony.

"It's inside me?" she asked. "No . . . no, it's me. I feel it." She brought the knife closer to the girls.

A sudden pounding on the door, and a voice shouting, "LET ME IN! BRAD, IT'S PHYLLIS!"

Annie was momentarily distracted, and Brad took the instant to leap toward her, wresting the knife away. Her hand remained suspended in the air, her expression blankly confused.

The pounding continued, and Brad ran to the front door opening it, seeing Phyllis wearing a dark wig and wide-rimmed glasses.

"*It's Annie!*" he exclaimed. "*And the girls, too!*"

"Oh my God, they're all chipped!" Phyllis rushed past him, a palm-sized black box in her hand, a small red indicator light glowing on its side. She ran down the hall to find Annie and the girls in the bedroom. She set the box on the bed and sat down beside it, an anguished look on her haggard face. She watched Annie and the girls intently.

Now Annie leaned her head back against the wall, an expression of utter relief rising on her face, her eyes closed. Sighing, she wrapped her arms tightly around the girls, who had stopped crying.

"It'll take a while for the hormones, the drugs, to clear from their system," said Phyllis. She removed the glasses and wig. "They're still watching you. But the guy posted at the back of the building went to take a break, and I sneaked in."

"What is this?" asked Brad, touching the box.

"A cell phone jammer. Jams the chip signals. It took me a while to realize that's what I needed, I was so whacked out, I couldn't think. And it took a while to find one. It's a bootleg unit from Hong Kong. They're illegal, but there's a place in Providence that sells them under the table. I could only get two. They gave me another source to get them in Boston, but I haven't been able to contact them yet."

Brad was barely listening, having sunk down onto the floor, tightly hugging Annie and the children. Their warmth, their softness gave him such comfort. After a long while, he helped them up. He lifted each of the girls into their beds, covered them up, and kissed them gently. Then he embraced Annie, tears filling his eyes. He introduced Phyllis, and Annie nodded a greeting, her head still nestled on Brad's shoulder. When she finally lifted it, an expression of fury had replaced relief.

"They did this to us? It was the chip?"

"Yes," said Phyllis. "And to the girls, too."

Annie gasped in realization, then cursed, "*The God . . . damned . . . nanny!*" in a rage-filled whisper. "She took them to have it done after they fell asleep. She drugged them!"

"What do we do now?" asked Brad.

"I think you call Lundgren," said Phyllis pacing the room. "Tell him you give up,"

"*What? Never!*" exclaimed Brad.

"Fake it. You have to. It'll give us a little time. But not much. I don't think they realized I had a jammer. My chip doesn't have GPS, so they wouldn't notice. But since yours does, they could know the moment your signal stopped. Annie and the children, too. However, hopefully they're not paying much attention to your GPS signals right now, since they have surveillance on you. And if you call Lundgren, they might relax the surveillance long enough for us to get away."

Brad nodded slowly, absorbing what she had said. He took a deep breath, went into the kitchen and picked up the land-line phone, punching in Lundgren's number.

"Okay, okay, stop it! Stop it now! I'll do what you want," he declared to Lundgren. "But you also have to tell the people outside to leave. I want to make sure my family's safe." He listened for a moment, then hung up, announcing "He'll do it."

"Yeah, well, that's what he claims." Phyllis moved to the window, peering out between the blinds. "The car's leaving with both of them," she finally said. "Look, the jammer's only a temporary protection. The

GPS, the reservoirs, the sequestration . . . they're only disabled as long as the jammer's on. We've still got these chips inside us."

Embracing Annie, Brad said to Phyllis, "Okay, let's get Annie and the kids safe. We have friends in New Hampshire, Bob and Ella McNeil. They'll take them, and they'll be safe there. Then I'll come back with you and we'll figure out something."

"No," said Annie firmly, her expression one of smoldering anger. "*We'll* come back."

CHAPTER 17

It was midnight when they drove down the long, darkened drive-way to the Colonial-style house hidden in the trees, whisking over the drifts of leaves that marked a New Hampshire fall. Brad rang the doorbell three times, waiting long minutes before Bob McNeil answered the door. The puffy-faced young man wore a dark blue robe and a confused, sleepy expression.

"Brad? What are you doing here?"

"Bobby, I'm really sorry to wake you, but we've got kind of an emergency."

Bob was joined by his wife Ella, a petite woman with short brown hair, who stood behind him, also puzzled. She wrapped her red silk robe tightly around herself against the cold breeze streaming through the doorway.

"Are you all right?" she asked, with a puzzled shake of her head.

"Well, again I'm sorry to wake you, but we were on the road, and, uh, we've had an emergency. You were closest. We need to leave the girls with you."

"What?" asked Bob, his expression confused. "I don't understand. What kind of emergency?"

Brad paused, trying to assemble the story they'd concocted, when behind him, Annie said, "I just got a call. It's my mom . . . she's had an accident and she's in the hospital. We've got to go straight to see her."

Phyllis appeared behind them, and Bob and Ella peered at her suspiciously. She still wore her tattered clothes, and her hair was still unkempt. Brad introduced her as a friend of theirs, in turn introducing Bob and Ella to Phyllis as Brad's BU classmates. But Bob and Ella remained in the doorway, their expressions dubious.

"An accident?" asked Bob. "I'm so sorry. What kind of accident? Will she be all right?" The question was part sincere concern and part a veiled test, conveying his doubt.

"Car accident," said Annie. Her nursing experience kicked in, augmenting the lie. "She has a broken pelvis and a concussion. She's in intensive care. We have to get to her. And it means heading for Syracuse. We don't want to take the girls because . . ." Annie searched for a reason. " . . . we'll both be at the hospital, and we'd feel better if they were with you." She realized there was a gap in the story and tried to fill it. "Phyllis needs to be dropped off at the bus station; she won't be going."

Bob and Ella backed away, opening the door. Brad and Annie fetched the sleeping girls from the car and carried them into the house. They followed Ella upstairs to the spare bedroom, next to the McNeil boys' room. Meanwhile, Phyllis fetched the girls' backpacks and left them in the room.

"Uh, I'm leaving this here, too," said Brad pulling out one of their two jammers, with its glowing indicator light. He plugged its charger into the wall and left it on the bedside table.

"Oh?" asked Bob, who had come up after them. "What is it?"

"Backup hard drive. Stuff for my articles and a book I'm writing. I want to leave it someplace safe, since we'll be spending a lot of time at the hospital."

"He had an expensive laptop stolen with important files on it, and he's been paranoid ever since," said Annie. They tucked the girls in and went downstairs to the entry hall.

"Yes, and if you take the girls out, it would be great if you take the hard drive with you. I admit I'm paranoid."

Bob shook his head in sleepy puzzlement. "Sure, sure, no problem."

"Thank you so much," said Brad. "We wouldn't impose on you like this if it wasn't an emergency."

"Can I offer you coffee to go?" asked Bob. "Let's go into the kitchen, and make some and give you a thermos." Brad nodded, and they left the women and went together into the kitchen, where Bob's tone changed.

"Look, Brad, this is weird, showing up this late at night, and leaving the girls, and all. And that woman, Phyllis. Pal, she's a little sketchy. I've known you long enough to know that something else is going on here."

Brad slumped tiredly against the kitchen counter as Bob made coffee. "Bob, there's trouble. Please don't tell Ella. It's best for her. You've got to trust me. I can only tell you it's about a story I've been working on."

"The Fallon biography? I read about it on the BU journalism blog."

"It's better if you don't know. We talked about whether to tell you. If you don't know, you're safer. And so are the boys. Look, Bob, you and Ella are the girls' godparents. And if we don't come back . . ."

"*Jesus Christ, Brad!*" exclaimed Bob in a frightened whisper. "*If you don't come back? What the hell?*"

"Just take care of the girls. And don't let them out of range of that box."

"Jesus! Jesus! The box? What *is* that box?"

"A jammer. And your cell phones won't work anymore. Expect that."

Bob shook his head and stared silently at Brad, his concentration interrupted only by the gurgle of the coffeemaker indicating that the pot had finished brewing. He said nothing as he poured the coffee into a thermos and handed it to Brad. Finally, his straightened posture told Brad he'd made a decision.

"Just tell me, is there danger to us?"

"Not as long as that jammer is on."

"I'm trusting you Brad. And it looks like maybe I'm trusting you with *our* lives, not only the girls'."

"Honest to God, Bobby, this is important. I wouldn't be asking you to do this otherwise. It's not just our lives. It's *many* lives at stake."

Bob took a deep breath and embraced Brad. They walked back out to the hallway and Bob replaced his look of concern with that of a gracious-but-sleepy host.

"Okay, you guys want to get on the road, so we won't keep you. You take care!" The last sentence was said with a little more urgency than usual.

Brad, Annie, and Phyllis said their goodbyes, got in the car, and sped away, Annie wiping away tears.

They wound along the dark country roads back to the freeway, and had just crossed the border into Massachusetts when Phyllis, riding in the back seat, erupted in a string of *"Shit, shit, shit, shit!"*

Startled awake, Annie twisted to find out what was wrong.

"The jammer! Its battery died! The indicator light's out! We need to get a battery or plug in the charger!"

Brad slammed the accelerator down, and the car surged forward to eighty-five miles an hour. He prayed that there were no cops out late at night. Five miles to the next exit!

They made it to the sign that read two miles, when a smothering wave of black depression engulfed him. He slumped over the wheel, his knuckles white with the force of his grasp. His despair became suicidal. How easy it would be, he thought, to swerve off the overpass they were on, to smash through the guardrail, to slam into the pavement below, to end this hell.

Next to him, Annie had curled into a fetal position, quivering, whimpering. And in the back seat, Phyllis had begun to moan softly to herself, *"No . . . no . . . no . . . no . . . no!"*

Brad reached toward Annie and to his relief, her hand grasped his. She was fighting the hormone-fueled depression! Like him, she could withstand the onslaught, now that she knew she was being manipulated by the bastard Lundgren. Her hatred trumped her fear.

The exit loomed out of the darkness, and he whipped the car onto it, and down the ramp to the surface street, running a red light, skidding into a right turn and swerving into a McDonald's parking lot. They staggered into the restaurant's fluorescent glare, and the late-night customers in line shrank away from the demented-looking trio. Brad ran along a row of booths, seeking an electrical outlet.

When he found one next to a booth, he commanded the teenagers there to leave. One of the teens, a hulking boy in a backward baseball cap and a football jersey stood up, clenching his fists, ready to resist. He towered over the slightly built Brad. But Brad grabbed him by his shirt and shoved him across the room into the drink dispenser.

He turned to the others, wild-eyed, and shouted, "GET THE FUCK OUT, OR I WILL BEAT THE SHIT OUT OF YOU!" The manager, a pudgy man in a white shirt and black tie, appeared just as Phyllis plugged in the jammer, and the three of them slumped into the booth, their agony thankfully subsiding.

"Sir, what are you doing? I'm going to have to ask you to leave, or—"

"No problem, sir," gasped Brad, recovering his composure. "We'll leave shortly."

Annie, waved her hand in apology, her terror-stricken expression giving way to relief and rationality. "Please forgive my husband. When we were passing the booth, the young man used a profanity toward me. My husband lost his temper."

"Well, you burst in here like you were nuts."

"We just got a call with some bad news. My husband's distraught. His mother . . ." Annie let her voice trail off, not exactly specifying what the bad news was.

"Oh . . . well . . . go ahead and have your meal. And I'd appreciate it if you'd keep it down." As the indignant teens continued their protest, the manager waved his hands in dismissal and pointed them to a booth across the room.

To give them time in the restaurant, and time to think, Phyllis got in line and ordered hamburgers, fries, and coffees.

At a nearby table, a tattooed teen uttered a puzzled "Hello?" into her cell phone, as she lost her signal.

Phyllis returned shortly with the food, shaking her head. "They know where we are. They began to receive GPS signals from your chips when the jammer went off. They know your car. We have to get off the freeway. I just don't know what to do next."

"Well, clearly we have to do something permanent to disable these chips," said Annie. "I don't know about their structure. What are they, exactly?"

Invigorated by the food, the coffee, and the relief from the hormonal and drug assault, they fell into a long discussion about the chips. Phyllis described in as much detail as she knew about the nanoelectronics and the nanofluidic systems in the chips, and how they controlled the hormone and drug reservoirs.

Leaving Phyllis and Annie in deep discussion, Brad went to a nearby QuikMart, taking care to stay within the jammer's range. He bought enough batteries to keep the device going for weeks, as well as maps of Massachusetts and New Hampshire. They would need the paper maps, since their own phone signals were being jammed. He also grabbed energy drinks and pills with the highest caffeine levels he could find, to keep them alert.

Shortly, they had climbed back into the car and were speeding away from the 93 freeway, winding their way along the darkened back roads toward Boston.

• • •

"Okay, we know they were off ninety-three when their GPS signals showed up," said the muscular young mercenary wearing the Coronado Security jacket. He tapped the projected display showing a map of the freeway exit.

Nine other men, similarly dressed and wearing pistols and wielding assault rifles, sat on folding chairs in the Burlington warehouse of Coronado Security. Behind them sat a phalanx of black SUVs.

"They must have gotten a jammer," continued the mercenary, "and they must know we pinpointed them when it quit on them. They must have switched it back on, because the signals are gone. But they're almost certainly headed for Boston." He scratched at his face stubble reflectively for a moment. "But they won't be on the freeway."

Tapping a key on the laptop connected to the projector, he zoomed the map in on the area between New Hampshire and Boston.

"They don't think in strategic terms, so they almost certainly don't realize there's a choke point here, where there are only four likely roads to Boston. So, we station two-man teams on each of those roads, and we intercept them. You have the car make . . . Subaru Outback, dark gray . . . and the license."

"To be clear, what's the action here?" asked a burly crew-cut man cradling an MP5K submachine gun in his lap.

"Capture if feasible. Otherwise, terminate."

• • •

Despite downing large quantities of caffeine, Brad was fading. He nodded at the wheel several times, and the car swerved off the road the right tires bumping along the grassy shoulder of the country lane.

Finally, he reached a village green in one of the rural towns they had been passing through, and gave up. He pulled the car over and slumped over the wheel. Annie and Phyllis had fallen into an exhausted slumber, so he didn't want to rouse either of them to drive. But the vicious mix of anxiety, fear, and depression that he had suffered had left him soul-deep weary.

What's more, the lack of sleep had brought hallucinations. A shadow on the road had become a boulder. He'd almost swerved off the road before he realized what it was. The flash of a streetlight shining into the passenger side transformed into some shadowy animal crouching there. He'd startled for a moment, losing control of the car.

He climbed out of the car, gently closing the door. A walk in the brisk night air might help. It was three a.m. and the village green was deserted, so he felt comfortable leaving the car, while staying within the jammer's range.

The walk cleared his head enough so that he could begin to consider their situation. It had been four hours since the jammer quit. Maybe twenty minutes before they could get it working again. Plenty of time for Lundgren's mercenaries to pinpoint their location and organize to track them.

Walking along the sidewalk, crunching through the autumn leaves, he pondered what to do. They were going back to Boston. But for what? What could they do? He realized they were blundering ahead with no plan. They had to stop. They had to think. And they had to do it with clear heads.

Across the green sat a small bed and breakfast, a spare revolutionary-era house with thick gardens and a driveway to a parking area hidden in the back. He returned to the car and eased it around the green to the front entrance, so as not to wake the sleeping women.

Climbing the steps to the porch, he found a printed sign that said to ring the bell after ten p.m. He did so, and after many minutes, a sleepy, disheveled elderly man in a white bathrobe appeared. Brad apologized profusely for the late hour, and said he'd almost had an accident, he was so tired. Could he and his wife and friend possibly have rooms for the night? The man was surprisingly friendly, admitting that he'd just been up for one of his multiple nightly trips to the bathroom and was awake, anyway. Brad arranged for two adjacent rooms on the second floor in the back and pulled the car out of sight behind the house.

He awakened Annie and Phyllis, explaining the situation, and they readily agreed that it was a good idea to get a night's sleep in real beds and have a morning with minds refreshed for planning.

Nestling into the high antique four-poster bed, Annie fell instantly into an exhausted slumber. Brad watched her lovely face, as she settled back into sleep. He was both sad and angered at the horrible ordeal she'd suffered. And even though his caffeine level was still high, he managed to settle into slumber himself, the glowing indicator light on the jammer resting on the nightstand fading into darkness.

Five miles down the rural road toward Boston, two men sat in a black SUV parked behind a screen of trees, positioned to afford a clear view of the road. One man, the burly crew-cut man with dark face-stubble, slept. The other, a wiry, dark-haired man in a tan Coronado Security jacket watched the road for a dark gray Subaru. Each held a compact machine pistol fitted with a silencer.

• • •

"One big problem is, our chips don't have an off-switch," said Phyllis over eggs and waffles the next morning. She whispered to Annie and Brad, so the other guests in the sunny dining room of the B&B wouldn't hear her. "And a chip can't be located in the body without a radio-frequency scanner programmed to its specific ID code. And even when it's located, the only way to remove it is surgery. So, it's usually just left in the body."

"Any way you can get into the lab, to get those codes, or a scanner, or *anything* that would help?" asked Brad.

Phyllis stared down at her coffee. "My access card was deactivated the minute I disappeared. And there's heavy security, and my computer password wouldn't work even if we got in. The best thing I can do right now is to get more jammers, to try to help as many other people who have the version two chip. I want to try the place in Boston that's supposed to have them. I'll need to make a landline call from here."

Annie had remained studiously silent during the breakfast, her face showing an intense concentration. Finally, she spoke up. "You said last night the chip had conventional electronics in it."

"Yes," said Phyllis. "They're nanoscale, but they still have electronics."

"And there are metals in them?"

"Sure, both in the electronic components and the nanofluidics. They've got copper and iron oxides."

Annie smiled a knowing smile. "Well, then, I think I may know how to deactivate the chips, wherever they are in the body. We need to get to Boston General."

"What do you mean?" asked Phyllis.

Annie started to speak, but Brad held up a hand. "Wait . . . before you say anything, think about this. We're all chipped. You know what those chips can do to us. If they catch any of us, they could make us tell whatever we know. So, Annie, if you don't tell us what you're thinking of doing, we can't tell them."

Annie nodded, a frustrated expression on her face. "Okay, okay. I'll keep it to myself. But I'll need to make a call from a landline, too."

As they got up from the table, Brad said, "I know one thing we can do. They probably know our car. I'll tell the innkeeper our car is having problems and ask to leave it here for a while. I'll find a rental place."

• • •

"What the hell happened?" demanded Lundgren, pacing the floor of the conference room off the main laboratory.

"We watched all the roads in the choke point said the sandy-haired mercenary, unzipping his Coronado Security jacket and leaning back in his chair. "The car didn't pass. Either they're still in New Hampshire, maybe northern Massachusetts, or—"

"Or, they were smart enough to change cars, get on the interstate, and whizz right past you."

"That's certainly a possibility."

"Their signal's still gone," said Beale. "Hasn't come back since last night."

"Well, stay at the choke points," said Lundgren. "Tell your people to look for, not just their car, but any other vehicle that passes with three people in it."

"Any change in the orders?" asked the mercenary.

"Perhaps a bit of a reordering of priorities," said Lundgren. "Shoot first."

CHAPTER 18

Brad paced back and forth in front of the B&B, waiting for the Enterprise rental agent to deliver the car. He continually scanned the village green, scrutinizing each vehicle as it navigated the square. One of them might contain the mercenaries who were surely after them. But all seemed peaceful. A young mother out for a morning jog pushed her baby stroller ahead of her. A couple of retirees emerged from a quaint country store across the street with morning coffee and strolled over to sit on a bench to enjoy it in the crisp morning air. How strange it was to watch such a bucolic scene when he and the others faced such horrors.

Phyllis and Annie were still inside, finishing breakfast, amid the other guests' complaints that the Wi-Fi wasn't working, and neither were their cell phones.

As he scanned the traffic, he mulled over their strategy, or lack of it. He fetched a paper map of New Hampshire and Massachusetts from the car and sat on the steps, unfurling it. They were traveling a rural road into Boston, to avoid their pursuers. Good idea to avoid the interstate.

But then there was a problem, he realized. On rural roads, they drove slower. Anybody watching for them would have a better chance of seeing them, even in a rental car. Driving seventy on the interstate would actually be safer, given they'd now be in a car that wasn't his Subaru.

He had an idea of how to make it safer still. He strolled over to the country store and picked up a modest disguise. A baseball cap would hide his red hair, and sunglasses would help obscure his face. Once equipped, he returned to his station in front of the B&B. There, his plan grew even more elaborate.

A gray Ford Fusion pulled up, driven by the Enterprise agent. Fortunately for Brad's plan, he was a slim young man about Brad's build. Annie and Phyllis emerged from the B&B, and got into the Ford.

"Say, I wonder if you could do me a favor," he said to the young man.

"Well, depends on what you need."

"Well, my Subaru's parked around back. It's been giving me a little trouble. I'll follow you to your lot. Then could you keep our car and drop it off at a garage for me?"

"Well, we don't—" began the young man.

"Is there a repair shop down the road that way, toward Boston?" interrupted Brad pointing the direction they would have otherwise traveled, had they continued on back roads.

"Well, not really. Not until the next town. There's a Subaru dealer there."

"Tell you what. I'd like to use that one. I'll make it worth your while to drop it there. And maybe drive as fast as you can, without breaking the speed limit. The car's hesitating at high speed, and you could describe the problem to the mechanic."

"Gee, well, I don't know—" began the young man, suspicion tingeing his voice. But Brad interrupted in a most effective way. He pulled out his wallet and began to count out twenty dollar bills until he reached two hundred dollars.

"That car is kind of my baby. And I'm in a hurry . . . business . . . so it would be great to get the repair problem off my plate."

The young man's doubts evaporated at the sight of the bills, and he eagerly agreed. So, they signed the papers, and the three followed the young man in the Ford to his lot. After getting an okay from the manager, Brad watched with smug satisfaction as the young man sped away in the Subaru down the state road.

Five miles down that road, a black SUV accelerated from a parking lot and sped after him. The young man watched with growing anxiety as the big car loomed to within inches of his bumper. On a wooded stretch of road, it abruptly swerved into the left lane, slammed its massive bulk into his left rear fender, and spun the little car around, bringing it to a stop. Two men piled out of the SUV, appearing at the car's windows brandishing automatic weapons.

The young man's eyes grew wild with panic, as he looked down the barrel of one gun, then the other. One of the gunmen spat a curse, and they both jumped back into the SUV and gunned it away, leaving the young man clinging to the steering wheel to steady his trembling hands.

• • •

Brad maneuvered the gray Ford through the narrow streets of the Boston suburb of Somerville, past rows of weather-beaten houses and apartments. Phyllis and Annie peered out the windows, trying to decipher their addresses.

"Here!" said Phyllis. "He's expecting us."

After cautionary block-circling to check for tailing SUVs, Brad wedged the car into a parking spot, and they walked to a white house with peeling wood siding, nestled behind a thicket of overgrown bushes. They climbed the worn porch steps and Phyllis rang the bell.

From behind the door came an annoyed voice. "You've got a fucking jammer on! Turn it the fuck off!"

"We can't," said Phyllis.

"Why the hell not?"

"Just open the door. Let's do some business. You've got jammers, and we've got cash."

Brad pulled a fat envelope out of his jacket pocket. He'd taken the risk of withdrawing as much money as possible from a nearby ATM, since he'd given the Enterprise agent all his cash. Even though Lundgren's men might pinpoint them, they would be long gone before the mercenaries could have arrived.

A metallic clinking of locks being undone emanated from the other side of the door. It opened to reveal a skinny, bearded man wearing a faded t-shirt and jeans, and a sullen expression. He held a lit cigarette in one hand and a pistol in the other.

"What's with the gun?" asked Phyllis, backing away and holding her hands open.

"Believe me, I've got lots of them. And if you're fucking with me, there's a guy in the back with a big one who'll be happy to take care of you."

"We only want the jammers," said Brad. "Here's the money. We'll take whatever you have."

"Okay, come in. I'll get them." He turned and walked away, leaving the door open.

Phyllis started to enter, but Brad stopped her. "Something smells funny here. This guy . . . he's . . . I don't know, something's just funny."

"We've got to take the chance," whispered Phyllis. "Those are my friends at the lab who have those damned chips implanted in them. Who knows what Lundgren would do to them if he got desperate? And if we give them jammers to block the chips, they can help. When they find out the death that's inside them, they'll help willingly."

Brad shook his head in sad acquiescence, handing her the cash.

"I'll go in alone, okay," said Phyllis. "We need to separate anyway, to make sure all of us aren't caught." She took a deep breath, entered the house and closed the door. After a long moment, she appeared with two jammers, different models with antennas jutting from them.

"It's okay," she said, handing the jammers through the door. He's getting more from the back. You take these. Go ahead. I'll be okay. I've got enough money to get the other units and check into a hotel. I'll be at the Sheraton Boston."

She closed the door a little too quickly, and Annie and Brad looked at each other in puzzlement.

"Something is wrong," whispered Annie. "She was scared."

"Well, something's been wrong for a week. I'd be scared, too. Look, I think we need to leave, whether she's okay or not," whispered Brad. "We have to think of the girls. We're all in danger until we finish this."

Annie finally nodded her head in reluctant assent, and they hurried down the steps and back to the car.

• • •

"Why should we go to Lisa Fallon?" Brad shook his head in doubt, as he maneuvered the car through Somerville's narrow streets. "It's dangerous as hell. And we barely escaped ourselves. All that's keeping us safe is these jammers." He rested his hand on one of the small black boxes perched on the car's console, its red light glowing reassuringly.

Annie placed her hand gently on his. "She deserves to know what happened. I just know if you died, I'd want the truth about how. And maybe she knows things we don't. After all, she was Marty's wife, his closest confidant."

With a sigh, Brad signified his resigned agreement and pulled into a service station.

"Well, okay, she may know something that could help. Maybe she'd have information to convince the FBI and Pritchett. My credibility is pretty well shot."

He entered the small gas station store, taking care to stay within range of the jammer still in the car, and paid in cash to activate the pump. As he filled the car, he slumped against its side. A deep fatigue permeated his body, like the aftermath of an electric shock—remnants of the soul-deep emotional trauma that he had suffered over the past days.

He managed to recover himself, finished filling the car, and checked his phone for the number of the Fallon mansion. Back in the store, he gathered up an armload of snacks and water, to mark himself as a good customer, worthy of a favor from the pudgy young man at the register.

"Say, my cell phone's dead," he told the clerk, as he settled payment for the gas and the snacks and water. "Mind if I use your land line for a local call?"

After some hesitation, the clerk gestured to the phone behind him, and Brad circled behind the counter and made the call. The phone rang and a female voice answered "Fallon residence."

"This is Brad Davis. I was working with Marty on his biography. Can I speak to Lisa?"

"She's not available. This is her sister Julie. Look, I'm sure you understand, but—."

"Julie, I was there when Marty died. I need to tell her things she'll want to know."

There was a long pause. "This can't wait? She's in terrible pain. This has been a severe shock. She wants to be alone with the children."

"It's urgent. She'll want to know what I have to tell her."

"She doesn't need more pain now. I'll tell her about you later, when she's recovered. That's all I can do. Goodbye."

"Wait! Wait!" Brad agonized over what to tell this stranger. Meanwhile, the gas station clerk was drawing his finger across his throat, signaling Brad to hang up. Fortunately, Julie had stayed on the line.

"Really, Mr. Davis. She needs to rest."

"I'll tell you what. Put the phone down. Go tell her I'm on the phone. Tell her that it's about Lawrence Lundgren." Brad prayed that Lisa had thought Lundgren as arrogant, perhaps even as suspicious, as he had.

"Buddy, you'll have to hang up," said the clerk. "I've got customers." He approached Brad, his hand out for the phone receiver. Brad thought a moment, then cradled the phone between his ear and shoulder, dug in his wallet and came out with a twenty dollar bill. He slapped it into the clerk's hand.

"That do it?"

The clerk's expression hovered between surprise at the bill and suspicion of anybody who would fork over money just for a phone call.

"Is this something that's hinky?" he asked.

"No. Just a family issue that I need to get settled. And for twenty bucks, could you put a little distance between us?"

The clerk shrugged, pocketed the bill and went off to ring up a six-pack of beer for a customer. Brad suspected that the clerk just might tell somebody about the odd encounter, and he glanced up at the store's camera. He was on video.

"Hello, Brad?" It was Lisa's voice.

"Lisa, there's a lot you don't know about Marty's death, the company, what they're doing. I was there."

"Brad, you need help. Lawrence told me you've been acting erratically, that you were institutionalized . . . and did drugs . . . I don't think—"

"I was affected by the chip. I need to tell you—"

"Brad, I can't help you. You do need to get help. I hope you do."

He could tell she was on the verge of hanging up. "Wait, just listen! He was murdered! I saw it!"

"I have to go."

Brad felt a hand on his shoulder, and he turned to see Annie. She motioned for him to give her the phone.

"Lisa, this is Annie Davis. I'm Brad's wife. Listen, please. He did suffer a breakdown. And he was drugged. It *was* due to the chip. You have one in you, right?"

"Well, yes, but I'm sure—"

"And the children?"

There was a long pause. "Well . . . yes."

"So do I. So do my children. We were affected. It was horrible, the depression, the hopelessness. The chips are dangerous, even deadly. Lawrence Lundgren and his people did something to the chips . . . added a chemical control capability without telling Marty. So they killed him. You have to see us."

The store clerk approached, his hand out asking for the phone. Brad slapped three twenties into it, and the young man shrugged and backed off. Still, he looked suspicious, and Brad was certain the security tapes would be saved, and perhaps even shared with the local police.

"Well, I hope this isn't just shared paranoia," Lisa said finally. "Where do you want to meet?"

"It can't be your house," said Annie. "The security people are Lundgren's. It has to be somewhere you would normally go. They can track you. Your chip probably has GPS."

"*Track me? Jesus! Let me think!*"

"And you can't tell anybody what we're telling you."

"The children's school. I'll tell them I'm going to see their teachers. To get their homework. And to have time alone."

"Good. Here's Brad."

Brad took the phone and got directions to the private school in Weston. Lisa also gave him her cell number. Back in the car, they maneuvered through Somerville's narrow streets onto the 90 freeway and toward Weston. Rather than park at the school, they pulled off onto the side of a country lane near it. Carrying their two jammers, they made their way cautiously through the leaf-littered forest behind the school, peering around for any sign of a security detail that might precede Lisa.

The school was a pin-neat complex of gray-shingled buildings, nestled in the woods. Looking as calm and collected as they could, they strolled among the crowds of children changing classes and entered the white-columned building marked Administration, asking whether Lisa had called.

"Indeed," said the trim young woman behind the desk. "She said that you are parents of prospective students, and she wanted to introduce you to the school. She'll meet you in the Fallon Family Building."

The assistant directed them across the flagstone courtyard, and as they walked, a black SUV pulled up the long drive. Behind the wheel was the muscular, sandy-haired security man with the stubbled face! As Annie and Brad ducked quickly into the building, he pulled into the parking lot choosing a distant spot, apparently trying to hide his presence.

They peered out the window at the main drive as Lisa arrived, seemingly unaware of her shadow. They watched her climb out of the BMW sedan and make her way slowly toward them, her grim expression portraying a woman who had suffered a grievous tragedy. She checked in at the administration building and crossed the courtyard to the building housing the conference room. Her expression didn't change when she found them there.

"You have something to tell me," she said flatly.

"You're being followed, but that's the least of our problems," said Brad.

• • •

"You've got to see this!" exclaimed the technician, calling Beale to him and tapping the computer screen. "I just got an alarm. We've lost Lisa Fallon's signal."

"Where was she?" asked Beale, frowning at the map showing Boston's western suburbs.

"At the kids' school when the signal quit."

"GPS glitch?"

"Not likely. She wasn't going into a tunnel or anything."

"It's one of those jammers, goddamnit! She must be with the Davises!" Beale took out his cell phone and punched in Lundgren's number, informing him of the situation. Lundgren, in turn called the Coronado Security operative.

"It's Lundgren. Where are you?

"Sitting in the parking lot of the kids' school," the stubbled man answered. "She said she had to go there to pick up their homework. And to give herself a break."

"The monitors have lost her signal. It must be one of the jammers Phyllis Kelley had. She's almost certainly with Brad and Annie Davis."

"What are your orders?"

"Move in. Take control of the situation. Extreme measures if needed."

"Sir, it's a school. There are children."

"I said take control of the situation."

· · ·

If Lisa Fallon was bereft before, now her soul was smothered in abject fear, after what Brad and Annie had told her.

"Dear God, this is all true?"

"Yes," said Brad. "As horrible as it sounds . . . as just plain crazy . . . it's all true. We must stop him."

"Well, I don't know what I could do. Marty didn't talk to me in great detail about Lawrence. He knew Lawrence was somewhat aggressive, but *this!*"

"Anything . . . anything you can tell us would help."

Annie, who was keeping watch out the window, interrupted. "The security guy. He's coming this way!"

Sure enough, the mercenary was making his way up the driveway, his expression determined.

"I can deal with him," said Lisa, starting to open the door. But Annie stopped her.

"You can't. He works for Lundgren. Does the school have enough security to stop him?"

Lisa nodded coolly. "Children of some of the most prominent families in Boston go here. The gym teachers are ex-military. So are the security men. They keep the weapons out of sight, but they're well-armed."

"Alert them. We've got to get away," said Brad. He handed her a black box with its glowing red light. "This is a signal jammer. It will make you and the children invisible to their tracking. And it will block the effects of any chemical attack. You should take the kids and get as far away as possible. We've got to try to get away from him. They've already tried to kill us."

Lisa took the box, and shaking her head, went to a wall phone, punching in a number.

"This is Lisa Fallon. I'm in the conference room. There's a very suspicious man walking up the drive. He's been following me. You need to do something."

Immediately, the school public address system clicked on, and they heard "Code 300. Front entrance."

In an instant, teachers began herding children who were outside into the building, and locking the doors behind them. Four athletic-looking men in gym clothes appeared, striding down the driveway to meet the mercenary, just as two men wearing blazers with the school emblem appeared, carrying large cases. They positioned themselves behind the large oak trees flanking the entrance. Looking as casual as men out for morning air, they leaned against the trees, cases at their feet in easy reach, intently watching the approaching intruder. Each casually reached into his jacket, leaving his hand resting there.

"You can go out the back door and into the woods," said Lisa. "I'm going to take the children and fly to a lodge we own. And I've got security people I can trust. I only wish I could help."

"We just want you and the children to be safe," said Annie, as they turned to go.

Lisa peered upward, her expression one of dawning realization. "Wait! Maybe I can tell you something useful. About China. Marty told me that Lundgren was insistent on fast-tracking their marketing in China. He even wanted to set up an R&D facility. But Marty didn't think it was a good idea, since the Chinese government is so authoritarian, and they steal technology."

"That helps!" exclaimed Brad. "You and the children stay safe!"

As they ducked through the back door and sprinted toward the woods, they could hear coming from the school entrance the sounds of heated arguments, as the men confronted the mercenary.

• • •

Brad dropped Annie off at the front door of the spare brick and glass building that was Boston General's suburban medical imaging center. He anxiously circled the block, watching for following cars, while Annie met whomever she had planned to meet. He'd emphasized again that he didn't want to know. If he was caught, at least she could have whatever treatment she was planning.

After half-an-hour, Annie emerged through the double glass doors and quickly slid into the car, hugging him with relief.

"I think this will work! We have an appointment tomorrow. It's off the books. I know the head nurse. We were in school together."

"She can be trusted?"

"Sure. It's a big favor, but I helped her with a serious problem in school. She'd gotten into drugs, and I took her to get help before she got caught. She cleaned up."

"Okay, let's meet Phyllis at the Sheraton."

Soon, holding the jammer, Brad and Annie walked cautiously through the lobby of the huge downtown Boston hotel. They passed guests lounging in the padded chairs. A young woman leaning against a paneled pillar asked a puzzled, "Are you there?" into her cell phone, as the jammer knocked out her signal. Brad felt only slightly guilty. They found a lobby phone and asked the operator for Phyllis's room.

The phone rang and she answered with a tremulous "Hello."

"You okay?" asked Brad. "You sound stressed."

"Wouldn't you be? I'm up here with this jammer, hoping that they haven't figured out how to pinpoint jamming."

"Yeah, I guess."

Phyllis gave them her room number, and they went to the floor and knocked on the door. Brad and Annie looked at each other in silent puzzlement, as it took uncomfortably long for Phyllis to open the door. Brad took Annie's arm, and was about to tug it in a *let's-get-out-of-here* gesture. Finally, Phyllis appeared, her face ashen, and ushered them into the living area of a suite. She glanced pointedly at the closed door to the bedroom.

"You okay?"

"Yeah . . . sure . . . of course. It's good to be off the street. I hope you don't mind my spending your money on a suite. I thought you might like to rest here, as well."

But strangely, even given the respite from the trauma she'd undergone, Phyllis's haggard, fearful expression showed no relief.

"So, here's what we're planning—" Brad began, but strangely, Phyllis brought her finger to her lips to silence him, gesturing with her head at the bedroom door, and mouthing "*They're here.*"

Brad gave her a quizzical look.

"Before we talk can we order room service first?" she asked. "I'm starved."

"Sure, of course."

Phyllis sat down on the couch and picked up the phone, leafing through the hotel guidebook to the room service page and punching in the room service number.

"Take a look; see if you want anything," she said. As they ordered food, she began to write with a trembling hand on the hotel notepad:

"*Jammer guy turned me in! L's thugs in bedroom! Trying to hear what you know before they take you!*"

Annie quietly gasped, but recovered and lied, "Well, the girls are safe. We put them on the plane to California."

"Great," said Phyllis, continuing to scribble: "*Chipped me: version 2.0. Lethal reservoir! Go along with me!*" She slashed three urgent underlines beneath the last sentence.

"So, what do you think the next step should be?" asked Brad.

"I think we go right to the source, to the lab."

"Really? You think that's wise?"

"I've got a friend who can get us in. That's where we can gather the evidence we need."

"Okay, sure. I don't have any other play."

"Right, we do need *evidence*," said Phyllis, emphasizing the last word as she pulled a bundle of rolled-up toilet paper from her pocket and pressed it into Brad's hand. He unrolled the flimsy tissue, seeing a list of scribbled names.

Phyllis continued: "The best evidence would be the names of people in the first trial, the ones who disappeared. I could probably remember *some of them* . . ." She pointed emphatically at the list ". . . but we'd want the whole list."

"Well, I left my notes, recordings, and other stuff with a friend. How about we pick up the material and meet you near the lab tomorrow afternoon? We'll bring it with us."

Phyllis urgently motioned for them to leave. They rushed to the door, opened it and were out, as they heard Phyllis continue to talk as if they were still there:

"Sure. Bring everything, and once we download the data from their server, we'll take it to—" The door closed, and Brad and Annie stood in agonized indecision, his arm around her.

Annie shook her head emphatically. "We have to leave!" She extricated herself from his embrace and pulled his arm, gently at first, then harder. Finally, he relented, and they both rushed for the stairs. They'd been forced to abandon Phyllis to whatever fate the men decided for her.

CHAPTER 19

S am Pritchett almost missed seeing Brad and Annie in the Starbucks among the morning crowd. They had slouched down into armchairs in an inconspicuous corner, as far from the windows as they could get. He folded his lanky frame into a chair and leaned forward, sipping his latte.

Around them, puzzled people tried to use cell phones that had lost signal, or laptops whose Wi-Fi had failed. The manager moved out from behind the counter, shrugging his shoulders at the complaining people and offering free coffee drinks to the disgruntled crowd.

Pritchett's impatient scowl told them what was coming next.

"Okay, time's run out," he said. "I gave you the corporation list a week ago. My editors want to know how this list connects to NeoHappy. Do these bumps in product sales have to do with the Happy Ratings? Is there hanky-panky going on?"

"Look, I can't tell you yet," said Brad. "This thing has gotten much bigger than when I first talked to you. I need your help on something else. It's part of this."

"Damn, Brad, you keep asking and not answering. Tell me the story . . . *now!*"

Annie held up her hands in caution, saying, "Understand this. Our lives are now at risk, and more importantly, the lives of our children. You just have to trust us that you'll get the whole story when we can give it to you, okay?"

Pritchett leaned back, his expression softening.

"Your children? You're not just shining me on?"

"No! Absolutely not!" exclaimed Brad, pulling out the list Phyllis had given him. "To show you how dangerous this thing is, here's a list of people to check out. One of your police reporters should do it. We think they're either dead or missing."

Pritchett took the small roll of toilet paper, unfolded it and scanned it.

"Jesus. Do you realize how goddamned strange this is getting. I mean, *really*, Brad. Clandestine meetings in a coffee shop. And now you hand me a wad of toilet paper with a list on it."

"Just check them out. And I need your advice on what proof I need to take this to the police, the FBI, the SEC, the FDA, and anybody else who needs to know."

"Well, for one thing, you probably shouldn't hand them anything written on toilet paper."

"Yeah, yeah, but seriously, what do I need?"

"Well, you sure as hell can't go to them with vague suspicions and lists of corporations who had good product sales and people who died, or took a vacation without telling anybody. You need incontrovertible financial records. And better still, you need audio . . . or better, video recordings of these people confessing their sins."

"Okay, I can try for that."

"But remember, these corporate types are smart bastards. That's how they got where they are. They're smart enough not to blurt out their crimes. And even if they do, they've likely got plans to evade or obstruct investigations. You've got to be subtle, to try to outwit them."

Failing to notice the frustrated people around him, Pritchett took out his phone.

"Let me call our head police reporter. Ask him for his advice." He paused, scrutinized the screen, then uttered a curse.

"Your phone won't work," said Annie.

"What? Why the hell not?"

"We can't tell you," she said.

Shaking his head, Pritchett copied the list into his laptop, gave Brad the toilet paper, then stood up to leave.

"Well, shit. I just hope to hell you two aren't totally loony, and have gotten me to go down a rabbit hole with you."

• • •

Annie pushed through the glass doors and emerged from the Boston General medical imaging center. She smiled cautiously, handing Brad a hospital badge.

"Just put this on and walk in past the reception desk. Don't stop, even if they ask you to. Follow the signs that say 'MRI suite.' Ask for Elaine Goforth. She's the radiologist who runs the machine. Do what she says. Then come back."

Brad did as he was told, and within thirty minutes, emerged, his face still grim. Annie drove the car up and stopped just long enough for him to slide into the passenger seat.

"You're done?" asked Annie.

"I'm done. But I don't know whether it worked or not. Annie, I don't know whether I can take what'll happen if it doesn't work."

"Okay, then you take the jammer. I'll test whether the chip's deactivated."

Brad smiled ruefully, shaking his head. "Sweetheart, you know it would hurt me more if you were hurting. And you need to make sure the girls are protected if their jammer fails. Drop me off in Chelsea. I'll show you where. Take the jammer with you. Whether your idea worked or not, I won't need it. Hug the girls for me."

"Brad, be careful. I can't lose you! God, this is so terrible!" She wiped away tears as she drove, and when they reached the office building in Chelsea, she threw her arms around him, holding him for a long time. "Will we get out of this?"

"Yes. I'm sure we will. I'm sure he'll help."

"But you said last time he threw you out."

"Sweetheart, your job is to get the girls, and if this works, get them to the imaging center. I'll wait an hour to be sure. Then I'll call on the McNeils' landline if I'm free."

Taking a deep breath, wiping her eyes and setting her jaw, Annie dropped the car into gear and sped away toward the freeway that led to New Hampshire.

Brad stood for long minutes outside the building, steeling himself against the devastating emotions that would tear at him if the chip unleashed a blast of hormones. Or just as devastating, for the appearance of the mercenaries who could track him if the chip was still active.

He leaned against a car and tensed, waiting to learn of his fate.

. . .

Beale hovered over the technician, angrily commanding him to switch from one person's signal to another.

"So, you acquired Annie Davis's signal for ten minutes, but then lost it?"

"Right," said the technician. "She must have gone out of range of the jammer."

"Where was she?"

"A hospital clinic in Newton . . . Boston General."

"Maybe one of them needed medical attention. For some effect of the chip."

"Should we tell Mr. Lundgren?" asked the technician.

"Hell, no! I've learned not to go to him with questions. He wants answers. And since our operative at the school is now sitting in the Weston police station explaining himself, we have no one watching Lisa Fallon."

"Damn!" Exclaimed the technician. "It's the Davis girls! Their signals are back."

"Okay," said Beale. "Take advantage of this window."

"But they're just little girls."

"We hit them once before. Do you want to tell Lundgren we missed a chance?"

. . .

Gregor Kalinsky grunted in disgust, preparing to slam the company's office door in Brad's face.

"You are back? You think I don't mean it when I say I will not answer any more questions?"

"You know Marty Fallon is dead?"

Kalinsky opened the door a bit wider, his scowl softening to sadness.

"*Da, eto ochen' pechal'no* . . . uh . . . sorry. I talk Russian when upset. It is very sad about Marty. It's terrible. I love Marty. But you don't care. All it means is that you are out of job. So, you—"

"Lundgren killed him."

It took a moment for the news to sink in. The red flush of rage rose on Kalinsky's bearded face. He whipped the door back against its hinges, the crash bringing startled gasps from the programmers in the room behind him.

"*ETOT UBLYUDOK!* HOW DID THAT BASTARD . . . HE CAN'T . . ." He didn't finish, but slammed his fist against the door and stalked away into the office. Brad took it as an invitation to enter. He followed Kalinsky to his cluttered private office, where the big Russian impatiently waved for Brad to come in, shutting the door behind him.

"Okay, how does he do this? Kill Marty. You don't bullshit me. You tell me whole focking story about this focker."

Kalinsky slammed his large body into his recliner, gripping its arms in barely contained fury. Brad proceeded to tell Kalinsky what he had uncovered—the crooked financial dealings, the secret laboratory, the control chip, the experiments on unknowing subjects, Bell's attempted suicide and ultimate murder, and finally their own agonizing torture from the chip.

Kalinsky sat in a smoldering rage for a long time, his chest heaving, glaring at Brad. But Brad knew the anger was not directed at him.

"What you want?" he finally asked coldly.

"I need you to help me get the evidence that I can take to the police, to the FBI."

"We can focking do that," snarled Kalinsky. "I have people who can do that. I can do that."

"I have a problem. All my notes and data are in our apartment. There's critical material I should have uploaded to my cloud drive."

"*Nyet*. Bad idea using commercial cloud drive. It be hacked. We have done it for NSA. I give you instructions on uploading to our site on the Darknet."

"Darknet? The one criminals use?"

"*Da*, for drug-dealing, arms trading. But we are not criminals. Not now, anyway. We good guys. I will get you a little gadget you will find useful. Then we will go get focker Lundgren."

CHAPTER 20

"This is weird," said the lean, dark-haired mercenary into the cell phone.

He sat in the driver's seat of the dark blue van with the Parker Plumbing sign. Beside him sat another thickly muscled ex-Marine, his head shaved bald. He had binoculars trained on Davis's apartment building from their inconspicuous spot in the side street.

"What's weird?" asked Beale over the phone's speaker.

"I just got eyes on Brad Davis. He's hiding behind a fence down the block from the apartment. But my cell phone's still working. So, he doesn't have a jammer, but you can't see his GPS signal, right?"

"Nothing," said Beale. "Maybe it's the GPS chip. We need to examine that chip. If possible, we also need him alive. But if not . . ." Beale didn't need to finish the sentence.

"Yeah. Okay by me." The driver turned to his bald partner and shrugged offhandedly. "Hey, a little wet work, a lot more money. Take the front. I'll circle the van around to the next street and come up from the back."

The bald-shaven mercenary slipped out of the van, keeping his jacket closed to hide the shoulder-holstered nine-millimeter pistol. He sprinted to the front of the building taking a quick look through the glass door into the downstairs hallway. He ducked through the front door, backing into a small alcove containing a wall of mail boxes. He pulled out his pistol and screwed on a silencer, chambering a round and clicking off the safety. He nestled the pistol under his coat, should anybody come in to check their mail.

Periodically glancing out of the alcove, he could see anyone who came in the back door and up the back stairs. He waited.

After a few minutes, he heard somebody come through the back door. He heard the elevator door slide open, and a quick look around the corner told him it was their target getting on. He waited for his partner, and when he heard the back door open again, knew he should take the elevator up. His partner would take the stairs to box in their quarry.

They reached the third floor together, with the dark-haired mercenary moving to the door to the Davis apartment, while his partner remained on watch over the other three apartments on the floor.

The dark-haired mercenary listened at the door, gingerly tried it, and finding it locked, took out a set of bump keys used for lock-picking. Choosing one that matched the Schlage door lock, he inserted it, and deftly gave it a series of sharp taps with his gun butt until he detected the latch open and could quietly turn it to unlock the door. He screwed a silencer on his pistol, and quietly chambered a round, motioning to the other mercenary to join him.

They burst through the door, slamming it back against the wall, and dashed down the hallway, stopping at the bedroom. There, Brad sat at his desk, his fingers on the computer keyboard. They leveled their pistols at him, and he turned and regarded them with a cold stare.

"You want to die here or go with us?" asked the dark-haired mercenary quietly.

"Easy answer," said Brad. "Go with you. You're too late, anyway. I'm done here." He stood and raised his hands.

Saying nothing, the lean mercenary slammed him onto the bed, wrenched his hands behind his back, and bound him with a plastic zip tie. The mercenary punched in a number on his cell phone. He reported the capture, shaking his head as he hung up.

"Beale says he's still not getting a GPS signal from the guy's chip," he said to his partner. Then to Brad, "Too bad, pal. Guess they'll just have to cut that chip out of you and find out what went wrong. That'll hurt."

• • •

Annie gripped the wheel of the rental car, as she eased it cautiously up the long driveway to the McNeil house. She constantly checked the rear-view mirror, taking several deep breaths, trying to calm herself. She was desperate to see her babies, but felt the dark weight of dread, knowing that dangerous men were on the lookout for her. And there had been no call from Brad telling her that her idea had worked; that their chips were deactivated. She dared not switch off her jammer to test the possibilities, shuddering at the memory of the vicious, suffocating shroud of despair that had nearly driven her mad. And she had to stay in control for her babies.

She saw no headlights behind her, no strange cars waiting in the driveway, so she slid out of the car and sprinted to the door. Bob McNeil answered the doorbell with a fearful expression on his face.

"God, Annie, I'm so sorry," he said.

"Bob? What do you mean?"

"Okay, most importantly, the girls are okay now. But this morning, we heard them crying. We ran into their rooms, and they were crouched in the corner, sobbing. They were beside themselves. I checked the box, and one of our boys must have played with it when we weren't looking. It had been unplugged, and the battery ran down and it was off. My God, they were so . . . I'm *so* sorry."

Ella joined him, her panicked expression mirroring his. "We think they're fine, but—"

Annie rushed past them up the stairs, followed by Bob and Ella, and into the guest room, to see the reassuring glow of the jammer indicator light. Each girl was curled up in a twin bed, the covers up to their chins, sleeping, their faces so sweet in repose. She sat down on Sarah's bed, gently caressing her lovely face. Her cheeks were stained with tears, and her body periodically shivered from crying. Little Sarah would probably not realize what was happening, but did Sally? She moved to Sally's bed to find the little girl curled in a fetal position. Her eyes opened, she realized her mother had come and leaped up, her little arms encircling Annie's neck.

"Mommy, I was so scared. Then I was so sad. What happened? I'm so glad you're here!"

Annie hugged her child tightly and kissed her on the forehead, the neck, the cheek.

"Yes, sweetheart, I'm here. I'll make sure that never happens again." She turned to the McNeils. "Please don't blame yourself. It was an accident. I'm deeply grateful for what you've done. Now we have to leave. Otherwise, you'll be in more danger. Did you get a call from Brad?"

"No," said Bob. "We haven't heard from him."

At the news, Annie shook her head in anxiety.

Bob continued. "Look, can you tell us what's going on? Can you tell us what that box is?"

"It's best you don't know. We *have* to go. Brad is depending on us. I'm not sure . . . I haven't heard from Brad . . . but I think we have a way to save the children from what you saw."

"Thank God!" exclaimed Ella. "Whatever it is, it's horrible." She moved quickly to pack the girls' backpacks. She unplugged the jammer, making sure its red light still glowed brightly.

"Bob, do you have a gun in the house?" asked Annie.

"Well, yeah, a pistol I bought Ella, for when I'm out of town."

"I'm going to have to ask you for it."

Bob nodded and disappeared down the hall into the master bedroom. He appeared with the semi-automatic pistol, handing it to Annie.

"Do you know how to use it?"

Annie nodded, efficiently popping out the clip, checking the bullets, slapping it back in, chambering a round, and switching on the safety.

"I learned in Afghanistan. All ER personnel carried sidearms. We were in a forward position." Her expression became cold-bloodedly determined. "We had a saying that sometimes the best patient care is killing the enemy."

She slipped the pistol into her pocket and returned to the bedroom, enfolding Sally in her arms and carrying her out. The little girl wrapped her arms around her mother's neck, laying her head on her mother's shoulder. Bob followed her down the stairs, cradling the sleeping Sarah. They buckled the girls into their car seats, and tucked blankets around them against the chill autumn night. She stowed the jammer in the front seat, as Ella appeared with a bag containing extra batteries.

Annie turned to hug the two friends. Tears ran down Ella's face, and she said, "You call us when you can. Let us know that you're okay. And we will go *anywhere*, do *anything* to help."

As Annie climbed into the car, Bob and Ella stood with their arms around each other for support. She turned the car around and drove down the long driveway to the dark country lane. She stopped before entering the road, switched off the engine and lights and peered into the darkness in both directions. No sign of a car. She listened to the still night. No sound of an engine, or voices, or the rustle of someone moving in the fall leaves.

She turned around and checked the children. Sally had gone back to sleep, and Sarah's eyes were closed, their angelic faces at rest. She reached back and tucked the blankets more tightly around them.

Consulting the paper map, she plotted the route back to Boston that would keep her on back roads. She pulled out and accelerated away, the car's headlights lighting the narrow, wandering asphalt road flanked by thick trees. She passed a driveway, but intent on the road ahead, she didn't notice a black SUV pulling out behind her, its lights off. The SUV waited until she had rounded a curve to turn on its headlights, following her.

After several turns, checking her rear-view mirror, Annie glimpsed the flash of headlights. Her heart began to pound as she sped up, while knowing she couldn't take too many chances, given her precious passengers.

The driver of the SUV was under no such restrictions, and apparently realizing that she had seen the tail, gunned the massive vehicle, swerving through curves until it pulled to within inches of the car's bumper.

Annie swerved into a turn and careened into a hard right onto another road. The SUV did the same, switching on its brights to flood the car with light. From the back seat, Annie heard Sally whimper. "Mommy, you're driving fastest. I'm scared."

"It's okay, sweetheart. You're safe. Mommy is just going fast to get us to a good place fast."

But with a jarring thud, the SUV rammed the little sedan and she uttered an involuntary cry, as the car jerked forward, snapping her neck back. She struggled to maintain control, skidding to the left and correcting. She couldn't go faster. The risk was too great of slamming into one of the massive oaks flashing by on either side of the pitch-black road.

She saw the SUV's lights shift to the left, as it swerved into the oncoming lane and accelerated up to her rear fender. She felt the impact of the SUV slamming its massive bulk into the fender. The children screamed in fear; the landscape whirled past the windshield, as the car skidded around. With the violent, sickening crash of crumpling metal, it slammed sideways into a tree.

The burly crew-cut man climbed out of the SUV and walked toward the smashed car, shining his flashlight into it and pulling his pistol. He heard the children sobbing, saw the small form of a woman slumped over the wheel, her curly blond hair hanging forward over her face. He shrugged. *Too bad. The woman was dead but the mission was still successful. They'd have the kids.*

But the woman abruptly lifted her bloodied head and turned toward him, her eyes gleaming with hatred, her jaw clenched in rage.

In one lightning move, she brought up the pistol and fired.

• • •

Brad sagged into the chair, moaning, his head lolling back, his eyes closed, his hands bound behind him.

"Feeling unwell?" asked Lundgren. He stood over Brad, waving away the two mercenaries guarding him and motioning for Beale, at the back of the room, to step forward. He whispered to Beale. "Looks like just the GPS failed. We've still got control."

"I'm not sure," began Beale. "We think—"

"*It's just the GPS,*" snapped Lundgren, as if his declaration would make it so. "Look at him, for God's sake. We kept his chip reservoir inactive, so he'd have a good store of hormones. And now that we have released them, look at him with just small doses. He's overwhelmed.

Besides, we've had *no* chip failures in tests. We're going ahead with this demonstration."

Lundgren then addressed a well-dressed Asian man—who, like Lundgren, was resplendent in a bespoke suit.

"This subject has a version two-point-one chip, and we have him under complete control. I can show you what we're capable of making him do."

"Yes," said the man. "It would be of interest to see that." He sat down in a chair across the windowless room and crossed his legs.

"Bradley, this is Mr. Zhu," said Lundgren, with a tone of patronizing sarcasm. "Mr. Zhu is from the Chinese Ministry of State Security. I just want you to understand that there is absolutely no way anyone can stop this research. You see, Mr. Zhu has agreed to facilitate his country becoming our new development and beta test site. His country has no problem recruiting large numbers of people to enable full-fledged deployment, and in secrecy. In return for the development and field trials, we've agreed to let his country be the first customer—"

"For an exclusive term of five years," broke in Zhu. "But you say we shall see a demonstration?"

"Certainly," said Lundgren. He nodded to Beale, who shook his head doubtfully, but spoke into his cell phone.

"Initiate the self-destruct sequence," instructed Beale.

Lundgren turned to Zhu, "Sir, you will see that we've formulated a sequence of hormonal bursts that quite reliably trigger a self-destructive act. The subject feels deep depression, hopelessness, and utter panic; and the combination produces an irresistible desire to escape those feelings . . . permanently."

"OH, DEAR GOD!" gasped Brad. One of the mercenaries snipped off the plastic cuffs and grasped his head as it pitched forward. "I . . . I . . . CAN'T . . ." As Brad alternated groans and screams, Lundgren placed a pistol on the table.

"Brad, do you see this? It's a way out. You can end the pain. Go ahead, Brad. End the pain." Then to Zhu. "This will show you how powerful the chip is. He will use the weapon on himself."

"He knows it is loaded?" asked Zhu. "I do not want a demonstration in which the subject does not really believe he will die."

With an expression of mild exasperation, Lundgren nodded to Beale, who took up the pistol, held it before the moaning Brad, chambered a round, and placed it back on the table.

"You see, Brad. This is your way out."

Brad crawled to the table, haltingly pulling himself up. He reached for the gun with a trembling hand, grabbed it, and staggered backward into the corner. He slowly raised the gun to his head.

Then his demeanor abruptly changed. He stood up and smiled, aiming the pistol at Lundgren. "Sorry to disappoint you . . . *Larry*," he said sarcastically. "I'm actually not feeling that bad."

"WHAT THE HELL?" shouted Lundgren. "Beale, what's going on? He's not affected at all. He's normal."

Beale merely raised his hands and shrugged, his face registering an I-told-you-so expression.

"There's only one bullet in the gun," said Lundgren to the mercenaries.

"Hmm," said Brad coolly. "I guess that means I only have one target, and that's you *Larry*. Either of those guys moves, and you get it in the chest."

Pausing for an instant, Lundgren gestured for the men to lay down their weapons, which they did. Brad instructed the two to slide their weapons across the floor to him. He picked one up, quickly checked that the safety was off, and brought it to bear on the men.

"You see, *Larry*, I have a *very* smart wife," said Brad. "She figured out that since the chip was electronic, exposing it to a high magnetic field would fry it, just like it would fry any other electronic device. Did you happen to know that an MRI scanner generates a massive magnetic field? My very, *very* smart wife knows."

"Kill sequence," hissed Lundgren, and Beale repeated the phrase into the cell phone.

Brad flinched, but just for effect, quickly resuming smiling. "Still alive! Looks like my chip is totally toast. The succinylcholine reservoir doesn't work. I should also tell you that all of this encounter has been on camera." He pointed to his belt buckle. "A very technically savvy fellow I know is sitting down the road watching this and recording it."

Lundgren showed surprisingly little emotion at the news. "Tell your friend that lives will be lost if he disseminates that video. And lives will be lost if you do not do precisely what I say. Lives that are dear to you."

"Who?"

Lundgren picked up a tablet computer and slid it across the table to Brad. Keeping an eye on the mercenaries, he picked it up.

"You will see two dots on the map of New Hampshire. Those represent your children. Those dots appeared last night. We have operatives there now. Hand one of these gentlemen your guns, or Mr. Beale will call them and tell them the children are of no use to us."

"*Jesus!*" breathed Brad. "*My children! You can't—*"

"Of course I can."

His body slumping in defeat, Brad handed the guns to one of the mercenaries.

Lundgren turned to Zhu. "As you can see, sir, there are still technical issues to be worked out. The first chips . . . the ones that are in millions of people now . . . didn't have enough electronic components to be affected by magnetic fields. But we suspected that the new chips would. But we couldn't test this vulnerability until we were in clinical trials, and the chips were actually functioning in living bodies. Fortunately, Mr. Davis has provided us a test of that problem. Once we extract the chip from him, we can figure out how to harden future versions, and your colleagues can proceed with clinical tests of those."

"These are not major problems," said Zhu. "Our army technology division is expert at hardening electronics. And we have an excellent electromagnetic spectrum-warfare capability. We can make the chips invulnerable to jamming."

"That's what we were counting on," said Lundgren.

The mercenaries grabbed Brad's arms, and Beale stepped forward with a syringe, plunging it into Brad's shoulder.

As a fog of unconsciousness enveloped him, Brad could hear Lundgren talking to Zhu.

"It should be a straightforward surgical procedure," said Lundgren.

"And if there are complications?" asked Zhu.

"Actually, we are only mildly interested in seeing him survive."

CHAPTER 21

"What the hell happened here?" asked the New Hampshire state patrolman, climbing out of his cruiser, donning his wide-brimmed hat.

He surveyed the scene on the country road in the morning light. The thick forest lining the narrow lane reflected the swirling lights of an ambulance and four patrol cars. He shook his head at the crumpled gray sedan jammed against the tree and the body lying beside it, with two white-coated EMTs bending over the corpse.

"Road rage?" he asked

"Well, there's more," said the sheriff's deputy who met him. "That's why we asked you guys to come in. This kind of thing is beyond us."

They walked over to the car.

"Okay, this guy was shot once in the chest. Car's a rental. Agreement in the glove box says it was rented to a Bradley Davis of Boston. But the thing is, we're worried about the possible kids."

"Kids?"

"Yeah, we found toys in the back."

"Jesus. That *does* make it a different situation."

"That's still not all. Another guy was cuffed to the steering wheel. He's not talking. We cuffed him and put him in the back of our car."

"Identification?"

"Here's his wallet. His ID says Coronado Security. Same as the deceased. Both guys are probably ex-military. They both have shoulder holsters. Empty."

"Who the hell could take on a pair of ex-soldiers? And presumably take their vehicle. What were they driving?"

"The guy won't say. Maybe he killed the other guy, and somebody handcuffed him to keep him here. Or more likely the guy Davis did it and took their car."

"Likely. We'll do a GSR test on the prisoner, anyway, to see if he fired a weapon. I'll transport him to the station. You secure the scene. I'll call forensics, the coroner. We'll contact Boston PD to locate this Bradley Davis. We'll put out a bulletin about possible kids missing. We'll see what Coronado Security has to say about these two. And we'll see what we can get out of this guy."

Together, they hauled the wiry, dark-haired man in a tan Coronado Security jacket out of the deputy's cruiser. The two patrolmen took another try at asking him questions, but the man remained steadfastly silent. They deposited him into the highway patrol car, and the patrolman radioed the information to his station, still sorting through the facts of this very strange case.

• • •

Annie crouched behind a car that was parked in a conveniently remote spot in the apartment parking lot, grasping the bumper to steady her jitters. Her experience in Afghanistan and the hospital ER, gave her the fortitude to steady herself against the memory of the night before. The sight of the man approaching the car holding the pistol. The heart-rending sounds of her babies sobbing. Their shriek at the gunshot. The stunned look on the man's face as blood oozed from his chest before he crumpled to the ground.

Her military training and a burst of adrenaline had enabled her to bolt from the car to get the drop on his partner sitting in the SUV. He had shown considerable respect, given that his partner was lying dead from her bullet.

Now, she had to recover herself to complete her task. She couldn't let the girls see her frightened. They'd been through enough with the crash, the gunshot, her shouting, and being carried to the black SUV with their eyes covered.

Now, they were settled again, sleeping fitfully, buckled into their car seats. She recited to herself the calming mantra she used during a medical emergency at the hospital. *Be cool, be efficient, save lives.* She was used to blood, used to seeing the consequences of violence. But not used to visiting it upon another human. But she had saved the girls. She had to concentrate on that.

Recovering herself, she stood up and scanned the lot again. It was still empty of people, as the morning light was just overtaking the night. But still she had to work quickly, to make sure the SUV wasn't stopped by the police. Using a screwdriver from the SUV, she removed the license plate from the car. She quickly swapped it with the SUV's.

As she worked, she mulled over the unsettling discovery she'd made while searching the SUV—a footlocker holding a cache of weapons, radios, and other equipment that soldiers would carry. These were soldiers! That made her certain she had to take every action necessary to evade the police. Soldiers knew how to monitor police scanners, to use their skills to find her and the children. She'd added to that footlocker one of the guns she'd taken from the men, slipping the other into her jacket pocket. She would carry two. She had no idea who else was following her, but her training had taught her to always have adequate firepower.

She also suffered under the burden of dread that she still had no idea where her husband was, or if exposure to the MRI had inactivated their chips. He purposely hadn't told her what he was planning, and she admitted to herself that it was just as well.

Even though the reach of these men seemed frighteningly long, she had one advantage. There was *nothing* she would not do to protect the girls. And there was *nothing* she would not do to find Brad.

The license plates switched, she climbed into the SUV, checking the batteries on the two jammers. Both were low, so she switched off one to save it.

Just as she was starting the SUV, Sally was waking up, yawning and stretching.

"Mommy, where are we?"

"We're back in town, honey."

"Whose car is this?"

"It's somebody we know.

"Is it time for school?"

"We're taking some more days off. Would you like breakfast?"

"Pancakes!"

"Absolutely, sweetie. I saw a place driving in. We'll go there."

The thought of a brightly lit restaurant with a bustling morning crowd gave her some comfort. Soon Sarah, always the late-rising sleepyhead, would be stirring, too. And that little girl was always ravenous in the morning.

By the time they reached the restaurant, Sarah was awake chattering about pancakes; and the breakfast was, indeed, a welcome, bright beginning for the day. Annie needed the girls to be in a good mood, because she would still have to put them through another scary experience—even if she was still not sure it worked.

• • •

"Annie, I'm just not comfortable with this." Elaine Goforth sat at the small control panel of the MRI scanner, her dubious expression portraying a person teetering between two distressing alternatives. "Look, you won't tell me what's going on. You want me to put your children into the scanner, and that could be traumatizing for them. Putting you and Brad in was one thing. But kids? This is different. I just feel I have to tell my supervisor."

Annie hugged the two girls to her side, as they happily played with toys from the pancake restaurant. "Please, Lainie. You know the magnetic fields are harmless. I'll be in there with them. And I've explained to them what's going to happen." She gestured at the window into the machine room holding the massive donut-shaped scanner. And you know I wouldn't put my babies through anything I didn't have to. Please!"

"Tell me why. *You tell me why.*"

"Lainey, that would put you in danger. Trust me. I know this is weird. But just like you did with Brad and me, just switch the machine on. They don't have to be scanned. Just slide each girl into the chamber and then out with the magnet on. That won't even show up on the log."

Elaine stared at her for a long moment, then finally shook her head in reluctant agreement and motioned for them to enter the scanner room.

• • •

"You are goddamned well kidding me!" Beale exclaimed into the phone. "Jesus!" Then, to Lundgren, sitting beside him in the van, "The dumb shit is in jail!"

Beale pulled the van off the freeway and into the parking lot of a Burger King, so he could concentrate on the call. But first, he went around to the back of the van and opened the doors just enough to make sure their bound captive was still unconscious.

"Put him on speaker," demanded Lundgren. Beale did so, and from the van's speaker came the voice of one of the mercenaries they had sent to capture the wife and children.

Even over the phone, the mercenary's voice exuded anger at his situation, at Beale, at Lundgren.

"Hell, we chased after her, and the bitch wouldn't stop! We had to do a tactical ram to stop the car. It crashed, and Al went to get the woman and kids, while I stayed to give us a quick extraction. I hear a shot, and I'm thinking Al had to take action. I really didn't want to see a dead woman, so I sat there. The next thing I know there's a gun to my head. This woman was fucking crazy!"

"And this crazy woman took your SUV, weapons and all. And left you there handcuffed."

"I told you she was crazy. Get me a damned lawyer."

"We will," said Lundgren. "Keep your mouth shut!"

"Of course."

"Any idea where she is now?"

"No. But check the tracker on the SUV. That'll find her."

Beale ended the call and muttered several more curses under his breath. He called Coronado Security, getting through to the technician monitoring the surveillance teams. He muttered more curses. "He said there's no signal from the SUV. It must be in range of a jammer."

"Tell them that," instructed Lundgren. "And tell them she's got an arsenal. And she's killed one of their guys. And they should shoot on sight and say it's self-defense."

"But she's got the kids with her."

Lundgren cocked his head in indifference. "Collateral damage."

CHAPTER 22

The first sound invading Brad's drug-shrouded conscious was a male voice rising above the drone of an engine. It was Beale talking to somebody. Brad forced himself to open his eyes and take a deep breath, shaking his head to clear it of fog. He peered around to see that he was in the cargo space between the back door of a van and the second row of seats. He heard Lundgren's voice answer Beale. At first, he was too foggy to grasp what they were saying.

His memory began to return—of the needle jab and the captivity before it. He *had* to free himself from the anesthetic's grip. He struggled toward alertness, realizing that his wrists were bound behind him by something that cut into them. Plastic zip-tie cuffs. He shook himself again, to full wakefulness, helped by the pain of inadvertently knocking his head against a metal box. He could see that it was a toolbox, in the alternating light and darkness of streetlights passing overhead. Maybe it held some tool he could use to free himself.

As he gathered his wits, he listened to Beale talk, then Lundgren answering. He monitored their talk intently, not only to hear what they were saying, but to ensure they didn't hear him moving around in the back.

"You really think it's worth it to take him to an OR, to try to do the surgery and keep him alive?" asked Beale.

"Remember, the surgery serves two purposes," answered Lundgren. "One, we get the chip. Two, we do it without anesthetic, so he'll be willing to tell us everything to escape the pain. We need to know who was at the other end of his video feed. Whether that person would take the video to the police."

"Well, we need to finish this fast. Lot of logistics needed to transition the work to China."

"Yes, indeed. Worth it, though. A good environment."

"Zhu agreed on the whole package? Signed the agreement?"

"Yes. They've got one-point-six million soldiers, and a huge subjugated population. He guaranteed they would all be at our disposal. And sufficient funds and facilities to perfect the chips."

"And then?"

"Let the Chinese have the chip technology, and come back here and submit it for FDA approval."

"And give the Chinese the red and blue chips, too?"

"For the right price. Those are the ones they want most."

"Well, we sure couldn't get them approved in the US."

"Probably not. And, of course, Marty would never have allowed it, either. Fortunately, neither he nor the FDA will have a say."

In the back, Brad realized with a mental *aha!* that he didn't need any tools to free himself. He had freed himself from plastic zip ties several times before. He'd learned the trick from a magician he'd interviewed for an article on the technology of magic. Now to see if it would work on these cuffs. He rolled onto his side, so he could hold his wrists away from his body. He slapped his tightly bound wrists as hard as he could against his lower spine, enduring the shooting pain. Nothing.

"And you're sure about Phyllis Kelley?" Beale asked.

Lundgren waved his hand dismissively. "Soon she'll be just another data point. And as for Davis, I haven't told you, but I instructed Coronado to make it look like he killed their operative at the crash site. They're very clever that way."

Hearing the plans for Phyllis's and his future, Brad redoubled his efforts. He had to escape! He had to take the chance that Annie had rescued the children and they were safely protected by a jammer. He needed to find his family!

The desperation gave him the utter determination he needed. He slapped his wrists against his back even harder. Still the cuffs held. He could feel the slickness of blood wetting his wrists.

"Damn," he heard Beale say, and the van slowed. The engine noise abated, allowing him to hear the whoosh of traffic on a freeway. A traffic tie-up. That was good! This was his only chance!

One more time, ignoring the pain, he viciously whacked his wrists against his back, and the cuffs popped open. He listened. Beale and Lundgren continued their talk. They hadn't heard anything. What to do next?

The tool box! He ever-so-quietly unlatched it and raised the lid. By the faint light coming through the van's rear window, he could make out pliers, wrenches, a mallet. He pulled out the mallet and stuffed it into his belt. He found a Phillips head screwdriver! Perfect! It reminded him of another article on tire technology he'd written for a car magazine. Tires were weakest on their sidewalls.

He pulled out the screwdriver and reached up to the van door handle. He knew that the instant the door opened, they would detect it by the light from outside, and the louder traffic sounds. So, he would have to move quickly.

He shoved open the door, dropped to the ground, ducked under the back of the van, placed the tip of the screwdriver against the inside sidewall of the right tire and whacked it hard with the mallet. It sank into the thin rubber there, and he yanked it out, relishing the whoosh of air escaping. He quickly did the same with the left tire, producing a similar whoosh.

Alarmed voices rose from within the van. A loud honking behind him made him whirl around to see an alarmed middle-aged couple in a silver sedan, reacting to his sabotage.

Bursting from the back passenger door of the van came a mercenary, the same lean, dark-haired man who had abducted him. Brad hadn't even realized he was in the van. He'd apparently been sitting in the back seat, leaning forward listening.

The mercenary held a pistol, and as he rounded the back of the van, Brad slashed the mallet down on his hand, knocking away the gun. He smashed the mallet into the man's face, unleashing a gush of bright red blood from his nose. Another blow right between the eyes sent his head flying back.

Brad leaped between the stalled cars, sprinting away from the van, crouching low. The van was in the right lane, and his plan was to sprint over to that side of the freeway and down the side. But that side was a sheer drop! He'd have to escape all the way across the other side of the freeway, through speeding traffic!

He ducked behind stalled cars, hurdled the guard rail between the two sides of the freeway, and leaped onto the other side, where traffic rushed past unabated.

He dodged past one oncoming car, barely missing being struck. A truck skidded toward him, the driver desperately trying to control it. He sprang past the truck and reached the outside lane on the other side of the freeway, stopping abruptly as a bright red car slammed on its brakes and barreled past, tires screeching. An explosive pop sounded behind him, and a hole blasted into the car's side window. He looked back to see the mercenary, nearly blinded by blood, holding his nose with one hand and shooting with the other.

Evading two more cars, each of which was struck with a bullet, he reached the shoulder on the other side. He turned back to check whether anybody was following him, seeing that the mercenary had been stymied by the cars and trucks speeding past and the bleeding nose.

With considerable satisfaction, he bellowed back, "YOU DON'T 'FOCK' WITH A SCIENCE WRITER!" before sliding down the highway embankment and onto a residential street below.

• • •

Brad sat in the coffee shop staring grimly at the disposable cell phone. He'd tried to call Annie over and over, desperate to hear her voice, to find out whether she and the girls were safe. But no answer; just her voice mail. He'd hung up each time without leaving a message. They had agreed not to leave a voice or text trail, given that either of them could end up captured, as he had been. But he could call the McNeils, so he punched in their number, and Bob answered.

"God, Brad, what's happened to you?" he asked.

"I'm okay. Where are Annie and the children?"

"We don't know. They left here last night. Brad, the jammer quit for a while. It was all my fault. The boys played with it."

"What happened? Bob, what happened to them?"

"It was horrible, Brad. The girls were crying. I feel so terrible. But we got it back on, and by the time Annie got here, they were better. I am *so* sorry."

"So, she's got them. Thank God. Look, Bob, you've done everything for us. Don't you feel sorry. I want you to—"

"Brad, I've got to tell you something else. Something that has us really scared for Annie and the girls. She had taken my pistol. Then we saw on the news this morning there was a car crash near here. A man was shot. Another man was arrested. We saw the footage. The car was your rental! Your face is on the news! They think you were driving the car!"

"Jesus!" Brad lowered his voice to an urgent whisper, so the other coffee shop customers wouldn't hear. "What else? Any mention of Annie and the girls?"

"No. But I don't think the police are releasing all the information. Brad, they may have been taken. We just don't know."

"Well, if she calls, give her this number. Tell her I'm okay. I'm going to the police. We'll finish this!"

Brad considered what to do next, looking around the coffee shop to make sure nobody was staring at him. Fortunately, he had a fairly standard-looking face. He'd have to do something to change his appearance. Not a beard or mustache. He chuckled wryly to himself. He'd never been able to grow a decent version of either one. Maybe now was a time to see what he'd look like in a fake. He also realized his clothes were pretty grungy from wallowing around in the back of a van and sliding down a freeway embankment. He'd go back to the Walmart where he'd gotten the phone and buy clothes and something to make him look different.

Walmart actually did have fake beards and mustaches. It was close to Halloween. But Brad didn't think he'd look particularly convincing as a pirate or backwoodsman. So, he finally decided on a version of a disguise that had worked before—a Red Sox baseball cap, reading glasses, and a more reputable-looking shirt, pants, and jacket. He changed into his new clothes in the bathroom, went outside and called Kalinsky.

"You are on news, all over," said the Russian. "Where are you?"

"You have the video?"

"What? You think I chicken-shit out? Of course I got video of big focker and all his other fockers . . . until he smash your little camera after they knock you out."

"And you didn't give it to the police?"

"'Course not, what is name I should call you . . . *dumbass?* Yes . . . dumbass, I already send some people of mine to find you. But now you have found yourself. Where are you? I come to get you. Stay put."

Brad gave his location and killed time wandering the aisles of Walmart. He felt a pang of anguish passing the toy aisle, remembering the girls running up and down one like it, chattering, giggling, and trying to choose from the brightly colored display. He remembered how he and Annie would set an "absolute" limit of one toy each, with the one who relented first teasing the other for being a pushover.

• • •

Within an hour, Brad had been picked up by Kalinsky in his black three-ton Cadillac Escalade, which was pulling up to the modern gray stone building that was the Boston Police Department headquarters. Brad rode in the back seat; up front sat Kalinsky and a wiry driver with a buzz-cut, whose arms were festooned with tattoos. Kalinsky introduced him merely as Mark.

Brad had been startled to see the massive chauffeured vehicle pull up to the Walmart entrance. Somehow, he'd figured Kalinsky would drive an old rattletrap of a car littered with fast-food wrappers and computer parts.

They walked together into the headquarters, and Brad approached the desk sergeant sitting behind the bulletproof glass.

"I'm Brad Davis. You're looking for me in connection with the car crash in New Hampshire. So are the New Hampshire state police. More importantly, we have information about a major corporate crime."

It took only seconds for the sergeant to grasp what he was saying. The cop tapped a command into the computer and stared at the screen for a moment. Transferring his stare to Brad, he picked up the phone and mumbled something into it.

Within moments, three uniformed cops appeared from the inner office, accompanied by a burly, balding man in suit and tie, wearing a badge on a lanyard around his neck. One of the cops grabbed Brad, spun him around, and snapped cuffs around his wrists, over the bloody welts left from the plastic ties.

"*What the hell?*" exclaimed Brad.

"*What the fock?*" bellowed Kalinsky simultaneously.

"You have the right to remain silent . . ." began the red-haired man, launching into the recitation of Miranda rights.

They hauled Brad through the door, and Kalinsky followed shouting in Russian what was surely a string of obscenities.

They were both led into an interview room, and Brad was shoved into a chair. Crowding in with them were a uniformed cop, the burly, balding man, and a short, curly-haired man in a suit. The two suited men sat down across from Brad and Kalinsky, the burly man setting a laptop onto the table.

"What is this?" demanded Brad. "I came here to give you information. Why are you doing this?"

"I'm detective Shawn," said the burly man. "This is detective O'Hara." Then to Kalinsky: "Are you his lawyer?" His tone was dubious, as he coldly regarded the disheveled, bearded bear of a man.

Kalinsky paused only a beat before answering. "*Da*, I am lawyer. I am great focking lawyer, so you better not pull any bad shit."

Shawn turned to Brad. "Where were you last night?"

"I was being held captive by Thomas Beale and Lawrence Lundgren of NeoHappy, Inc. I came here to report their crimes."

Shawn shook his head and checked the laptop. "The state police in New Hampshire report that a witness has identified you as being the man who left the scene of a car crash and murder in a stolen SUV. And the car was rented in your name."

"As lawyer, I say that is all total *bullshit*," growled Kalinsky. "You listen to what he has to say."

"Look, I wasn't driving the car," said Brad. "My wife was. She may have had our children with her."

"Yeah, well, I'm told there were toys in the car," said Shawn. "Where is your wife now?"

"I don't know. She's missing."

"But the witness identified you. You're not saying she killed the man."

"If she did, he deserved it. Let me tell you what's really going on."

For the next hour, he explained his involvement with NeoHappy, the deaths of Fallon and Bell, and what he and Bell had discovered about Lundgren's crimes. As a climax, Kalinsky showed the video of Lundgren implicating himself and drugging Brad.

Shawn sat back shaking his head in puzzlement and looking over at O'Hara, who's expression portrayed similar confusion.

"Look, I'm not saying I believe any of this," said Shawn. "But we checked you out. You don't have a record. And it sounds like they've got pros, maybe mercenaries, handling their security. Okay, that does suggest the so-called witness could have been a fake. So, here's what we're going to do. My partner will start verifying what you've told us. I'm going to make a call to the FBI and get them involved. We'll see where this goes." He gestured for the uniformed cop to remove Brad's handcuffs.

Brad rubbed his wrists, still bleeding slightly. "Fine. Check it out. We need to stop these people."

The two detectives left Brad and Kalinsky sitting in the interview room, staring at the mirrored window.

"Looks like we've finally got some action," said Brad.

"Yes, action. But what kind?" asked Kalinsky darkly. "I never get good feeling around cops."

Shawn returned, holding a sheaf of papers. "Okay, we've got a team that will meet in the FBI offices. New Hampshire has jurisdiction over the crime there, but it looks like the feds will be investigating your allegations about NeoHappy. If you'll come with me, we'll go meet with them."

He led them to the garage, where he opened the back door of a squad car. "I need to transport you in this vehicle, for your safety."

"I have car," said Kalinsky. "We will follow."

"That's just it," said Shawn. "Whoever might be after you . . . if your story is true . . . likely knows that car. Send your car out as a decoy, so if you're being tailed, they'll follow it. We need to take every precaution, if these people have security people as dangerous as you say."

Kalinsky paused for a long moment, regarding Shawn with a suspicious scowl. Finally, he made a cell phone call, speaking in Russian.

"Nobody else is coming with us?" asked Brad. "No escort?"

"It's best if we keep this low profile," said Shawn. "It's early in the investigation, and we don't want to draw attention."

They climbed into the back of the squad car, and Shawn drove them out of downtown, east toward Worcester.

"What's out here?" asked Kalinsky.

"We're setting up in a special operations center outside the city," said Shawn. "It's better security." He exited a freeway into an isolated warehouse district, pulling up in a parking lot. He sat waiting, silently, peering around.

"Okay, what the fock is going here?" growled Kalinsky. "This is out in boondocks."

Shawn still said nothing, but got out of the car, walking around the front. Brad and Kalinsky simultaneously grabbed for the door handles on their respective sides, realizing that the back seats of squad cars were effectively jail cells.

A dark gray van pulled up, and Brad recognized it as like the one in which he had been held. Four men in Coronado Security jackets got out, just as a black SUV pulled up holding four more. Brad recognized the familiar faces of the mercenaries who'd taken him prisoner.

"Jesus, Gregor . . ." he began, but Kalinsky held up a hand.

"I am not surprised," he said coldly.

Shawn talked to one of the Coronado men, spreading his hands in pleading. The mercenary nodded back, and Shawn slumped slightly. He came back to the car and opened the door.

"You're going with them. Look, I'm sorry to have to do this. They chipped my daughter. They told me how Marty Fallon died. If I don't do this, they'll do the same thing to her. And there's nothing I can do but do what they say."

"This is shitty thing you do," said Kalinsky. "It is also really big focking mistake, you know that?"

Brad moved to pull himself out of the car, but Kalinsky restrained him. "You and me, we stay here for a while. Wait until is all over."

"Until *what* is over?" Both Brad and Shawn looked puzzled, but Kalinsky merely chuckled and patted Brad's shoulder.

The rumble of multiple engines grew in the distance, and a phalanx of three black Cadillac Escalades roared into sight, skidding around to encircle the mercenaries and the squad car.

Kalinsky leaned back in the seat. "I am from Russia, you know," he explained matter-of-factly. "I have distrust of police. So, I made . . . arrangements."

Shawn went into a defensive crouch and drew his pistol, aiming it at one of the SUVs, as did the eight Coronado Security men. But their confidence drained away, as a gang of scruffy, lean tattooed men leaped from the Escalades and crouched behind the doors, leveling assault rifles at them. From one of the Escalades emerged Mark, leveling a twelfth assault rifle at the mercenaries.

"These are *my* security detail," said Kalinsky to Shawn through the car window. "You see, they don't like idea of me and my friend being taken. Hey, dirty cop, you go with sons of bitches and leave us. We don't shoot you full of holes so your mothers don't recognize you."

For a long, tense moment, the two groups faced each other, weapons aimed.

"Oh, I forget to tell you, dirty cop," chuckled Kalinsky from the squad car. "I also employ really good snipers. They already have rifles trained on you. Do you want to die with head shot or chest shot? Ask your friends the sons of bitches and let me know. I tell the snipers. I have them on speed dial." He pulled out his cell phone, waving it in the air.

Shawn gave the lead mercenary a look of desperation. Finally, the man muttered a curse, holstered his pistol, and waved for the others to do the same.

Leaving Shawn standing alone and bereft, they climbed into the vehicles and sped away. Shawn raised his hands, and Mark relieved him of his weapon, and reached under Shawn's coat to take his handcuffs. He bound Shawn's hands behind him and shoved him to his knees.

"Please, please!" said Shawn. "My daughter! They'll kill her!"

"No, they won't, at least for the time being," said Brad. "They'll need something to hold over you. Look, I'll make you a deal. You don't say anything to anybody about this, I'll arrange for the chip to be neutralized. I know how to do it. And you stall the investigation into the shooting in New Hampshire."

"I can't possibly do that. It's their jurisdiction, and—"

"Just stall it. We'll tell them everything at the appropriate time. But not now. You understand?"

"Sure, sure, okay," said Shawn. "But you know they've likely done this to others in the department . . . in the FBI . . . anybody in law enforcement."

"Gregor, ask one of your men to go with him to pick up his daughter," said Brad. "Arrange to have her scanned with an MRI machine."

"Oh, sure, MRI, of course!" exclaimed Kalinsky. "What an idea! That would fock the chip up good." Mark uncuffed Shawn, and Kalinsky instructed one of the men to follow him to his daughter.

Brad scanned the surrounding rooftops. "How did you get the snipers in position so fast?"

Kalinsky laughed and aimed his bulk in the direction of the Escalade. "Oh, I am just focking with sons of bitches' heads. I got no snipers; just really big balls!"

They climbed into the Escalade, and with Mark at the wheel headed to Kalinsky's to figure out how to find Annie and the children.

"See why I like big focking SUVs?" asked Kalinsky. "They look real scary when they show up. Especially when they carry guys like mine with Kalashnikovs. They are good boys. You should get to know them, now that you working with us. Guess how they are named. This is Mark Makers," he said, reaching over and jovially slapping the lean, young driver on the shoulder.

"They are Russian, too?" asked Brad.

"*Da,* we are all Russian hackers. We work for Organizatsiya . . . what you call Russian mafia. We steal credit card data, hack corporate computers, sell trade secrets, and all like that. Then Russian government want me work for them. I hate how focking Russian government hacking America, fixing elections. So, we all want out. Then we get our chance. When my guys hacking into some computers in Middle

East, they find evidence for terrorist plots against America. We tell US government about plots. They catch guys who are going to bomb US. We save lots of lives. So, CIA, they tell me, they give us all asylum, make us citizens. They ask us to become their own secret computer hit squad . . . ethical hackers, they call us . . . white-hat hackers. We look for terrorist plots. We embed spyware in foreign computers. We fock bad guys . . . even Russian government . . . before they fock innocent people in this country."

"But how did the Russians let you out?"

Kalinsky chuckled. "My guys are very, very good hackers. We plant logic bombs all over in Russian computers. Any of us harmed, we trigger them, bring down mob, bring down government, even bring down rich oligarchs."

Brad's expression became one of puzzlement. "But what about their names, like Mark Makers? Isn't there a whiskey, Maker's Mark?

"Well, we are having big focking celebration in this bar to sign the citizenship papers. I tell guys they need new names, because they can be tracked down. We are very, *very* drunk. They all decide they need American names. Whiskey is American drink. Not vodka; that is Russian. So, Mark sees bottle of Maker's Mark on shelf. He decide to name himself after that bourbon. But he switch the name around; he like it better that way."

"And so, they all named themselves after whiskeys?"

"*Da*, most of them. Remember, we are very, very drunk at the time." He began to tick off more names on his pudgy fingers:

"There is Johnny Walker. He take that name because he was once communist party member. Johnny Walker *Red*. Get it!" He gave forth another deep rumbling laugh. "Then there is Jim Beam, Jack Daniels, Chivas Regal, Cutty Sark, I. W. Harper. And there are the three Glens . . . Glen Livet, Glen Fiddich, and Glen Morangie. Only name that is not all scotch is Vladislav Ballantine. He decided to keep first name because he got it from grandfather. Of course, there is Bacardi. He take only one name."

"That's a rum."

"He like rum better than whiskey. Besides we are running out of whiskey names. Only other possibility is Wild Turkey, and he does not want that name. Anyway, by time we sober up, we have already sent in citizenship papers. So, guys decide, what the fock! They keep the names."

Kalinsky's expression became serious once more.

"Now, we got to figure how to tell everybody about focker Lundgren and his guy Beale."

"Don't worry. I've got a friend in the newspaper business who'll take care of that," said Brad. "But first I have to find my family."

• • •

Annie picked up the jammer, giving the sweetly sleeping girls one last look. This would be the test. She was taking a desperate chance to find out whether her idea for rendering their chips harmless had worked.

It had been a long, fearful wait before she could do the test, and she tried to hide that fear from the girls with a pasted-on smile. As usual, Sally had fallen asleep immediately, but Sarah insisted she needed to stay up a while to sing a lullaby to her new doll. It was eleven o'clock before Sarah finally drifted off, both girls wearing new frilly nightgowns, and cozily nestled together in one of the two queen beds in the motel room.

Annie knew better than to try to sleep in the same bed with them. They were nocturnal wiggle-worms, and all too often she'd end up with a foot kicking her stomach or a smothering head of baby hair in her face.

She smiled at the memory of their nighttime antics, as she made sure they were sleeping peacefully. She hoped the trauma of the last few days hadn't scarred their little souls with fear. But her own dread had remained, even grown worse. She feared not just for her girls and herself, but for her missing husband. Was he free of the chip, or God forbid, dead from its effects!

Now, making sure that the jammer beside the girls' bed was plugged in and operating properly, she walked out the door holding the other one. She had chosen a motel room on the highway side of the complex, so that she could keep that door always in sight, making sure nobody went near it. She'd also taken care to park the stolen SUV around back in a shadowy corner of the parking lot.

Carrying the jammer and her cell phone, she walked across the front parking lot to the road, looking back often at the door behind where her daughters slept. She crossed the road to the Cracker Barrel on the other side, and kept walking. The door had shrunk to a tiny rectangle, but she could still see it. This was a good place; almost certainly beyond the range of the girls' jammer.

She took out her cell phone, holding it in front of her, steeling herself for the agony that might engulf her. She switched off the jammer. Her cell phone now showed a signal, so if her chip was active, she would soon know it. She waited for the hormonal assault, as an active chip would do its masters' bidding—blasting her with devastating doses of chemical from somewhere inside her on a venous wall.

Nothing! No feeling of fear, of hopelessness! She felt okay! She waited ten minutes more. She allowed herself a long moment to enjoy the moment of relief, of triumph. Now she knew she could go back and turn off the girls' jammer without risking them being assaulted by waves of depression and panic.

But first, she had to call her husband. She punched in a number. A voice answered "Hello."

"Hello," she said back. "I'm looking for Brad. This is his phone, right?"

"Indeed it is."

"Is he there?"

"He's indisposed at the moment."

"Who is this?"

"Is this Annie?"

"Who is this!"

"Annie, it's Lawrence Lundgren."

"WHERE THE HELL IS MY HUSBAND!" She bellowed, startling a group of restaurant customers walking to their cars.

Lundgren took a long pause. "We have him. Unless you come in, and bring the children . . . well . . . it would be unfortunate."

Annie's mouth was open, but no sound came out. She felt rising within her the same cold fury she had felt before she pulled the trigger to kill the man threatening her daughters. She channeled her fury into measured, icy words. "You . . . do . . . not . . . harm . . . him. I will kill you if you do. You know I have killed."

"I do, and I have no doubt you would do it again," said Lundgren smoothly. "Annie, all we want to do is to extract your chips, which I promise we will do painlessly. We need to study them. Then, we will release your husband, and you all can be on your way."

Annie's mind swirled with a turmoil of fears, plans, contingencies. Above all, she had to protect the girls. But she also had to rescue Brad.

"Okay, you can have my chip. But my daughters are totally off limits. You'll just have to settle for Brad's and mine. I'll call back with where and when to meet."

"No. We will tell you—"

"My chip, my terms," she interrupted. "I will call you." She hung up, hoping her insistence would give her an upper hand. She slipped the phone into her pocket, and hiked back to the motel. Sally had kicked off her covers, and she pulled the blanket over her sleeping form. Sarah also still slept peacefully. She crawled into the other bed, the burst of adrenaline from challenging Lundgren preventing her sleeping at first, but finally falling into an exhausted slumber.

The next morning, as the girls ate pancakes at the Cracker Barrel, she called Enterprise Rent-A-Car, ordering a van to be delivered to the motel. The van arrived in an hour, and Annie directed it to the where the SUV was parked. The rental agent got out and gave her the keys, so she could drive him back to the Enterprise lot.

"Oh, could you do me one favor?" she asked smiling.

"Of course, ma'am," the rental agent said brightly.

"This locker in the back of the SUV. I can't lift it. Would you please put it in the back of the van?"

He obliged with some effort, saying "Wow! This is heavy! Books?"

"No, just my assault rifle collection," said Annie.

The rental agent laughed, shut the van doors and they installed the girls' car seats, buckled them in, and headed back to the lot to finalize the rental.

CHAPTER 23

Annie had settled on a plan, and it could require violence. So be it. They had brought it on themselves.

Tucking her pistol into her waistband, she climbed into the back of the van, opened the footlocker, and lifted out an assault rifle. It was an M4 carbine, the same kind she'd trained on in the Army.

Her muscle memory of that training took over. She popped out the clip, finding it empty. Rummaging in the footlocker, she found the ammunition case, pulled out the cartridges, loaded the clip and slapped it back into place. She pulled back the bolt, feeling the solid clunk of a round being chambered, then made sure the rifle was on safety.

Rummaging through the footlocker, she also found more ammo magazines, loading them.

A wooden box in the footlocker was filled with small, black cylinders labeled "Model 7290 Flash Bang, 1.5 second delay." She'd trained on fragmentation grenades, so she could operate these. Just pull the pin, and after one-and-a-half seconds, a blinding flash and deafening bang would render the enemy temporarily disoriented.

So, she was well stocked with weapons, ironically those that she had taken from the very mercenaries who would be her targets.

She had been thinking far more clearly all morning, now that she and the girls were free of the frightening grip of the infinitesimal chips that now rested inert somewhere in their bodies.

First, she had figured out how to keep the girls safe—her most important objective. And where would they be safest? *School, of course!* The place was designed to protect children.

So, her first stop after getting the van had been to drive them to school. She had parked the van out of view of the street. Reluctantly stowing the pistol beneath the seat, she had walked them into the principal's office and explained that they hadn't been in school because of a family emergency. She then escorted the girls to their respective classes, kissed them goodbye as calmly as she could manage and returned to the van.

At first, sitting alone in the van, she had been haunted, almost paralyzed, by the horrible memory—the man with gun in hand approaching the crashed car, the children screaming in fear. The pistol in her hand, an extension of her fury. The explosion of the shot. The look of shock on his face when the bullet slammed into his chest. The red stain spreading on his chest as he collapsed. His lifeless eyes. And the heart-rending sound of her girls screaming.

But she had recovered her resolve when she thought of what those monsters had done to the girls and Brad. Now, she stowed the rifle and grenades back in the footlocker, climbed into the front seat, took a deep breath, and called Brad's cell phone.

As she had been examining and loading the assault rifle, she had figured out a meeting place. She made the call.

"Yes, Annie," said the voice of the hated Lundgren.

"Okay, I'll meet you, so you can take my chip. But I want to talk to my husband first."

Lundgren paused. "He's under anesthesia. His chip has been removed. He's fine."

Annie bowed her head in thought, finally saying "When we meet, I want to see him awake and well. Otherwise—"

"Oh, he certainly will be."

"I will meet you in Hopkinton State Park. In the parking lot at Main and Birch. Get out and show me Brad. Then, I'll come with you."

Until now, Annie had never thought of the park strategically. But it was perfect—isolated, thickly wooded, and the layout well-known from their picnics there.

But when she ended the call, her resolve seemed to seep out of her. She began trembling, her eyes filling with tears. But again, she steeled herself. She drew on her nurse's training, her Army training. She willed a cold-blooded calm to take over.

• • •

"There's no need for me to go," said Beale.

"No, of course not," said Lundgren. "That's what we pay these people for."

He flipped a hand at the mercenaries. The two who had abducted Brad stood in the conference room of the laboratory administration building—the muscular balding ex-Marine, and the lean, dark-haired mercenary. The latter wore a bandage over his nose, where Brad had smashed him with the mallet. A third, their leader, was the muscular, stubble-faced man who had until recently been the chief guard for Fallon and his family.

They were dressed in jeans, sweatshirts and dark jackets, the better to blend into the woods that would be the site of their next operation.

"What's your objective . . . specifically?" asked the leader.

"Specifically . . ." said Lundgren, smiling tolerantly at the dense underling. " . . . we want the chips, of course. It's imperative that we know what components were damaged, so we can harden them."

"And the woman?"

"Alive, if convenient."

"And the children?" asked Beale. "If they're at the meet site?"

Lundgren shrugged. "Alive . . . again, if convenient."

"Children?" asked the leader, his tone sharp with incredulity.

"They won't likely be there," said Beale. "Just the woman."

"You know she has our ordnance cache?" asked the leader.

"Jesus, she's a nurse," hmphed Lundgren. "She won't know what the hell to do with your *ordnance*."

"A nurse who was in the Army in Afghanistan."

Lundgren waved his hand in dismissal. "All the better. She's seen what can happen in a firefight. She'll go along."

The leader shook his head at Lundgren's willful mix of ignorance and arrogance. But he was paying big, so they would carry out the mission. And after all, it would be three men against one woman.

• • •

The weather was perfect—an overcast gray, with a chilly fall drizzle that would keep the park deserted of joggers and picnickers. And the mid-week day, Wednesday, meant that most people were at work or school.

Annie needed absolute isolation, given the potential for a noisy confrontation, perhaps involving gunfire. She sat waiting, crouched on a picnic table from which she had a clear view of the parking lot. Her van was parked a quarter-mile away, pulled off the road where she could execute a quick getaway.

The faint hiss of tires on wet pavement and the low thrum of an engine penetrated the sound of the falling rain. Annie stiffened, ready-ing herself for what would come next.

A dark blue van with a Parker Plumbing sign pulled slowly into the parking lot. Its engine shut down, and it sat silently, no movement inside.

She stood up from behind the picnic table and walked toward the van, stopping beside a large oak, her hands making fists at her sides.

"Where is he?" she shouted. "Show him to me."

There was a long pause. The driver-side door opened, and a wiry, dark-haired man with a bandage on his nose climbed out and walked toward her. At the same time, the van's side door slid open, revealing a large bald man, who stepped out, remaining beside the van.

"We'll take you to him," said the dark-haired man.

"*Bullshit!*" exclaimed Annie. "*I told you to bring him.*"

"We couldn't. He's recovering."

Annie noticed that the bald man had moved toward her, one arm behind his back. Her experience reading body language as an ER nurse, told her these two were tensed to act. It was an ambush!

Annie whipped her hands out and flung two small canisters arc-ing into the air toward the two men. For only an instant, they froze, peering up at the two canisters—a reaction Annie had counted on. People tend to reflexively lock their eyes on moving objects. But Annie knew not to.

She ducked behind the massive oak as two blinding flashes lit the overcast forest, along with two ear-splitting blasts.

The two men staggered back, throwing up their arms, but quickly recovered to draw their weapons. The dark-haired man whipped a pistol from behind him, leveling it at Annie. And the hulking bald man pulled up the assault rifle he'd hidden behind his back.

But Annie had already retrieved the assault rifle she'd concealed behind the tree and leveled it at the men. Ducking behind the tree, she fired a volley of short, precise bursts of fire that sent the exposed men scrambling for the van. Her aim was good, and the bald man grabbed his leg, slamming to the ground, grunting in pain. He recovered, rolled over and sent a burst of automatic fire that blew chunks of wood from the tree and the picnic table.

The wiry man ducked behind the front of the van, leveled the pistol at Annie and fired round after round that slammed into the tree.

But Annie had already ducked to the other side of the tree quickly flinging two more grenades, aimed precisely to land beside the prone bald man and behind the van. Again she ducked behind the tree, a lucky decision. Her back against the tree, she spied movement deep in the woods behind her. Another mercenary!

Flipping the rifle onto full automatic, she sent a lethal fusillade of bullets ripping through the forest, slamming into trees, and producing a loud pained grunt from the dark form behind one of them. She moved forward to find a man in a camouflage jacket slumped on the ground, groaning in pain. She reached the man and rolled him over. He was a sandy-haired man with face-stubble.

He panted in pain and clutched his side, where a spreading blood stain soaked his shirt.

"Get up," She commanded.

"Yes. Don't—"

"Kill you? I'm not going to kill you. Get up and walk toward the van."

The man complied, crouched over in pain, as he stumbled out of the woods.

The prone bald man leveled his rifle at Annie, but seeing his wounded comrade, pitched it aside, and sat up, grimacing, his hands held high.

"Come out with your hands behind your head!" commanded Annie of the man at the van, and the wiry, dark-haired mercenary obeyed, one arm hanging limply at his side, blood flowing from a shoulder wound.

Annie instructed them to lay face-down on the ground, hands behind their heads. Clicking the rifle to single shot, she took careful aim and blew out three of the van's tires. She stayed at a safe distance from the men, leveling the rifle at them.

"Here's your choice. You tell me where my husband is, and I leave you here with your cell phones, so you can call whoever you need to. But if you don't tell me, I take your cell phones and leave you with the van. It's isolated out here, so if I were you, I wouldn't depend on somebody having heard the noise."

"*Fuck you!*" breathed the stubble-faced man, as he bent into a fetal position.

"Oh, and as an ER nurse I can tell you that one of you has a wound that will kill him in about half-an-hour without treatment."

"Which one?" asked the bald man, clutching his leg.

Annie shrugged. "That's for me to know, and you to find out."

The men lay in silence for two minutes. Finally, the stubble-faced man spoke up. "Okay, look, we don't know where he is. That's the truth. He got away."

"So Lundgren was lying?"

"Yeah. That's why he didn't let you talk to your husband."

Annie smiled grimly and began to back away into the forest, and toward her van. "Just stay where you are until I'm gone."

She ducked into the forest, sprinting for a quarter-mile through woods parallel to the road, emerging at the van, starting it up, and speeding away.

She had just reached the Massachusetts Turnpike heading into Boston, when her phone beeped. *Lundgren,* she thought, answering without looking at the calling number

"*Dammit, you tried to kill me, but I got your men first, you son of a bitch!*"

"Annie, it's Brad," she heard that wonderful voice declare. "Are you all right? Are the girls all right?"

"*Oh, dear God, Brad!*" she choked out. "*Oh, my God, yes!* The girls are fine! Our chips are deactivated! Until just now, I thought he had you."

"No, actually, we have him . . . by the balls!"

• • •

"Can we pick the girls up now?" pleaded Brad. "I really need to hug them!"

"Sorry, Daddy," said Annie, smiling for the first time in a week. "The school might get suspicious if we picked them up early, after they'd been gone for days."

She gripped his hand. They hadn't let go of one another since their emotional reunion at the car rental lot, where Kalinsky and Brad had picked her up when she had returned the van. They'd also stopped at the cell phone store, where Brad had deactivated the smartphone in Lundgren's possession and bought a new one for himself. Now they sat in the back seat of Kalinsky's Escalade, on their way to the *Boston World*. Behind them sat two of his men, whom Kalinsky had introduced as Mr. Beam and Mr. Daniels.

Kalinsky was still celebrating Annie's achievement. "You have swiped large box of weapons from sons of bitches! *Amazing!*" he exclaimed over his shoulder from the front seat. "I hope you and Brad are not looking to be Bonnie and Clyde. I read about them. They are crazy gangster couple."

Brad shook his head in amusement. "Believe me, Gregor, we'd just as soon that this nightmare was over, and Annie can go back to nursing and me to writing."

"We have checked police scanner," said Kalinsky. "There was report of gunshots at park. They found Coronado Security van with flat tires. But no sons of bitches with bullet wounds."

"No surprise," said Annie. "I left them their cell phones, as part of the bargain to tell me about Brad."

They pulled up to the two-story glassed entrance of the *Boston World*, entering its lobby, where Sam Pritchett stood waiting impatiently. He hurried them to a large conference room, where seven editors sat waiting around the conference table. Pritchett introduced them as editors of the *World*'s business and metro sections, the managing editor, the executive editor, and two newspaper lawyers.

"We've done the investigation you asked," said Pritchett. "The people on the list you gave me . . . they've all either just vanished or died of what looked like accidents . . . falls, car accidents, and so forth. The police said—"

"We can't trust any cops," interrupted Kalinsky. "Cops are in their pocket."

He and Brad went on to tell about being kidnapped by Shawn, and the threat Lundgren had made against the detective's daughter. Annie also told them about the gunfight in the park. The metro editor ducked out of the room, declaring that he would dispatch a crime reporter to investigate.

"The problem is we couldn't find any connection between these people and NeoHappy," Pritchett continued. "I know they signed NDAS and were told to keep their involvement in the clinical trial confidential, but still—"

"Look, we've got proof," interrupted Brad. "We've got the video you wanted."

Kalinsky opened his laptop and connected it to the room's digital projector. The group watched with amazement Brad's encounter with Lundgren, Beale, Zhu, and the mercenaries. One editor mouthed a 'wow' when the video showed Lundgren sliding the pistol across the table, bidding Brad to commit suicide. Others shook their heads in stunned wonderment.

Once the video ended, the tone of the discussion changed drastically. Now the group fell to an excited discussion of how to break the story, interrupting one another and finally dispatching Pritchett to contact NeoHappy for comment. They summoned the health and science editor to plan coverage of the clinical angle of the story. And the multimedia editor arrived to upload the video to the *World*'s web site.

Amid the chatter, Kalinsky had risen to pace at one end of the room, muttering darkly, while Brad sat with his arm around Annie.

"What is it, Gregor?" asked Brad. "We've got him. What's the problem?"

"Focker is too smart. He is not going to be taken by surprise. He will be steps ahead."

"You've got that right," said Pritchett, who had just reappeared in the room. "I contacted his office, and they said he's unavailable. I found the number of their limo pool and told them I was an assistant trying to get him his briefcase. They said he was already at Hanscom Field. He's got a private jet. I looked it up and got the make and the tail number and called the airport flight desk. They said he'd taken off."

"*China!*" exclaimed Brad. "You saw the guy Zhu on the video. And remember what I heard in the van? He's got to be headed for China!"

"Told you! Told you!" exclaimed Kalinsky, continuing to pace, is face reddening, gesticulating angrily. "Focker is gone!"

"Yes, but not necessarily out of reach," said Brad. "What kind of jet and what's the tail number?"

"Gulfstream, N754T," said Pritchett.

Brad took out his smartphone and tapped commands onto the screen. "I'm checking FlightAware for their position," he said. After a few moments, he looked up from the phone, a pleased expression on his face. "They're heading west toward Cleveland. Let's see if we can spoil their plans."

He punched in 911. "Hello. Listen, a buddy of mine just called. He was at Hanscom Field getting ready to taxi out in his plane, and he saw a Gulfstream taking on luggage. It was a bunch of boxes. They dropped one, and my buddy saw bags of white powder spill out. Yes. Yes. He said tail number N754T. No, he'd rather not be identified; y'know drug dealers and all."

He ended the call, saying to Pritchett and the editors, "It's one of the few advantages freelancers have over staff reporters. We can bend the rules a bit. Check on the flight later. Maybe it will have been forced down. But of course, if Lundgren has the police department in his pocket, the response to my nine-one-one call might be . . . well . . . postponed."

As Kalinsky, Brad, and Annie left the building, Brad made follow-up calls to the DEA and FBI. Back in the Escalade, he continued to scrutinize the smartphone screen.

"Damn," he said, showing them the US map. The map's airplane icon had veered north. "He's changed course for Canada. That'll mean the DEA will have to coordinate with the Canadians."

"Could he escape?" asked Annie.

"He could. Then he'd be free to do whatever the hell he wants. That includes eliminating anybody here who could implicate him."

"Phyllis?"

"I mean *everybody*," said Brad shaking his head, considering the magnitude of the potential tragedy. "We need to neutralize all those chips. We need a better way than an MRI machine."

"How the hell could that be possible?" asked Kalinsky.

"An EMP generator. Electromagnetic pulse. It destroys any electronic device it's aimed at."

"You know where to get such device?"

Brad punched in a number as he answered. "I know how to get one built quick. There's a company I profiled for the *Boston Business Journal*. Called Megamag."

"Are they as good at making those machines as we are at hacking?"

Brad smiled at Kalinsky's oblique boast. "Close, Gregor. Pretty close," he said.

CHAPTER 24

"Damn," said Lundgren, scanning the refrigerator in the Gulfstream's galley. "That dolt of a pilot forgot to load the Cristal." An annoyed look on his face, he chose a lesser champagne, grumpily pouring himself a glass and sat down in one of the jet's tan leather armchairs.

"I'm terribly sorry," said the copilot, appearing from the adjacent cockpit. "We'll be in Toronto shortly. I'll have a case waiting there."

"Just have them load it into the other plane," said Lundgren. "And please, will you make sure all the other provisions are as specified? We have a long flight from there."

The copilot nodded his head, his face stoic to mask his irritation, and left.

"You're sure we have to switch planes?" asked Beale. "It's a pain in the ass."

"Oh, I can absolutely guarantee you the authorities have begun a search for this plane. The one we're taking is a charter by one of my shell companies, not traceable to me. We don't want any . . . inconveniences. You've finished uploading the data to the Darknet site?"

"Yes. We're the only ones with the login and password. I've deleted all the data at the laboratory. And I've done a digital shredding, so it can't be recovered."

"And have you *deleted* the other data repositories?" he asked, raising an eyebrow.

Beale's expression became a cold-blooded mask. He understood that Lundgren meant killing people.

"I installed a timer code in the central chip control software. It will trigger the succinylcholine reservoirs in their bodies in . . ." Beale paused to look at his watch ". . . five hours. We'll be beyond extradition. There will be no institutional memory of the projects." Like Lundgren, he was avoiding mention of the mass killing of the laboratory scientists.

Lundgren smiled and sipped his champagne. "Eliminating the 'institutional memory.' Interesting way to put it. When we get there, you make sure the cargo is transferred onto the other plane," he commanded.

"Of course."

"Remind me, how many chips did you end up acquiring?"

"A hundred thousand of the version two-point-one chips. And a hundred each of the two Zombie chips. That's all we could get fabricated in the short time we had after finalizing the designs."

Lundgren shot Beale a sour look of utter distaste. "Dammit, don't call them Zombie chips! That's trivializing them. They're much more significant. They constitute a stunning advance in regulating human behavior. Call them red and blue chips, as I told you."

"Okay, so we have a hundred each of the *red and blue chips*," declared Beale with sarcastic emphasis.

"And the miniature injectors?"

"Completed and tested," said Beale. "We tried one on an employee. He felt only a small discomfort, like a splinter."

"Good. Now, send an e-mail to Zhu. He has agreed to field trials of the new chips, but tell him I want to make sure they start as soon as the facility and the subjects are in place. That will really demonstrate the technology's potential to the Chinese. And tell the director they must plan for those subjects to be confined for the duration. We'll need especially sturdy confinement for the red chips."

"True. Control is one thing; compulsion very much another." Beale opened his laptop and began to type.

"Yes . . . compulsion," said Lundgren sipping his champagne. "Quite a new and interesting paradigm. Y'know, perhaps I should be the one to choose the subjects for the blue chips. Handsome young women who can be appropriately . . . tested."

Beale bent over his laptop, typing, to keep himself from uttering an epithet reflecting his opinion of Lundgren's arrogance.

• • •

The three black Escalades pulled up just out of sight of the guardhouse on the road into NeoHappy's clandestine laboratory.

"You are certain the Phyllis Kelley woman is in there?" asked Kalinsky.

"Almost," said Brad. "They had her in a hotel room, last we saw her. But they would've wanted to move her to this secure facility."

"Those Coronado Security guys would certainly be here," said Kalinsky. "With son-of-a-bitch Lundgren gone, they would be told to guard laboratory, I bet."

"Yeah, and knowing Lundgren, my bet would also be that they're going to do more than guarding. He'd want the place shut down. And he wouldn't want Phyllis or the others talking."

"Jesus!" said Annie. "You're not saying he would—"

"Kill everybody? Yes, he and Beale likely would," said Brad. "I'd bet they're all chipped like Marty was; like I was. He's a textbook sociopath."

"And lab people are all witnesses," said Kalinsky. "They have knowledge about chips, about Lundgren. They will be killed once Lundgren in international air space, where he could not be intercepted, and then in China, where he could not be extradited. That's what bastard people in Organizatsiya would do."

"Can you get some cameras on the lab, so we'll know what's going on?" asked Brad. Kalinsky nodded and issued a command into the phone, which was conferenced to all his men. Shortly, he touched the screen on the Escalade dashboard to bring up a shaking image from a camera being carried through sun-dappled fall foliage.

Brad and Annie leaned forward to peer over his shoulder at the scene. Kalinsky touched the screen again to bring up a second, more stable image of the guardhouse. Two men in Coronado Security jackets manned the booth—one sitting inside, and the other pacing back and forth beside the gated chain link fence. Kalinsky switched back to the first scene, which showed guards parked outside the main entrance to the sprawling laboratory building.

"We need to get in there fast, get past the guards," said Brad.

Kalinsky looked over at Mark, his round, bearded face breaking into a sly grin. "Say, Mark, let us do same thing we do to get into that big computer company in Taiwan. Remember? Is your girlfriend available and willing? She was *so* helpful last time."

Mark Makers grinned, and made a call, explaining to his girlfriend what was needed. And Kalinsky announced into his phone, "Guys, we need whole car full of pretty girls. Who has prettiest, bravest girlfriends?"

He listened, as the sounds of loud arguing issued from the phone. "Okay, okay . . . enough! You *all* have pretty and brave girlfriends. Cutty, Chivas, Vladislav, you call girlfriends. Tell them to meet Mark's girlfriend and come here fast."

"Well, whatever you're planning, we'll also need help on the inside," said Brad. "Let me try something." He punched in the laboratory's main number and put the phone on speaker.

"Warehouse," answered the female voice he'd heard before.

"Listen carefully. This is Brad Davis. I've been investigating what you're doing there. I believe you are all in grave danger. Lawrence Lundgren and Thomas Beale are leaving the country. We're not sure what orders they gave the Coronado Security people guarding you, but we believe they mean to do something drastic."

"Sir, this is a warehouse. We don't—"

"Look, just go to the supervisor there. Tell him you got this call. Tell him to look into it. Have him call me back at this number. We are trying to help you."

The voice on the other end of the line began to stammer. "We . . . uh . . . are a warehouse, and—"

"Just do it! *I think they mean to kill you all!* Call me back at this number. Don't let the guards hear. We want to help you."

He ended the call, saying to Kalinsky and Annie, "I hope she does what I asked. With luck, we'll have help inside. With bad luck, I've alerted the guards that we're here."

Kalinsky began to position his men for the next step in his assault on the lab. He dispatched four to circle the building, saying cryptically, "Sometimes we don't use doors."

The camera-carrying Harper moved into position across from the laboratory's main entrance.

Meanwhile, Brad, Annie, and Makers led I.W. Harper and Bacardi through the woods, settling in with them as near to the guardhouse as they could safely get. As they crouched behind the boulder with the men, the steady thumping bass beat of music arose from down the road. The beat grew louder, revealing Cindy Lauper's song, "Girls Just Want to Have Fun," emanating from a silver Mercedes that sped into view. The car stopped at the guardhouse, and four buxom young women emerged, giggling and singing, their skimpy shorts and halter tops showing more skin than was prudent for the crisp fall weather.

Makers smiled broadly. "That is my girlfriend driving! Lovely, yes?" he whispered.

The two guards seemed not to notice the seasonal fashion discrepancy. The pacing guard walked up to the car, smiling. And the mercenary in the guard house, fairly leaped from its shelter to approach the car.

One of the girls stretched languorously, showing a lithe, long-legged body. Holding a small black object inconspicuously at her side, she strolled around to the back of the car, opening the trunk and bending in, showing a shapely bottom that drew the guardhouse guard's rapt attention. He circled back to the trunk, but in an apparent growing suspicion, placed his hand on his pistol.

Each girl suddenly jammed a black box into a guard's neck. With an electrical crackling sound, both men collapsed in quivering heaps. The other two girls wrenched the paralyzed guards' arms behind their backs and expertly zipped their hands together with plastic cuffs.

Mark, Brad, Annie, and the others raced to the car and dragged the inert guards into the woods. Mark gave the driver a kiss and a hug, and the girls piled into the car and, tires squealing, executed a fast U-turn and sped away. The sounds of "Girls Just Want to Have Fun" faded away down the road.

"We have access," said Kalinsky into the phone, and the Escalades pulled up to the now-empty guardhouse.

Brad's phone rang and he answered to hear a voice that identified itself as the laboratory supervisor. He put the phone on speaker.

"*What do you mean we're in grave danger?*" asked the quavering voice.

"Lawrence Lundgren and Thomas Beale have left the country by now. We believe they mean to do you all harm. Are you chipped?"

"Well . . . yes. But they are the newest versions. They're more stable."

"Marty Fallon had the newest version."

"*Jesus! He's dead!*"

"He was murdered by Lundgren and Beale using that chip. It contains a reservoir of succinylcholine. I was there. I think you all are next."

"Oh, my God, what can we do?

"Where are the Coronado Security people?"

"All over. They came in this morning. They said Tom Beale instructed them to come in because of a security breach. And we found that all the research data had been erased from our servers."

"They're really there to clean up after Beale triggers your chips. After you're dead. Listen, get all your people to a safe place. Tell the Coronado people you're having a staff meeting."

Kalinsky leaned toward the phone. "We will give you fifteen minutes. Then we are triggering an explosion to breach the back of the building. Our people will enter there, and at the front."

"I have an electromagnetic pulse generator with me," said Brad. "It can neutralize your chips. I'll need to reach you as quickly as possible."

They heard urgent chatter in the background, then the supervisor returned. "One of the techs says he just found some kind of countdown in the control code. There's only a little over an hour left."

Kalinsky, leaned forward, his voice urgent. "Can't you just shut down control computer?"

"The tech tried to interrupt the sequence, and even shut down the computer. But when it came back up, the countdown continued. He says the control server is off site. We don't know where. *It can't be interrupted!*"

Brad repeated his instruction to the supervisor, then hung up. "We've got to go now!" he said to Kalinsky.

Kalinsky punched a number in on his phone, and gave the instruction, "Go!"

After a few seconds, they heard the jarring thump of a distant explosion.

"Guys have breached wall in back," said Kalinsky. "We hit front now!"

The Escalades accelerated down the entry road toward the building's entrance, where half-a-dozen Coronado Security men crouched behind their SUVs, leveling assault rifles at the approaching vehicles.

They unleashed a fusillade of gunfire, peppering the SUV with bullets. As Brad leaped over Annie to protect her, he realized that the impacts were not penetrating the SUVs.

"Bulletproof," shouted Kalinsky over the explosions of gunfire. "I have bulletproof cars, because some people do not like me very much."

With that, he and his men piled out of the Escalades, and from their cover behind the vehicles began to return fire. Their bullets ripped into the Coronado vehicles, bursting tires, shattering windows, pocking doors with bullet holes. A Coronado man spun around, blood spurting from his shoulder. A Kalinsky man bellowed in pain, grabbing his thigh.

But as the battle grew in intensity, Brad sat still behind the SUV, a look of concentration growing on his face. "Jesus," he said to himself. "I should have thought of that!"

"What?" asked Annie from the floor of the SUV.

"Gregor, ask for a truce."

"Truce? We don't ask for truce! We kill these bastards!"

"I think I can get us in without more bloodshed. I realized something."

Kalinsky shrugged and shouted for his men to stop firing, leaving only the continuing gunfire from the Coronado men.

Brad stripped off his sport shirt, pulled off his white undershirt and slipped his sport shirt back on. He gingerly stood up behind the SUV and began to wave the undershirt.

"Brad! They'll shoot you!" exclaimed Annie, reaching for him.

But the gunfire abated, then stopped.

"You're in danger!" shouted Brad.

"No shit!" shouted a voice from the Coronado men.

"Are you chipped?"

"Yeah . . . so?" answered the man.

"When?"

There was a long silence. The Coronado mercenaries were apparently trying to puzzle out Brad's angle.

"They said our chips were outdated," finally came the reply. "Last week they put in new ones that worked better."

"Do you know how Marty Fallon died?"

"The news said it was a heart attack."

"It was a succinylcholine injection. *From his chip! The same chips that are in you!* Lundgren and Beale did it. We think there's a countdown going on right now. Less than an hour from now, when it reaches zero, the laboratory workers will all die the same way as Fallon. *So will you!*"

"*Son of a bitch!*" exclaimed the voice. "What can we do?"

"I have a device to fry the chips. EMP shockwave generator. You lay down your weapons, we'll inactivate your chips. Then you leave. All we're interested in is saving the workers."

"*Bullshit! It'll kill us!*"

Brad did not reply, but circled quickly to the back of the SUV and hauled out a large black box with a silver parabolic dish at one end. One of Kalinsky's men helped him carry it into the no-man's-land between the two rows of SUVs.

"This is the generator. It's the only way you'll stay alive. Leave your guns and come forward. We'll treat you and let you leave. Do this or die."

"Is that some fucking death ray?" shouted the Coronado man.

Brad flipped a switch on the generator, triggering a rising whine as its capacitor charged. Brad stepped in front of the reflector as a loud lightning-like crack emanated from the box.

"See? That's it. No danger. It'll save your life. In any case, we'll let you leave."

After a long moment, the Coronado men began to step forward, laying their weapons aside. Shortly afterward, more emerged from the building.

A series of loud electrical crackles pierced the air, as the generator repeatedly charged and discharged for man after man. As the line of men took the treatment, Brad called the supervisor, asking about the countdown.

"Forty minutes! Please hurry!" he was told.

With Kalinsky's men training their guns on them, the Coronado Security men climbed into their SUVs and sped away. Kalinsky's men hauled the EMP generator into the building, where they were met by the frightened supervisor, his face damp with the sweat of fear.

"Oh, God, please hurry!" he pleaded.

They found the laboratory workers huddled in the large lunchroom, and Brad plugged in the generator so it wouldn't depend on its battery.

On large monitor screens, the supervisor brought up the countdown timer and the alphabetical list of laboratory workers' names, showing in red.

"Red means their chips are still active," said the supervisor. "The techs have set the display so the name turns blue when a chip is deactivated and there's no more signal from it."

Brad asked the workers, one by one, to crouch in front of the parabolic mirror, making their bodies as compact as possible, so the narrow beam would be more likely to target their embedded chip.

The room echoed with the whine of the generator charging, and the loud crack of its discharge, as it sent bursts of electromagnetic waves into their bodies.

"Thank God you're here!" Brad heard a voice behind him exclaim, and turned to see Phyllis, her slumped posture and haggard expression portraying the trauma of her captivity. Brad briefly hugged her, and Annie took her to another room to give her a checkup.

"Fortunately, she has an old chip," Brad told Kalinsky. "She's safe."

Kalinsky received a call from his men patrolling the building for remaining Coronado Security men. He pronounced the building clear.

"Thirty minutes!" declared the supervisor, as the countdown timer continued its inexorable march to zero.

Brad did a calculation, with an agonizing result. Each cycle of the generator took roughly a minute. There were some fifty people. Some would die. He enlisted Kalinsky to help move people into position as quickly as possible.

"*Clear!*" the supervisor would declare, as a name on the list switched from red to blue.

"Twenty minutes!" the supervisor announced, although every eye in the room was riveted on the timer and the list.

Still too many red names! Twenty eight! Now they only were up to names beginning with L. Brad had to take a chance.

"Double up!" he exclaimed, and Kalinsky helped arrange two people one in front of the other, so the electromagnetic pulse would pass through both.

"Ten minutes!" exclaimed the supervisor.

The doubling didn't work! The second person's name didn't turn blue on the list.

"Closer!" commanded Brad. "Hug one another!"

They did so.

The generator emitted its crack and two names turned blue!

"Thirty seconds!"

Three people left! Only one more cycle possible! A young woman whose name badge read "Elizabeth Zachary," would die unless he could think of something.

"Triple!" exclaimed Brad. "We have to try three people at once." As the generator emitted its rising, charging whine, the last three people huddled together in front of the parabolic dish as tightly as they could. The young woman in the back was sobbing. Abruptly, the man with the name Evan Yancey on his ID badge, who was in front, leaped behind Zachary, possibly giving his life.

The supervisor counted down the seconds to zero. "Five . . . four . . . three . . . two . . ."

With a sharp pop, the generator emitted its last pulse. All eyes watched on the list.

All three names turned blue! Sighs of relief, laughter, crying, and loud applause. The people crowded around Brad and Kalinsky, hugging them and slapping them on the back.

Annie appeared at the door, her face stricken with shock.

"Oh, Brad," she cried, her voice breaking. "They chipped Phyllis again. She must have been unconscious. She didn't know. She's dead. I couldn't do anything. I couldn't help."

Brad enfolded her in his arms, as she cried softly. "But she wasn't on the list."

The supervisor slumped into a chair near them, his head in his hands. "I think I know why. We just developed a control algorithm that used a portable device. Tablet or smartphone. She must have been controlled that way, separately from us. She wouldn't have been on the main list. Dear God."

"Fockers!" spat Kalinsky. "The evil fockers."

But Brad couldn't let the workers dwell on Phyllis. "Look, we don't know what other traps he set. This whole building could be rigged. You have to get out now!"

Supporting one another after the ordeal, the laboratory workers began to stumble out of the lunchroom, down the hall, and out the front door, some pitching their badges and white coats aside as despised emblems of their work. The supervisor turned to Brad and Kalinsky, his hands outstretched in supplication.

"We were pawns," he said sorrowfully. "We thought we were keeping the work secret because of industrial espionage. Please, let us go!"

"It's not for us to say," said Brad. "The best advice I can give is to wait for the police and the FBI. Cooperate fully. Tell them everything you know."

His arm still around a bereft Annie, Brad made a call to Pritchett. Pritchett answered, and they had a brief conversation.

He ended the call and announced, "The *World* is breaking the story this afternoon. I told Pritchett to call the police, the FBI, everybody who should be called. They should get out here. He also said the Canadians lost Lundgren and Beale at the Toronto airport. The plane had landed half-an-hour before the RCMP reached it. They think Lundgren and Beale got out in another plane."

"He cannot get away with this," said Kalinsky.

"He won't." Brad hugged Annie closer, his voice coldly determined. "We're going to China."

. . .

"*Oh, hell no!*" declared Kalinsky. "You are not going to China with me! You stay here with little girls. I take some guys, we go after those two *ublyudki* . . . bastards . . . we take care of them good."

They sat in Kalinsky's office, the door closed, while outside in the main room, they could hear the urgent clamor of Kalinsky's people gathering intelligence on Lundgren's whereabouts and what he was doing in China.

"We've talked about it," said Brad, holding Annie's hand.

"We realized that we need to do this," said Annie. "I called my parents in North Carolina. We didn't tell them what we were doing, but that we had urgent business that needed both of us. We asked them to take the girls. Mom is flying up tonight, and I'll meet her at Logan Airport, so she can take them back with her. They said they'll be happy to keep the girls as long as necessary."

"Revenge," declared Kalinsky. "You want revenge. Let *us* do that. We know how."

"Yes, revenge is part of it," said Annie. "But we want justice. We're committed to that. And, Gregor, we also bring skills and contacts that you and your men don't have."

"Skills? You two are writer and nurse."

"I'm an Army nurse with battlefield training. You can use somebody who's medically trained. And weapons trained."

"Well, true, you did put some serious firepower on those fockers at park."

"And I've been in battle," said Brad. "Two tours in Afghanistan. And, I have a contact in China who will be invaluable."

"Contact?"

"Yes, Ping Pong."

"Hah, that is game with balls. He has balls?"

"That was his nickname when he was at BU with me in the science writing program. His name is Peng Pyang, and he's a tech writer in Beijing for American magazines. He knows the tech scene there. He also has contacts in the black market."

"Then you tell me where to find him. We work with him."

"Gregor, you know he wouldn't trust you. I have to be there."

Kalinsky scowled at them. "You have daughters. Beautiful daughters. You cannot leave beautiful little girls."

Annie's face grew grim. "Gregor, we talked long and hard about this. We talked about what would happen to the girls if we . . ." she could not finish the sentence.

Brad took up the argument. "We decided that if Lundgren and Beale unleash this technology on the world, it would be catastrophic. And our girls would have to live in that world."

"Besides, you need us as a couple," argued Annie. "I mean look at your guys. They kind of stand out, tattoos and all. Can you blend into the crowd like Brad and I can . . . a couple of American tourists just seeing the sights?"

"Fock!" muttered Kalinsky in surrender. "You two have good arguments. But you should know that we will be on our own. I have talked to my contacts in State Department, in CIA. They say they cannot be involved. They tell me that if their official guys are caught trying to stop Lundgren, it will be major diplomatic incident. Only thing they can do is make cover story for us as civilians. But if we are caught, they will not admit we were operating as spies. And Chinese will just make us disappear."

"We know that," said Brad. "We understand the risks."

"Okay. I call guy at State Department. I tell them to start putting together our covers. You are still focking crazy."

"Probably," said Annie.

CHAPTER 25

Their entry into China seemed routine . . . at first.

Brad, Annie, and Kalinsky inched slowly back and forth in the long winding queue for foreign visitors that snaked through the sterile, cavernous Beijing Airport.

"This should go okay," whispered Kalinsky. "I just got text message from contact in State Department. They have finished our cover, and it will not be questioned."

They reached the desk of an unsmiling Chinese immigration officer in the official gray uniform. He scrutinized their passports and inserted each one into a small black scanner. But when he looked up at them, his expression grew coldly suspicious, and he pressed a button on his desk. Four policemen emerged from a nearby door, wielding assault rifles, and one of them stepped forward.

"You will come with us. Now!"

"What for?" asked Kalinsky. "We are here on US State Department business."

"Come!" he commanded, as the policemen all brought their rifles up to their chests, in preparation for aiming them. Brad raised his palms in agreement, and the policemen marched them away from the immigration line to the alarmed murmurs of the crowd. They were escorted through

a side door, down a long deserted hall lined with windowless steel doors. The leader curtly waved them through one of the doors and into a room bare except for a metal table and five folding chairs.

Kalinsky subtly brought his finger to his lips and rolled his eyes around the room. Brad and Annie understood that it meant the room was monitored. For an hour, they sat silently with grim stoic expressions, trying to keep their breathing steady, their hearts from pounding. Brad held Annie's hand, as Kalinsky began to pace the room. Their thoughts were as one: they were prime candidates for being disappeared into China's prisons. It was what happened to people suspected of espionage, even Americans.

The door swung open, and a spare middle-aged Chinese man entered, followed by two armed guards who took up stations by the door. He wore the dark green uniform of a Chinese border policeman, complete with epaulets, and with a stiff, formal bearing. Saying nothing, he took off his cap and placed it precisely on the table, sitting down and opening a notebook. Not acknowledging their presence, he studied its pages for long minutes.

"You are holding us with no cause," Brad finally said.

The officer looked up, scanning impassively from one to the other. "We have cause," he said in barely accented English. "You are coming from the US, not for pleasure, but on government business. Your visas were rushed through. We want to know why you are here and how long you will stay."

"We don't know how long we stay," said Kalinsky, sitting down and leaning toward the little man, scowling. "As for why—"

"And you are Russian, sir. Why are you coming from the US? We have many questions, and I think we will hold you here until they are answered."

Kalinsky stood, towering over the officer. "I am American citizen, naturalized. And you focking—"

Brad interrupted him, sensing that Kalinsky was about to go off on a wild-bull rant. "Are our visas in order?"

The officer paused for a long time before admitting, "They *seem* to be."

"And as for our business here, it is the State Department's business. By definition, it is diplomatic and thus a matter of diplomatic immunity.

You would not want our detainment to become an incident that was reported up to your superiors. Our ambassador values our country's good relationship with the People's Republic."

The policeman stiffened almost imperceptibly. The reaction told Brad the tack he should take. He scribbled some numbers on a sheet of paper from his notebook, ripped it off and slid it across the table. "Here is the ambassador's personal cell phone. Could you please call him and tell him that the people whom he requested to come immediately on embassy business are being detained?"

The policeman left the paper sitting between them, glaring at them, then abruptly snatched up his hat, positioned it precisely on his head, got up, and left.

Within ten minutes, the security policemen entered and ushered them back to immigration. As they walked, Brad took out his phone and covertly tapped out a quick text message. Within twenty minutes, they were through the airport and had boarded the sleek train that sped into the city's center.

Again, Kalinsky touched his lips with his finger, whispering, "Our delay might well have been to give them enough time to put surveillance in place."

So, they sat quietly, watching a Beijing cityscape flow by—a succession of sterile, monumental high-rise buildings that dwarfed the flowing crowds of people going about their business, walking, biking, and occasionally riding in cars. The train slid smoothly into Dongzhimen Station, a stark gray box set among the skyscrapers. Two security guards in blue uniforms walked past with their dogs. The men eyed the trio suspiciously, but passed on to patrol the station.

"We should walk a bit," said Brad. "We need to talk outside, where we won't be monitored." They exited the station, finding themselves engulfed in Beijing's notorious, choking, eye-stinging smog. They rolled their suitcases through packed crowds of Chinese, many wearing surgical masks. Overhead hung an oppressively claustrophobic gray sky.

As they walked, they passed a slim young Chinese man wearing dark blue coveralls. He put away his tablet computer and rose from a bench, threading his way through the crowd, keeping up with Brad, Annie, and Kalinsky.

"How did you know number of ambassador?" asked Kalinsky.

"I didn't," said Brad. "I made it up. Okay, what the hell is our cover story for being here?"

The young man drew closer, walking ahead of Brad, then slowing to let Brad pass him.

"I am sorry," Kalinsky said. "But I did not really know our story until we get into airport. My friends in State got us the visas and said they would take care of story. It took them time to build cover. We are officially here to do specialized work on embassy computers. They had to get word out that computers had glitched and consultants needed to be brought in to fix and upgrade."

"And of course unofficially they want us here to stop Lundgren," said Brad. "Something they can't do because he's not even here . . . officially."

The young man briefly moved up beside Brad, then melted away into the crowd. Brad looked straight ahead, but nodded. Annie glanced over at the young man, and gave a subtle smile.

"So what about this Ping Pong person?" asked Kalinsky. "He will help, eh? When will we see him?"

Brad unfolded a piece of paper in his hand and read it. "We will meet him tomorrow in the National Stadium."

"He told you that?"

Brad leaned in to whisper to Kalinsky. "That was a friend of his, in the baseball cap. He gave me a note. Peng can't send texts himself. He's being monitored. And even his friends are wary."

Kalinsky chuckled. "Sneaky little man. I like him already."

The contact made, they hailed one of the small yellow-striped taxis and crammed themselves and their luggage into it.

Kalinsky instructed the driver to go to the Park Plaza Science Park Hotel. "We will be close to Lundgren, I am sure," said Kalinsky. "He will be working somewhere near university. There is nanoscience center here that he will need."

"So, basically, we've narrowed down the search from billions to millions," said Brad. "We've got our work cut out for us."

The taxi pulled up to the high-rise hotel, and they strode past the massive steel-clad columns and into the atrium lobby, not noticing the three black BMWs that pulled up around the hotel, watching all the exits.

• • •

"I think they're all alive," muttered Beale, scrutinizing his tablet.

"You *think?*" demanded Lundgren. "You goddamned *think?*" He pitched his linen napkin onto the plate and got up from the table, striding over to the floor-to-ceiling glass wall of the penthouse dining room. He glared out over the landscape of sleek high-rises that comprised Zhongguancun, the Beijing suburb that was the Chinese version of Silicon Valley.

"All the lab workers' signals just disappeared from the tracking system," continued Beale, tapping the tablet, his brow furrowed. "Their vital signs didn't go to zero, which would have indicated they died. Their signals just disappeared. Serially, not all at once. But I know the system is functional, because one did go to zero. Phyllis Kelley."

"One? One out of fifty!" Lundgren exclaimed. "So much for eliminating institutional memory. You managed to only take care of one out of fifty?"

"Well, somehow, they found out what we planned to do. And somehow, they must have known to get access to an MRI machine, or—"

"Somehow? Isn't it obvious? *It was Davis!*" Lundgren held up his own tablet to show the home page of the *Boston World*. The headline read "NeoHappy Secretly Tested Deadly Control Chip." Lundgren scrolled through the lengthy article, which featured the video Davis had taken of his captivity. Lundgren spat a curse and slammed the tablet onto the coffee table.

"I read it last night." Beale stood up from the table to join Lundgren at the window. "It doesn't say anything about the lab workers. Or about Davis or his wife."

"Well, it wouldn't. The FBI, the CIA, the Boston police . . . they've got them, and they'll bargain with the lab people to make a case against us."

"But they can't possibly reach us here."

"Not a wise assumption. I want you to ask our contact in the Ministry to look for any out-of-the-ordinary visitors from the US and to monitor embassy activity. They'll be willing to do that. After all, we still hold all the cards. They don't have their hands on the sequestration technology much less the red and blue chip technology. And they won't. And we have the chips themselves."

"So, we begin?"

"Yes, we begin."

• • •

"The girls are fine," Annie reported to Kalinsky the next morning, as they rode to the US Embassy in a taxi. "We called them last night. They sounded happy. My mom and dad are spoiling them rotten. But I had to be careful about explaining to my folks what we were doing, given the news stories."

"The little girls deserve lots of happy," said Kalinsky. "They have been through so much. And we are here to make sure nobody ever goes through that again."

Brad nodded in resigned agreement. "As much as we miss the girls . . . as much as we worry for their safety . . . you're right."

The taxi pulled up to the black steel gate of the US Embassy complex, a fortress of concrete boxes designed to protect against any assault. The Chinese paramilitary policeman at the gate checked their credentials and waved them through.

On a side street, a black BMW eased up to position itself for a view of the front gate. Its occupants radioed in their position and settled back with the bored patience of any loyal enforcer of a repressive regime.

Brad, Annie, and Kalinsky made their way through the surrounding fortress of concrete buildings to the glass high-rise at the center of the embassy complex. At the entrance, they were greeted by a slightly paunchy middle-aged, blue-suited man who introduced himself as Adrian Allen, a technology attaché.

They shook hands, and Brad started to speak, but Allen put a cautionary finger to his lips. "We're so pleased you could come," he said, pronouncing his words a little too succinctly, as if into a recorder. "Our computer system has given us serious problems, and we'll appreciate any help you can give." He then led them silently to a secure conference room.

"We're rather careful here," he said, closing the door. "Perhaps it's an abundance of caution, but there is the reality that someone may be listening. The Chinese have made quite remarkable strides in their eavesdropping technology . . . and of course their hacking ability." He offered them coffee, which they gratefully accepted, still adjusting to the twelve-hour time difference.

As they settled into chairs, Allen said in a more low-key conversational tone, "As you may already have surmised, I'm your CIA contact here. I can provide some limited support, but you need to be seen as operating outside our imprimatur."

"Yes, that is what we expected," said Kalinsky. "We are prepared to be left to hang out to dry."

Allen ignored the sarcasm. "We have ourselves a bit of a quandary. We could only get you into the country quickly on the pretense of an emergency with the computers. But the minute you entered the country the Chinese Ministry of State Security somehow got you on its radar."

"We noticed," said Brad. "We were singled out at immigration."

"Ah, indeed, that is a sure sign."

"Does *he* know we are here?" asked Kalinsky.

"Lundgren? Probably not. We can likely depend on the various arms of the Chinese government not communicating well with one another. Thank goodness their paranoia even runs to suspicion of each other."

"What do they say about Lundgren and Beale?"

"Nothing, and we haven't asked. Better to pretend we don't know they're here, although they likely know we know."

"Any leads about where they are?"

"Well, it makes the most sense that they've got working relationships with the National Center for Nanoscience and Technology. But I'm sure that's very much under the table."

Kalinsky got up to pace the room. "So, is our job to make relationship over the table, to find them out."

"Look, we need mobility," said Brad. "Chinese security will follow us from the hotel and camp outside the gates. We'll need to evade them."

"I understand," said Allen. "We know how to smuggle you out during the day."

Kalinsky shook his head. "Well, it had better be foolproof, or we could be disappeared if they catch us in city. Oh, and we will not be only needing daytime mobility. We need to operate at night."

"Well, I'm afraid we can't help you there," said Allen. "If you need to move about after hours, it would be best if you made your own arrangements to evade any surveillance."

"Again, we are hanging out there, eh?" said Kalinsky, notching up his sarcasm. "What we need are dependable crooks."

Brad nodded. "We might be able to supply those. I'd bet Peng knows somebody."

Allen smiled wryly, shaking his head. "We don't need to know about that. In fact, we don't *want* to know. But you *must* stop this technology from falling into Chinese hands. I've read the brief, and the potential is frightening. Superhuman soldiers, remote executions, population control. The Chinese would readily apply this. And, they'd sell it to their allies. Imagine what North Korea would do with such technology."

"Don't worry. You will have deniability," said Kalinsky, his Russian accent sending the last word rolling richly off his tongue.

"What do you hear from the FBI, the CIA back home?" asked Brad.

"Quite a lot, actually," said Allen. He held up a thumb drive. "This is a copy of the report that arrived in the diplomatic pouch yesterday. The NeoHappy scientists whose lives you saved were most forthcoming. Especially after they were given immunity."

"Gregor should review it," said Brad. "He knows more about the system than us."

With that, Allen handed the thumb drive to Kalinsky, who said, "*Da*, I will spend time analyzing. There are no doubt clues in here about what they are up to."

"Anything about us in the media?" asked Annie. "We're not aware of any mention of us."

"So far, the *World* has kept its word and you remain anonymous sources," said Allen. "And our own media sources indicate no other outlet is onto you yet, either."

"Good," said Brad. "We need to start our work here."

. . .

A knock on his door prompted Kalinsky to haul himself to his feet, a scotch in one hand, a tablet computer in the other. He peered through the peephole, let out a grunt of relief and threw open the door.

"You were gone an hour!" he scolded Brad and Annie.

"Romantic walks around the area take time," smiled Annie. "Especially those meant to recon who's watching us."

"Three surveillance cars, black BMWs," reported Brad. "Three guys in the lobby, in case we go our separate ways. When we took our walk, two followed us. The area is too open to lose them on foot. We think we can lose them in the subway. We managed to do some shopping in stores they couldn't follow us into without being obvious. I got some local clothes and other stuff that will help us blend in, disguise us."

"You two are sneakier than I thought." Kalinsky plopped back onto the easy chair and waved the tablet.

"We already know just about everything in this report. But the FBI did get new information out of scientists. They said that Lundgren and Beale took all of the data. And they took many thousands of the control chips, the version two."

"Jesus," said Brad. "Obviously, they mean to do mass testing, then."

"But something new, something that makes me worry." Kalinsky leaned forward, waving the report, his eyes narrowing. "They also took many of a totally new kind of chip we didn't know before. What they call the Zombie chips."

"What're those?"

"The scientists didn't know what they do. Beale designed them himself. Turned them over to the fabrication techs, and he gave them code name Zombie. The fabrication people said there were two kinds. And both kinds had much more complicated reservoirs, for holding different drugs, probably. But same kinds of sequestration chambers as version two-point-oh chips, for extracting and storing hormones from the blood."

"So, what would you guess they're for?" asked Brad.

"Well, they hold more drugs . . . add to that the hormones, and you have more control over any poor focker with chip inside him. But Beale, he erased all the plans, so all we have is description of chip structure from techs."

"Two kinds of chips," mused Annie. "That implies you're trying to control two kinds of behavior. You'd have to figure out what kinds of drug- and hormone-induced behaviors they might want to control."

Brad sat down beside her on the couch. "All this makes it even more important that we find Lundgren and Beale now." He waved a slip of paper. "I got a message from Peng. He's set a time for our meet this evening at the National Stadium."

At six p.m. that night, the unmistakably rotund, bearded Kalinsky, emerged from the hotel elevator and paraded ostentatiously through the stark, geometric lobby and out the front door. A small nondescript Chinese man emerged from the bar and followed him.

Shortly afterward, two people exited unobtrusively from separate elevator cars. One was a young woman with short dark hair, wearing a dark coat; and the other, a slim young man in a knit cap with glasses carrying a shoulder bag. They also left separately, attracting far less attention than Kalinsky.

Lounging at the bar, the two remaining Chinese agents were not even bothering to watch the elevators. Rather, they were intent on a map on a tablet computer screen set on the bar. It showed two flashing, stationary red icons inside the hotel, and a third advancing slowly down nearby Zichun Road. The two men sipped their beers, and one made a quick call on his cell phone. He reported with certainty that Brad and Annie were still in the hotel. After all, the tracking chips that had been implanted in their clothes in the airport baggage area still showed them in their room.

So, the Chinese agents sat comfortably in the bar having a casual, confident chat over the phone with their colleague who was following Kalinsky. The large Russian towered over the Chinese pedestrians, striding along the busy street for several blocks before reaching a taxi stand. He climbed into a taxi and instructed the driver to pull away for what the puzzled cabbie would believe to be a wandering drive through the city with a bored, rich tourist.

CHAPTER 26

Brad and Annie followed the busy flow of the tightly packed crowd of Chinese out of the subway station to see looming above them the massive, bulbous Beijing National Stadium. Trying to look like rubbernecking tourists, they chatted among themselves about its nickname, the Bird's Nest, gesturing at its bowl shape and crisscrossing filigree of woven girders.

They also continually scanned the crowd for anyone who seemed to be paying particular attention to the two westerners amid the crowd of Chinese. But aside from a few sidelong glances, they seemed to attract little notice. To stare was not only impolite, but politically unwise in China.

"These crowds make me nervous," said Annie. "I keep thinking there's somebody among them following us. I wish we could have met at a restaurant."

"Believe me, this is the best way," said Brad. "I've done enough meets with confidential sources to know that a crowd means that it's harder to connect Peng with us. The Ministry of Public Security police could detain him. And he's got to have the freedom to do the snooping we need."

As the massive stadium loomed before them, Brad located the ticket office and picked up the tickets that Peng had left for them. They entered the stadium, walked beneath the labyrinth of burnished steel girders and into the cavernous, sprawling open arena. They stopped and marveled at the arresting sight on the field of an artificial craggy mountain surrounded by a snowy slope populated by skiing Chinese.

Brad chuckled at the sight. "I'd read they had a big problem filling the stadium for sporting events, so they made it a slope."

They sat down in the largely empty stadium, and immediately began to search among the sparse, scattered spectators for their friend.

They waited for an hour, and were prepared to abandon the meet, when Brad felt a tap on his shoulder. He turned to see a young woman dressed as an usher. She handed him a note, smiled, said a few words in Chinese, then left.

"It says I'm to go to an arena entrance on the other side of the stadium," said Brad, reading the note.

"We'll go together," said Annie. "A foreign man alone looks more suspicious than a couple of tourists."

Their arms around each other, conspicuously smiling and chatting, Brad and Annie made their way up the steps and into the cavernous stadium hallway, walking among the square support pillars. They passed the section entrances, seeking the one designated by Peng. But just as they were approaching their destination, they heard a familiar lightly accented voice behind them.

"Do not turn around, my friends. I almost didn't recognize you in your disguises! Just keep walking to the pillar ahead. Then walk around it and go back the other way. Then stand behind the next pillar."

"What's wrong?" asked Brad, without turning his head.

"I have a shadow. Most journalists have plainclothes shadows, especially me because I am reporting for American publications on technology. But my shadow likes skiing, so he has his mind on the skiers, and that gives me some room to maneuver. He is maybe a hundred yards behind me. I have just come out of the stadium for a pee and a smoke, so I shall go into the *yù shì* . . . the bathroom . . . then come out and lean against that same pillar. You stay out of sight on the other side.

After he makes sure I am just smoking, he will duck into the arena to watch the skiers. So, we can talk until he comes back."

Annie played her part well, gesturing at the soaring steel architecture, and seeming to guide Brad around the pillar to see more of the structure. They walked to the next pillar, trying to pick out the internal security operative following Peng. He might have been the small, fidgety man with a bowl haircut, but they couldn't be sure. If so, he passed by them without a glance. They stopped behind the next pillar.

After a short moment, they heard Peng's voice on the other side of the pillar.

"I am so happy you are here! You are looking well!"

"Well, we wish it was a pleasure visit. You've seen the papers about the NeoHappy chip?"

"God, yes! Wow! You were involved?"

"We were right in the middle! I asked them to keep our names out. I was writing Fallon's biography. I saw him killed. Annie and the kids were chipped. And now Lundgren is here in China." Brad quickly explained how he, Annie, and Kalinsky had tracked Lundgren and were trying to stop him.

"What do you need? *Anything*, my friends."

"We have no idea where he is, but we think he might be connected with the nanoscience center."

"I know the center. They've got biological testing facilities."

"We don't want you to be directly involved. We need people who are unofficial, who are . . ." Brad paused, trying to think of a word.

"Pirates," said Peng.

"Pirates?" asked Brad.

"There are many people here who make and sell pirated goods. They work out of the Zhongguancun market. They mostly sell DVDs. He's set a time for our meet this evening."

"Well, we need a top-level guy . . . somebody who's smuggling sophisticated machines, like for making chips."

"That's tough," said Peng. "I'll try. But listen. I've got to warn you. Some of them are actually moles for internal security. They'll be perfectly willing to sell you out, get you sent to a Chinese prison. And some of them are violent criminals who'll disappear you. I'll try to find somebody dependable. But I can't guarantee."

"Well, do the best you can."

"Okay. Meet me in the market tomorrow night at seven p.m. I should have a contact for you by then. But you're right. It's the only way I can think of to get the inside—" Peng stopped in midsentence. *"Oh shit!"* he exclaimed.

"What?" asked Brad.

"My shadow's here!"

"Peng? Are you all right?" whispered Brad urgently around the pillar. But the journalist didn't answer. They waited a long moment, then as casually as they could, strolled out from behind the pillar. Glancing over toward the nearest arena entrance, they saw Peng in heated conversation with the small fidgety man in the bowl haircut. He was flanked by two security guards.

Not looking back, they made their way quickly out of the stadium and toward the hotel.

"God, I hope we haven't implicated him," breathed Annie, as they entered the subway.

• • •

Lundgren peered into the cell in the Jia building of Qincheng Prison, nodding his head in approval. The cramped rubber-padded room held only a single low bed and a toilet. All the corners within the cell had been rounded and smoothed.

"You see, there is no possibility that an inmate may harm himself," said the squat, gray-suited warden, waving with stubby hands. "Lighting is recessed and hardened, so no possibility of electrocution. And the single window is reinforced."

Beale stepped inside the cell, inspecting its interior. "We require constant video surveillance of each cell. All two hundred. With video recording. We need a full record of the subjects' behaviors."

The warden frowned. "We have no such system. Too expensive." He swung the iron-plated door shut with a solid clank and pointed to peepholes at toilet level and eye level. "However, we have excellent views of the prisoners. Our guards are very assiduous about maintaining surveillance."

"Install a video system," instructed Lundgren. "Your superiors will pay for it."

The warden nodded and shrugged at the mention of his superiors in the Ministry of Public Security. Whatever they approved, he would agree to, he had learned in long years of service.

"And how about the controlled transport of the subjects?" asked Beale.

"Oh, we can transfer them wherever you wish."

"I emphasize *control*. Some of the subjects, mostly men, will require particularly strong restraints. They will be very, very violent."

"They can be sedated," said the warden. "And anyway, the inmates we are providing for your testing are naturally docile. After all, they are not violent. They are only prisoners who are enemies of the state because of agitation."

Beale shook his head decisively. "They will be extremely violent, very strong in the physiological state we will induce. But at no point should any subject be given any drugs of any kind. They must be only under the influence of the drug regimen we are testing."

"Ah, well, then we will devise a method for secure transfer. Our people have experience in these matters."

"And for those subjects we will need a facility for taking blood samples, testing reactions, and measuring muscle strength and other physical capabilities while the subjects remain fully restrained."

"We have no such room."

"I noted you had a cafeteria. That will do. You won't need it for meals. The subjects will be fed in their cells. They will remain in the cells except for testing."

"They will require exercise."

Lundgren smiled wryly. "They will receive plenty of exercise."

"And their diet?"

"They are to be fed very well. The best quality food. The best nutrition. I want no nutritional or sensory deprivation to affect the data.

And they are to be given any entertainment . . . books, videos, and so forth . . . that they wish. You will monitor all those requests, as well."

Again the warden frowned, but said nothing. These inmates would be treated like none he had managed before. An odd combination of total control and pleasant amenities.

Lundgren strolled down the hall, still issuing instructions. "And for our testing of another cohort of subjects, we will require ten private apartments with bedrooms and bathrooms."

The warden couldn't suppress a puzzled look. "The cots we have are quite adequate. I am not sure I understand what kind of testing will require private apartments."

"You don't need to understand. Just provide large comfortable beds with linens meticulously laundered. And those rooms will have a completely separate video surveillance system."

"Well, staff quarters have become available, since the new Yancheng Prison was built and staffing here was reduced."

"We will see those now," said Lundgren. "And do you have the files of the candidate subjects?"

The warden handed him a thumb drive. "There are six hundred files here. You will almost certainly find a sufficient group for your needs."

Lundgren handed the thumb drive to Beale. "I have made it clear that none should possess any criminal pathologies."

"As you specified, all are otherwise physically healthy and psychologically normal . . . except of course for their antisocial political activities."

"We will give you the list of our chosen candidates over the next few days. Begin transferring them in immediately," said Lundgren.

He and Beale proceeded to inspect the staff quarters, with Lundgren dictating the extensive remodeling that he would require. The warden dutifully typed the instructions into a tablet computer, as he had been doing all morning.

Finally, Lundgren and Beale strode out of the prison through its pagoda-like portico, entered their limousine, and sped away.

The warden watched them go, took out his cell phone and punched in the top number on his directory. He frowned during his short conversation with the person at the other end. He nodded his head submissively and emphatically declared over and over "*Wǒ tīngdédǒng*" (I understand). He ended the call and peered down the road where the limousine had gone, muttering "*Sīshēngz*" (bastards) under his breath.

• • •

"*Got DVD! New DVD!*" exclaimed the hawkers outside the sprawling warehouse that was the Zhongguancun electronics market. The young men eagerly waved copies of the latest movies, as they repeated their spiel in Mandarin, switching to broken English when they saw Brad and Annie approach.

"*Have good quality!*" shouted one.

Another chimed in, "*Cheap! First-run movie!*"

Brad and Annie strolled casually along the row of folding tables to the north entrance, peering through the glass doors into the bustling mall to see a sprawl of open stalls with glass cases tended by clerks selling all manner of electronics.

"We're early," said Brad. "Let's take a quick walk through, just to scout."

"*DVD!*" shouted a voice behind them, but continuing in a near-whisper. "You should not go in, Brad and Annie. You should come with me."

They turned to see Peng Pyang wearing a red Boston University baseball cap and a Star Wars t-shirt that said "Forces is to be Made!"

"Peng!" exclaimed Annie. "We were worried that you might—"

He shook his head emphatically. "I'm known around here. Let's go quickly. There's somebody you need to meet. A source. We have to move fast, to watch for a tail."

Peng scurried off, his head low, weaving deftly among the thick crowd of shoppers streaming along the wide boulevard. He accelerated to a sprint, ducking around the sometimes startled pedestrians. Brad and Annie kept up the pace behind him, following the baseball cap, almost missing him ducking through a small shop festooned with fake designer handbags.

They followed him into a narrow, dark alley. Peng stopped for a long moment and peered back through the shop. Seeing nobody following, he urgently motioned Brad and Annie into a blue motorized three-wheeled cab, its passenger compartment shrouded in canvas.

They had just squeezed into the seat, when the cab lurched away, zipping onto a main avenue, weaving at breakneck speed among the swirling confusion of cars, bicycles, motorcycles, and people. As the little cab swerved precariously through hairpin turns, Brad and Annie could make out that they were leaving the electronics malls behind and entering a labyrinth of dark, narrow streets lined with battered, anonymous warehouses. Annie squeezed Brad's arm in an unspoken warning. Was Peng inadvertently leading them into a trap?

The cab slowed, and Peng urged them, "Okay, we get out. Hurry!"

Brad and Annie stumbled behind him out of the still-moving cab, and it accelerated away with a throaty rattle of its motorcycle engine. They found themselves standing before a metal warehouse with a truck-sized overhead steel door, beside it a smaller human-sized door. All was dead quiet. Twin surveillance cameras, their red lights glowing, were aimed at them from over the doors.

With a metallic creak, the smaller door opened, and a hulking Chinese man with the build of a wrestler stepped out, looking them up and down with fathomless obsidian eyes.

"I must leave you here," said Peng. "I will have no knowledge of this place. You understand?"

Brad nodded, and peering up and down the street, Peng hurried away.

Brad and Annie now stood alone, facing the massive Chinese man. Their military training kicked in, and they scanned the area for means of escape if necessary.

The huge man waved his meaty hands at Brad, to indicate that he needed to check Brad for weapons. Brad stepped forward and raised his arms, glancing back at Annie, who moved around to position herself to attack the man, should it be necessary.

But he only did a routine pat-down of Brad's chest, back, waist, crotch, and legs. He then turned to Annie, who frowned at him and cocked her head in a universal I-dare-you expression. He looked back at Brad, who smiled ruefully and shook his head in warning.

"I don't know if you understand English, but if you do, I should tell you that you don't mess with her."

The slightest smile flickered on the huge man's round face. He paused a moment, then nodded in respect and jerked his hands outward in a gesture that she should take off her coat. She did so, pirouetting slowly around to show that she was neither armed nor fitted with a recorder.

The man pulled open the door and led them inside, where they walked among towering shelves of pallets of consumer and industrial electronics. Brad recognized not only the expected televisions and audio components, but high-end semiconductor fabrication machines.

"That's a two-hundred-thousand-dollar CT scanner," whispered Annie, pointing at a large crate labeled with a GE logo.

They reached a door at the back of the warehouse where two more men waited, each equipped with both holstered pistols and assault rifles. The big man gestured for them to enter, but stayed outside.

They pushed through a steel door to find themselves in a thickly carpeted, walnut-paneled waiting room. A voice from an inner office said, "Please, do come in."

They followed the voice, unprepared for the sight of an elegantly furnished room with a red silk-brocade-covered sofa and wing chairs, a massive, ornately carved walnut desk, and French impressionist paintings on the walls. A dapper middle-aged Chinese man in pinstriped suit stood and walked around the desk. A Bach concerto played quietly in the background. A large bouquet of roses on a side table gave forth a faint aroma.

"Won't you have a glass of wine?" asked the man in perfectly accented English. "I have found a perfectly delightful Chilean pinot noir." He stopped and shrugged apologetically. "Oh, pardon me. I did not introduce myself. I am Mai Tou-Ning." He extended a small, manicured hand, which Brad and Annie both shook.

"I'm not sure how to say this, but you're not what we expected," said Brad. "Our friend Peng Pyang said we would meet a pirate."

The man settled into a wing chair, gesturing for them to sit on the sofa. "I do not know such a person," he said simply, a wry smile betraying his fib. "I am a businessman. And as such I provide products to whomever wishes to buy them."

"Okay, we'll say you don't know Peng," said Brad. "But if you don't mind us getting straight to our point, we need to know about the purchase of certain nanoelectronic and nanofluidic fabrication equipment. Machines like electron beam lithography machines, focused ion beam systems, chemical vapor deposition machines, and so forth."

The small man shrugged and smiled politely. "As I have said, I am a businessman. It's not good business to talk about a customer . . . that is, if such a customer existed."

"Do you have a wife and children?" asked Annie, leaning forward.

"I do," said Mai, his smile fading into puzzlement. "Of what relevance is that?"

With that, Annie launched into a long, impassioned telling of their story and the horrors they and their young daughters had suffered. Brad told of Lundgren's and Beale's killings and their attempts at mass murder of the laboratory technicians. Mai sat and listened, folding his hands together as if in prayer, his increasingly grim expression revealing the impact of Brad's and Annie's words.

Brad finally stood and paced the room, telling Mai, "These are the evil men who are now planning to spread this malignant technology to your country, your people. Do you want to be known as someone who aided them, even if only by providing equipment?"

Mai remained silent for a long while, his lips pursed, his jaw set. Finally, he said quietly, "I have heard . . . mind you, only *heard* . . . of attempts to procure such equipment." Falling silent once more, he rose smoothly from the chair, went to his desk and scribbled a note, handing it to Brad.

"Thank you," said Brad, reading the note and giving it to Annie. She read the address on the slip of paper, and nodded in thanks.

Mai returned to his chair behind the desk and nodded a silent goodbye. The meeting was over. The office door opened, filled by the looming presence of the massive guard, who had apparently received some signal from Mai to appear.

"You have never visited this place," he said emphatically. "You do not know me. Should I ever discover that you have told anyone otherwise, there will be . . . consequences."

Brad took Annie's arm, and they glanced at each other to confirm that each understood the implication of Mai's statement. Finally, they both nodded in agreement and turned to follow the mountain of muscled flesh that was the departing guard.

Mai stood looking after them for a moment, his face settling into an impassive mask. He crossed to a wall and pressed a button, triggering a paneled door to glide open revealing a bar. Its back-lit glass shelves held crystal decanters, a wine rack, and liquor bottles. He chose one of the wine bottles, pulled its cork with an ornate silver corkscrew and poured a generous amount of red wine into a stemmed goblet. He sat down in the wing chair, taking a sip and setting the glass down.

His expression still matter-of-fact, he took out his smartphone and touched its screen to make a call. He waited for the party to answer, taking another sip of wine.

Not bothering to identify himself, he said simply, "I've just had some interesting American visitors. Have you heard of Bradley and Annie Davis?"

• • •

"Are these the Americans you have been seeking?" asked the deputy assistant to the minister of state security, handing Lundgren three folders.

Lundgren flipped them open one by one, his expression darkening with each folder. After scanning the final dossier, he slapped the folder shut and handed all three to Beale, who also began to leaf through them.

"How the hell did they get in?" demanded Lundgren. "I thought you Chinese had a well-controlled country."

"They were admitted as technicians for the US State Department," said the deputy assistant—a wisp of a young man whose obsequious stoop marked him as one who would always be a minion. He ducked his head in apology, rubbing a sore spot on his arm. He had apparently jabbed himself on some sharp object as Beale had met him at the entrance to Qincheng Prison. "We cannot—"

"Arrest them," said Lundgren. "Just put them in some hole somewhere, so I don't have to bother with them, anymore. I want a meeting with the minister, not a flunky. This is clearly an underhanded attempt by the US government to stop us. I want assurances that it will go no further."

The deputy assistant registered only the slightest annoyance at being called a flunky. He knew his place. He tried repeating the excuse.

"Ah, but they are listed as official contract employees of the State Department. There would be serious diplomatic consequences. We cannot—"

"Fuck diplomatic problems! Find a way. Charge them with smuggling. Charge them with trying to steal secrets. You Chinese can always find a way to do what needs to be done. I have clinical testing to do."

Lundgren turned away, striding from the warden's office and down the gray-painted prison hallway, followed by Beale, who was still examining the dossiers. Then Lundgren stopped so suddenly that Beale walked on for a few steps before realizing he had continued alone.

A smile rose on Lundgren's face, and he returned to the office, where the little deputy assistant sat at a scarred wooden desk, beginning a phone conversation.

"On second thought, I want them here," said Lundgren. "We can use them to answer certain clinical questions."

Behind him, Beale also slowly began to smile and nod, as the implications of the idea dawned on him. The little deputy assistant peered back at them with an impassive expression that, for him, was a carefully sublimated signal of frustration. Lundgren ignored it, turning and gesturing for Beale to follow him.

"I don't trust the Chinese to get those three. Let's hedge our bets, shall we? A first field test of the red chip? Put some subjects out there to do the capture."

"*Field test?*" whispered Beale urgently, striding alongside him. "*Jesus, Lawrence, we don't know what the hell will happen! The subjects might just go randomly berserk!*"

"We motivate them to do as we instruct," said Lundgren, shrugging his shoulders. "Have the warden identify subjects with families. We insert the red chips. We tell the field subjects that if they follow our instructions, their families will be rewarded. If not, their families will be punished. A good experiment. It will yield important data about whether their intellects remain intact enough to modulate their actions."

"And if they still go nuts and kill people?"

"It's China, for Christ sakes! The government kills people all the time." He stopped at the entrance to the monitoring room. "Did you chip that lackey?"

Nodding, Beale brought out his smartphone and tapped the screen to bring up a map. "Yes, as he was coming in I jabbed him. And it's active. He's leaving the prison." A small red dot was making slow progress through a diagram of the building.

"A good test of the subcutaneous insertion. It won't give us the control capability of the venous insertion, but it will do what's necessary."

"Yes, and the advantage is that all he felt was a bit of discomfort during the insertion. The needle is so small, it just feels like a little prick."

"So, with a little prick, we now have chipped a little prick," said Lundgren, smiling at his joke. "Let's hope we have the same success with the minister."

• • •

"You saw this man? This pirate?" asked Kalinsky. The large Russian had abruptly appeared at their side, as they emerged from the subway, like a plus-sized ghost. They wove their way through the nighttime crowd of Chinese as they talked, keeping their heads close together, trying to keep their voices from being heard by any eavesdropping security men who might have embedded themselves in the throng.

"You lost the tail?" asked Brad.

"Hell, I lost tails every day in Moscow," chuckled Kalinsky. "These teeny little Chinese men, they are so easily fooled!"

"Peng connected us with a guy who seems to be one of the pirate bosses. He traffics in all kinds of electronic goods. But he said he hadn't had an order for the instruments we're looking for. But he did give us an address." Brad produced the slip of paper for Kalinsky to scrutinize.

"No. No. We don't go here yet," he announced. "We get CIA people to tell us about it first. Tell us what they know."

"I'm not so sure we involve them," said Brad. He spoke at a normal volume now, because they were now alone, having ducked into a darkened side street. "We can't wait until they run this information through all their intelligence folderol. We might just miss a chance."

They passed a narrow, deserted alley, when the headlights of a van suddenly switched on, bathing them in the glare. Blinded, they heard the metallic clunk of the van doors sliding open, the heavy scuffling of large bodies leaping from it. Then an animal sound they had never heard before. A fearsome, deep, breathy grunting.

The van's headlights showed the silhouettes of men running toward them. But not really running. Rather loping toward them with a hulking near-animal stride.

"What the—" Brad began to say, but Kalinsky grabbed both him and Annie and shoved them away from the approaching men, turning to challenge whoever the assailants were. Realizing the threat to Annie, Brad grabbed her and they ran headlong from the danger they did not understand.

"YOU GO!" bellowed Kalinsky behind them. "THIS IS SOMETHING THAT FOCKER—" but his voice was cut short by the thud of fists impacting flesh, the grunts of struggling men. Brad heard a feral growl that he knew must have come from Kalinsky, but had never imagined the man could emit such an enraged sound.

After running half a block down the main road toward the hotel, Brad stopped and grabbed Annie's shoulders, looking into her surprisingly calm eyes.

"You go as fast as you can back to the hotel! Call Allen. Get some CIA people, Marines . . . whoever the hell they can send. I'm going back."

"And do what?" challenged Annie. "There looked to be half-dozen of whoever . . . or *whatever* . . . those were."

"I don't know. But I have to! He saved *us!* We have to save *him!*"

Annie took a deep breath, nodded her head, and bolted away.

Brad rushed back toward the alley, scouting for some kind of weapon along the way, still hearing the sounds of combat. He found a length of iron drain pipe hanging loose against a building and wrenched it free. He flattened himself hard against the brick wall of the building, quickly looking around the corner into the alley. The headlights of the van revealed a vicious struggle in the distance. He could still hear the sickening sounds of fists slamming into flesh, although the animal-like grunts that came with each impact sounded like no humans he had encountered.

Wielding the pipe, he leaped into the alley, running toward the headlights, grasping the pipe, prepared to smash it into whatever it was that had attacked them. But as he approached, he heard the metallic sounds of the van's doors slamming shut, the van's engine racing, the whine of a transmission propelling the van in reverse.

The headlights shrank away down the alley until they reached another main road, then swerved, as the van backed out, lurched forward, and sped away.

The only remaining sound was the low thrum of the city. Brad approached the spot where the vicious fight and abduction had taken place.

He slumped against the building in despair. In the dim light of the alley, on the pavement he could see dark, glistening patches of blood.

CHAPTER 27

Adrian Allen sat behind his desk in the embassy, waving his small wrinkled hands in frustration. "So, you don't know who took him," he said.

"No," said Brad, holding Annie's hand, sitting across from him.

"And you don't know where they would have taken him."

"Well, no."

"And our field agent confirmed there was a great deal of blood on the street. So, you don't even know if he's alive."

"He's alive," said Annie firmly. "That man just doesn't die."

"But you don't know."

"*He's alive!*" Annie exclaimed, desperation tingeing her voice.

"And you'll recall that since you're here as private contractors, we can't really demand any kind of official State Department inquiry. He's just a private citizen who was mugged."

"An *American* citizen!" exclaimed Brad. "Well, then, how about this? How about we contact his people back home. How about we tell them he's missing. Do you know who those people are?"

Allen's deep, abrupt frown told them he was perfectly aware of the capabilities of Kalinsky's men. "We will do what we can . . . within the limitations we face as an embassy."

Brad and Annie stood up together. Brad leaned forward over Allen's desk, thrusting his face toward Allen, his jaw set.

"Look, you're CIA. Your job is to solve problems like this. But just so you understand, we're not waiting on whatever the hell you do."

"Look, that's—" began Allen, but Brad and Annie had already left.

They returned to the empty embassy office that had been their room for the night, after they had been picked up by an embassy car and driven there, hiding in the back seat to avoid the inevitable Chinese surveillance. They sagged into two chairs, neither having slept.

"Do we really call Gregor's men?" asked Annie "What would they do? What *could* they do?"

"We don't have a choice. You know how loyal they are to him. They will have to be told. And besides, knowing those guys, they will make anybody who harms Gregor pay holy hell."

With that, Brad picked up the office phone and punched in the international number to the US. Maybe the Chinese would be tapping the phone, but given the names Kalinsky had bestowed on his men, the Chinese would only think some American was ordering whiskey. Lots of different brands.

• • •

A taxi dropped Brad and Annie off in a deserted warehouse district in northeast Beijing and the nervous driver accelerated immediately away from the disreputable part of the city.

They ducked close against one of the soot-encrusted brick buildings, feeling not only the cold of the gray morning and its enshrouding smog, but the visceral chill of anxiety about their situation. They had waited two days in the embassy, frustrated and worried. Only a cryptic text message from Kalinsky's men instructed them to come to this deserted place at this time.

"This is just screwy," whispered Brad. "What the hell are we doing here? We have no idea what these people are up to."

"Well, we know they're loyal to Gregor," said Annie reassuringly. "We know that they would do anything to save him. I just have this feeling that they've done what's needed."

A low rumble from down the narrow street grew to become the roar of an approaching truck, a large one. A massive Chinese army transport loomed into view, and pulled to a stop.

"*Oh, shit!*" exclaimed Brad. "*They've found us! They're after us!*" He and Annie sprinted away down the block, acutely aware that they had no escape route—no side streets, no doorways—to duck into. They had been lured into the perfect trap. Behind them, they heard the scuffling sounds of troops exiting the truck, a telltale rattle of metal signaling the hefting of rifles.

"*Wait!*" shouted a voice from the truck. "*It is us!*"

Brad stopped, puzzlement on his face. He *knew* that voice. The last time he heard it was from the driver's seat of Kalinsky's SUV.

Annie had the same reaction. She clutched Brad's arm, and they turned to face the truck. "Mark?" she asked. "Is that you?"

Before them stood a platoon of uniformed Chinese soldiers, heavily armed. Brad and Annie almost turned to flee again, when they recognized that these Chinese soldiers weren't Chinese. They were the scruffy-looking Russian hackers that were Kalinsky's "guys". And their leader was Mark Makers!

They turned to hurry back toward the truck.

"How the hell did you—" Brad began, but Makers waved his hand in modest pride.

"Oh, at one time we have done much business with our Chinese friends. In fact, you visited one of our best trading partners . . . Mai Tou-Ning. He called us after your visit to ask about you, and we confirmed that you were telling truth. So, he was willing to smuggle us into the country and equip us. He is not a particular friend of the government. He is shocked by their collaboration with Lundgren, even as ruthless as that government is."

"But the truck, the uniforms?"

"First, we need to check something." Makers took out a small wand, flipped a switch on its side, and began to scan it over them, as he said, "Mai has many useful sources of supply in the army. And we are willing to spend much money on equipment like this gadget." He finished his scan and asked the quizzical couple, "You have been wearing clothes bought here?"

"Yes, when we go out at night," said Annie. "And we change at the embassy before we're smuggled out for the day. We wanted to blend in. We bought everything in the local stores."

Makers laughed wryly and shook his head. "It was a very fortunate choice. Your American clothes have been bugged with GPS chips." He smiled. "The Chinese were no doubt fooled into thinking you were spending much time in your hotel room. Like honeymooners."

"God, that's how they found Gregor," said Annie. "He was wearing his own clothes."

They turned gratefully to greet Kalinsky's men—including Johnny Walker the Red, Jim Beam, Jack Daniels, Chivas Regal, the three Glens, and of course Vladislav Ballantine.

They all climbed back into the army truck, and the vehicle navigated its ponderous way through the narrow side streets into a warehouse nearby. The windowless brick building had been transformed into a staging area, complete with trucks, weapons, computers, and large-screen displays.

"What next?" asked Brad. "How do we find where they have taken Gregor? And where Lundgren is?"

"Both are at same place," said Makers, bringing up a map of China on a display screen. "Mai has told us that Qincheng Prison has been destination for much computer equipment, security cameras, and so forth. And his source in army said prisoners are being shipped in."

"What's unusual about that?" asked Brad.

"Prison was being shut down. No need for lots of new equipment or new inmates, unless they were doing something different. Like testing chips on prisoners."

"Then we need to see this place. You could break in. Save him. Get Lundgren."

"Is a problem, though." On the large screen, Makers brought up a satellite image of the prison. "Complex is surrounded by flat farmland. No cover. Even though we are in army truck, they would see us coming. And we don't know how security systems are set up; or where the guards are."

"You need somebody inside," said Annie.

"We will send one of us."

"That won't work," she said. "You're Russian. They'll immediately figure out you're connected with Gregor. And they'll know one of you being here means that you're all here. They'll expect a raid, then. It needs to be somebody who Lundgren doesn't think has any backup. It needs to be Brad and me. They won't harm us; he needs to know what we know."

"*Never!*" announced Brad, grasping Annie's shoulders. "I'd never let you go in there. We'd both be in danger. It should just be me. The girls need you."

"You need *me*," said Annie, with a finality that allowed no debate.

• • •

Lundgren sat at the control room's instrument console scrutinizing the first test results, as Beale watched the technicians enter data into the computers. Beyond the window of the small room, the guards were wiping up the blood splatters and pools, and the bits of red tissue remaining in the test chamber, after the bodies had been removed.

"Solid data," pronounced Beale, scrutinizing the columns of numbers. "We've got a statistically significant dose-response curve. And it's clear that weight and muscle mass do make a difference."

The door clanged open, and the warden stalked into the room, his jaw clenched.

"This will stop now! I have just returned to find that you are conducting the most barbaric of experiments. Twelve men dead! What are you doing?"

Lundgren looked up calmly from his chair. "We told you that we would be testing these chips."

"Physiological tests! Behavioral tests! Not like this! You are—"

"These *are* behavioral tests," said Beale, still examining the screenfuls of data. "Performance tests can only be done with . . ." he shrugged his shoulders ". . . performers."

Lundgren stood, and in a patronizing tone that a parent might use to explain a concept to a child, said, "You do not need to know the details. Let us just say these red chips create a physiological state that your government would find highly useful in military application. The chip engenders properties of strength and aggression. We need to measure that strength and aggression, but how do you take measurements on an animal . . . which is what these subjects become? And, we need to measure their cognitive functioning as well, in the context of a battle to survive."

"I didn't give you control of these people to kill them!"

"Unfortunate incidents. But clinically useful. We need to have autopsies, anyway, to look for any pathologies caused by the chips. Dr. Beale is performing those."

"And some don't die," said Beale, in an obviously insincere reassurance. "We give those that survive the best of medical care. Of course, it's because we need to measure their physiological resilience."

"Resilience!" hissed the warden. "These are not gladiators! These are political prisoners—"

"True, that is a complicating factor. Which is why we now have procured another very interesting test subject," said Beale. "He is no political prisoner. He is a former Russian mobster, very strong, very aggressive. And a brilliant computer hacker. He will give us data points we could not have gotten with these . . . ordinary . . . subjects."

"He's a bit damaged at the moment," said Lundgren. "He was difficult to subdue. He actually injured our field subjects, who were under the influence of the red chips. It shows what he can do under normal circumstances. That test, by the way, showed that chipped operatives can be released and controlled in the field. But in a few days, we plan to place this new subject in the test chamber, chipped, and proceed to the endpoint."

"Endpoint!" exclaimed the warden. "You will make him fight until he dies."

"A necessary data point," said Lundgren, moving toward the door. "But warden, I must leave you now. I have a rather more pleasant series of clinical trials."

"The women. You are raping the women."

"Oh dear no," smiled Lundgren. "They are freely participating . . . that is as freely as is possible given the blue chip cocktail."

"What terrible drugs are these, in this *cocktail?*" asked the warden.

"Again, warden, details you do not need to be told. You do your job of managing the prison, and please leave us to our work."

"Well, you shall not proceed further with these experiments as long as I am in charge of this prison."

"Easily remedied," said Lundgren, staring coldly at the warden. The warden stalked out slamming the door behind him. "I shall be in the master bedroom," said Lundgren, following the warden out.

Lundgren walked down the hall and crossed to the adjoining wing, where he met a guard who opened the door to the richly appointed bedroom. A young woman lay on the bed, covered by a white silk sheet that draped itself over her naked body. She turned her head toward Lundgren, her eyes glassy, her lips parted seductively. She smiled a wan smile.

"Good evening," he said smoothly, shutting the door behind him.

• • •

The next morning, Brad and Annie, wearing their own GPS-chipped clothes, moved quickly out the hotel entrance and into a limousine that accelerated away from the hotel and wove its way through the thick traffic. It sped down the broad avenues and through the gates of the American embassy. A black BMW gave chase, maintaining a discreet distance.

After fifteen minutes, a battered laundry truck drove slowly out of the gate, lumbering along the wide boulevard and into an alleyway.

As they crouched in the back of the van moving slowly along the boulevards of Beijing, they felt it suddenly lurch to a halt. They heard guttural shouted commands in Mandarin outside, and after a moment, the rear doors slammed open to reveal the gray Beijing morning and three soldiers, their submachine guns leveled at Brad and Annie.

"Chūqù! Jǔ qǐ shǒu lái!" shouted one of the guards in Mandarin. Then, in English. "Get out! Hands up!"

"Please! Please don't hurt my wife!" pleaded Brad, waving his hands above his head.

The soldiers slammed him against the side of the van, patting him down for weapons. Annie let out only a small cry, as they searched her. Their hands bound behind them, they were dragged past the army truck, and to their surprise, thrust into a black limousine.

The army truck cranked up its engine, and rumbled away, the limousine accelerating in the opposite direction.

Alone in the back seat, Brad and Annie gave each other looks that blended anxiety with triumph. Brad decided to try some provocation.

Drawing up his legs, he gave the closed partition between the front and back seats powerful kicks. After two such blows, the partition slid open, and a nine-millimeter pistol thrust itself at them. Behind that pistol appeared the face of Thomas Beale.

"You'll want to settle down," he instructed. "I don't necessarily have to bring you in completely intact."

"We figured it was you," said Brad. "We've been looking for you."

"Well, now all three of you have found us. You'll be seeing the Russian shortly. But perhaps not under the circumstances you would have wished."

"What do you mean by that?" demanded Brad, but Beale said nothing, closing the partition.

The limousine sped down the long straight highway, heading north out of the city across flat farmland toward the bleak, brown landscape of a low mountain range. The car reached a compound of high brick walls, whose color blended into the desolate surroundings. Coils of razor wire topping the massive walls conveyed the futility of escape. But to Brad and Annie, they also conveyed the futility of anybody attempting a rescue assault—even Kalinsky's very capable reformed thugs, whom they knew were following them.

The limousine passed through a village of small houses flanking the compound, turning into a broad drive, blocked by massive steel gates flanked by two guardhouses.

The driver let down the limousine window and spoke authoritatively in Chinese to the guards, and the large gates swung slowly open.

"Damn big gates," whispered Brad to Annie.

"Yeah . . . looks like getting out of this place will be all up to us."

CHAPTER 28

S oldiers hauled Brad and Annie, their hands still bound, out of the limousine, and dragged them along behind Beale across the compound and toward a three-story brick building.

"This is Qincheng Prison," said Beale over his shoulder. "The Chinese government has given it to us for our clinical testing. Very secure."

"Clinical testing of what?" asked Annie.

"You will be told. In fact, you will be part of our trials. A statistically useful part."

Beale led them into a room with a row of computers along one side—manned by technicians busily typing at keyboards. The other side wall was hung with large-screen monitors showing multiple angles of a large chamber with two steel doors. The wall across from the doorway consisted of a large observation window into the chamber.

The soldiers shoved Brad and Annie into chairs facing the window, binding them to the chairs with plastic zip ties. Behind them, they heard the door to the room open and shut.

"It is good to see you again, especially in these circumstances. Well, actually, *useful* is more the apt term."

At the sound of Lundgren's voice, both Brad and Annie twisted in their chairs to glare with utter hatred at the man whom they had vowed to destroy. He had moved up to stand easily beside them, dressed in his usual meticulously tailored suit, looking coolly into the chamber behind the window.

Brad was the first to give voice to his rage. "You *murderer*. You *coward*. You—"

"Yes, yes, I realize what you think of me," said Lundgren with a dismissive tilt of his head. "But what we are doing here is far more important than any personal animosities. We are developing technology that will profoundly impact humanity; that will have untold benefits—"

"*Benefits?*" interrupted Annie. "Benefits to you and Beale and to the tyrants you're working with. The world knows about you, and you will be stopped."

"Well, not by you, it appears. In fact, your presence here will actually advance these studies considerably. I wanted you to understand thoroughly what we're doing. Not because I much care that you know. But your complete understanding is necessary for you to be useful subjects."

"Subjects?" asked Annie. "I don't—"

"Just observe our next clinical trial, if you will."

Lundgren motioned to Beale, who instructed the technicians to bring up images on the large screens of a set of graphs, prompting Annie to say, "Those are physiological data. EKG, blood pressure, EEG—"

"Indeed," said Lundgren. "And you'll notice there are two sets of data." He waved an index finger at one of the technicians, who pressed a button to slide open one of the doors in the chamber.

Kalinsky emerged, stalking through the door, his powerful wrestler's physique apparent because he wore only a pair of shorts. White electrodes were attached to his chest and his now-shaved head. But he was not the gruff-but-amiable Kalinsky Brad and Annie knew.

Now, his clean-shaven face showed undirected, smoldering rage. His eyes, those of a predator, darted back and forth searching for prey. His large hands repeatedly clenched into fists, then unclenched into claws.

"The electrodes transmit the subject's physiological data to our computers," explained Beale, nodding to a technician, who signaled back with a brief thumbs-up.

"GREGOR!" shouted Brad. "IT'S US! WE'RE HERE!"

"He can neither see nor hear you," said Beale. "Soundproof, one-way shatter-proof Lexan. Otherwise, the distraction would interfere with our data. But he'll hear me now."

With that, Beale leaned over and pressed a green button on a console, announcing into its microphone,

"*Gregor. He's coming to kill you! He is going to try to kill you!*" Kalinsky shook his great head back and forth, peering madly around as if not understanding the source of the voice.

The other door slid open, and a small, wiry Chinese man burst into the room, circling Kalinsky in a feral crouch. His savage wild-eyed expression marked him as another one under the influence of the same drugs as Kalinsky. He wore the same array of electrode patches.

The two locked gazes of pure animal hatred and lunged at one another, Kalinsky grabbing for the man's throat. But the smaller man was quicker, evading Kalinsky's grasp, reaching up to claw at his eyes, trying to blind him. His fingernails opened a gash under Kalinsky's right eye, producing a trickle of blood down his face.

Kalinsky whipped around as his opponent circled behind him, clutching the man's arm, wrenching the man toward him, clutching that arm in a death grip, reaching down for the man's leg with his other hand, hoisting the man into the air and with a massive thrust, slamming him into the wall. The man collapsed to the floor, and Kalinsky did not hesitate, but lunged forward, bringing his bare foot up, trying to crush the man's chest against the floor.

But the Chinese man recovered enough from the impact to avoid the crushing blow, grabbing Kalinsky's leg hoisting it up and causing the huge Russian to fall backward, slamming into the floor. The little man struggled to his feet, stumbling slightly and went again for Kalinsky's eyes.

But Kalinsky reached up and grasped the man's head between his huge hands, rolling over and standing up, hoisting the man by his head. The man's hands tore ineffectually at Kalinsky's arms in a feeble attempt to loosen their vice-like grip. But his flailing had little effect.

The sounds of their struggle played through a speaker into the control room, and now Brad and Annie heard Kalinsky's guttural growl as he slammed the man's head into the Lexan wall.

Annie screamed and averted her eyes, as Kalinsky repeatedly smashed the man's skull against the window, leaving it smeared with blood and brain matter. The EKG trace on one of the computer screens flatlined.

"WHAT ARE YOU DOING TO THEM!" bellowed Brad. "THIS IS BEYOND INHUMAN. YOU ARE MONSTERS!"

"True, it is not a pleasant sight. But you need to go beyond the obvious, here," said Lundgren coolly, pacing behind Annie and Brad. The chamber door opened and Kalinsky released the shattered corpse of the Chinese man and, his face a blank mask, lumbered away through it.

"What you have seen is a demonstration of a stunning new technology," continued Lundgren, as Beale busied himself with the technicians analyzing the data. "It is unfortunate that we had to use violence as our measurement parameter. But it gives us unequivocal data points as to the efficacy of the control system. This system can just as well be used to reduce social unrest, increase satisfaction . . . in other words to enable authorities to produce a more productive state in its citizens."

Annie had recovered herself enough to ask, "This chip. What is this *ungodly* chip?"

"We call it the red chip, for obvious reasons. It releases into the bloodstream precisely measured doses of hormones, anabolic steroids, and a derivative of PCP . . . what people call 'angel dust'. We created that drug ourselves to maximize aggression. These chemicals, together with a metabolic-enhancing drug, create a state of rage. It's like what is colloquially known as 'roid rage. But more than that, it's a rage coupled with an extraordinary strength."

"Jesus," whispered Annie. "And you're putting this in humans? You're having them murder one another?"

"We need to measure that strength. But how do you take measurements on a violent animal . . . which is what these subjects become? And, we need to measure their cognitive functioning, as well, in the context of a battle to survive."

"Why are you showing us this?" asked Brad. "Is this some sick, arrogant boasting?"

"Not at all," said Lundgren. "I wanted you to understand very clearly what we are about to do to *you*. You see, we plan to red-chip you and see the effect of an encounter between you and Gregor."

"*Oh Jesus!*" cried Annie. "*Oh, please don't. You don't need to do this.*"

"Indeed, we do," said Lundgren. "You see, until now, all our data have been taken in . . . well . . . *contests* between subjects who don't really have any emotional connection with one another. So, we can't really measure the cognitive influence of that connection on the red chip's power to compel action. For you, Annie, we have a similar plan."

"You're going to put *her* in there?" gasped Brad. "*No, please! Just me! Just put me in there!*"

Lundgren smiled, as if indulging a child. "No, of course, not. There is another chip, we call the blue chip. Let me show you." He gestured to Beale, who brought up a video recording on the large-screen monitors. Multiple scenes of bedrooms appeared, with naked Chinese women lying on large beds, glassy eyed, squirming sensuously. Soldiers appeared in the frames, stripping off their uniforms. The women would grab at them eagerly, wrapping their limbs around them, drawing them into vigorous sexual coupling.

"That is rape!" exclaimed Annie, straining at her bonds. "Those women are being raped. You are making them into sex slaves."

"Well first of all, that is not our intention. True, they are highly sexualized, but their sexual behavior is merely an indicator . . . way to measure the performance of these control chips in evoking a pleasurable feeling. We can provide the Chinese government a version of this chip engineered to instill a profound sense of pleasure in their citizens . . . a pleasure cocktail, if you will."

"A cocktail is a drink. You are creating a horrific brew of drugs," said Annie.

"Perfectly acceptable drugs, but ones that synergize to produce a stunningly strong sexual urge. And we use this as an observable output. For these experiments, we combine hormones and the sex-drive enhancer, Libialis—"

"—which was banned in our country, because—"

"Because of its hypnotic effect? That was merely the bureaucratic nonsense that the FDA is well known for. That side effect that caused them to reject the drug are the very properties we find valuable. The effect needs to be irresistible, as will the pleasure induced by future versions of the chip, using other drugs. And so far, it seems so in these subjects.

But, Annie, we have a problem in testing this chip. The effects are much more difficult to measure than those of the red chip."

"*You are measuring by raping these women!*" exclaimed Annie, but Lundgren ignored her outburst, and continued.

"You see, we cannot be sure these women are acquiescing simply to gain favor, to avoid punishment. After all, some of them have been prisoners for many years. Ah, but we now have a more realistic test subject to measure the effectiveness of the blue chip. Our new subject is a woman who has a close bond with a husband . . . who has normal interpersonal relationships, and so forth."

"Yet another rape victim? Who?"

Lundgren smiled down at Annie. "The subject is you."

. . .

Brad struggled furiously to escape the chair in the treatment room. A Chinese technician pressed buttons to activate the injector that would plunge the needle into his vein. He strained to hear any sounds that would tell him what was happening to Annie, who had been dragged into another room. Each of them had cursed Lundgren and Beale, begging them not to chip the other.

Beale entered to join the technician, and Brad repeated, "Don't do this to my wife! Please! You don't need to do this!"

They ignored him, the technician going about the business of tightening the strap that bound his head to the operating table. The technician pressed a final button to launch the needle into his vein. This time there was no anesthetic, and he felt the sharp pain of the needle penetrating his neck. He felt it withdraw.

After a minute, the technician said, "Okay, good chip," in his thick accent. "Put him out?"

"Absolutely, as usual," said Beale. Then to Brad: "We're sedating you because we've occasionally had initial leakage of the drugs from the chips. And those subjects have become violent immediately, and . . ."

Brad didn't hear the rest. His consciousness faded, as the technician pressed another button, and the enveloping fog of anesthetic took effect.

He woke up in a small padded cell, lying on the floor, wearing only shorts. He shook his head to clear himself of the anesthetic; he guessed Propofol. Annie had told him about the drug. It put people to sleep immediately, but they woke just as quickly. Beale and Lundgren would want him fully alert.

He was beginning to examine the wireless monitoring electrodes attached to his chest, when a vicious, blind, paranoid rage erupted within him, a volcano of hatred. With a violent grunting, he leaped to his feet, his hands forming into fists, and began to stalk back and forth across the small room.

Somebody wanted to kill him! *Somebody* hated him! He didn't know who. And he hated back, wanted to kill; wanted to rip into flesh, to tear sinew, to destroy this unknown threat.

"Brad? Brad?" asked a voice over an unseen speaker. He was so immersed in his paroxysm of hatred that at first he didn't recognize his own name. But then he looked up in vague recognition.

"Who . . ." grunted. "Who are you? What do you want?"

"He's going to kill you, Brad! He's out there! He's coming for you!"

"Huh? Who . . . who are you talking—"

"The door will open. You will see him. He is coming for you."

The door Brad hadn't even noticed slid open, and through it, he could see an outer chamber with a mirrored wall and a man about his size crouched in the corner, poised to spring.

Brad had to attack first! He exploded through the door, leaping at the man, who sprang at him at the same time. They slammed together in the middle of the chamber, tearing at one another, slashing with their hands. Pummeling with closed fists. They rolled around the chamber, each intent on the other's death. Brad managed to haul the man up and slam him face-first into a wall. He encircled the man's neck with his arm, grabbed one hand with the other, and began to choke him.

The hated man would die! The threat would be gone! He felt life leaving the man's body, as it began to slump to the floor.

Then the rage left him, evaporated, leaving only an emptiness. Another feeling replaced it; one of peacefulness, satisfaction. He released the man and stumbled back. The man collapsed to the floor, his breath returning in gasps.

"Brad, it's done," said the voice. "You're fine. You've proven yourself. Return to the small room. Go back now or you will feel the rage again."

Brad realized with dull horror what he had almost done. Almost killed someone. A stranger he didn't even know. Not knowing what to do next, he obeyed, slowly walking back into the cell. There, he slid down tiredly into a corner, leaning his head back against it, closing his eyes. He looked up when another door opened and Beale entered. Brad knew he was free of restraints; that he could try to overpower Beale and the technician behind him. But it was a purely theoretical idea. He didn't have the strength of will to overpower anyone.

Beale stood over him, smiling a disgustingly complacent smile. "Your red chip is functioning well, Brad. This was a good test. But it was only an initial test. You'll be taken to a cell to rest. You'll get food, water. You'll have plenty of time to recover. Then, we'll see what happens when you and Gregor meet. You're an important data point, Brad. A critical measure of whether you can cope with moral quandaries. Would you defend yourself against a friend? Or conversely, would you kill a friend? Or would your friend kill you?"

Even from the depths of his fatigue and hopelessness, Brad managed an answer.

"Fuck you."

•   •   •

Lawrence Lundgren hmphed sarcastically to himself when he exited the limousine in front of the building housing Chinese State Security. It was a rather unimpressive gray colonnaded building topped by a small dome, which reminded Lundgren of a rather pedestrian copy of the Capitol Building in Washington.

He was met by the same obsequious deputy who had delivered the papers to him at the prison.

"Is the minister ready?" he said. "I've come a long way. I would like to get this business concluded."

"Oh, yes, of course," replied the deputy as he escorted Lundgren to the minister's office.

Lundgren scanned the office with some disdain. It was like the rather spartan Chinese private jet he'd had to endure to get to Wuhan, seven hundred miles south of Beijing. There were the gray walls and the standard heroic paintings of Chairman Mao and other former holders of the high government posts. Lundgren noted gaps in the row, no doubt due to some of the ministers being imprisoned or executed. He wondered whether one or another of those ministers might end up as one of his experimental subjects.

The minister of state security entered—a small, squat man who nevertheless carried himself with authority befitting his enormous power. Lundgren did not bow; a sign of his annoyance and a distinct rebuke to the minister. However, he did shake hands, Lundgren applying a much firmer grip than he usually employed. In fact, the minister grimaced slightly, withdrawing his hand quickly and moving to his desk to avoid appearing weak.

He motioned for Lundgren to sit in an ornate Chinese antique chair with carved serpents as arms. With the minister's assistants arrayed behind him, he began to speak in Chinese, his voice emphatic. He paused, and the slim man who was his interpreter began to translate.

"We understand that you are making great progress and that you have been given the resources that you need. Is that true?"

"To some extent," said Lundgren. "Regarding the payments into my account . . . you will ensure that they are not late and comprise the full amount that we agreed upon."

The minister ignored Lundgren's instruction about the payments. "Sir, there are concerns. The warden has lodged a formal complaint against you for what he calls inhumane experiments. Do you understand what I am referring to?"

"Unfortunately, the warden does not truly understand the nature of our work or the need for the experiments. I would require that you replace him with someone who does."

After the translation, the minister shook his head. Then, with a wave of his hand, he dismissed his assistants, who scurried from the room. Now they were alone, except for the interpreter. The minister scratched the side of his face with his index finger, a characteristic Chinese gesture Lundgren recognized as denigrating.

"Mr. Lundgren, I do see the need for your experiments. But the warden, you should know, is the brother of a close friend of the premier. He will not be replaced. And if he decides to complain to his brother, it goes directly to the premier. And your experiments, no matter how necessary, will not continue."

"You understand the significance of our work to your mission to strengthen your military, to maintain the submission of your people?"

"Of course."

"Then you will make the matter go away."

When he heard the translation, the minister scowled, shook his head and muttered an answer that translated as, "You have no power here! You are here at my tolerance!"

"Would you please call your deputy in?"

The minister paused, looking at his interpreter, who translated the request.

"Why?" asked the minister through the interpreter.

"His presence is important for you to understand my position."

With a puzzled expression, the minister waved his hand, and the interpreter departed. Lundgren and the minister regarded each other in dark silence until the young man arrived.

"You are in good health?" asked Lundgren of the young man.

"Yes," he said. He turned to the minister to translate the question. The minister gave Lundgren another quizzical look.

Lundgren took out his smartphone and told the young man "Please tell the minister that a chip was injected into you when you were at the prison. And that a moment ago, when I shook hands with him, I inserted the same chip into him."

The young man raised his hands in puzzlement. "When? What does this mean?"

"Please relay the message."

The young man did so. Upon hearing the translation, the minister rose from his chair, his face flushing with anger.

"Do you understand?" Lundgren asked the minister. The minister knew enough English to nod his head.

Lundgren touched a button on his smartphone, and the deputy assistant abruptly staggered against the desk, clutched his chest and doubled over, collapsing to the floor, dead.

Wide-eyed in shock, the minister bellowed a command that brought the interpreter rushing into the room. The interpreter saw the deputy assistant, knelt to the floor and began to weep, sobbing words in Chinese.

To the interpreter, Lundgren said, "Please tell the minister that this death will appear to be natural, a heart attack, not attributable to me. Also, tell him we have full control of his chip. Please tell him that I also have agents who can easily do the same to his friends, his family . . . anybody associated with him. If you handle my problem to my satisfaction, minister, you will also have this technology at your disposal. If you do not, well . . ."

Leaving the sentence unfinished, Lundgren exited the room and the building, climbing into a waiting limousine to take him to his flight back to Qincheng Prison.

CHAPTER 29

Annie sat slumped over on the small cot in the cell where she had been locked after being chipped. She wore the gray shapeless dress given the other prisoners, her feet shod in the same thin slippers. Her curly blond ringlets, greasy and unkempt, cascaded over her downcast face, shrouding it.

At the sound of the door being unlocked, she looked up dully, and her glassy eyes registered recognition only when she saw who had entered: Lundgren.

"How are you?" He asked smoothly. "I would have liked to have been here when you were chipped. But I did see the video, and the effects when it was activated. How do you feel?"

"I . . . I feel . . . different," she mumbled. "I have . . . I feel a need."

"For what?"

Annie shook her head and furrowed her brow in deep confusion. "For . . . you. I don't understand. I hate you . . . no . . . I *hated* you." She buried her face in her hands.

"Do you want me?"

Annie paused for a long moment, raising her head to stare blankly ahead. "Yes, I do. I want you."

"And what about your husband?" Lundgren swiped a finger along the wall to make sure it would not soil his suit, then leaned against it, folding his arms. This was a fascinating test.

"Brad?" She nodded her head vaguely. "Yes. He's . . . he's my husband."

"But how do you feel about him?"

Again, a long pause and a slow shake of her head. "He is not you. He could never be you."

"And what do you mean by that?"

"I want to give you what you deserve. You . . . deserve what I can give you." She began to nod her head slowly in certainty.

"Indeed, that is true. Shall we get together now?"

With a halting gesture, Annie smoothed back her dirty hair. She looked down at the plain dress, attempting to smooth it out with tentative hands.

"I'm not prepared for you," she mumbled. "I want to be prepared for you. I want it to be . . . special. For you."

"How?"

Annie waved her hands over her body in an encompassing gesture. "Bath . . . hair . . . dress . . ." She looked at her nails, ragged from struggling with her captors ". . . nails."

Lundgren smiled. This was a significant piece of data. This subject's cognition was asserting itself over the blind lust they had observed in the other subjects. This could mean that, while the subjects would yield to the chip's irresistible control, they would not be total automatons. Her sexual performance with him would reveal the extent of her cognition. He smiled smugly at the prospect. She was a beautiful young woman. And he was human. And this man Bradley Davis had been a major annoyance. He decided that their first sexual congress should, indeed, be a momentous event. She should be as enjoyably alluring as possible.

"Very well," he said magnanimously. "I will see that you receive what you need to prepare yourself. Then, we can have our first . . . encounter."

"Thank you." Annie smiled wanly, her eyes still staring blankly.

Lundgren made his way back to the control room, where one of the large monitor screens showed Annie still sitting quietly.

"She wants to be fixed up?" asked Beale, as they watched the inert form, still slumped on the cot.

"Yes. But more significantly, she wants to make herself attractive to impress the alpha male."

"And that would be you?" Beale asked, with a touch of sarcasm.

"That would be me. It shows strategic intent. Allow her to bathe. Have someone call the village. Bring in people to dress her, do her hair, manicure, and so forth. Let's see how this behavior plays out. I will test her once she's ready." He turned and left.

"Alpha male," muttered Beale after him, the sarcasm now slathering his words.

• • •

Mark Makers, surrounded by the other men, crouched beside the Chinese army truck, hidden deep in a thickly wooded ravine. He spoke in Russian. "Any way to get in?"

"We scouted the full perimeter of the prison," said Chivas Regal. "We took the whole night to do it. No obvious weak points."

"And the guards?"

"They're strategically placed," said Glen Morangie. "They look like regular army." He smiled and chuckled. "But like most guards, they are complacent. They've lapsed into a routine. I've recorded the routes, the timing of their passing, when they change. We have an opening there."

"Why the hell can't we use these uniforms, this truck, to bluff our way in?" demanded Cutty Sark.

"Then what?" asked Makers. "We have the prison layout, but we don't know where people are . . . where Gregor, or Annie, or Brad are. We don't know their condition. We'd be going in blind. So, we send in a scout; somebody to reconnoiter, to set things up."

"How do we do that?" asked Sark.

"Jack and Jim know Mandarin. And Jack is Uzbek. He looks close enough to Chinese to fool them as a soldier. Jack delivers Jim to them as somebody suspicious he captured."

"Yes, I can look Chinese," said Jack Daniels. "Jim, can you look suspicious?"

"Fuck yes!" exclaimed Jim Beam in English. "I look suspicious my whole life." He moved to the truck to exchange his uniform for civilian clothes.

An hour later, a People's Liberation Army truck approached the prison main gate, and the guards snapped to high alert. They leveled their assault rifles at the truck, the sergeant in charge bellowing a command to "*Tíngzhǐ!*"

The driver waved a hand out the window, shouting in Mandarin "Comrades, we have captured a suspicious person."

However, the dialect he spoke was Beijing Mandarin, not local, so again, the sergeant bellowed, "We will fire upon you, if you do not stop!"

The driver stopped at a respectful distance from the gate, climbed from the truck and went around to drag a manacled prisoner from the other door and walk him toward the guards.

"We were on our way north near the prison, and we saw this man run into the woods. We tracked him and found that he carried a knapsack with night-vision binoculars. We will leave him with you to interrogate and continue to look for any accomplices."

After a long moment staring at the prisoner, the sergeant waved his men to lower their weapons and directed two to take him. The sergeant radioed news of the prisoner, and following the sergeant, the guards walked him through the gate and across the courtyard.

A satisfied grin on his face, Jack Daniels climbed back into the truck, turned it around and accelerated away down the road, before the prison guards thought to check the truck's back.

"I am no spy!" protested Beam, as he was hauled into the administration building. "I am only a camper . . . well, to tell the truth, I am a thief. But only a thief. I was looking for houses in the village to rob. But only that, I promise!"

With some satisfaction, Beam saw that he was being taken into the administration building and into the warden's office. There, the guards slammed him into a chair, and waited with the sergeant for the warden to appear. After fifteen minutes, the rotund warden came into the office and walked around behind his desk, glowering at the prisoner.

"You *will* tell us your purpose here and who your accomplices are," he commanded in Mandarin, sitting down at his desk. "That is a foregone conclusion. Whether you tell us immediately, or after we have done considerable harm to you, is up to you."

"Do you speak English?" asked Beam.

The warden's brow knitted in consternation. He stared at Beam for a considerable time, deciding how to answer. Finally, he said, "Yes."

"Do your guards speak English?" Beam knew he was risking his life with this plan. But he was perfectly willing to be tortured, or even die, if there was a chance to save Kalinsky and the others.

"No, no English," answered the warden.

"Then make some excuse for us to speak English. I have things to tell you that you will want to know, and only you."

Again, a tense silence while the warden considered his situation. He knew that his sergeant was a ranking member of the local chapter of the Kuomintang, the ruling party. So, the sergeant would readily report any departure from party doctrine—even speaking English to a suspicious prisoner. But this prisoner seemed more than a random captive.

Finally, the warden declared to the guards in Mandarin, "This prisoner seems more able to explain himself in English. I will tolerate this, but only if he is forthcoming. Sergeant, you will contact our interrogators. Tell them that unless I am completely satisfied at this man's explanation, we will consider him an enemy spy and that they will have full authority to use whatever means to elicit information from him."

The tough language seemed to satisfy the sergeant, and he left to carry out his assignment. Only the two guards remained, and the warden considered them loyal enough to him not to question what they might see or hear.

"What do you have to tell me?" asked the warden in English.

"You have a man here, a Russian." Beam knew enough not to use Kalinsky's name, which would be recognized by the guards.

"What if we do?"

"Do you know what is going on here? Do you know what they are doing to him? To the other prisoners in your care? These people who are only political prisoners?

"I do."

"We are here to stop it. To rescue all the victims of this horror. This technology they are developing is incredibly dangerous. It will take China—and the world—into a darkness worse than the Cultural Revolution."

The warden stiffened, but tried to hide his tension from the guards.

"The Cultural Revolution? I hated it. My father and mother were arrested then. They went to a labor camp. They died there. I went to a reeducation school. But as much as I might agree, there is nothing I can do."

"Please try. For your sake, for the prisoners' sake. For your country's sake."

"The guards, most of them, are loyal to the state. I do have some people I can trust. But the minister of state security has given Mr. Lundgren and Mr. Beale total authority."

"I'm not asking you to do anything now. At least not anything overt. Have the guards take me to a cell, but over a route that allows me to scout the compound. And if possible, have one of your loyal men unlock the cell. Right now, we have no plan. But we are hoping something will happen that gives us a chance."

The sergeant returned, as the warden was considering the request. In Mandarin, he instructed the sergeant, "This man has told me a story that I need to have checked out. Take him to a holding cell, but do not interrogate him until I find out more. Also, make sure he sees the experiments that are taking place here. That should frighten him enough to loosen his tongue. So, take him through the clinical areas before you put him in the cell."

The sergeant saluted, and left with the guards and the prisoner. The warden took up his phone and punched in the number of another sergeant, a boyhood friend from the same village whom he could trust. He gave a brief instruction, asking his friend not to question it.

After the lights went out that night in the cells, Beam's door would be unlocked.

• • •

"They are both in good shape?" asked Beale.

"Vital signs are good," said the technician, scanning the screens in the control room. "They've been fed and are rested."

Lundgren scrutinized the video displays showing Brad and Kalinsky pacing back and forth in the cells that led into the test chamber.

"I don't want either to know who his opponent will be until they confront one another," he said. "I want to see their reaction. But do give them the standard threat warning. I want to see whether they can process the dissonance between that warning and the fact that they recognize a friend."

"And the drug levels?" asked the technician.

"Crank them all the way up," said Beale. "I want them absolutely mad with fury, maximum strength."

"One of them will not leave alive," said Lundgren simply. "Make sure of that. I want a definitive endpoint so we can see the other's reaction. That's good data we need."

"And if they're too exhausted to make a kill?" asked Beale.

"I noticed that the guards' rifles had fittings for bayonets. I assume that means there are bayonets available. At the end of the match, put one bayonet in the chamber. One of them will surely use it on the other."

"We'll be ready shortly, then," said Beale.

"Wait an hour," said Lundgren. "I have another rather significant experiment to conduct personally. Record my session as usual, but don't display a live feed, if you please."

• • •

Lundgren stepped into the bedroom, wearing an anticipatory smile that was perhaps more self-satisfied than usual. He was even more pleased when he saw Annie standing beside the bed.

She wore a low-cut royal blue silk nightgown that accentuated her smooth, milky skin and the womanly curves of her petite body. Her blond hair was done up in a mass of soft curls, revealing the delicacy of her neck. She wore just enough makeup to bring out her fine features; and her subdued red lipstick accentuated her sensuous lips. Her lips were parted in anticipation.

Her eyes showed the same slightly glassy look as the other women he had tested; her expression the same vacancy that marked the effects of the drugs released by the blue chip.

"You look quite beautiful," said Lundgren.

"For you," said Annie. "This is for you."

Her silken voice had the same honey-rich timbre he had heard before. But gone was the slight roughness from the trauma of being captured and chipped. She was committed, he thought, ready for him.

She approached him and embraced him, holding her warm body close against his. He allowed his hands to slide slowly, enjoyably, across her soft flesh beneath the nightgown. She took a small step back, and with her left hand on his shoulder, began to loosen his tie with her manicured right hand.

"May I?" She asked with a submissive lilt to her voice.

"Indeed, you may," he answered. He noted with some scientific precision that she was arousing him in a deeper way than had the other chipped women. Perhaps it was a difference in how the drugs affected her; perhaps a difference in culture, or in her higher cognitive function. He would have to analyze further . . . but later . . . much later.

She continued to undress him with her right hand, slipping off his coat, then unbuttoning, unbuckling, and unzipping, until he stood before her, naked, becoming aroused. She stepped around to the other side of the bed, slowly slipping the gown off her shoulders and then allowing it to drop to the floor. He saw with deep appreciation that her pert breasts, her flat stomach, her slim, shapely legs, were still firm and trim, even after bearing two children. He deeply enjoyed the sight, becoming even more aroused.

She pulled back the bed covers on her side and lay gracefully and voluptuously onto the bed, her smile inviting him to do the same. He laid down beside her and began to caress her body, hands sliding over smooth, flawless skin, free of the intervening nightgown. She drew the silk sheet up over their bodies.

"I want this to be memorable," she whispered. "I want you to never forget me. I want to be in your mind forever. So, please let me start . . . down there."

He nodded his permission, and she moved her head beneath the sheet down toward his waist. He ran his fingers through the soft blond curls of her head.

Amid his delicious, enveloping lust, he realized that this was a very special trial. She was using conscious strategy to captivate the alpha male.

She was showing high-level cognitive function. But again, that analysis would wait for later, as he felt her head move lower. He awaited the exquisite feeling of her lips that was to come. But her head reappeared, coming up to kiss him deliciously, her left hand beneath the covers, caressing his genitals.

"Relax. Put your arms up," she said, taking his arms and gently moving them above his head, pressing her breasts luxuriantly against his face "You'll feel it more."

He did so willingly, and once more she began to slide her body downward. Her lips reached the level of his ear.

"Did you know that I'm a very good actress?" she whispered.

Lundgren smiled, anticipating a worthy performance. He clasped his fingers behind his head.

"Uunnhhh!" he grunted, as a searing pain shot from his genitals, beyond any he had ever imagined. His mouth flew open, but now his throat had constricted with the agony, so that the only sound he could manage was a guttural, stifled scream. His hands flailed impotently over the bed, his eyes bulged in shock. He began to bring them down, to clutch this creature that was bringing him such utter torture.

"Keep your hands behind your head," Annie whispered, her voice now utterly cold-blooded. With that command, his pain intensified, if that was possible. Grunting again in agony, he complied immediately, and the pain abated enough to convince him that his only choice was instant, total obeying of her commands.

"Please . . . please . . . please . . ." were the only words he could manage. The pain intensified and his mouth went agape, his words becoming again a series of guttural sounds.

Annie whispered, "If you haven't realized already, those are my nails digging into your scrotum, squeezing your testicles." She smiled as she spoke, acutely aware that any monitoring camera would show Lundgren in apparent ecstasy at whatever she was doing with her hand beneath the sheet.

"No . . . please . . . no . . . pleeeeaaase!"

"My nails are tipped with pieces of blade that I broke from the razor I was given to shave my legs. The blades are firmly attached with the glue the manicurist used on the acrylic nails. Now . . . *this is for what you did to my children.*"

A new wave of pain brought him to whimper, *"Oh, God . . . oh my dear God!"*

". . . and *this is for what you're doing to my husband.*"

Yet another peak of agony made him begin to sob piteously.

Releasing her grip only slightly, to allow Lundgren to recover his faculties, Annie whispered, "I am a nurse. I have assisted on many surgeries. I know precisely the force needed for a sharp instrument to slice through tissue, specifically your scrotum. If you do not do exactly as I say, I *will* tear off your balls. As you lay there bleeding, I will then rip off your penis. I will dispose of those organs in the toilet, so you will have no chance of any restorative surgery. Do you understand?"

Lundgren jerked his head "yes," tears welling in his eyes, beads of sweat rising on his brow.

"I see an intercom beside the bed. Does that allow you to talk to the control room?"

"Ye . . . yes. Please!" He began to unclasp his hands, but a vicious squeeze on his testicles made him instantly reclasp them.

"I will allow you to reach over very slowly and push the button. You will then repeat exactly what I whisper into your ear."

"Yes! Yes!" he panted. He reached slowly for the button beside the bed—ever so slowly, because she gave his testicles a painful cautionary squeeze, digging her razor-tipped nails into the soft flesh of his scrotum.

"I want to try an experiment," she whispered.

"I want to try an experiment," he dutifully repeated into the intercom.

"What?" answered Beale's voice. "What do you mean?"

"I want to see the husband's reaction to her, and vice versa."

"I want to see the husband's reaction to her, and vice versa," Lundgren repeated.

"But he's being readied for the test with Kalinsky."

"Postpone it. Bring him here."

"Postpone it. Bring him here."

"But he's in full drug-delivery mode," said Beale.

"Inactivate his chip."

"Inactivate his chip."

"Really? But the drugs will wear off. And we won't have any control."

"Do as I say," whispered Annie. *"You stay in the control room. Have the warden bring him."*

"Do as I say," repeated Lundgren. "You stay in the control room. Have the warden bring him."

"The warden, why him?" asked Beale.

"I have my reasons.

"I have my reasons," repeated Lundgren in a barely managed authoritative tone, releasing the button. Then, to Annie, *"Please, please—"*

But she only tightened her grip.

They laid there for ten minutes, Annie watching with quiet satisfaction the soul-deep suffering that contorted Lundgren's face. He was now sobbing even harder.

The door was opened by a guard, and the warden wheeled Brad in. He was plastic-cuffed to a wheelchair, his expression still registering a smoldering inchoate anger from the lingering effects of the drugs.

"Brad!" cried Annie. "Brad! Are you okay?"

Seeing his wife in bed with Lundgren, Brad bellowed in rage and struggled to tear himself from the cuffs. Blood began to well on his wrists where the cuffs were slicing into them."

"Warden, don't let him loose!" exclaimed Annie

The warden hauled Brad back against the wheelchair, the expression on his face mixing disgust and total puzzlement. "Mr. Lundgren, this is yet another outrage—"

Now it was Annie's turn to look puzzled. "Warden, are you saying you object to this experimentation?"

"Yes, I—" The warden realized that Lundgren was in pain. "Mrs. Davis, what is going on?"

With that, Annie folded back the covers to reveal Lundgren's flabby, pale body, and her taloned fingers clutched his testicles, blood flowing from his scrotal sac and staining the white bed sheet.

"Ha!" Exclaimed the warden, his face breaking into a grin. "You literally have this creature by the balls!"

Annie shushed him. "So, you are on our side?"

"Absolutely!" exclaimed the warden. "Just tell me what to do to help you."

Brad's expression relaxed as he began to realize the situation. He took a deep trembling breath to calm himself, to try to overcome the drugs' effects.

"Sweetheart!" he mumbled, a drug-affected slur in his speech. "You've been busy!" He managed a faint smile.

Chapter 30

"I am so sorry," said the warden. "I tried to stop this man's madness, but I was overruled by the minister of state security. He has control over my prison."

"Well, as you can see, I have control over him," said Annie, covering herself with the bed sheet, but pointedly leaving Lundgren exposed. "You can release my husband. He's okay now, right, Brad?"

Brad nodded slowly, glaring at Lundgren. The warden snipped the plastic cuffs that bound Brad to the wheelchair, and he rose to his feet, breathing deeply and rubbing his face to continue clearing his head.

"You trust your guard?" he asked the warden, his voice still slurred. "Have him cuff this . . . man." He said the last word with disgust, gesturing offhandedly at Lundgren, who remained stock still, lest his testicles be torn away.

"There is something else you should know," said the warden as he opened the door to summon the guard. "One of Kalinsky's men is here. He was brought in by People's Liberation Army soldiers who found him apparently spying on the prison."

The guard entered, his eyes widening at the sight of Annie grasping Lundgren's bloodied testicles. At the warden's instructions, he rolled the naked Lundgren on his side and bound his hands behind him. Annie released her grip, triggering a thankful gasp from Lundgren.

"Oh, dear God!"

Wrapping herself in the bedsheet, she rose, declaring, "Brad! If one of Gregor's men is here, they all must be!"

Brad rushed to embrace her. "Bring her some clothes. And bring Kalinsky's man."

The warden nodded, saying, "I will also tell those I trust that we will move soon to take the prison." He left, and Brad and Annie continued their embrace, ignoring Lundgren, who continued to gasp pitiably.

"Oh, sweetheart, I was so scared!" exclaimed Annie. "For you . . . for Gregor. I didn't know whether I could carry this off."

"Well, you did. Are you all right? Did he hurt you?"

Annie smiled. "Well, I broke a nail."

Brad smiled, too, holding up her bloodstained hand. "Before we do anything else, we do need to get you some nail clippers."

They were still enfolded in each other's arms when the warden returned with Jim Beam, his hands cuffed. The guard immediately sliced away the plastic cuffs, saying, "We had to do this to get him through the prison."

Beam spied Lundgren, bound naked on the bed, his crotch bloody, and erupted a hearty laugh.

"I didn't know what to do next," he said. "But it looks to me that you figured something out pretty good!"

"It was Annie," said Brad. "She was . . . um . . . very handy."

"Well, my dear husband gave me the idea," said Annie, waving her razor-taloned hand at Beam. "Something he said a long time ago . . . that we had him by the balls. By the way, pack his testicles in ice to stop the bleeding."

The warden directed that ice be fetched and applied, as he handed Annie a set of clothes. Holding her hand aloft to avoid wounding herself, she moved into the bathroom to put them on.

"You are both okay?" asked Beam. "Is Gregor okay?"

"I don't know. They were about to have me fight . . . probably Gregor," said Brad. "But then they took me out. Beale may be getting suspicious. We need to move quickly to save Gregor. Are the others here?"

"All of us. Dressed as PLA soldiers. Mark has satellite phone. I can tell him what's going on."

"Go!" said Brad.

• • •

At the prison gate, the sergeant bolted from the guard house, snatching up his rifle as he went, and ordering the other two guards to do the same. To their dismay, accompanied by another guard, walking freely toward them without any restraints, was the man who had been a prisoner only the day before. The guards chambered rounds and leveled their weapons at the spy.

"He has been cleared," declared the approaching guard.

"What do you mean?" asked the sergeant. "He was clearly planning something."

"We are releasing him. He is free to go."

"*No no no*," declared the sergeant, shaking his head and aiming his weapon at Jim Beam. "That does not sound right."

The rumble of an approaching vehicle arose behind the sergeant, and the army truck they had seen the previous day roared up to the gate. The same man was driving. The sergeant whipped his rifle around to aim it at the truck, and the other two guards did the same.

A phalanx of soldiers piled out of the truck, dressed in PLA uniforms, but definitely not Chinese.

"These are not ours!" exclaimed the sergeant to the other guards. "This is a trick! You are to—"

But his command was interrupted by the butt of a rifle slamming into his skull.

He collapsed to the ground, as the prison guard confiscated the rifles from the other two guards. Jim Beam beckoned urgently to his comrades.

"Please hurry, my slow friends! Gregor is somewhere inside! Come!"

• • •

Thomas Beale was oblivious to his surroundings, as he leaned over the technician's shoulder, intent on reviewing the data from the last trials.

He didn't notice that the large-screen display showed an empty cell where Kalinsky had paced only moments before. He finally did look up at the monitor, jerking upright, his brow furrowing at Kalinsky's absence.

"What the—" he began, when the door to the control room burst from its frame, one hinge ripping away, to leave it skewed crazily against the wall. Kalinsky filled the door, his face contorted in a mad rage.

"*Hello, focker!*" he growled, lunging at Beale, slamming him against the technician, crushing the technician's rib cage against the computer console. Kalinsky grabbed Beale by the throat, lifting him bodily and hauling him across the room to smash him against the wall of monitors, ripping them from their mounts and sending them crashing to the floor. The Russian hoisted one of the shattered monitors and heaved it against Beale's face, sending a gush of blood from his nose. Kalinsky placed his massive body astride Beale, and drew back his fist for a blow that would have smashed Beale's skull into an unrecognizable mass of bone and brain tissue.

But two sets of strong hands grabbed Kalinsky's arm, barely restraining it from that death blow. Two more of Kalinsky's men, clutched him around the chest and neck, hauling him struggling off Beale.

"*UBLYUDOK! YA UB'YU TEBYA! VYRVU TEBYA NA CHASTI!*" Kalinsky bellowed, wild-eyed, spittle flying from his mouth, attempting to reach Beale, who dragged himself across the floor to the corner of the room, cowering.

As Kalinsky struggled against the men holding him back, Mark Makers appeared, standing over Beale.

"He says he will kill you . . . tear you apart. He can do that, you know. You need to do two things, or we let him have you."

Beale nodded, wide-eyed, panting in fear and wiping the streaming blood from his nose.

"You need to shut down all the chips in the prison. And you need to give us the information we need to access your data on the Darknet server. I am correct that you have stored all the data on the Darknet?"

Beale hesitated, shaking his head. "I can't . . . Lawrence—"

Makers chuckled. "He is no longer in charge. He has been . . . well . . . neutralized." He turned to the men barely able to hold back Kalinsky. "Okay, then, release him."

"No! No!" Beale hauled himself up and shoved the unconscious technician away from the console.

With Makers and I.W. Harper watching closely, he typed in commands to inactivate the chips. Kalinsky's struggles began to wane, but his men still held him in a combination of restraining hold and warm embrace.

"Now the Darknet access codes," commanded Makers. "Write them down. Give them to Harper."

Beale hastily scribbled a string of numbers and letters on a piece of paper, and Harper moved to another console and began to access the data.

"Gregor, calm down. Are you okay?" It was Annie's voice. She and Brad had entered the room, and she placed a hand on Kalinsky's sweating cheek.

At her touch, Kalinsky slowly began to relax, shaking his great bald head. He seemed to emerge from the fog of rage, regarding Annie with dawning, joyful recognition.

"*Golobushka! Sweetheart! You are safe!*" His men released his arms and he bear-hugged her, lifting her off the floor. He spied Brad standing behind Annie. "I hug you, too, dear friend . . . but later. Guys, I am okay. I will not kill focker Beale. I am feeling better."

"It will take a while for the drugs to wear off, Gregor," said Brad. "Give yourself some time."

"I have no time. We need to act."

"We are all here, Gregor" said Makers. "The chips have been inactivated. Harper is accessing the Darknet data."

Kalinsky stood and rubbed his face blearily, then scanned the room, gathering his wits and creating a plan. He began issuing orders.

"Tell Ballantine to come and check the chip controller system. I want to make sure all chips inactivated. And find where all other chips are stored."

"The warden is helping us," said Brad, who then briefed Kalinsky on all that had happened in the prison.

When he got to the description of Annie's clawed attack on Lundgren's scrotum, Kalinsky loosed a gale of roaring laughter so overpowering that he had to grab the door frame for support. Annie held up her taloned hand, and he took it very gingerly and danced her around the room.

She extricated herself, gave him a warm kiss, and announced that she needed to go get a nail clipper and help give medical treatment to the released prisoners.

Vladislav Ballantine arrived and sat down at the control console. After some minutes, he reported, "There is still one chip active," he announced. "It is off site."

"Mr. Beale? What do you know?" questioned Kalinsky, threat tingeing his voice.

"The chip is in the minister of state security. Lundgren chipped him."

"Damn!" exclaimed Brad. "That explains why they had control of the prison. It's time to contact Allen in Beijing. We need the CIA."

• • •

Lawrence Lundgren looked far less imposing without his bespoke suit and precisely knotted tie; and Thomas Beale looked powerless without his lab coat. Now, he and Beale wore the same threadbare gray shirts and pants that their prisoners had worn. Both sat slumped on the same cot in the cell that had held Annie. Lundgren shifted uncomfortably, his aching testicles a reminder of their humiliating imprisonment by Annie's clenched, razor-tipped fingers. The only difference between them was their bandages. Lundgren had a bulky ice pack covering his crotch. Beale's face was bandaged.

Beale breathed with some difficulty, having been diagnosed by Annie with three cracked ribs.

Kalinsky opened the cell door and regarded the two battered men with great satisfaction. Behind him stood the three Glens—Livet, Fiddich and Morangie—and Bacardi.

"My two focking friends," he addressed them jovially. "We have found the chips and the injection room, and we are going to give you both a present! Your very own chips!"

"Please don't do that," pleaded Beale. "We'll cooperate. Please—"

"This is absurd," interrupted Lundgren. "You have us in your control. There is no need—"

"Oh, there is *every* need," countered Brad, stepping in beside Kalinsky. "I need . . . the prisoners need . . . we *all* need to see you experience the same terrible fear that you inflicted."

With that, the three Glens hauled Lundgren and Beale into the treatment room, where each was injected with a version 2.0 chip. Even as they recovered from the shock of having their own chips inserted into their bodies, Kalinsky added even more dread to their lives. He held up a smartphone, its screen showing the names "Beale" and "Lundgren," with matching countdown clocks and twin on-screen buttons.

"Mr. Harper, he has developed this for me. He is very smart computer programmer. You see, we don't know what will happen down the road. So, he programmed your chips with countdown timer. If I do not press button to signal chips every two hours, succinylcholine is released, and you are dead meat, as Americans say."

"No!" shouted Lundgren. "THIS IS INHUMANE!"

"Not nearly as bad as what you have done," said Brad. "Just a little payback, and also a way to ensure you don't escape. In fact, it's a way to ensure that you 'voluntarily' return to America for trial."

"Oh, goodness me," said Kalinsky with mock surprise. "I have forgot to press button." He held the phone's screen close enough for Lundgren and Beale to see that the latest countdown was reaching ten seconds, then nine, then eight . . .

"GOD, DON'T!" Shouted Beale.

"Let me see . . ." said Kalinsky, his face clouded with comic puzzlement. ". . . how long should I wait? Should I see how close I can get to zero?" He did wait until one second before elaborately pressing each button. "Okay, two hours to go, now. I just hope I don't forget. Or maybe that Harper has made some mistake in the programming."

Lundgren and Beale slumped against the wall of the treatment room, their heads bowed, tears tracing a path down Lundgren's face.

CHAPTER 31

"Congratulations to you all," said Adrian Allen, surveying the control room. He was accompanied by three CIA agents, all dressed in dark gray suits. "This is an amazing achievement! You have done the impossible, stopping this terrible technology from spreading."

"Most of the prisoners have recovered from the effects of the chips . . ." said Annie, ". . . although some still have serious injuries from the fights Lundgren and Beale forced them into."

"And we have access to the data on the project," said Kalinsky, now dressed in his usual t-shirt and jeans. "It was on Darknet server."

"Well, you have saved not only China, but the world from this abomination," said Allen. "You have given us a major intelligence asset. And you have given us the minister of state security."

"We found all the chips stored in one of the cells. We're about to destroy them, except for the two we implanted in Lundgren and Beale. We figure it's a foolproof way to control them."

"Ironic justice. Good idea," said Allen, smiling and nodding. Then, his smile seemed to become forced, maintaining a mask of amiability, but his brow furrowing slightly. "Um . . . about the remaining chips. I'd ask you not to destroy them. We'll take care of them. And we'll take the access codes for the Darknet data. And the code for the minister's chip."

"You are wanting all the stuff?" asked Kalinsky. "Hell no! You are wanting for your purposes. You are not—"

But Brad laid a hand on his shoulder, saying, "Sure, we understand completely. We'll provide everything as soon as we can gather it."

"I will focking not—" began Kalinsky, but Annie laid her hand on his other shoulder, saying, "We will agree, but there's a pressing problem we also need to deal with. The prisoners, the warden, the guards who took our side . . . their families . . . their lives are all in danger from the government once this gets out. They have helped us. They deserve—"

Allen gave an offhanded shrug. "Well, I wish there was something we could do, but unfortunately that's out of our hands. We'll just take Lundgren and Beale and arrange for their transport back to the US to stand trial. It'll take some doing with the Chinese government, but we do have the minister of state security . . . well . . . on our side."

"Sure," said Brad. "Well, let us just get things going, and we'll be back." He and Annie all but dragged Kalinsky from the control room, as Allen and the other agents began scrutinizing the data that Harper was displaying on the glowing screen.

Once they were out of earshot, Kalinsky growled, "*This is bullshit!*"

"Absolutely," said Brad. "They want the data, the chips, Lundgren, Beale . . . and they want to turn it all to their advantage. So, this is what we do . . ."

• • •

Brad, Annie, and Kalinsky stood at the prison gates and watched the three black SUVs accelerate away, carrying Allen, the CIA agents, Lundgren, and Beale.

"Did they look happy?" asked Annie.

"Oh *da*, they look very happy," said Kalinsky.

"How long to do think that happiness will last?" she asked.

Brad smiled and took Annie's hand. "Until they find out that the vials in those crates are filled with plain water, not water containing chips. And until they find out that Harper gave them bogus Darknet access codes."

"Giving them Lundgren and Beale . . . are you sure that was a good move?" asked Annie.

"Sure," said Brad. "Those two are nothing but excess baggage to us here. And they will even be useful to us if they are with the CIA. They'll keep both the CIA and the Chinese preoccupied. Both still think Lundgren and Beale have the technology. And those two are not about to admit otherwise to anybody. They'll think that keeping the CIA believing they have the technology will get them benefits. And, they think if they somehow escape, the Chinese will give them asylum."

Behind them, Kalinsky's men were hauling cardboard boxes into the courtyard and piling them onto a stack of wood. Gathering around them were the still-recovering prisoners who had suffered so horribly from the effects of the chips that those boxes held. Some were able to walk, others hobbled, and a few were pushed in wheelchairs.

The men signaled to Kalinsky that the last box had been deposited. Cutty Sark hefted a five-gallon can of gasoline up to the pile and doused the boxes thoroughly. He stood back and nodded to Kalinsky.

"They should all do the honors. Tell them," Kalinsky said to Daniels, who translated the instruction to the prisoners. Each had been given matches, and together they sent dozens of lit matches arcing toward the pile, triggering an explosive flame that began to transform the boxes into black, flaming lumps. The prisoners cheered, some sobbing, others still grim-faced with anger.

The warden approached Kalinsky, Brad, and Annie, and warmly shook their hands, but with a shadow of worry on his face.

"We cannot stay here any longer. The people in the town . . . the families of the guards we hold captive . . . they are calling and asking about their relatives. We are giving excuses, telling them that the guards had to work extra shifts. But we must leave, and very soon. My loyal guards and their families must go. They will be imprisoned, killed."

"And the prisoners *all* have to go, too," said Annie. "If they are captured, the Chinese will operate on them for their chips. We need to get them all out."

"I understand," said Kalinsky. "Harper examined the data on the prisoners. To remove chips, people were murdered, dissected. The same would happen to all of them. But I do not see how we could take everybody." He waved his hands around in a futile gesture. "Look, there will be hundreds of them. How can we possibly—"

"We must do it," declared Brad. "After all the horrors we've seen, we can't let this go on."

Kalinsky beckoned to his men to gather around them. "Then we have no choice. You will not like what must be done."

CHAPTER 32

F ive rifle-wielding Chinese PLA soldiers in bulletproof vests and riot helmets burst into the warehouse. They found it seemingly empty except for a group standing at a large table in the center. The soldiers leveled their rifles at the group and cocked them, the metallic sound of rifle bolts reverberating in the vast space. With one soldier keeping his rifle pointing at the group, the other four fanned out to search among the warehouse's rows of empty shelves.

"Hey, is nobody home but us!" exclaimed Kalinsky, raising his thick arms in both greeting and surrender. "It is safe, okay? These guys safe, too." He gestured at Jack Daniels, Jim Beam, and I.W. Harper, who stood behind him. He turned the other way, gesturing at Brad and Annie, who were bound in chairs, furious expression on their faces. "And you can see these people are not threat, eh?"

The five soldiers surrounded the group, one shouldering his rifle and proceeding to frisk each man.

"I am sorry that my friends cannot get up," said Kalinsky, gesturing toward Brad and Annie. "I bring them here because I cannot trust them to be anywhere else. They do not like my plan. You see, they still do not believe China should get chip technology. And, of course, that I should get money."

"Goddamned right, we don't like your plan," muttered Brad. "This goes against everything we've worked for!"

"Survival of me and my men is what I work for," said Kalinsky, turning to the soldiers. "Tell minister please come in. Meeting will be worth his while . . . *guaranteed*."

One of the soldiers issued a curt command into a microphone attached to his vest. After a long moment, ten more soldiers entered, followed by five men in gray suits. The minister of state security stepped forward.

Speaking through his interpreter, he said, "You have blackmailed me to be here. You have said you know about my chip." The interpreter hesitated before saying the last word. His worried look betrayed his knowledge of the implications of the minister's chip.

"I have not meant to blackmail you. I just told you fact—that we know about chip and we have control of it." He beckoned Harper forward and took a smartphone from him. The minister stiffened. "There is button here on screen." Kalinsky moved toward the minister, and with a snap, the soldiers brought their weapons up. Kalinsky hesitated, smiling. The minister gestured for him to approach, and the soldiers lowered their weapons.

"I see the button," said the minister. "What do you mean to do?"

Kalinsky pressed the button, and the minister visibly flinched.

"Your chip has been inactivated. Permanently. You are no longer in any danger. I do this as a gesture of good will."

"DAMMIT, GREGOR, WHAT HAVE YOU DONE!" exclaimed Brad.

Kalinsky ignored him. "Just to make sure for yourself, undergo an MRI or have an EMP generator give you an intense electromagnetic pulse. Both are harmless to your person. That will fry the chip, preventing any possible reactivation. But you can be sure that I have done the same by pressing button."

The minister frowned in puzzlement, but uttered a terse "Thank you. Now, what do you want?"

"To give you everything *you* want . . . for a price."

"What do I want?"

"The chip technology. The technology that Lundgren and Beale have brought here but have not shared with you."

"They are working on perfecting it. Once done, we will have it."

"They are not able to work on anything. They are in CIA hands."

At this revelation, the minister issued an order in guttural, emphatic Mandarin to one of the suited men, who bolted away.

"How do you know this?"

"You are too late. They are undoubtedly in the American Embassy by now. The best you can do is attempt to make sure they stay there. They did have the access code for the Darknet server where all the technology data are stored."

"*Did* have?"

"We got it from them and changed it. And we can give you new code."

"Again, what do you want?"

"The same payment you were offering Lundgren. Three billion yuan. I believe that's five hundred million dollars, yes?"

The minister paced back and forth for long moments before turning back to Kalinsky.

"We wait," he announced through the interpreter. An assistant fetched a chair, and the minister sat down across from the group. He busied himself for half-an-hour making phone calls and issuing orders, while Kalinsky paced. Jack Daniels periodically whispered into Kalinsky's ear, translating what the minister was saying. Brad and Annie continued to glare at them, straining against their bonds.

The warehouse door opened, and the suited man reappeared, carrying a briefcase. He whispered something to the minister, and the minister announced through his interpreter, "We have tracked US embassy vehicles to the prison and back to the embassy. There is evidence that Lundgren and Beale were in the vehicles going to the embassy. We have increased surveillance on the embassy to make sure they do not leave. And we have issued a formal protest to the ambassador."

Kalinsky laughed. "So, basically, you are protesting the kidnapping of two Americans who you do not even acknowledge are here in first place. My dear minister, we are your *only* shot at getting technology. What about our offer?"

The minister stared at Kalinsky coldly, at one point glancing pointedly at the soldiers with their assault rifles. Finally, he said curtly, "The money is agreed to."

"Good. We are also in deep shit with American government. We also need a way out of China for me and my men."

"With three billion yuan, you cannot charter your own plane?" the minister asked after hearing the translation.

"Not one that won't be stopped. We want your government to provide a plane, specifically a Boeing 747-400."

"That is a big airplane. Just for your men?"

"We need room. We are big men. There is a remote entrance to the main Beijing Airport runway. It is a dirt road leading off East Sixth Ring Road through a warehouse complex. You will have plane waiting on runway beyond fence, and we will board it. Your soldiers will provide cover."

The minister said nothing, his expression impassive, but gestured for his assistant with the briefcase to come forward. The assistant opened the briefcase to reveal a laptop computer. The minister issued a command, and the interpreter said, "Prove you have access code. Allow my technicians to inspect the data."

Kalinsky shrugged in assent and motioned Harper forward. He sat at the table and keyed in the access codes, and the laptop screen filled with window upon window of intricate chip diagrams. Three of the minister's men took over, examining one window after another, nodding and chattering to one another.

"Stop this now!" demanded Brad. "Gregor, you simply cannot allow them access to this technology!"

"Shut up!" commanded Kalinsky. "They meet my price, I give them data. No skin off me."

One of the technicians reported to the minister, and he declared, "It looks legitimate. But here is our requirement. We transfer funds to your account. You immediately allow us to change access codes so you no longer have ability to alter or erase."

"Hah! And then you take us all into custody? No focking way! Here is counter-proposal. We are all on plane. We are on runway, ready for takeoff. Runway is clear. Right then, you transfer funds, we give you access codes, and you can change them right before we take off. Even you would not bring down a plane at your biggest public airport."

• • •

Lawrence Lundgren winced slightly, as Adrian Allen entered the bedroom where he was being kept. Lundgren shifted in his chair, wincing again, still feeling the effects of the Davis woman's vicious assault on him. None of these people's crimes against him would go unpunished. And this CIA toady could be the instrument of that justice.

"The codes he gave us were bogus," said Allen. "We tried them and got no access to the data."

"And you're surprised that Kalinsky double-crossed you?" asked Lundgren sardonically. "Fortunately, we have a copy of all the data in the cloud. We would not be foolish enough to only have one." Lundgren assiduously maintained his confident air. He could easily conceal that they had nothing, and could assume that Beale was not stupid enough to confess it. Lundgren had unfortunately ordered that only one copy of the data be kept. It seemed like the wisest move at the time.

"Okay, then, you need to prove it by giving us a look at those data," said Allen.

Lundgren gave a sardonic smile. "Well, you wouldn't even know what you were looking at. You need to bring in somebody with . . ." Lundgren was about to say "intelligence," but he reconsidered ". . . expertise in nanotechnology."

"Nevertheless, you need to show us that you have what you claim."

"But you need to address a serious problem first."

"And what is that?" asked Allen.

"The Davises, Kalinsky and his men, the Chinese prisoners. They all present problems of different sorts. Most serious is that Kalinsky and his men have access to their copy of the data. You know he will likely try to sell it . . . perhaps to the Chinese . . . perhaps to the highest bidder."

"So you would suggest—"

"I would suggest that you find some way to neutralize all of them. You would be a hero for preventing the technology from falling into the wrong hands. And, of course, Dr. Beale and I would provide the technology to you, making your stock rise even higher."

Allen regarded Lundgren silently for a long while, his expression reflecting a man deep in thought. Then, still saying nothing, he turned and left.

Lundgren chuckled, as he reached for the glass of wine to toast himself. He would be in prison for the rest of his life. But his enemies would be dead.

• • •

The Beijing industrial area was deserted, when the battered van pulled up to the brick building, slamming into reverse and backing quickly up to its door. Two men quickly hauled a five-foot, army-green aluminum box out of the van's back and into the building. Clutching an aluminum briefcase, Adrian Allen watched the process, and even though it was night, and the street was dark and deserted, he nevertheless peered intently into the gloom, searching for any telltale movement. Finally, satisfied that the transfer had not been seen, he slipped through the door into the building.

Inside, four Chinese dressed in nondescript gray overalls stood waiting to receive the box. One of them unlatched it, opening the lid to reveal the launch tube of a loaded Stinger missile.

"You have used these before?" asked Allen.

Without answering, the man lifted the launcher from its box and inspected it, finally hefting it expertly onto his shoulder in a firing position. The act revealed the tattooed symbol of the Chinese gang *Zun Tong* on his wrist.

"This works?" he asked.

Allen frowned. "Of course, it works. Do you think we'd give you a nonfunctioning missile?"

"This could be a sting," said the man, smiling at the almost-joke. "You hire us to do this. Then you give us shitty missile. We are captured. We are fucked."

"And then you tell them who hired you, and *we* are fucked, too," retorted Allen. He handed the briefcase to the man. "This should persuade you."

The man opened the briefcase and riffled through the thick bundles of hundred-yuan notes.

"Almost persuaded," he said, handing the briefcase to his comrade. "You want us to shoot down aircraft?"

"Yes."

"Where? When?"

"We don't know yet."

"*You are fucking me!*"

"No. But we want them to die on Chinese soil. We do know that our targets will be flying out of the country at some point. We have people monitoring them. We'll know where and when, and we'll contact you." He held out a cell phone, and the man laughed and refused it.

"We give you a phone, not other way around. That way, we know it is not bugged." He took a disposable phone out of his pocket and handed it to Allen.

"And how do we know this one isn't bugged?"

"You are smart CIA guy. You'd find any bug."

"One more thing. We'll want you to hit the plane on the runway. Before it takes off. That way, it'll look like a bomb, not a missile. Less suspicion on us."

Again the man laughed. "And you think nobody will see missile contrail?"

"We're hoping the takeoff is at night."

"And then people see missile flame. This is one big possibility of fuckup. Big risk."

"There's enough money there to take the risk. And there's a second briefcase for you when the job is done."

"No. Price double. I tell you where to bring second briefcase right now. Then two more after. Who are these men we are to kill?"

"You don't need to know."

"We do need to know. You see, Mister CIA agent, if this thing cause our organization problems with Chinese government, it is big problem for our business. We don't like problems with our business."

"Well, they're Americans."

"What Americans?"

"Gregor Kalinsky, his men, and Bradley and Annie Davis. Actually, we suspect the Chinese government wouldn't have a big problem if they were killed."

"We will check them out. If we decide no problem to us to take them out, then they go down. If not, we keep missile. It bring good money on black market."

His jaw clenched, Allen turned and left without a word, followed by the other two men. Once they were back in the van, navigating the deserted streets toward the CIA safe house, where Lundgren and Beale were captive, Allen began to give instructions.

"The Chinese still think Lundgren and Beale are in the embassy. Keep up that ruse. Once we get their immunity agreement in place and they give us access to the technology and the code for the minister's chip, fly them the hell out of here. Whatever goddamned rock they want to crawl under, let them. Make sure it's an untraceable goddamned rock. How are your eyes on Kalinsky?"

One of the CIA agents made a brief call on his cell phone. "We temporarily lost them in Beijing. But we've reacquired. They're headed back to the prison."

"Good. Nice to be able to track a target so easily."

• • •

In the darkness, the PLA army truck's headlights illuminated the gate in the chain link fence that led to the airport runway. But beyond lay total blackness.

"They have focked us," muttered Kalinsky, climbing out and pulling his pistol. Harper followed him, bringing up his assault rifle.

Abruptly, they were bathed in the glare of five sets of headlights and engulfed in the roar of five army trucks bearing down on the fence. They could not see beyond the glare, but they heard the unmistakable sound of troops unloading.

Kalinsky and Harper both flicked the safety off their weapons.

Three figures appeared silhouetted against the headlights, and they walked slowly toward the fence. They approached close enough that Kalinsky and Harper could make out that they were the minister's computer technician and two of the assistants who had been in the warehouse.

"Turn off headlights," instructed Kalinsky. "I want to see who you have brought with you."

The technicians shouted a command, and one by one, the Chinese trucks' headlights blinked out. Kalinsky could make out in the dim light of his truck's headlights, a mass of dark figures. He recognized them as armed soldiers.

"Come ahead," said Kalinsky. "But keep soldiers back."

The technician and assistants approached the gate, slipping through it.

"The plane is as you requested," he said, gesturing at the gleaming body of a 747 sitting half-a-mile away on a taxi-way. "And now, let us complete the transaction."

"No. We load plane first." Before the technician could object, two of Kalinsky's men emerged from behind the truck and flung the gates wide. A long line of buses appeared, rumbling through the gateway and onto the tarmac.

"What is this!" exclaimed the technician, as the Chinese soldiers moved up to block the buses. "You said your men were to go. Who are these people?"

"New part of deal. We decide. Is minor thing, right? Do you really care who is on big damned plane?"

"The minister must be consulted."

"This is something you do not bother minister with, given that he wants chip technology."

The Chinese soldiers took up positions blocking the gate, their rifles trained on the buses. The buses lurched to a stop. "This was not part of the deal!" exclaimed the technician.

Kalinsky moved threateningly toward him, bellowing, "WHAT THE FOCK DO YOU CARE! MOVE THE FOCKING SOLDIERS, OR WE TURN AROUND AND LEAVE, AND YOU GO TO FOCKING LABOR CAMP! YOU WANT FOCKING LABOR CAMP?"

The technician blanched and turned to an urgent chatter with the other assistants, both of whom shook their heads vigorously in dissent. But the technician spat out what was likely a curse in Mandarin, and gestured emphatically at the soldiers.

The signal was apparently one of permission, for the soldiers lowered their weapons and parted their ranks to allow the buses to pass. Still, the technician took out a cell phone and began an urgent conversation, his tone portraying dual fears—of losing the deal and of being sent to a labor camp.

Harper, his assault rifle still held at the ready, took up a position at the gate, waving for the buses, driven by other of Kalinsky's men, to accelerate through. Kalinsky boarded the last bus through, and they sped to the plane, with Kalinsky's men rushing 340 people out of the buses, up its steps, and through its door. Finally Brad and Annie, their hands still bound, were herded into the plane by Ballantine, his rifle at their backs.

To the Chinese pilots' surprise, Ballantine and Bacardi charged into the cockpit, ordering them to leave. Pistols were displayed in their holsters and the pilots ducked their heads and complied quickly, turning over the plane to the two, who took the controls and began checking the instruments.

The Chinese computer tech stood with Harper and Kalinsky at the bottom of the stairs. One of his assistants took out a laptop, and with Kalinsky peering over his shoulder, typed in instructions to transfer three billion yuan from the Bank of China.

After a moment, Kalinsky looked up from the computer screen and nodded his permission.

"Okay, the money is in our Dark Wallet. Give them code."

Harper provided the pass code to the technician, who took over and typed it into the laptop. He watched as the screen showed masses of scrolling data and diagrams.

"You happy?" asked Kalinsky. "Now your government can build chips, control enemies, control your people."

The technician merely smiled at the prospect of a reward for his fine service.

Satisfied with the data access, the technician changed the access code and handed a slip of paper containing it to one of the assistants. With an emphatic shout, he ordered the soldiers to depart, and the 747 began to run its engines up to full roaring throttle.

• • •

The muscular Chinese gangster shoved open the rusty window of the warehouse, sighting in on the plane a mile away. He hefted the Stinger missile launcher onto his shoulder. The second member of the two-man team called out the targeting coordinates to zero in on the plane.

Squinting through the eyepiece, the gunner centered the sighting system's reticle on the plane, activating the infrared tracking signal. The launcher emitted a series of beeps, quickly transforming into a steady tone signaling that the missile's tracking system had identified and acquired the target. Both men tensed, preparing for the explosive ejection of the missile from its launch tube, the blast of its ignition as it sped toward its target, and the massive explosion of a jumbo jet loaded with fuel and passengers.

But their preparations were interrupted by three metallic clicks—sounds of the bolts of three assault rifles being thrown—that caused them to freeze.

The three Glens—Livet, Fiddich and Morangie—emerged from the shadows, their rifles aimed at the gangsters' backs.

"Too bad, you did not do your homework on our boss," said Glen Fiddich. "Kalinsky, he always have aces up sleeve. And we are those focking aces! Shut down missile, or we shut you down."

The two gangsters gingerly switched off the launcher, its targeting tone dying.

Fiddich ripped the launcher from the ganger's hands, and Livet and Morangie slammed the butts of the rifles into the gangsters' foreheads, knocking them cold. They bound the two unconscious men with plastic zip ties.

Fiddich hefted the Stinger appreciatively, saying, "Gregor is very clever. Now we have missile for his plan."

• • •

"Are we in international airspace?" asked Brad over the excited babble of the prisoners and guards they had rescued.

"Yes, my friend," said Kalinsky.

With that, Brad twisted around in his airline seat and with a few quick slaps of his wrists popped loose the plastic cuffs that bound him. He gently lifted Annie and with a pair of scissors that Makers handed him, snipped her cuffs.

"I am surprised you didn't cut cuffs yourself," said Kalinsky grinning at Annie. "Those fingernails."

"Gave myself a manicure," she replied. "I prefer not to injure people when I shake hands."

"Except for Lundgren, but you didn't shake his hands. You shook his *glands!*" Kalinsky laughed heartily at his joke. He turned to Brad. "Should we tell everybody?"

"Sure. They'll be very happy."

With that, Brad and Kalinsky made their way from the top level of the 747 down the stairs and to the front, receiving handshakes and cheers along the way. Kalinsky clicked on the intercom.

"As you know, we are safely away from China." He paused to wait for the cheering to subside. "We have all kinds of news to tell you that will make you very happy. I will tell you first that I had very terrible plan. I wanted to give focking chip technology to Chinese in return for your freedom. But this sneaky person Brad, he come up with better idea. I let him tell you." He handed the handset to Brad.

"True, Kalinsky's best computer hacker did hand over access codes to the data on the chip technology."

A sudden, shocked murmur spread through the plane, as those who understood English translated for those who did not.

Brad continued. "But he very cleverly and subtly crippled the data, so it will be useless."

Visible expressions of relief appeared on the group's faces.

"Kalinsky sold this crippled technology to the Chinese for a considerable sum. As a result, Kalinsky's computer expert, Mr. Harper, is now setting up bank accounts for each of you. Every man, woman, and child will receive a million dollars."

That statement was received by cheers and shouts of joy, and Brad had to wait for a long moment to continue.

"Mr. Harper will hand each of you an account number and will show you how to access your money." He smiled at Kalinsky. "Mr. Kalinsky is arranging for each of you to have new identities. And we will settle you and your families anywhere in the world you wish."

Cheers, hugs, kisses, and tears greeted the two men as they made their way through the entire plane, greeting the refugees. Finally, they returned to the 747's upper level, to the quiet corner where Annie waited for them.

"Okay, tell me exactly what you did to that software," said Annie.

Kalinsky poured himself a scotch from a small airline bottle, took a healthy drink and explained, "Me, Harper, and my other hackers went through whole database very carefully. We find little nooks and crannies where we can change numbers, move decimal points, and so forth. Chinese will try for months to make chips work. They will spend millions on equipment. We make it so that chips *almost* work but not quite. Finally, they give up. Minister of state security probably lose his job and go to work camp."

Kalinsky chuckled, raising his glass in an expansive gesture. "And what do you know? A year later, a virus will pop up in their computers. It was hidden in chip data that they download. Very nice friend at CIA give us the same virus they use to fock up Iranian computers. This virus send tons of data to CIA and totally fock up Chinese computers."

"And the chip technology? It's going to disappear?"

"Oh, yes. I tell director that nobody gets that data. We make sure even faulty Chinese data will erase itself after a while."

"So you've settled things with the CIA?"

"Oh, we are in great shape," said Kalinsky. "I call director in Washington. We are good friends after we found that terror plot. I tell him we focked up chip data, we hide virus. I tell him what idiot Allen did. And even though idiot Allen bring them Lundgren and Beale, he will no doubt find himself posted to place that either very, very cold or very, very hot."

"You told him Allen tried to have us shot down?" asked Brad. "And that we have the Stinger."

"Well, actually not," answered Kalinsky, an oddly merry lilt to his voice.

"What! What did you do with it?"

"Well, we leave it there, where Chinese gangsters will find it. They think we have to abandon it, to leave quick."

"What the hell, Gregor, you—" Brad began, but Kalinsky wagged a finger at him while taking a sip of whiskey.

"Oh, not to worry, dear friend. We do a little fixing on it first. The three Glens, they have experience with missile electronics."

"What do you mean?"

"Well, you know how missile is supposed to go *whoosh* . . . fly out of launcher and then go *boom* . . . hit target?"

"Yeah."

"Well, the Glens, they rewire missile to go *boom* before it leave launcher. Whatever gangsters . . . or terrorists . . . try to use it, will not be happy at all when that happen."

"So, the gangsters either kill themselves or make enemies of some very serious terrorists!" Now Brad poured himself a whiskey, and smiling and shaking his head, toasted Kalinsky.

"*Da*, and that focker Allen will have a bunch of nasty enemies. And CIA big brass happy because bad guys get taken out with their weapon!"

"And they will take care of the refugees?" asked Annie.

"*Da*, they absolutely ready to. I tell director I bring him biggest intelligence coup in decades. The prisoners know more Chinese secrets than anybody can imagine. We land at Edwards Air Force base, and CIA people debrief them, give them their new identities. And of course, CIA get big publicity coup, too. They take credit for catching Lundgren and Beale."

"And you, Gregor?" asked Annie. "Where are you in all this?"

"Oh, I am never here. My men are never here. We go back to my little company in Boston. CIA leave us alone to do our work."

"Really?" she asked incredulously. "You don't want any credit?"

"Nah. I want you and Brad to be big stars. You deserve it. You save me. You make this possible. Now I go drink with my guys." Kalinsky heaved his bulk out of the airplane seat and went off in search of his men.

EPILOGUE

Brad wrinkled his brow in annoyance. He could never get used to having makeup applied, no matter how many television interviews he'd given.

"Look, it's just to keep the shine down," said Annie, smiling puckishly. "You don't want to be shiny, do you?"

A final pat of powder on his face, and the two of them took their place on the couch of the network morning show. Annie settled herself down with some awkwardness, given her pregnant belly.

Shortly, the smiling host, a well-coiffed blonde woman, appeared, greeting them warmly and chatting, before the red light of the camera flicked on.

After an introductory video on their adventures, the host turned to them and said, "My God, what a story! Your ordeal was horrible. Given the suffering of you and your family, would you go through it again?"

"*No!*" they exclaimed in unison, with Brad continuing. "Given what happened to our girls, we would never dream of getting involved like that. But given what needed to be done to stop this monstrous technology from being disseminated, we had to do it."

"And I take it you agree with the President's decision that any further such nanochip work be placed on a par with the control over nuclear weapons, and be conducted by a special agency with heavy oversight."

"Completely," said Brad. "Like so many other such technologies, great care must be taken to guide its use."

"A personal question: Have you recovered from the trauma?" asked the host.

"Well, yes," said Annie. She patted her belly. "As you can see, we're moving on with our lives, expanding our family."

"Boy or girl?"

"Boy," said Brad, smiling and taking Annie's hand. "We decided to find out."

"In fact, we've already named him," said Annie. "Gregory."

The host smiled, but leaning forward, her expression grew serious for the next question.

"Now, even though your book together tells the incredible story of what you went through, there are things that you decline to reveal. For example, you don't reveal the identity of this mysterious man you call the Bartender. He was key to coming through this ordeal."

"Absolutely," said Brad. "But he and his colleagues wish to remain anonymous, and we will always honor that wish. But suffice it to say they are heroes and patriots. The Bartender also happens to be our guardian angel."

"But you two shouldn't minimize your own courage in stopping Lawrence Lundgren and Thomas Beale. People are saying that your bestselling book, the planned movie, and all the other rewards are very much deserved."

"Well, thank you," said Brad. "Now, we just want to settle down for a while and try to get back to something of a normal family life."

"That might be a bit difficult given your amazing story. And how you overcame what looked like insurmountable odds. For example, I think the most . . . well . . . extraordinary part is how Annie . . . uh . . . subdued Lawrence Lundgren. That was quite resourceful."

Brad and Annie smiled at the host's reluctance to detail what his wife did to Lundgren in bed.

"I think the best way to describe that incident," said Annie, "is that I saw an opportunity and grabbed it."

"Yes, she came through in a clutch," added Brad.

The host laughed, as did the other people in the studio. "But to be serious, do you see a lesson in all this?" he asked.

"Yes," said Brad. "Annie and I have talked about that quite a bit. We also talked to historians, ethicists, and others with a thoughtful perspective on what those people did. And we've realized that there are profound questions that need addressing about these potentially intrusive technologies. Like when does knowledge become control? And when does that control become corrupting? As technology insinuates itself more and more into our personal lives . . . like those chips, for example . . . we'd better answer those questions before more such tragedies happen."

www.ingramcontent.com/pod-product-compliance
Lightning Source LLC
Chambersburg PA
CBHW020236260626
47156CB00002B/702